No Turning Back

by
Katie Vorreiter

NO TURNING BACK BY KATIE VORREITER
Published by Cross & Dot Editorial & Publishing Services

ISBN: 978-0-9985253-0-3
Copyright © 2016 by Katie Vorreiter
Cover design by Dineen Miller
Cover images: woman—Fotolia / © Doreen Salcher; flames—AdobePhoto /
© Sergey Nivens; bars—123RF.com / © Igor Stevanovic
Text separator image by Freepik

Printed in the United States of America

Praise for No Turning Back

A debut novel offers a prison thriller leavened with Christian philosophy ... The author turns San Quentin into a character, graphically changing it into a foreboding setting for the civilians stranded there. She challenges the concept of who is a good guy and who a bad guy, as some of the prisoners aid the church group members caught inside. Vorreiter has created characters that readers should care about, regardless of their backgrounds. She transforms a prison into a place where Livvy, Tobin, Lucas, and others are born again, learning better ways to cope with their lives. **A propulsive action tale augmented with worthwhile character development.**

—*Kirkus Reviews*

No Turning Back is a terrific suspense novel that feels incredibly real. 1 petite blonde opera singer + 5000 rioting San Quentin inmates = 5001 reasons not to fall asleep tonight. If you can't handle gut-wrenching suspense, don't read this book.

—Randy Ingermanson, author of *Oxygen*

Wow! *No Turning Back* is an excellent debut novel. Part prison thriller, part romance, all fun. You won't want it to end.

—Rick Acker, author *Death in the Mind's Eye*

A tense and exciting thriller with wonderful characters. Nothing like getting trapped in a prison in the middle of a prison uprising!

— C. S. Lakin, author *Someone to Blame*

This is a page-turner. As romantic suspense, inspirational-style, this one could raise your hair and keep you up all night.

—Anne Baxter Campbell, author *Blessed by Time*

No Turning Back is not a book to begin if you have anything else to do—like go to work, feed the kids, or flee a burning building. You will not be putting it down. Vorreiter drops her heroine, alone and terrified, into the midst of a San Quentin riot, and proves that there is no prison so dark, or pit so deep, that God's redeeming hand cannot reach it. A heart-stopping read, and an amazing debut novel.

—Cathleen Armstrong, author *Welcome to Last Chance*

To

Nicole Jolyn

You've been by my side since we were nine,
even when we were on different continents.
For some reason, you've always believed in me.
You have been my biggest encourager and greatest
contributor on this writing journey,
not to mention in much of life itself.

I love you, Nico.

Chapter One

The man in second row center stared at her. Fleecy hair swept back and angular jaw set, he was a clean-shaven version of Michelangelo's God. And beneath craggy white brows, his dark eyes glinted at Livvy Fischer.

Livvy clenched her fists, digging the nails of her ring fingers into her palms. Of course he stared. Giordano Landucci, music director and principal conductor for Opera San Jose, generally stared at auditioning sopranos.

But, seated in the front left row of the auditorium, Livvy wasn't singing.

Tamping down panic, she attempted a neutral, pleasant expression as she watched the mezzo-soprano on the stage of the historic California Theatre. But Livvy couldn't concentrate on the *Carmen* aria. "Love is a rebellious bird"? *Psht*—Bizet made the heartless sound so beautiful. "When will I love you? Good Lord, I don't know. Maybe never, maybe tomorrow. But not today, that's for sure." Opera wasn't short on mind games. At least Carmen gave a guy a heads-up: you didn't get that in the real world.

Livvy could feel Landucci's gaze burn the side of her face as he continued to focus his attention on her instead of on the mezzo. He must have known who she was. Any casting assistant worth their salt would have checked out Livvy's credentials. And a quick web search would have yielded the articles: *Oh, that soprano* ...

Did they invite her to audition out of curiosity? Because of the hair-raising story that still circulated the opera world?

Of course not. They were professionals, their time precious. They invited her because she was qualified.

Livvy caught herself breathing short. That wouldn't do. She'd never been this nervous at an audition before—nervous for days before, sure. Anxious for days after, yes. But invariably, once inside the hallowed halls—be it practice room or center stage—the adrenaline would kick in: *Get me up there. Let me open my mouth and let it out.*

But what if it wouldn't come out? What if her ability to become the character—to mine her emotions and offer them up to the audience—was gone? Vaporized like smoke, her opera career vanishing along with it.

Dear God, what was I thinking, coming here? I'm not ready. It's too soon. She itched to sprint from the auditorium in her three-inch Christian Louboutin knockoffs. But no way could she tell her sister she'd wimped out.

Stop it. Be present.

I am *being present. I am presently going to dissolve in sweat. Going to seep into the burnished gold carpeting. Soak down the sloped floor to the orchestra wall and drip, drip through cracks and seams to the pit below, where I'll leave a stain. The stain known formerly as up-and-coming soprano Livvy Fischer.*

"Livvy Fischer?" The casting assistant read from her clipboard.

Livvy started. Rose. Gave the assistant what she hoped passed for a smile. She strode—nay, *glided*—to the stairs and ascended the stage, Landucci's eyes following her all the way.

When taking the stage in an audition, Livvy typically felt certain the directors and conductors focused on one thing—her size. Certainly not all sopranos were as amply proportioned as the stereotype, but Livvy's tiny frame raised at least eyebrows and often questions. Did she have the lung capacity to project unamplified over a chorus and a full orchestra to the farthest reaches of an opera house?

At this point in an audition, she typically anticipated blowing their socks off.

Not today.

Today she didn't anticipate getting the weight of the past off her chest long enough to draw breath, much less blow off any socks. She hadn't been on stage since that dreadful night.

The archetypal conductor, Landucci exhibited focus and intensity. At his right presided Lisette Garofoli, Opera San Jose director, founder, champion, and patron saint. All class and elegance, the world-renowned former soprano proffered a genteel smile. "What will you be singing for us today?"

"I'll be singing 'Sempre libera,' from *La Traviata*."

"Verdi it is." Landucci nodded at the pianist, then waved Livvy on. "When you're ready."

Livvy drew herself up and smiled at the accompanist. The familiar music cued, and somewhere within Livvy, Violetta reawakened.

"Sempre libera degg'io folleggiare di gioia in gioia ..." The theatre lay at Livvy's feet, resplendent in gold and ornamented with cast-plaster details and stenciled ceilings. Would she earn the chance to sing here for a full house?

She imagined the musculature of her torso—abdominal wall, back, diaphragm, and intercostals—all working in harmony, empowering her lungs to marry sound to breath, to infuse the air of the auditorium with her voice. "Free and aimless, I frolic from joy to joy, flowing along the surface of life's path as I please."

Yeah, right. "Free and aimless" just meant naive.

Focus, Livvy!

The Italian tasted exotically familiar to her mouth. Like the memory of a tropical fruit. *"Nasca il giorno, o il giorno muoia ..."*

Move, Livvy! Don't just park and bark. If they wanted a potted plant, they wouldn't have hired an accompanist.

Livvy's body kept going, moving, singing. But her brain jumped the tracks. She couldn't keep herself present.

When the aria ended, the theatre seemed to hold itself in check until the last strains faded. Livvy held her ground, poised, while her all-important audience of two remained impassive.

"You won your district in the National Council Auditions, two years ago," Landucci said.

And here we go ... Livvy nodded.

"Yet you didn't go on to compete in the region finals. Why is that?" he asked.

So many responses prepared, practiced. All partial truths. She had decided to go with "family emergency."

"I had ... I injured my vocal cords. Smoke inhalation."

Neither Landucci nor Garofoli looked as surprised at this information as Livvy felt upon disclosing it.

Please keep it at that. That's all I can speak to right now.

Ms. Garofoli's gracious smile was a lifeline. "I can hear the work you did in Milan. Your pronunciation is impeccable."

"Thank you." Movement caught Livvy's eye. The curtain of the Juliet balcony, stage left, fluttered.

"Well then, let's hear from a different language. What's next?" Landucci asked.

Livvy glanced from the conductor back to the Juliet balcony. Was someone up there? Watching her?

Landucci made a slow, exaggerated turn to follow Livvy's gaze.

Livvy's face flushed hot. "'Silver Moon,'" she blurted. *"Rusalka."*

"Very nice." Ms. Garofoli leafed through pages of what must have been Livvy's resume, bio, and repertoire list. "Who coached you on the Czech?"

"No one," Livvy answered. Garofoli lifted an eyebrow. Impressed? Doubtful? "I learned it by ear when I was a kid, listening to my parents' bootleg cassette of Renée Fleming." A wistful smile snuck out at the memory. "I wore out the tape, rewinding and fast-forwarding, imitating her."

Livvy smoothed her already sleek sheath dress. *Okay then.* She nodded at the pianist. And plunged into panic.

Bad, bad choice. Of all arias, why had she chosen this one?

Scenes played themselves across her mind. Not of the opera world where her mind was supposed to be focused but the real world. Long hours perfecting the aria. Recording a demo with the help of her Number One Fan. The world of possibilities opened by that demo. The world of torment created by that fan.

Livvy willed herself to focus, to stop the wild thoughts. An audition for Opera San Jose's Resident Artist Program was not the time to sing on autopilot. And definitely not on an autopilot gone haywire.

But anyone could be watching her right now—not just from the Juliet balcony but from literally all around her: the projection booth in front, wings behind, catwalks above, traps below the floor ...

Livvy's heart began to race—that anomalous rhythm that had become terrifyingly familiar. And once the racing heart started, there was no stopping or controlling a full-blown attack. Oh not now, please! *Jesus, you created my heart to beat at its own perfect pace!* Not this.

Livvy's back dampened. Was the front of her dress soaked with sweat too? Then her throat began to close, the precious airway constricted. Tears sprang to her eyes. *Where are you? You designed me to sing!*

Landucci frowned. Garofoli's eyes widened in alarm.

Livvy closed her eyes, put her hand to her throat. Gasping, she turned upstage, her back to her judges. The accompanist stopped playing, Dvořák obscenely extinguished.

Trembling, Livvy teetered on her heels. The pianist shot to his feet, bench screeching across the stage floor. Livvy waved him off. Then ran off. Ran stage right, into the wings. Ran blind and breathless, down stairs, through hallways, and out the door marked *Emergency Exit Only: Alarm Will Sound.*

Chapter Two

Livvy stopped sobbing by the time her afternoon shift at Cuppa Joe started. As she tied on her apron, Charlie gestured at her puffy eyes. "What gives?"

"Allergies," she replied. No doubt he saw right through her, but she appreciated that he left it alone. She was steaming milk when her phone began to vibrate text alerts.

Grace.

There was no way she could tell Grace about the audition while at work. She'd lose it again. And no one wanted their barista blubbering in their pumpkin-spice latte. Her sister would have to wait.

But Grace would not wait. The text notices stopped. The calls started. Livvy turned off the phone.

"Hey," Charlie called over his shoulder. "The new Michel Gondry premieres Friday. You wanna go?"

Livvy shrugged. "I'm not sure the risk of a *Green Hornet* outweighs the promise of an *Eternal Sunshine of the Spotless Mind*."

"Ah, come on. Live on the edge." Charlie tapped grounds out of the portafilter basket. "Life is short."

Tell me about it. It's short and passing me right by. I can't get it together enough to do the one thing I love, the only thing I'm trained for and good at. Plus, Grace is married and I don't even have a guy on the horizon. Well, other than Charlie. Sweet, persistent, and directionless good-time boy.

"You gonna stay home and wash your hair?" Charlie gave her a dejected pout.

"Oh, not the wounded puppy!" Livvy snapped her towel at him. "I can't take the wounded puppy."

"And don't I know it." Charlie grinned, then jerked a nod toward the counter. They had a customer.

Ahhh ... Mr. Venti Black, two ice cubes. Lucas. Glory hallelujah, there'd be at least a ray of sunshine in her day.

"Hi, Livvy." Lucas's grin included his eyes.

"Hey, Lucas. The usual?"

"Yep, thanks." Lucas waved at Charlie. "Hey, Charlie." That was one of the cool things about Lucas—he remembered their names and actually seemed to like talking with them. Lots of great regulars frequented Joe's, but not many felt like friends. Plus, it didn't hurt that Lucas was sort of Chris Pine meets a young Michael Weatherly.

Livvy rang up Lucas's coffee while he poured in his two sugars. "Got it just right?"

"It's a delicate balance," Lucas replied. "What's your bevvie of choice, Livvy? You a nonfat-latte gal? Or are you all about some frou-frou chai drink?"

"Currently I'm into the espresso macchiato."

"Whew. You like 'em strong."

"Yup. Like my men." Livvy winked. *Ahhh*, she made his dimple come out. "Did you know that *macchiato* means *marked* or *stained* in Italian? The bit of milk marks the coffee."

"Didn't know that. I only just stopped saying *expresso*."

Livvy laughed. "I think that's partly why I like the drink. Most days I feel a little macchiato myself."

Lucas's brows went up.

Livvy's cheeks flushed warm. "Weird, huh."

"Not at all. Very profound. What does that say about my venti black with two ice cubes and two sugars?"

"That you tackle a lot, but can't take the heat?"

"Interesting." He stirred. "I guess that's better than being a *doppio*."

"Definitely." Livvy flashed him a smile and glanced around the café. It was slow today. *Stay*, she willed to Lucas.

"So what else do you like, Livvy? You have any hobbies?"

Livvy shrugged. Frowned. "I guess you could call singing a hobby right now." That's about all it was.

"Yeah? Cool. You'll have to give us a solo sometime." He straightened as if to go. Then he paused. "Hey—my church is starting to plan our Christmas program. There's a meeting Sunday for anyone interested in singing." It was a statement, but he said it like a question.

"Yeah? What church?"

"Willowvale Bible Church. Off Lincoln."

"I know that one. I've heard good things about it."

"Really? Glad to hear it. Services at nine and ten thirty. The choir meeting is at ten thirty."

"Good to know. Thanks." Livvy watched Lucas leave, her spirits lighter than they'd been in a long time. Lucas didn't wear a ring. But did he have a girlfriend? He'd merely been a customer to flirt with. But if he was a Christian ... There was nothing sexier than an eligible guy with a passion for Christ. Was that weird? Livvy's conscience often pricked over that one. If a guy got all fired up about Jesus, it was between him and the Lord, right? Who was she to get in on that?

She'd just have to go on Sunday and see what she could get in on.

><del><-/\-></del><

They all noticed. A cocked head, an inclined ear—obvious signs. Caught up in worship, Livvy'd forgotten herself and indulged her soprano range. But stolen glances from other pews grounded her with an unspiritual thud. One lady—a youngish, redheaded Judi Dench—actually did a full torso turn to appraise Livvy.

Too loud.

Livvy wanted to swallow the notes back down. Used to be, she could hide behind a hymnal. But like so many churches these days, Willowvale Bible Church projected the lyrics on a screen. Livvy shifted her attention onto the God to whom she sang.

Close your eyes. Focus on the words. On him.

No good. Livvy's eyes flew open. Anyone could be watching when she stood defenseless like that. Her fingers began to chill. She needed to get out of there. Why had she sat in the middle of a row? *Calm down.* Only a few minutes remained. If she walked out now, every last person would look at her.

Livvy made it through the service and forced herself to stop by the multipurpose room for the Christmas program meeting. She wouldn't feel so naked participating in a choir, right? She'd blend into the group of people. Dip a toe back into the water.

Judi Dench made a beeline for her. "Have we met?" She proffered a manicured hand and gracious smile. "I'm Joan."

"Hi, I'm Livvy." She glanced around the room. No Lucas. "A friend told me you may be putting together a choir for your Christmas program."

"You're in the right place, and you have a beautiful voice!"

"Thank you."

"Just so you know—before we talk about Christmas today, we're going to have a brief meeting about next week's outreach. Say"—she wagged her index finger at Livvy—"you should consider coming with us. You can get to know some of the worship team.

There's a softball team and—oh! Here's our fearless leader now."

"Pardon me, 'scuse me. 'Scuse me, pardon me." A stainless-steel coffee urn weaved through the crowd in their direction, deftly supported by tan muscular arms.

"Pastor Lucas!" Joan called.

The urn turned, and Lucas appeared. "Just a sec, Joan. Hey, Livvy! You made it." He deposited the coffee on the refreshment table, which gave Livvy a moment to muster a nonchalant expression.

Pastor Lucas? Mr. Venti Black, her flirt obsession, was a pastor? Good grief—had she said or done anything embarrassing?

"You've met?" Joan asked.

Livvy nodded. "Lucas is the—person—I told you about. That invited me today." She turned to him. "I didn't know you sang."

"I don't." He waved off any such misconception. "I'm here about next Sunday's outing."

"I was just telling Livvy about it," Joan said.

"Oh, great! You in?" He grinned down at Livvy, his left cheek pulling back a dimple.

Softball was about the only sport in which Livvy did not embarrass herself. "Sounds fun."

"Oh! There's Cathleen." Joan waved across the room. "Cathleen! Excuse me, Livvy. Nice talking with you." Joan disappeared into the crowd.

"I didn't get any particulars yet." Livvy had a hard time holding Lucas's gaze. Lame. Why did his being a pastor tie her tongue?

"We meet here at twelve and pile into vans."

Livvy nodded, mute. How embarrassing. He could probably hear her heart beat.

"Oh, and let me give you a website." Lucas fumbled in his pocket, then swiped a stray bulletin off a table. Livvy handed him a pen. "You'll want to take a look at the dress code."

"Dress code? For softball?"

Lucas shot her a glance as he wrote. "Oh! No. The softball is guys only. You'll be with the team in the chapel."

"Chapel? Joan said softball."

"Uh. Not." Lucas straightened and handed her the web address and pen. "We don't take women into the yard. But the chapel is safe. Joan leads worship teams in all the time."

Safe? The yard? Livvy glanced at his note: www.SanQuentinVisiting Guidelines.gov. Her jaw dropped. "Uh, I don't think ..." Lucas grinned and lifted an eyebrow. "... that should be a problem."

It was the dimple. Sucked her right in.

"Are you nuts?" Grace dropped to the park bench next to Livvy as a couple of moms with jogger strollers, tots, and even a leashed dog passed at a pretty respectable pace.

"I know, right?" Livvy sighed, lacing her running shoes.

"You're not really going to go, are you?"

Livvy stood and wedged whistle, pepper spray, and key into the waistband pocket of her running shorts. Grace often teased about such overkill when running with a buddy midmorning on the busy Los Gatos Creek trail. Then Livvy would contemplate the concept of *overkill*. To kill above and beyond what was necessary. And that line of thought left her nauseated and likely as not adding safeguards to her routine instead of removing. "Well, I'm kinda committed now."

"You should be committed. There will be murderers and rapists!" Grace rose with a frown and eased her right arm into a stretch.

"I know, I know. But I'd have like three hours round-trip in a van with Pastor Luscious. I mean Lucas."

Grace wouldn't be deterred so easily. "Liv. C'mon. It's me."

"I don't want to talk about that." Livvy rested her heel on the back of the bench and stretched gently. If she got all emotional, her gut would get too knotted for a run.

"Look, it's up to you. I'm not trying to talk you out of this, but it's a one-eighty from our last conversation. You can't get through your favorite aria without having a panic attack, and now you're singing in a prison?"

"Yeah, well, I'll be with a group this time. And I have to get past what happened." Livvy wondered who she was trying harder to convince. They broke into a light jog. "Maybe God's trying to tell me to trust him. He gave me a gift; he wants me to use it."

"You've used it plenty. And you can again. You need time to process—"

"I've had *time*, Grace. Lots and lots of time. What I don't have is some sort of 'process' that fixes anything." Livvy blinked rapidly. *No tears.*

"I just think that you'll know when you are ready to end your hiatus. It should be your choice and it should feel right."

Hiatus. Such a pretty word. More like *breach, rift, schism.*

"Yeah." When was the last time anything felt right?

"That's right, 'yeah.'" Grace always sounded so confident. "I have the benefit of wisdom that my age brings."

"Uh huh. Those eleven months you have on me make quite a difference."

"Darn tootin'."

"Just try to keep up, you old coot." They increased their pace in parallel strides.

"Hey! Respect your elders."

Livvy smiled. Then frowned. Grace was right. Clearly Livvy had no business singing in public yet. And of all places to face an audience—San Quentin?

Livvy was standing at the bathroom sink when the memory struck her like a blow to the chest. She dropped the brush she'd been holding.

No, not this apartment. He'd never been here. He'd never walked through these rooms, touched these things.

Still, she trembled violently. She fought the urge to throw the hairbrush into the trash. It wasn't the same one as before. It had never been violated like the items in her San Francisco apartment.

She stared long and hard at the mirror—not into it, not at her reflection. At the glass itself, the surface she kept obsessively clean, a tic she'd struggled with over the months since she'd entered the other apartment, the other bathroom, spotted the other mirror that reflected back her horror at the one word: *MINE.* The message he'd left for her, licked onto the glass.

Chapter Three

Monday evening, Lucas drummed his fingers on the back of his phone. He stared at the muted television without really seeing the Giants game.

It was just a phone call. A completely legit call to discuss Sunday's trip to San Quentin. A necessary call, actually.

Then why did warning bells reverberate in his head?

Well, *duh*, because his heart rate increased around this Livvy ... uh ... What was her last name? See—he genuinely needed to call her.

He flopped onto the couch.

You knew this day would come. It was inevitable, really. Still, it didn't track with all the hypotheticals. In seminary, they'd talked through various scenarios, covered pastoral boundaries, and discussed appropriate interaction with congregants of the opposite sex. He knew measures to keep things aboveboard if he suspected a member nursed romantic feelings.

But no hard-and-fast rules existed when it came down to his own feelings. For years he'd prayed for a godly wife. Trusted that she was out there somewhere. He believed God was preparing a special person to be his wife and him to be her husband. But unless that woman dropped into his life, divinely labeled "The

One," Lucas had to figure out how to balance integrity as a spiritual leader with actual romantic interaction. He felt like Road Runner with an anvil teetering above his head.

And here the day had come. Way to put himself in a pickle—invite the woman who upset his equilibrium to church in order to get to know her better and check out her faith. Which also put her under his pastoral umbrella. Did he get to claim some sort preexisting condition for their friendship?

What was it about Livvy anyway? Certainly she was attractive. But other attractive women attended WBC. He could hardly say her "inner beauty" appealed to him since he barely knew her.

Something about her eyes arrested him. She remained entirely *present*. Transparent. Without artifice or social affectation. She exuded almost a kind of vulnerability.

If she *was* especially vulnerable, it was critical that he remain completely above reproach. He couldn't exactly pounce the moment she stepped through the doors of WBC, could he? What if he creeped her out and she stopped coming? Stopped going to church at all?

Lucas rolled his eyes. *How about getting to know her a little bit before drafting your vows. Just take it slow—you have no idea how things may play out.*

He dialed her number.

It was just a phone call.

"Hello?" Livvy's voice sounded muffled.

"Hey, Livvy, it's Lucas. From WBC."

"Yeah! Hi." *Thump.* "Just a sec ... I'm in the closet."

Lucas quirked an eyebrow. "Is that a metaphor?"

She laughed. A nice sound. "No. Just getting my vacuum cleaner."

"Ah." He nodded, though of course she couldn't see him. "So, hey, the Department of Corrections needs to do a background check before they'll let you into prison."

"Wow, that's a sentence I would never have expected to hear."

This time he laughed. "Can I get some of your particulars?"

"*Okaaay* ... I hate broccoli, am mildly claustrophobic, and have a bad habit of getting popcorn all over the living room carpet."

"Hence the vacuum cleaner?"

"Hence the vacuum cleaner."

Man she was easy to talk to. So funny. He could picture her grin and those eyes that made him feel like they could practically dispense with conversation and communicate telepathically. He almost hated to get back to business, but when she stopped thumping around, he continued. "Okay, so noted. But what I need is your driver's license number, social security, and birth date. Nothing too painful."

"Well, actually, I've been trying to get ahold of Joan—"

"She tends to let her machine get it." Lucas said. "Did you leave a message?"

"Uh, no."

"She doesn't pick up unless she hears the voice of someone she wants to talk to. She's pretty good about returning messages though. And I'm sure she'll get right back to you—she's giddy about your soprano being the answer to her prayers." The last bit was true, of course. But he had to admit he'd thrown it in to emphasize *Joan's* eagerness that Livvy come Sunday.

An extended pause stretched from Livvy's side of the line. *Where'd she go?* "Anything I can help with?"

"Well, to be honest, I'm not so sure I'm the answer to Joan's prayers." Livvy drew an audible breath. "I don't think I can do it."

"Sing?"

"Well actually, maybe at all, yeah. But especially there. At San Quentin." She sounded like she struggled with more she wanted to say.

Lucas traced the discolored ring long soaked into his wood coffee table. "Ah. That's normal. It's typical to get the jitters the first time you go into a prison, but I guarantee you'll be every bit as blessed from the experience as you'll bless those inmates—or more."

"Yeah." She did not sound convinced.

"Look, I don't want to pressure you into something you're uncomfortable with. How 'bout I get your security clearance rolling, and you keep praying. See how the week goes for you."

"Sure thing."

"And in the meantime, if you want, we could grab something to eat and talk over what to expect on Sunday. Maybe that'll help make it less mysterious."

"'Kay, yeah. That sounds good." Livvy gave Lucas the information he needed.

He hung up, then palmed his forehead. What was he thinking?

No prob. He went to Ruby's all the time. Half of WBC did. He was practically guaranteed to see someone he knew there—it was the perfect spot to have a private meeting in public. And clearly Livvy needed to talk something through. Grabbing a burger was a good call.

Usually.

Livvy schlepped empty boxes to the recycling with particularly leaden feet. Long day. It had started well, with her resolve to appreciate having a job at all as well as the opportunity to work on her public-singing issues. Then Charlie had called in hungover. A detail that she neither volunteered to nor hid from their shift supervisor, Kimi.

Kimi groused through the entire afternoon about how her boyfriend wouldn't get off the couch and get a job, because he wouldn't do anything he considered beneath him. Which set off the "career-versus-job" tug-of-war in Livvy's head, and now she wouldn't mind never seeing Cuppa Joe again. And San Quentin? *Not.*

She eased into her Mazda, snapped the seat belt, and engaged the door locks. What a one-step-forward, two-steps-back day. Dad would say you could get further walking backward at such times. Livvy grimaced. Not sure Paul envisioned "running the good race" in reverse.

A glance at the clock quickened her pulse. Fifteen minutes 'til her meeting with Lucas. Err, *Pastor* Lucas. It was a completely innocent meeting. Just a pastor reaching out to talk her through a ministry opportunity.

No big deal. She'd just explain she didn't want to go to San Quentin. That she wasn't designed for prison ministry. And they'd talk about something else.

Like how God designed her to sing. How he didn't want her to bury her talent.

If he designed me to sing, why doesn't he take away the panic attacks so I can sing in front of people again?

Argh. She was a ball of tension. Heightened emotion was one thing, but when the feelings contradicted each other and scrapped it out in her cerebral cortex, it made for headaches, confusion, and crankiness.

She did not want to be cranky with Lucas. And she certainly wasn't going to unload all over him. She didn't need to dredge up her stalker or "the incident" and start crying in the middle of some diner. She needed to be fun and witty.

There was another one-two punch. What was she thinking—that this was some kind of date? It wasn't. It was not.

So what if she was attracted to Lucas? The first man she'd been attracted to since dating had been fun and low risk. It didn't matter—Lucas wasn't meeting with her because she was a woman, but because she might start attending the church he pastored.

Here was the place. A clean, well-lighted place. *Ack.* Livvy dug the nail of her right thumb into her left palm. She had Lucas's cell number. She could still call and—

There he was, walking into Ruby's. He spotted her. Waved.

Double ack.

Suck it up. Get in there.

Lucas figured Livvy for a soup-'n-salad girl. So he was surprised when she ordered a bacon cheeseburger with guacamole.

"If I have to be stuck in the body of a high-school boy, I can at least enjoy the metabolism," she said with a faintly green grin.

High school boy? Did the woman not own a mirror? None of the girls from his high school were woman enough to be in the same sentence with Livvy. Was she self-deprecating to be funny, or was her self-perception totally out of whack?

Lucas took a swig of root beer to clear his head and his throat. "So. You're not so sure about this whole San Quentin thing," he said.

"Yeah." Livvy swirled a french fry through a small pond of ketchup. "Did you know that in Italy they eat their fries with mayo?" Her nose crinkled a little when she asked a question.

"I'd heard something like that. Doesn't sound too appealing to me."

"It didn't to me at first either. But it's good. I like trying new things." She waggled her brows at him, which was the first thing he remembered about her at the café.

"*Aaand* ... that brings us back around to San Quentin." He took a big bite of his Reuben sandwich—if his mouth was full, she'd have to do the talking.

Livvy pursed her lips. "I guess it does." She sat back against the brown vinyl bench seat.

Be still. Let her open up. Since that went totally against his nature, Lucas had to school himself.

Livvy wrapped her arms around herself. "So. It's hard to explain. I grew up singing in public. My family had a worship ministry, and we were on the road almost every weekend, singing in a church somewhere, through junior high and high school."

"Cool." So she was steeped in worship, with a touch of evangelism. That'd work.

"And then I trained in classical singing—opera—and did pretty well with it."

"Wow. Opera."

Livvy eyed him with a wry grin. "I know, right? Not something a lot of our generation is into. But it's more than just large people in Viking helmets shrieking at each other."

"Hey, a little shrieking can be cathartic."

Livvy shrugged and spun the pickle wedge on her plate.

Give her a minute. Lucas stacked his onion rings in smaller and smaller concentric circles, like the baby toy. "On the phone you said you didn't think you could sing *there*, at San Quentin." Not a question really, but still wide open. He fought the urge to rescue her. To guess at what she was feeling or put words into her mouth.

"Yeah, I ... I haven't sung in public for a while." Livvy was pale now. "Something happened a couple of years ago. Kinda killed it for me. Oh!" She dropped her forehead into her hands. "That came out wrong."

"Do you want to talk about it?"

Livvy scrunched her face and shrugged. A clear nonverbal *no.*

"Don't you think fear is lack of faith?" Livvy asked. "That if I trusted God enough he'd get me through it?"

Lucas blew out a breath. She was asking good questions. Good, but not easy. "Well. There really is no faith unless there is doubt. No trust without fear. If we were secure, we wouldn't need to lean on God—it'd just be a walk in the park. As for the second question, I definitely think God can get you through anything.

That doesn't mean you need to *do* every scary thing, though."

"So how do I know if I'm supposed to go or not?"

"Honestly, I don't know if you're 'supposed' to go. I do know that you can do anything through Christ who strengthens you, and that if you go, God will be with you and will bring something good out of the experience for you."

Livvy blinked slowly and looked at him. No smile or frown, just a penetrating look of consideration. Lucas fought the urge to squirm.

"Yeah ..." Livvy drew out the word. "I've heard that before. I mean, there's Romans 8:28, of course: 'God works everything together for the good of those who love God and are called according to his purpose for them.'"

"But you don't believe it?"

"I do with my head. But I don't think I do in here." Livvy tapped her chest.

Lucas nodded. "Yeah. I get that."

"I mean, if God doesn't protect you from a terrifying situation and doesn't seem to be around much for the aftermath, what are you supposed to think? And does he *not* work things for good if you *aren't* fulfilling his purpose for you?"

She had the lightest, clearest blue eyes he'd ever seen, and right now they implored him for an answer even more than did her words and voice. Everything he had to offer her seemed a bit cookie-cutter when looking into those eyes. *Lord, give me wisdom. Let your Spirit speak through me with your perfect timing.*

Livvy wiped her mouth with a napkin and then groaned. "I just wish there were a rule of thumb for how long it takes for him to work things for good."

Lucas snorted. "Yup. You and Moses both. And Job. And Abraham and Sarah during their barren years ..."

Livvy's face shadowed.

Oops. *Truth.* His role was to impart hope and truth. "That's why God shares those people's lives with us. We see them wrestle with genuine problems, and we get to witness God's faithfulness to them."

"Well, I really hope I get to see things work together for good. I don't mean to second-guess the Almighty or anything, but honestly, I'm not wild about the resolution of my story providing people hope and comfort long after I'm gone."

Gone? Dead? "You planning on going somewhere?

Livvy squished a French fry into a waffle pattern with her fork. "You never know. Things can turn on a dime."

Lucas studied the top of Livvy's bent head. What had happened to this girl?

Chapter Four

Livvy stood in the church parking lot just before noon. *What am I doing here?*

She'd run home after service to eat and change into appropriate clothing. Closed-toed shoes: check. Modest neckline: check. Loose-fitting slacks: check. Moderate panic: check.

Okay, so she still didn't possess that peace that passes understanding.

Lucas rounded the corner of the classroom building, and Livvy's tune rose an octave. Wow. God knew what he was doing when he made that man. Decked out in his softball gear, Lucas walked with athleticism and confidence. His physicality was strong, but his grin kind.

Perhaps this focus was no more peaceful, but at least it didn't make her queasy.

"Hey, Livvy! Glad you made it." Lucas waved her over to a couple of blue passenger vans. About a dozen men sported baseball attire, and a handful of people wore muted church clothes like Livvy.

"Okay, pile in, folks." Lucas slapped a hood. "Rudy, Dave, you driving?"

Livvy didn't hear Rudy's or Dave's answer. Her focus

sharpened with a snap. *Hmm now.* How was she going to end up in the same van as Lucas? Let alone near him. What if the chapel group and the baseball team traveled in different vehicles?

"Livvy." Joan beckoned from the further van.

Three hours round-trip with Lucas—that was part of the deal. The compensation. Which van was he getting into?

She couldn't stand there like an idiot much longer. Certainly her face had already given her away. Had she glanced at him? Inched toward him?

Deer.

Headlight.

Splat.

"Do you get carsick?" some guy with bushy eyebrows and a bushy mustache asked her.

"Uh. No?"

"All righty. Sean—you take shotgun." Bushy guy, perhaps Rudy or Dave, swung into the driver's seat.

The number of people milling in the parking lot dwindled. Now Livvy looked like the new girl who had no one to sit with at lunch. She wouldn't be pitied. Chin up, she took a resolute step forward.

"Hey, Livvy, if you're going to ride with the ball players, it's better to do it on the way up than the return trip, if you know what I mean." Lucas pinched his nose and nodded toward the open van door next to him.

Sweet. An invitation, an excuse, and a seat in the same van as Lucas. She tried not to grin overly wide at his wit.

"Right." She pivoted and slipped in past him. The first seat was shorter than the other two. A mere two-thirds of a bench. And it was empty, with only her and Lucas left to take their seats. Woot! Livvy scooted across to the window. Lucas hopped in and slid the door closed.

"All set?" he asked the van's passengers at large as he dropped next to Livvy and buckled up. "Okay, Rudy. San Quentin or bust!"

So now what, girlfriend? Livvy got what she wanted. She sat close enough to Lucas to brush arms if she tried. Now she had to be articulate, if not witty, for the trip north.

You know—when Lucas said God would bring something good out of this experience for you, he probably wasn't talking about himself.

Right. Besides, she didn't know if Lucas was dating anyone. How could she glean that intelligence without being painfully obvious? Grace would be able to do it. She was as smooth as ice and twice as cool. Hence she'd already netted Stan-the-man.

Livvy snuck a peek at Lucas. Judging from his posture, he was a great deal more relaxed than she was.

"So, Olivia Marie Fischer," he said. "What brought you to San Jose anyway?"

Livvy started. How'd he know her full name? Oh yeah—her security clearance. "Uh-oh. The full name. Am I in trouble?"

"I don't know—you tell me. Anything you want to get off your chest?" He glanced at his watch. "You have about ninety minutes. That going to be enough? You can prioritize from most shocking sin to least, if you want."

He was joking, right? Was he digging? Wanting to know what she hadn't shared at Ruby's? *Keep it light.* "I thought sin was sin. No scale or degree."

"She shoots; she scores!" Rudy called over his shoulder and winked at Livvy in the rearview mirror. "Though your sins are like scarlet, they shall be as white as snow," Rudy said. "Isaiah something, something ..."

"Chapter one." Lucas turned back to Livvy. His earlier lighthearted tone now held a note of sincerity. "True, but some sins do cause more devastation than others."

Livvy tensed immediately as if she were abruptly immersed in ice-cold water. *Don't I know it.*

Willfully changing focus, she leaned into the window as the van merged onto the Dumbarton Bridge, the shortest and southernmost bridge over the San Francisco Bay.

She'd always liked the Dumbarton. Crossing low from the sloughs on the peninsula to the salt ponds on the east side, they left Silicon Valley behind, exchanging views of industrial corridors for wind-swollen sails and sleek-hulled kayaks. Today, with the sun high overhead in a faded-denim sky, the choppy bay skipped diamonds from peak to crest.

"Check out that guy." Lucas pointed through the window. Livvy looked from his muscular arm to the windsurfer he indicated.

The wetsuit-clad athlete made it look easy, wielding his sail like a matador's cape. Leaping foam, spinning 360s, he glided his board through pitch and yaw like a tango dancer with his partner. Then, crouched, he crested into a trough and shot up the other side. Impossibly up—board perpendicular to bay. Impossibly up—with enough air to clear sail and mast under him as he deftly flipped the nose of his board back down in the craziest of eights.

Livvy shook her head. *He's so free!* What a vast array of talents God gave man. She'd probably couldn't even stand up on that board. Yet people told her all the time they wished they could sing like her. And she'd felt blessed. She was her happiest when singing.

Used to be.

That was another thing he'd stolen from her. Her stomach clenched and breath shortened.

Stop it. Stop it, stop it. Livvy squeezed her eyes closed and ground her teeth.

"You okay?" Lucas asked.

She popped her eyes open and met his gaze. She almost felt like telling him about Wade. *C'mon. You're the only one milking this thing.* She was just freaking herself out at this point. The nightmares had almost stopped, yet she'd torture herself by replaying the whole thing during waking hours.

She shifted her gaze back out the window. "Do you windsurf?"

"Not well. Skiing's my thing."

"Snow, or water? Wait. Snow *is* water."

Lucas chuckled. "Downhill. I tried snowboarding a few times. But I'm a purist—give me two boards and point me down a mountain."

"So, as a pastor, working on Sundays, is it difficult to arrange ski trips with people who have Monday-through-Friday jobs?" *Like a girlfriend, hmmm?*

"Not really. Friday and Saturday are my weekend, so I can leave on a Thursday afternoon, beat the traffic to Tahoe and ski on Friday. I often hook up with friends on Saturday." Lucas stretched long legs between the driver and passenger seats. "You ski?"

"Never had a chance to learn."

"You should come up this winter sometime. I'll teach you."

No way! That sounded like an invitation.

"There's always someone from WBC trekking up who you can catch a ride with."

No way. Apparently the same invitation everyone got.

"Sounds like fun." Could she really do something that free? Let go of her rigid, double-bolted, controlled grip for a while? Maybe today was a step toward an increase in freedom.

"So you're new at WBC, aren't you?" Rudy asked.

"Yup."

"Where have you been worshipping?" Lucas asked. *Eek.* His tone was low key, but she felt a bit called out. If he was truly keeping track, she was going to lose some points.

"I haven't really settled anywhere since I moved to San Jose. My sister's church is cool, but it's in Fremont. I wanted something more local." There—true but vague. No need to volunteer that she'd spent more Sundays in her fuzzy slippers than in a pew since leaving her folks' house where she'd recuperated from her injuries. If not recouped her life.

"How long have you been on staff?" she asked Lucas. *Focus, please.* Is there a girlfriend or not? And be witty already.

"Coming up on three years. Seems like I just got there and like I've been there forever." He grinned, his dimple teasing her unabashedly.

Maybe pastors didn't even date within their congregations. Fish from the company pier? Poach from their own flock? Guess that would make her either a fish or a sheep. Attractive. Maybe she'd Google it: www.ethics_of_pastoral_romantic_overtures.com.

Livvy snickered. Lucas cocked his head in query.

"Hey, Luc," one of the guys called, "how's the shoulder?"

Whew. Saved by the bellow.

Her attention drawn to Lucas's shoulder, she watched him roll it and rub his trapezius muscle. He had strong hands, long fingers. *Wonder if he plays the piano.*

Out of the corner of her eye, Livvy caught Rudy watching her in the rearview mirror. He raised a furry eyebrow at her, then winked.

Cheeks infused with heat, she snapped her gaze back to the window.

"So, Livvy, how does your boyfriend feel about you going to San Quentin?" Rudy asked.

Smooth, Rudy. Helpful though—key data for release to the inquiring public. Note to self: add Rudy to Christmas card list. "There's no boyfriend to raise any objections."

"Ah. Right."

"My sister wasn't too wild about it, though."

"Afraid you'd find yourself an incarcerated husband?" Rudy's mustache lifted in a grin.

Livvy snorted. "Right. The odds of that are somewhere between zip and nil. Fan girls of incarcerated bad boys have serious issues they need to work through."

"You don't say?" Rudy's tone piqued.

"I do say. I mean, who are these women? I'm talking about the ones who start writing to men in prison and buy into their stories: They're 'innocent,' 'misunderstood.' 'Their mothers never loved them.' 'The devil made them do it.'"

Lucas arched a brow. "So there's no room for redemption?"

"Well sure, but that's about salvation. About forgiveness and a guy's relationship with God."

"But no chance for earthly happiness?" Lucas pressed on. "Can't a man change? Should we just throw away the key?"

"That's not what I said. You know what I mean. And I'm not talking about women who stand by their men but the ones who meet and marry guys already behind bars. That can't really be about love, can it? It's some codependent role-fulfillment thing."

Lucas shrugged. "Love has all kinds of faces."

Whatever. Was he taking a politically correct route? Maybe it wasn't cool for a spiritual leader to register an official opinion on wackiness.

"There she blows," Rudy announced.

They crested the Richmond-San Rafael Bridge, a stunning panorama before them. From the peak of Mount Tamalpais to the coastline, the Marin Peninsula hunkered in olive greens and biscuit browns, surrounded by shimmering blue.

And just to the left of the end of the bridge, where land met sea, lay San Quentin.

Not far west of the penitentiary, plunk in the middle of San Francisco Bay, sat Alcatraz, decommissioned prison-cum-tourist destination. What had smacked Livvy in the face the first time she saw Alcatraz was its austerity. The Rock was a stern place—beauty lay in its vistas, not in its aspect.

San Quentin, on the other hand, gleamed from a distance. White columned walls on a grand scale, set off by blood-red roofs and fronted by azure waters beneath a matching sky. Institutional, yes. Imposing, yes. But with a grand, fierce beauty.

The enormity of the complex drove home the enormity of the undertaking. Livvy began to get cold feet. Literally. Her body's typical stress response kicked in, reducing circulation, rendering her extremities glacial. She crossed her arms and shoved her hands in her armpits.

"Everything all right?" Lucas asked. Dimple-less, he turned toward her, giving her his full attention. It was so sweet of him, but the last thing she needed at the moment was attention.

Livvy nodded. Then shook her head. Maybe she should have ridden with the worship team after all. She was walking into the prison knowing no one in the chapel group but barely Joan. Lucas's presence in there would be so comforting. She'd even take Rudy.

"Hey, Rudy, how's your singing voice?" she asked. "Care to be my bodyguard in the chapel instead of playing ball?"

"Tempting. But my boys need me."

"You'll have guards with you at all times," Lucas said. "We haven't lost anyone inside yet."

"Right," Livvy muttered under her breath.

How to explain that it wasn't so much fear that the prisoners would *do* something to her as the reality of them looking at her? She'd been visually appraised, measured, bisected, and dissected by pew dwellers and audiences since before puberty. They created versions of her that weren't real. Today there would be murderers and rapists staring at her while she sang. Gooseflesh crept up her arms. *Ugh.* This was a bad idea.

"This is a bad idea." *Stink*—her voice shook. "Can I stay in the van?"

"If you do, Joan will figure out a way to get the van into the chapel," Lucas said. "You'll be okay. Just put one foot in front of the other. And repeat." His tone was light, but he watched her closely.

Rudy eased the van off the freeway, looping underneath to the prison entrance.

Livvy put her head between her knees. *Yea though I walk through the valley of death, I will fear no evil.*

Except I do fear.

Singing publically was laying yourself bare in front of people. Especially in worship—you sang as yourself, not embodying some role. Then people thought they *knew* you and that this knowing was mutual. That some sort of relationship existed.

Lucas bent over also, hands on knees. With the slightest pressure, he touched the back of his knuckles to the outside of Livvy's knee and whispered prayer for her. He prayed for peace, courage, compassion, and joy. She clung to his words like they were tethers to God himself.

Then the van came to a halt, and it was time to go to jail.

Chapter Five

Go directly to jail. Do not pass Go. Do not collect $200.

The two Willowvale Bible Church vans disgorged their passengers into a parking lot adjacent to the San Francisco Bay. A prevailing breeze, fragrant with evaporated sea, lifted Livvy's hair and stole down the back of her shirt.

Voices muted, everyone filed into the visitor reception building: a drab, oatmeal-colored structure outside a chain-link fence and gate. Their group was already pre-screened and on file with the prison. They'd check in here and proceed up the hill to the actual prison fortress.

This was such a bad, bad idea. Livvy actually felt like crying.

Something popped into her mind: *Hey* ... Lucas had said that sometimes they'd drive all the way up here, just to find out there'd been a disturbance or general lockdown and they weren't allowed in. Hope flared. *Please-oh-please, let prison be closed for the day.*

"Livvy," Joan called from the front of the line. "Let's check in our group together."

With heavy, cold feet Livvy plodded Joan-ward. *Like a prisoner to her execution.*

Whoa.

Hang on.

Her thoughts reverberated accusingly. Here she stood in the shadow of California's death row for male inmates. The largest death row in the nation.

You should be ashamed! Such a whiner. Her past was past. She'd been delivered from evil, yet she continued to wallow in the shadow of death by her own choice.

What did a lifer or condemned man have to look forward to within these walls? If nothing else, Livvy's presence and faithfulness was her act of worship toward her God.

I'm sorry, Lord. I'm willing. Help me with my unwillingness. I give you my fear.

Drawing a deep breath of salty air, Livvy lifted her chin and strode through the metal detector. As mandated—no underwire in her bra.

"ID please." The uniformed guard checked her driver's license against his list.

"How is it today?" Lucas asked the officer.

"Quiet. They were real squirrelly yesterday, but today's quiet." He nodded at Livvy. "I'll need your necklace, Miss."

Livvy blinked. An oversized brushed-nickel cross dangled on a long chain. "Oh, okay."

She'd left her purse in the van, but Joan signed hers over to the property clerk. The men ponied-up cell phones and billfolds.

Rudy passed Livvy a form. "Sign on the dotted line."

She skimmed: *promise to hold harmless ...* yadda, yadda ... *agree if I am held hostage, the prison will not negotiate for my release.* Wait—what? Seriously? She clutched the clipboard, but it was unable to keep her steady. She skittered a look at Lucas—the heck with cool. He caught her gaze and then winked. "Most of that stuff hardly ever happens." The dimple had no power to calm her. But when he mouthed "it's okay," her breath eased a fraction.

Sean gently leaned into her from the left. "Remember who's in charge," he whispered.

"The warden?" Rudy asked. "Governor?"

Right. Livvy shivered. "God was in charge when the Christians were fed to the lions, so how exactly is that supposed to help?" Still, she appreciated their efforts and renewed her resolve to give her fear to the Lord. She scrawled her signature on the bottom of the form and slid it to the officer.

A step out of the visitor center and *bada bing, bada boom*—she was in prison.

Well, not exactly. The group traipsed up the asphalt drive from the guard station to the east gate. Livvy walked silently, awed by the looming castellated building in front of them. She felt very small. Guess that was kinda the point.

Prison. Was this the kind of place Wade might have ended up, had he been arrested? If the police had been able to do something?

Lucas dropped back alongside her. "That's the armory." He pointed left at a white octagonal tower, long narrow slits up its sides. "Outside the walls, for good reason, obviously."

"Obviously." The tower was almost rustically lovely, with a glassed-in lookout at the top, encircled by a catwalk. Scruffy brush at its base and the sea beyond it—it looked more like a lighthouse.

People hustled this way and that in the staff parking area. Business as usual for many of them. What an environment to work in. Spectacular geography. Singularly oppressive.

Lord, we've fallen so far from your design. You didn't intend any of this for man. Killing, raping, robbing one another. Locking people up in cages. Hanging, gassing, electrocution, lethal injection ... Livvy shuddered.

Lucas gave her a somber look and took hold of her shoulder.

Okay, that's totally pastoral. No sparks there.

"Listen, I'm sorry if I pushed you into this. I thought you had a more standard level of heebie-jeebies. Do you want to take a minute and talk?"

They'd come to the massive entry. Joan walked over and twined an arm through Livvy's. "Almost there, dear. Let's stay together and stick with the guys."

Livvy lifted the corners of her mouth for Lucas. "I'm all right. Thanks though."

He nodded, looking unconvinced.

There were lots of guards here. Not unlike airport security, one officer double-checked items approved for entry, and another monitored a metal detector, scanning some individuals with a wand. Personnel in uniform or street clothes with name badges stood in line for processing like everyone else. Certainly security had to be thorough. Unbiased. But Livvy felt like a gangster's moll. Did anyone still sneak in metal files? Stash them in their shoes? Bake them in cakes?

"Ah—there's Dale." Joan waved at a man on the far side of the bars. Slight of build with steel shot through close-cropped dark hair, the man returned a smile with a surprising flash of warmth.

A few paces behind Joan and the others, Livvy walked into the sally port. About as big as her bathroom, the space was barred on all sides. The gate in front of them was locked. And then the heavy iron gate behind them clanged shut. Their very own little micro prison. But like a pen at the rodeo, the door in front of them opened, and they herded out of the sally port on the prison side of the entrance.

"Livvy, this is San Quentin's protestant chaplain, Dale Peake. Dale, this is Livvy." The chaplain's handshake was a touch point. A tether to solid ground. Livvy regretted letting go.

"And I believe you've met everyone else?" Joan asked Dale, indicating the three men from the worship team gathered behind her. "Todd, Anthony, and Hector." Nods all around.

A tall correctional officer waved all the WBC visitors into a single huddle. "Hello, folks. I'm Lieutenant Knox. Welcome to San Quentin. I know some of you have visited before and some are first-timers. If we all remember the ground rules, we won't have any problems."

Knox was a sinewy Woody Harrelson type, same thinning hair even. He was no *Cheers* Woody, though. Not an easy-going Billy Hoyle from *White Men Can't Jump.* You'd no sooner suggest Rogaine to this guy than you would Chanel no. 5.

"Do not give anything to an inmate—not a pen, stick of gum, or piece of belly-button lint. Under no circumstance should you give a prisoner your personal contact information."

Why on earth did he look at Livvy when he said that?

"Stay together, ignore the visitor-baiting, catcalls—"

Knox's words were cut short by a piercing alarm. Livvy jumped and grabbed Joan's arm. *Quick, back out through the port!* An emergency would curtail their visit after all.

Joan covered Livvy's hand with her own. "It's okay, this happens all the time."

The squalling ceased, and Lt. Knox started up again. "What you just heard was the sound of an officer's personal alarm. That happens from time to time. If it occurs while you're inside, simply halt and wait for it to stop. In the case of an emergency—shots fired, for example—hit the ground and stay there. If we are able to extract you, we will do so as soon as possible."

If?

Livvy's brows shot skyward. What did he mean *if?* She stood rooted.

A non-uniformed prison staffer greeted the softball team. They fell in behind their guide.

Livvy sucked a lungful of air. It would only be like ninety minutes. Then she'd be on the other side of the wall again. Yet her shoulders and neck were so taut she wondered if her vocal cords could even vibrate.

"How was your drive?" Dale asked Joan, pivoting to lead the way out-of-doors. Into the prison.

The east gate opened into a quadrangle courtyard, guarded by antiquated buildings. Over a washed-out canvas of creams and grays, the sky popped a vibrant blue. Slices of clean, bright green grass broke up the square, scattered with a few leggy palms, bristly evergreens, and manicured junipers.

As the softball team took a separate path, Lucas looked back. A smile as warm and sweet as hot apple pie lit up his face. No dimple. No playfulness. Just a gleam of sincerity that infused Livvy with confidence.

Only ninety minutes.

Bunched like sheep, the worship team veered right. With a jolt, Livvy realized that the men scattered around the quad, clad in blue pants and chambray shirts, were inmates. One knelt in a flower bed, weeding. Another swept. A few pruned. As she passed a raised pond, Livvy chanced to make eye contact with the prisoner cleaning it. His eyes crinkled with the hint of a smile, and he nodded to her.

The shriek of an alarm made Livvy jump again. Her heart raced, but the inmates were unfazed. To the last man, they knelt or sat on the ground. By the time the peals quit, Livvy's breath returned to normal. Everyone went back to his business.

Chapel wasn't due to start for another fifteen minutes, but there were about a dozen inmates already milling inside. Some stood talking in groups; a few sat in the pews. At least one appeared to be reading a Bible.

As with the inmate in the courtyard, the men projected a sort of welcoming respectfulness toward the worship team. Livvy rolled some of the tension out from her neck, through her shoulders, and out her hands. She could do this.

Once seated in the front row, Livvy listened to the influx of inmates behind her. She tried to picture them in Sunday-go-to-meetin' clothes: suits, ties, sport coats. Did anything in the racket differentiate them from any other congregation?

"Uh, s'cuse me." A voice broke her reverie. A young man stood before her on the other side of the wooden rail. His black hair was neatly corn-rowed, braids hanging about shoulder length. "Don't mean to disturb you. Just wanted to welcome you and thank you for coming." He held out a hand.

Livvy stood and shook his hand. "Thank you. I mean, you're welcome."

The man's wide smile was marshmallows against chocolate, and his eyes burned brightly. "You ever been to the Q before?"

"Nope," Livvy answered. "First time."

"Well, D.P.—uh, that's Chaplain Dale Peake—preaches a good sermon. You singing?"

"Yep." *Come on, girl.* You can do better than one-word answers. "I'm Livvy."

"Hi, Livvy. Name's Smitty. But you can just call me Smitty." He laughed.

"So," Livvy said. "Uh ..." Good grief—*What're you in for? How long you been locked up? How 'bout them Giants?*—what was a person to say? "Do ... do you usually get a pretty good turnout for chapel?"

"This is a real small group. West Block is on lockdown this morning. And of course, only GP has chapel privileges."

Livvy must have looked blank.

"General population," Smitty clarified, "the mainline prisoners. Which doesn't include the Row, obviously. Or Reception—which is newbies waiting to be mainlined into the Q and guys heading for other facilities. Then you've got those in Segregation for their own protection." He ticked them off on his fingers. "Snitches, gays, gang dropouts, and child molesters. And finally there's the AC, the 'Adjustment Center.' That's institutional whitewash if there ever was any, huh? That's for the bad aa—uh, attitudes—who can't get along with others. The biggest troublemakers."

"Ah." Whew, good to know that chapel was a privilege. No troublemakers here.

"So, anyhow, you might have between fifty and a hundred guys for chapel. All depends. This is real small."

Dale walked up. "Hi, Smitty. How are things with you?"

"Just fine, D.P. I got my hearing in ten days."

"Yep, I have it on my calendar. I'll be praying."

"Good, good. That's real good. 'The prayer of a righteous man availeth much.'"

"Absolutely." Dale patted the man on the shoulder. "What say we get this party started?"

Smitty tipped an invisible hat to Livvy and strode back a few pews.

Joan nodded at the worship team, who filed behind her up a couple steps to the platform. At the front of the chapel. The *whole* chapel.

The room was a sea of blue chambray and male faces. Livvy dug a fingernail into her palm. *None of these men can leave. They can't follow you home.* She scanned the crowd for friendly faces. Not too much eye contact. There was Smitty, grinning. The man at his side was impassive. All muscular intensity, he was a closely shorn Josh Holloway—square-jawed Sawyer from *LOST*. He contemplated Livvy with unconcealed directness, as if she were a portrait.

Livvy's shoulders tightened. She focused on the back wall. A large painting of the face of Jesus hung over the door. Bold swaths juxtaposed light and dark. This was a forthright Jesus, the kind of savior who could handle the stuff that would come up in this room.

Harmonizing on "I have decided to follow Jesus" grounded Livvy. The traditional hymn was a great first choice. Lots of people knew it, but if you didn't, it was simple to pick up.

Most, if not all, of the men in the chapel sang.

I have decided ...

Young and old, long-haired and bald, men of every size, shape, and ethnicity.

... to follow Jesus.

An ancient guy sang sitting in his pew, while those around him stood. How long had he been in prison? How much longer would he be? Would he die in here? Livvy could no more guess any of the men's crimes than they could read her sins on her face.

No turning back ...

Smitty had said the prisoners on death row didn't have chapel privileges. So none of these men faced execution. Livvy lifted her eyes back up to the portrait of her savior. *You know what it's like to be executed by the state.* Wonder if that made Jesus more compelling to guys like these.

... no turning back.

Clearly Jesus had a heart for the convicted. Possibly the first guy to arrive in heaven on Jesus's heels was the criminal on the cross next to him. Wild.

I can't believe I was so close to chickening out. Thanks, Lord, for giving me the strength to walk in here. Just like Lucas said you would.

Maybe the past could be the past after all.

Livvy returned Smitty's grin. *Whew.*

And then a piercing alarm wailed through the chapel, penetrating Livvy's skull, skewering the knot between her shoulders. She almost vaulted off the dais, her shriek lost in the din.

Chapter Six

Chapel worship ceased, and everyone remained stationary. Nobody else even winced as the alarm continued to shriek.

How could anyone live this way? It was crazy!

Sawyer leaned forward, elbows on knees, focused on Livvy. She didn't have anything to do but stand and wait for the alarm to quit. Not singing, just hanging out up there in front of everyone.

At the rear of the chapel, Lt. Knox held his radio to one ear and covered the other.

The alarm continued and continued. There was only sound—no movement, no rational thought.

And no change in Sawyer's stare. Conscious that many eyes were on her—and that she represented Willowvale Bible Church—Livvy leveled a gaze back at the inmate. *You cannot consume me.* She worked on a neutral, unexpressive face. Sawyer didn't blink.

Still the alarm pealed. They would be locked this way forever—him staring, her staring, and the siren wailing.

But Sawyer broke first. He snapped his head around to look behind. Still mute, and mostly deaf, Livvy followed his gaze. A group of men streamed in through the rear doors.

Click, click—her brain worked slowly. The men were rushing, agitated. Shouldn't they be down for the alarm? But there *was* a guard with them.

Click, click—a struggling guard.

With a gun. To his neck.

Livvy's jaw dropped in a silent scream, and she turned to run. Behind was a brick wall—with a plain wooden door stage left.

Pandemonium reigned now. Most of the inmates in the pews either hit the ground or shrank to the walls. Lieutenant Knox dropped his radio and put his hands on his head, fingers interlaced. The other guards followed suit as rioting prisoners swarmed them. Sawyer was clambering forward over pews.

Horror clutched at Livvy's throat, threatening her breath. Her blood had turned to ice. This could not be happening.

A front-runner broke off from the incoming mob, sprinting for the stage. His face was a leering swirl of color—something like a tribal mask stretched over his face. The sight of him propelled Livvy into panicked motion: evil sprinted toward her and it would devour her. A shrill cry burst from her throat—the sound lost in the siren.

"Go, go!" Livvy screamed at Joan and the men from the choir. She shoved and pulled them toward the stage door. Joan looked frozen to the stage, mouth agape, as Livvy had just been. There was no time! They had to run before they were overtaken.

Sawyer vaulted the rail in front of the first pew. He was up the steps before Livvy could gasp. And in one swift motion, he caught her around her waist and spun toward the eastern chapel wall. She screamed and clawed at him, adrenaline surging through her flailing limbs, but she may as well have been a big rag doll the way he swung her off her feet and carried her at a full run.

He dumped her at the foot of a tall frosted window and pawed at her. Braced against the wall, Livvy kicked back at his hands. *God help me!* He ripped off her shoe. Then he cocked his arm and slammed the chunky heel down on the windowpane. Again.

Hector, from the worship team, wasn't far behind, springing

down the stairs. The onrushing inmate also veered toward them. Livvy gaped at his masked face—no, it wasn't a mask he wore. All of his visible skin, including bald head, was tattooed. Livvy was slammed with a wave of nausea.

"Tobin!" the inmate yelled to Sawyer.

Crash. Tobin shattered the glass with Livvy's shoe. He whipped an eight-inch shard toward the two advancing men. "Back off!"

In a blink, he was down to a white tee, holding his long-sleeved denim shirt. He flicked the shirt across the sill.

Livvy pushed off the wall toward Hector. But she was yanked back—Tobin had a fistful of her hair. "I said, *back off!*" he screamed at Hector, pressing the shard to Livvy's throat. She grappled with his wrist, trying to pull the glass away. The scene spun in a dizzying blur of chaos and horror.

"This one is mine, Gant," Tobin snarled at the tattooed inmate.

A sickening heave and Livvy was pulled backward through the open window. The inmate inside—Gant—caught at the hem of her pants, and Tobin sliced the glass down on the back of his hand.

Gant snatched his hand back, cursing. His eyes met Livvy's in the fleetest of instants, and the naked hunger in his glare took her breath away.

Tobin swept Livvy up in a fireman's carry, his shoulder digging into her gut.

"Put me down!" she hollered over the still-pealing sirens and pounded on his back.

"Shut up!" he yelled. He ran north along a tall, narrow corridor between the whitewashed chapel and the towering concrete east wall.

Livvy screamed, wordless now, the pavement a blur below her bobbing hair.

"Shut. Up!" The inmate set her down at the corner of the chapel, some sixty feet from the window and another six from the prison's north wall. She wavered and almost fell. He clamped his hand over her mouth and peered around the corner to the left. The afternoon sun illuminated the top of the outer walls, but left Livvy and her captor in shadow at their base.

"You have to be quiet!" Tobin's gray eyes drilled into hers, just inches away from where she strained against his palm, sucking air through her nose.

"Here," he said, removing his hand. "Breathe. But be—"

Livvy bellowed and kicked.

Tobin clapped his hand over her mouth again. He checked behind them, then around the corner, and half dragged, half carried Livvy to the north wall. Another long, colorless corridor ran between the back of the chapel and the north wall. Tobin threw his back against the prison wall and sidestepped them along it. He kept looking up, to the top of the outer wall. A windowed platform extended past the top of the wall, hanging over the yard.

A guard tower! Livvy dug in her single shoed foot and thrashed, pulled, bit at the inmate. He held firm, and sirens continued to scream, drowning all other sound.

Livvy couldn't see anyone in the tower. But down the slope ahead of them, past the end of the next building, she could glimpse into the lower prison yard. Swarms of inmates ran pell-mell, while others huddled or lay on the ground, hands laced on their heads. Still more were brawling, in twos, tens, hundreds? One hulking prisoner slammed a pipe on another's head. The victim dropped to the pavement like an unstrung marionette. Blood gushed from his still figure, spreading a stain that gave no one pause.

Livvy's legs crumpled, and she all but hung from Tobin's grasp, staring at the madness. *Back, back! Turn around, get me out of here!* Her stomach heaved, and she choked for air.

Shots rang out—from overhead, from somewhere to the left, from across the prison—staccato slaps echoing off ancient stone walls.

Eyes closed. Don't see this. Not happening.

But a stranger's breath panted warm in her ear. A convicted felon pressed her against his chest with an iron grip. Livvy whimpered. Inaudible, her throat vibrated against the inmate's arm.

God, help me!

Lucas pressed back-to-back with his teammates in an inverted huddle. Many of the players from the San Quentin team surrounded them on the ball field, fending off on-rushing inmates. Lucas could hardly think over the shouting men and wailing alarms. His mouth was dry. *What has happened?*

Everywhere he looked, men were running, shouting, pushing, fighting. The only officers he saw were the ones rushing along the top of the perimeter walls. They had rifles and took aim at the chaos. Just who among the hundreds would they shoot? It was total pandemonium. His breath came in quick, short bursts.

Sean grabbed his arm. "What do we do?" he yelled. His freckles stood out against white skin.

How am I supposed to know? Lucas shook his head. "Listen to those guys!" He pointed at Roberto and Greg, the two inmates he'd known the longest and trusted most. Pitcher and first base.

Greg cupped hands around his mouth and hollered. "See the gate in the wall over there?" He pointed back along the north wall, the way the team had come down from the quad. There were huge double doors—yeah, the gate to the prison industries. Lucas nodded and gestured to the rest of his guys to follow. Boy did they stand out, a multicolored knot in a field of prison blue. Lucas was flooded with gratitude when he realized that the San Quentin softball team continued to encircle them, keeping in step, pressing on toward the gate.

Crack!

The officers on the wall had started shooting. Lucas ducked his head. *Dear God!*

Crack!

If possible, the men in the yard roared louder. Bodies crushed in on Lucas and his cluster of friends like a mosh pit at a punk concert gone terribly, terribly wrong. He lost sight of Greg, but there was Roberto. Lucas grabbed the back of Sean's tee and shoved him in the right direction. "Rudy!" he hollered at the retreating back of his shortstop.

Then he threw his arms up over his face. *What is that?* Caustic fog engulfed him, scorching his eyes and lungs. The pain was searing. He stumbled, would have fallen if bodies hadn't been packed so closely. His eyes and nose streamed, and even his skin burned.

That's what they'd fired. Tear gas. In his fight for oxygen, Lucas sucked huge breaths, filling his lungs with still more poison. He convulsed with coughs.

"Lucas!" Someone grabbed his sleeve. He yielded in that direction, allowed himself to be pulled. He couldn't see anything but a blurry kaleidoscope of shapes in motion. It hurt so bad. He coughed up mucus and fought his gag reflex.

His movement through the crowd hardly felt like progress, but he and those around him jostled, shuffled, and stumbled until he realized they were past deep center field—the opposite direction of the gate to the prison industries. He rubbed his face with his shirt. It didn't help the bite of the gas but wiped away tears and snot.

He squinted at the faces of those around him. One, two ... three ... Three WBC guys. There was Dave—four. Lucas made five. Even with his weeping eyes he could tell nobody else in the immediate area wore civilian clothes. Just five? He leapt vertically, looking over heads, sweeping his gaze across the open area between buildings and walls that was the lower yard. In the sea of blue, there was the occasional green smudge of a correctional officer's uniform. No other colors. Where was the rest of the team? Six men were missing. He was responsible for them. He brought them in—

Oh! Lucas bent double with visceral horror.

Livvy.

Livvy was here.

Oh, dear God. He couldn't even finish the prayer.

He cupped his face in his hands. Wait. The riot was probably contained to the yard. Livvy was safe with the choir group. The chapel was close to the east gate. They'd surely been ushered out of the prison at the first sign of trouble. Right? The correctional officers assigned to them must have gotten them out.

Oh please, God, protect us all. Keep the choir free from harm. Please keep Livvy safe. On the *outside* of the walls.

Lucas scanned around him for the inmate softball players. He didn't recognize a single face. He spun on his heel. Did a 360. Not only were there no San Quentin ball players to be seen, he and the WBC guys were encircled by a bunch of guys who looked a lot alike. All of them were white, bald, and tattooed, every last one branded with the number eighteen. That wasn't the most terrifying part. The most terrifying part was that the whole circle stood, arms folded across chests, facing inward. And those faces— they reflected nothing but hatred.

Chapter Seven

All the fight had drained from Livvy's body. She quivered and shook, adrenaline running through her veins as rampant as the prisoners through San Quentin.

"Listen to me!" The muscled inmate yelled next to her ear, over the siren's din. Then the wailing stopped, echoes receding across the campus. Finally. But new sounds bounced off the cell blocks, buildings, and walls. Men's voices. Screaming—in rage, urgency, exaltation, terror, pain.

Tobin relaxed his grip on Livvy a fraction and took his hand from her mouth. She remained quiet. She didn't want attention after all.

"Listen to me," he repeated. "We're going in there." He pointed up and across a sloping drive to a long two-story building.

"Let me go," Livvy whispered. "Please! Just let me go—I can get back to the entrance from here." Why, oh why, had she challenged his stare?

"No." Voice flat and even, he peered around the corner.

"Please! I won't tell anyone what you did. Please—just let me go!" Livvy backpedaled, but Tobin gripped her wrist.

"What I did?" He looked at her now. "You mean rescue you?"

"Rescue? That was a rescue?"

"What'd you think?" He straightened, lowering the hand grasping Livvy's. "You think I snatched you? Weren't we just singing to the same Jesus in there?"

Livvy opened her mouth. Then closed it. Was he serious? The guy seemed indignant. Hurt even. Her brain locked up. She looked at the ground.

At one shoed foot and one socked foot.

She snapped her head back up. "You grabbed me by the *hair.* Glass to my throat! 'This one is mine'?"

"Yeah. I improvised. You're welcome." He briskly rubbed his stubbled blond hair. "Look, we've got to get you out of sight. We're going in there." He let go of Livvy and pointed again.

"*You're* going in there. I'm going back to the front gate." Livvy turned on her heel.

"They'll have that covered! They'll grab you, and then you'll appreciate my gentle touch."

Livvy waved over her shoulder.

Tobin raised his voice in a hiss. "And that guy—Gant?"

Livvy paused.

"He's got a pretty bad track record when it comes to women."

Livvy turned.

"Trust me. There's no turning back. I'll find a place to hide you until they put down the riot."

No turning back. Riot.

"We don't have time for a cost-benefit analysis," Tobin hissed.

Somewhere a man screamed. A long, drawn-out, inarticulate scream.

Livvy bolted toward Tobin.

He held up a hand and checked the road. "Wait till I go, and stay with me. Keep your head down. We're heading for that door. Although I may have to improvise." He laced the last word with attitude.

He took Livvy by the elbow and broke into a run. Up the drive ten feet, now twenty. A few stairs up to a landing with a door. Tobin tried the knob and grunted.

"Stand back." He pushed Livvy to the corner of the cement platform.

Wham! He kicked the door.

It was so loud! Livvy tucked below metal railing, pulse racing. She was a sitting duck. One glance and anyone could see she didn't belong.

Though the prison reverberated with noise, Livvy could make out several hot spots. Prisoners on the top floor of the cell block facing the chapel quad hollered and banged on windows. Though out of sight up the drive and around the corner, there was clearly a mob in the quad—barring the prison exit.

Wham! The door showed shallow fissure lines but held firm. Again and again Tobin kicked, while Livvy tried to stifle her gender. She smothered her mouth with both hands to keep the shriek lodged in her throat from bursting forth.

"It's reinforced," Tobin said. "C'mon." He tugged her down the short flight of steps, and further up the drive, toward the quad.

"Wait!" Livvy hissed. "Where?"

"C'mon!"

Shouts and sounds of breaking glass carried from the clearing around the corner ahead. Livvy braced and pulled back against Tobin. "What are you doing?"

He turned and grasped her waist. "Improvising!"

He hoisted her above his head. "Grab on!"

Livvy pitched forward, flailing wildly. Tobin lurched a step backward. "Reach!"

Above her head was the balcony of a fire escape. She extended, fingers brushing cold metal. "I can't!"

Tobin shifted, getting her knee on his shoulder. Then the other foot on the other shoulder. "Stand!"

Livvy wavered. If she stood, reached, and missed, she'd take a nosedive on concrete.

"I've got you!" Tobin grasped her legs. Then he hoisted. Livvy held her breath and lurched. She grasped a rail. Tobin gave her foot purchase, and she grabbed hold with her other hand. He pushed up on her heels, and she clambered and hauled herself over the rail to the grated floor of the platform. There was a door. Locked.

No! God, where are you? She tucked her clammy hands into her armpits and choked back tears.

Below, Tobin leapt for the escape's support strut. Then he hand-over-handed to the platform floor, used his feet up the wall, and in less than a minute stood at Livvy's side.

This door yielded with just one kick.

Livvy dashed into an abandoned room. She started breathing better almost immediately, just having four walls around her. *Thank you!*

Tobin scrabbled with debris that littered the floor, piling it in front of the closed door. Then he turned and appraised Livvy. And kicked his pile back away from the door.

"When I leave, shove anything you can in front of the door. Then hunker down, stay away from windows, and don't let anyone in but me."

Any relief she'd felt from making it indoors evaporated. "Where are you going?"

"To get you some clothes."

"I'm only missing a shoe."

Tobin was expressionless. "I'm going to get you prison blues. So no one does a double take."

"No one's doing a single take! I'm staying in here."

He shook his head. "There's no telling how long this thing might last. Or who else will come crawling through here." He turned to leave.

"Wait!" Livvy clutched at the air in front of her. "I don't even know your name. That other prisoner called you Tobin."

"Yeah. Tobin."

"'Kay. Livvy."

"I know. Smitty told me."

"'Kay." Livvy didn't know what to say to keep Tobin from walking out the door. She just knew she didn't want to be alone.

"I'm coming back, Livvy."

"'Kay."

And he was gone.

She stood rooted, trembling and staring at the closed door: so little between her and the rage that burned out there. Throat constricted, she tried to swallow.

The small office had obviously been unused for some time. It was an ancient building—practically caving in. Livvy tugged some debris in front of the door. Part of a doorjamb and huge hunk of plaster. The pile didn't look like it would stop anyone. Slow them down at best.

She sank to the floor in the corner, a wall at each shoulder, clasping and unclasping her hands, trying to get them to stop shaking.

All in all, it had been pretty easy to get into this building. Anybody could.

She drew up her knees, hugging them to her chest. And she listened to the battle outside. The authorities were yelling over loudspeakers, bullhorns: "On your stomach, on your stomach!" Their voices were drowned by the growing syncopated pulse of helicopters. The throbbing crescendoed and sent tremors through the building's frame. Help was right overhead.

I'm in here!

What a difference just a few feet of wood, rebar, and cement made, separating her from help, closing her in.

No duh. It's a prison, genius. She pressed her face into her knees and began to sob.

><del>∞</del><><del>∞</del><

One of the inmates encircling Lucas and his teammates clenched a bat. The guy was totally ripped, a specimen of muscle definition. Fear knotted Lucas's stomach. He didn't think the guy was on the San Quentin team. Lucas had worked hard to get all the inmates' names down and at the very least remembered the faces that had been present for post-game devotionals on the bleachers. He'd never seen this guy before.

Lord, what do these guys want? Please deliver us from this evil!

The inmate jerked his head in the direction of a small modular building next to their huddle. One of the muscled inmates behind Lucas shoved him toward the structure. The other WBC guys were being similarly manhandled.

"What are you doing?" Lucas yelled, straining against the man pushing him. He fought to control his panicked thoughts. He looked to the walls. None of the officers seemed to notice this little skirmish within the madness. Were these inmates friend or foe? Being inside a building, out of the raging prison riot, sounded like a great idea. But so did staying in eyesight of the only visible officials.

Rudy gave one of the goons a two-handed shove to the chest. Another inmate grabbed him in a choke hold and dragged him to the door, which a third kicked in. That answered that. These guys were *not* looking to protect the outsiders. Lucas ducked under the arm of the henchman closest to him. But there wasn't anywhere to go. The crush of men closed off any escape route. The inmate swung Lucas around.

Then belted him.

Oh man! Fist to an eye still streaming from tear gas. Lucas staggered and almost went down. He cocked his elbow to strike back. *Are you kidding me?* he asked himself. *Look at that guy.* The inmate looked bred and built for fighting. *When's the last time I was in a fight? Third grade?*

Lucas lowered his fist. By now Rudy was in the building, and then Sean. The inmate with the bat turned his attention on Lucas. Lucas held up his hands. "Okay. All right. We don't want any trouble."

The five-member remnant of the WBC team regrouped inside what turned out to be a classroom. His muscles taut for fight or flight, Lucas spun to take in the situation. They outnumbered the three inmates that joined them, but others stood sentry outside the door.

Lucas eyed the men in blue. The word *prisoner* had taken on a whole new meaning.

Chapter Eight

With no clock in sight, Livvy measured time in panic attacks. So far Tobin had been gone about three. What if something happened and he wasn't coming back? Maybe he hadn't really planned to.

Why should she trust this guy at all? He was a convict. How easily he talked her into going with him! What a fool—just say you're a friend of Jesus, and Livvy will drop all defenses. Put her life in your hands. Didn't her experience with Wade teach her anything about wolves in sheep's clothing?

What if Tobin *was* coming back—with others? Livvy didn't even want to consider the kinds of crimes the men in here had committed. She dropped her forehead to her knees. *Lord, Lord! What should I do?*

Window blinds blocked the afternoon sun, and dust floated in the dim room. Livvy crawled to the opposite window, which overlooked the large prison yard. She peeked out at bedlam. Hundreds of blue-clad inmates swarmed the open space. There were skirmishes everywhere. The baseball field had been overrun. Clouds of gas billowed from canisters, creating random odd-shaped clearings in the pandemonium.

Livvy brushed the old bubbled pane with her fingertips. Where were Lucas and the team? They would have been right out there in the middle of the chaos! There were no signs of civilians.

A dozen or so correctional officers stood out, scattered through the crowd, identifiable by their dark-green uniforms. Some of the COs seemed to be rounded up and held, on their knees, by clusters of prisoners. Others were struggling—*oh!* A prisoner had a CO by the throat, up against a chain-link fence. Then a gunshot rang out, and for the first time Livvy noticed the gun walk around the top of the outer prison wall. It was lined with guards clad in riot gear, training scoped rifles on the yard. She looked back to the prisoner who'd been choking the guard. He was down, and the CO scaled the fence. Up and over—then a mob of prisoners on the other side pulled him off and into their midst, where he disappeared into a sea of blue. Several sharpshooters stood stock-still, trained on that area of the yard, but they didn't fire into the melee.

What happened to the guard? Livvy bit her lip and fought tears. Men and women like that put their lives on the line every day to protect Livvy and society from those who would prey upon them. Was he dead? *Let him be okay. God, please protect him.*

A flurry of activity at the northern wall caught her attention. A door in the wall stood ajar, rifle barrels protruding, and some correctional officers struggled with inmates in front of it. Livvy squinted. Looked like—yes: COs were fleeing through it. They received cover from the guards on the other side as well as the perimeter wall above them.

Go, go! An inmate tried to grab a CO, and a gunner shot at the ground between them. Livvy held her breath. Following each metallic crack, a cloud of dust and concrete chips erupted. Several inmates dove to the ground, clutching at places where they'd clearly been hit by flying debris.

Run, guys, run! Maybe the softball team had long since evacuated through there? A flicker of hope ignited in her chest. Somehow it would be easier to bear hiding through this uprising if she knew that Lucas and the team were safely out of the prison.

A police helicopter hovered across the yard, just outside the prison's western wall. In a larger orbit circled at least two network TV helicopters. How bizarre. Livvy belonged on the other side of this news. Tuning in with horrified curiosity.

Oh no. Grace! Their parents! Did they know about the riot yet? Maybe all this would be over before they had to know. They'd be panicked.

Livvy sank to the floor. What had the information officer at the visitor entrance said? There were currently more than five thousand inmates in San Quentin. Were they *all* loose? Livvy's stomach swirled with something the opposite of nausea. Quicksand sucked her down. The enormity of the crisis crushed her, suffocated her.

Could they be dead? Lucas? Rudy? Joan? Surely not. This riot had nothing to do with them. They didn't belong in the middle of whatever it was.

But they were. Smack in the middle.

And she already knew—other people's choices could suck you into a nightmare. Make you a party to madness.

A splintering crash shook Livvy's haven. She reached for a two-by-four among the debris. Someone was in the building.

Tobin crouched behind a dumpster, watching. A handful of inmates herded two COs, Dale Peak, and the remaining civilians from the chapel toward the old library.

Don't be a hero. You got the girl out of their hands.

Still ... the woman in the group was crying. She reminded Tobin of his aunt Lydia. He ground his teeth. Nothing he could do. He should get back to Livvy. Shouldn't leave her unprotected.

These guys are just a negotiating tool. They'll be all right.

Yeah. His gut wasn't buying it. Still, the head ruled. He couldn't afford to get mixed up in stuff. The best prison time was the least prison time. That meant doing your time clean. You didn't get involved in gang activity or prison politics. Kept your hands clean and head down and didn't give inmate or CO reason to take notice of you.

Best he could do now was watch and learn. He counted four civilians, the chaplain, two COs, and six inmates—three of whom carried correctional Motorola radios.

Sure enough, the inmates busted the library door and hustled their captives inside. Now they had hostages.

Tobin took a deep breath. This thing wasn't going to blow over quickly.

The building's aged floorboards conveyed the approach of intruders. At least two hushed voices carried through gaping joints and sagging joists.

In addition to the door Livvy'd come through, there was an internal door, presumably leading to a hall, stairs, other offices. Perhaps to a better hiding place? A nook. A crawl space.

Should she open the door? Could she? It might be locked or stuck. It would creak and give her away. Or she'd open it up right in the faces of a whole chain gang.

She should go back out the way she came. And cower on the fire escape. Drop to the pavement if she needed to, or retreat back inside.

Hefting her two-by-four, Livvy rose to a crouch. A sharp crack and strangled curse rang out right on the other side of the interior door. The hair on the back of her neck stood up, her throat constricted. *Jesus, help me!*

She crept to the wall behind the door. The handle turned—

looked like a full rotation—but the door stuck.

Thump! A shoulder thrown against it.

She had to take down at least the first guy. *No hesitation, girl. Swing hard.* Then there was no telling if surprise would give her enough time to whack a second guy. If there were three or more, she didn't stand a chance.

Thump! The door jumped open a foot. Behind it, Livvy held her breath, plank cocked like a bat in her sweaty hands.

C'mon in.

Or leave. That would be great. Leave.

The door swung further, almost squishing Livvy behind it. The arc complete, it began to close. There was definitely someone in the room with her.

Now, now, now! Livvy brought the two-by-four around with all her strength. *Slam!* It struck the edge of the door, the impact jolting up Livvy's arms and into her shoulders.

"*Yiii!*" a male screamed.

Livvy staggered, stinging from the blow. *Stupid!* She pivoted, following through with the board so that all the energy went around and up, up again.

A man slammed into her, pinning her to the wall, dark hair in her face. He bellowed, gripped her raised wrist, and spun her facing the wall. With hand wrenched behind her back, Livvy screamed. The two-by-four crashed to the floor and the man kicked it away. Livvy strained on tiptoe to relieve the torque on her shoulder.

Tears sprang to her eyes. Pain and terror. "Please don't hurt me!" left her mouth before her mind formed thought. "Please, please!"

"Stop! Let her go!" Another man urged.

Her captor released her arm.

Livvy spun. Smitty! The other man in the room was Smitty.

The man who'd disarmed her wore an olive and khaki

correctional officer's uniform. "You Livvy?" the CO asked. "Did I hurt you?"

Livvy rubbed her shoulder, then found her voice. "Not permanently. Smitty?"

"Hey, little lady. You picked a bad day to come to the Q. You okay?"

Livvy nodded.

"This here's Miles Navarrette, one of the good guys. We ran into Tobin. He told us where you were." Smitty held out a bundle in his arms. "We got some dress blues for both of you to blend in."

The CO didn't hesitate. He dropped his equipment belt with a rattling thud and ripped open his shirt, buttons flying. He had a blue shirt on before Livvy acknowledged Smitty's offering.

"Look, I appreciate the gesture, but I'll wear my own clothes, thanks."

"These'll fit." Smitty sorted out a white turtleneck, blue shirt, and jeans. "They'll be a little baggy, but, uh, that's probably a good thing."

"Look—no one's going to believe I'm a guy." Livvy hugged her folded arms.

"They will." Officer Navarrette finished buttoning his shirt and unzipped his pants. "You'd be surprised. This is so tore up most cell warriors won't look at you twice. You just need camouflage."

This is nuts! Livvy pivoted away from him as he whipped pants off and on.

"We won't look," Smitty said. "And you can put the turtleneck right on over that little shirt you got under your sweater."

"Camisole," the officer interjected.

"I'm not going to go outside!" Livvy said. "I'm staying right here."

A sharp creak made her jump. Whoever was in the hallway, on the other side of the thin wall, would certainly have heard her voice. Her female voice.

She grabbed the clothing from Smitty's outstretched hands and clasped it to her chest.

Officer Navarrette grasped the two-by-four as the door creaked opened. Smitty faced the entry, and Livvy read the threat level in his expression. The tension around his eyes eased. "Tobin."

Tobin eased the door closed. "Aren't you changed yet?" he asked Livvy. "Got you these." He handed her a knit cap and some tennis shoes. "C'mon. Let's get a move on." He stared at her, impassive, as if she was just going to strip in front of him.

"No."

Navarrette and Smitty looked to Tobin. Tobin looked disgusted. "I'm trying to save your lily-white skin here, diva. You mind not adding to the problems we already face?"

Livvy felt her cheeks flush. "You may be an alpha dog, but throwing me over your shoulder like a caveman doesn't suspend my ability to make my own decisions."

The CO crossed his arms and rocked back on his heels. Livvy wasn't sure, but she thought that out of the corner of her eye she saw him grin.

"Okay," Smitty held up his palms. "This is all pretty fast and crazy. Livvy, it's okay. Nobody's bullying you."

Tobin shot him a look of disgust. He briskly rubbed his crew cut, blond hairs springing back into place. "Nobody's coddling you either. You can be a prima donna on your own turf. This is ours. I suggest you trust us to help you."

Livvy clenched a fist, digging a nail into her palm. She remembered how clearly the green-clad officers stood out in the sea of blue on the yard. She nodded.

Smitty and Navarrette looked relieved; Tobin inscrutable. As one, the three turned their backs and moved away.

"Hear you executed pretty quick in the chapel, Tobin," Navarrette said.

"Yeah, you shoulda seen him." Smitty's voice. "Almost like he knew it was going to happen."

Silence. Livvy looked over as she buttoned her shirt.

"You know what I mean," Smitty said.

"I told you to stay home today, 'Rette," Tobin said.

"I've never faked a sick day in my life. I'm gonna start now, because you had a 'feeling'?"

"It was more than a feeling. Gant's been off. Expectant."

Another long pause.

"That was real quick thinking," the CO repeated. "But you're lucky a sniper didn't vaporize your cerebellum while you were running off with her."

"There was no way I was gonna let him ..." Tobin's voice dropped. Livvy missed what he said.

"Hey—did you guys see anyone from my church out there?" she asked. "We have a softball team here too."

Shuffling of feet and three noes.

"But the worship team might have made it out, right? They were headed for that door in the back of the chapel. They could've gotten out and to the east gate, right?"

"Livvy, we went around the back side of the chapel. Did you see any exits?" Tobin asked.

She shook her head, though the men were still not looking her way. Good. They didn't see her wince. She took a slow, steadying breath and blew it out gently. No good—blinking rapidly she held her breath to hold in tears.

"That door leads to a hallway," Tobin continued. "The only way out of the chapel is through the front door."

"Or the window," Smitty added.

Livvy stepped into someone else's jeans. Some man's, a convict's. Hands shaking, she could barely zip. "So, then, they were all captured by that group of prisoners?" *What was happening to them? What would the inmates do to Joan?*

Silence.

"I'm finished."

The men turned, but only Tobin faced her. "I'm afraid so."

"What will happen to them?" Livvy whispered, clutching a white sneaker.

"Hard to say," Tobin said.

"They probably won't be hurt," Officer Navarrette said. "Some prisoners will gun for COs. But civvies—civilians—are mostly leveraged as hostages."

"Hostages? For what?" She felt dizzy, knees weak.

"Negotiation."

"The prison told us they won't negotiate for us." Was it just an hour since she'd signed that paper? Two? If only she could warn that Livvy and the group that stood reassuring her.

"That's mostly accurate. But the eleven o'clock news is a powerful motivator for the warden to make things happen."

"What about that guy?" Livvy looked to Tobin. "Gant. Will he hurt Joan?"

"No." Tobin didn't hesitate, didn't blink. "He won't."

How she wanted to believe him. "How can you be sure?"

Smitty cleared his throat. "He's kinda got a type, you know?"

"A type?"

"You don't know Gant?" Navarrette looked incredulous. "Don't you watch the news? His case was all over it about eight to ten years ago. It still comes up all the time."

Livvy shook her head slowly, a new nameless apprehension growing in response to Navarrette's words and Smitty's awkward shuffling. "I was pretty sheltered. And on the road a lot. What about him?"

"He makes Hannibal Lecter look like a Boy Scout, that's what."

"You know who Hannibal Lecter is?" Smitty asked Livvy.

Apprehension birthed dread. "I minored in film. I did a term paper on the use of symbolism in *Silence of the Lambs*." She flinched. *Nice, college girl. Be all elitist in the face of your rescuers.*

"Don't worry about Gant," Tobin said. He swept the beanie off the floor and tugged it over Livvy's head. "Tuck in your hair."

Livvy did, mind racing. "Tell me about Gant."

"You can Google him when you get home," Tobin said.

Livvy raised her eyebrows. "You know about Google?"

"Please. We live in a prison, not on Mars." Tobin twirled his finger, indicating that Livvy should turn a 360. "Good thing your hair's so short." He dug in his pocket. "Take off your makeup." He handed her a plastic container of petroleum jelly.

"How did you think of that?" Livvy marveled.

The CO tossed her his uniform shirt. "Use this."

"Where'd you guys get all these clothes?" Livvy asked. "They're not your sizes."

Head down, wiping her eyelid clean, Livvy got that sense— everyone was looking at her funny. "What?"

"Borrowed them," Smitty said.

"They were just laying around." Navarrette's voice got gravelly.

Livvy looked up in time to see Tobin shake his head at the CO.

"Whose are they?" She pressed.

"Don't worry about it. The inmates issued these won't be needing them anymore," Officer Navarrette said. Livvy peered at him. He still wore his officer's boots. Above them, the cuff of his jeans was spattered with blood.

Livvy shook her head. *No. No way.* She was not wearing the clothes of a dead guy. Without warning her eyes burned and vision blurred. "I want to go home," she whispered. Like a child. Like a little baby.

The three men stood stiffly, hands in pockets, while Livvy wept. Like a child. Like a little baby.

Chapter Nine

Lucas wished he could ice his eye.

If you're going to wish for something, why don't you wish yourself outta here? What was it his mom used to say? "If wishes were horses, beggars would ride." Except she'd often add a "mister" to the end. Well, this beggar would ride on out of this mess, *mister*.

"What do you want with us?" Lucas asked an inmate, not sure he could take a grim answer. In addition to an *18* on his neck, which this bunch all had, the inmate also sported an *88* on the opposite side of his throat.

"Whatever your hide will get us," 88 answered with barely any inflection and no facial movement.

Well, that was a punch to the gut. Lucas crossed his arms over his chest to steady his hands.

Rudy sighed. "Lovely."

Sean sank into a chair. Dave and Jim followed suit. Rudy remained standing, staring down the inmate in front of him, a stocky guy with one long eyebrow. Rudy was big, with a colorful past. He could probably take one of the inmates. But not three. And honestly, Lucas didn't really know if the new Rudy would engage in a fight.

"Look," Lucas said, "this is a waste of time. The prison doesn't negotiate for hostages. It says so on the release we had to sign. You're not going to get anything for us."

One of the inmates snorted. Number 88 glared. "You let us worry about that."

"Sorry. I'm worried about it." Rudy spoke into Unibrow's face.

"Sit down," Unibrow replied. He eyed Rudy with something Lucas had seen before. Challenge. He was baiting Rudy.

Oh, Lord—be in this. Fight this battle for us. Lucas took a seat. *C'mon, Rudy, don't bite.* He tried not to play out what could happen if Rudy engaged.

Rudy glanced his way, and, with a narrowing of his eyes, he too lowered himself into a chair.

Lucas caught Sean's attention. Bloodshot and red-rimmed, Sean's eyes must've been a mirror of his own. "How're you doing, buddy?" Lucas asked him.

Sean shrugged. "What now?"

How am I supposed to know? Lucas thought again, fighting the irritation born of powerlessness. "Now we wait."

He dropped his head, shutting out the scene with a close of the eyes. *Lord, help the authorities put this conflict down quickly.*

Maybe the cops would bust through that door before long. The group would be reunited with the rest of the team and the chapel singers.

Lucas imagined what he'd say to Livvy. He clung to the hope that the chapel team had made it out. What kind of details would she get on the outside about the riot? Chances were the authorities weren't exactly issuing press releases right now. Livvy, Joan, and the guys were probably in some waiting room somewhere, wondering what the team's status was, wishing for updates. They'd probably called the church—if they were permitted to—to get a prayer tree started.

Doubt knocked on his ribs. What if she hadn't made it out?

What if she were being held somewhere just like him? Was she worried about him? Did she blame him for dragging her here?

What if she was already dead?

He snapped his head up and eyes open. No. She was alive and okay. He'd see her when this outrage ended—maybe just an hour or so.

Can't believe my biggest concern this morning was getting to sit next to her in the van.

Jesus said that no man would know the day of his return. That he'd come like a thief in the night. This wasn't the second coming, but it sure was a wake-up call. There was no use storing up anything in this life that Lucas couldn't take into the next. Every day was a gift. The heck with decorum, propriety, and all that: as soon as he got the chance, he was going to ask Livvy out. Make sure she knew his feelings for her were more than pastoral.

Rudy was studying him. Lucas raised an eyebrow.

"You're thinking about her, aren't you?" Rudy asked real soft.

Lucas could have asked who Rudy meant. But that was so yesterday. "Yeah."

Rudy nodded. "Me too. Don't worry. She's probably okay."

"Yeah."

Funny. Rudy had meant to be encouraging. Instead Lucas felt doubt rap again. *Probably?*

Tobin stole a sidelong glance at Livvy. She'd stopped crying a while ago, thankfully. Man, was that hard to watch. She was such a tiny little thing, especially sitting between Navarrette and Smitty.

"With any luck, you won't even need your disguise," Smitty told her. "We'll just hang out in here 'til everything blows over."

The four remained hunkered down in building twenty-two. Without warning, a chunk of plaster fell off the wall and exploded into powder when it hit the floor.

"The reports about San Quentin falling apart sure are right on," Livvy said.

"They built this building before Lincoln was elected president," Smitty said.

"Great. And this is our safe place?" Livvy muttered.

"You got someplace else in mind?" Tobin asked. Not that he had a problem with the attitude, exactly. He just wanted her to look at him. She did, searchingly. Dang. There was something wide open about her face. He thought about Gant, the butcher, touching that face, and his muscles tensed involuntarily. *Not on my watch.*

He turned to Navarrette. "Whadda ya got?"

The CO monitored the traffic on his radio. "I haven't been able to get a sit rep—nothing but a busy signal since it all went down. Each and every imbecile that ganked a unit is broadcasting, tying up the whole network. Can't reach Master Control or the ERT."

"Emergency Response Team," Smitty whispered to Livvy.

"Of course the battery's almost dead." Navarrette swore under his breath and shoved the radio aside. He started removing stuff from his duty belt and stashing things in his inmate clothes. A wad of keys. Silver whistle. Handcuffs. "Here." He held out a white canister to Livvy. "You hold onto this. It's OC spray. Just in case."

"OC spray?" Livvy rolled the can over.

"Pepper spray," Tobin said, watching her reaction.

Livvy bounced it lightly in her hand. "Oh. Mine is in a purple can."

Tobin wouldn't have figured her for a pepper spray carrier. She wasn't urban enough. Course, she was tiny.

Livvy shoved the spray deep into her jeans pocket. "Thank you, Officer Navarrette."

"The 'officer' isn't necessary, ma'am. It just puts a target on my back," Navarrette said.

"Okay." Livvy paused for a second. "How long have you been a guard here, Miles?" she asked.

Tobin mouthed "Miles?" to Smitty, who snickered.

"I don't actually 'guard,'" Miles answered, glaring at Tobin. "I'm assigned to the ISU—Investigative Services Unit."

"What's that?"

"We monitor gang activity, investigate crime scenes, combat in-prison drug trafficking. Basically anything that affects institutional security."

Tobin snorted. "How's that going for you today, 'Rette?"

Navarrette's nostrils flared. "Shut up and color, convict. We've been monitoring. You didn't give us anything to go on but your gut."

At least I gave you that *to go on. I stuck my neck out for you.* "The signs were all there, man." Tobin's voice rose. "Guys stockpiling food, low turnout for assignments and meals."

"Did you expect a lockdown based on that?"

"I don't know what I expected—for you to do your job, maybe. Least you could've done was keep out civilians."

Navarrette rose to his feet and stood over Tobin. "You're on thin ice. Think you can address me like that because I'm wearing your uniform? Think you're ready to try on mine?"

Tobin kept his butt on the floor. He hadn't kept a clean record in the Q this long by being baited toe-to-toe by anyone. Much less a CO. Still, Navarrette would hear him. "All right then. Act like a CO and get her out of here."

Navarrette narrowed his eyes. "At-ease the attitude, Tobin. I need to determine what's at play here—what turned this chicken farm into a total snafu. Things have been reasonably quiet between the gangs and between the races. I can't figure it—I'm dying to know what set this off."

"Bad choice of words, man," Smitty muttered.

Navarrette shot him a black look. "The scale of it—it doesn't make sense. Everything went sidewise in the yards and the gym at the same time. A coordinated guard grab." He walked to the window. "That takes joint command of various factions. And lots of silence."

"How come ..." Livvy squirmed, directing her question somewhere toward Navarrette's shoulder. "I mean—why didn't you guys just shoot people? Only the rioting ones, I mean."

Right. Just shoot the inmates. *There you go—if 'Rette's comment didn't clarify things enough, that'll help you remember your worth around here.*

Navarrette nodded at Livvy. "Logical question. I don't know if you've noticed, but COs don't carry guns among prisoners. The guys that do—on the wall, gun rails, and in special Ops—will drop an inmate if they can stop imminent harm or an escape, stuff like that. Our marksmen can turn a brain into pink mist from far, far away."

Livvy flinched.

Was that necessary? Tobin kept the thought to himself but rolled his eyes at Navarrette.

"But once we have multiple hostages and multiple sites—then it's up to command to order an armed assault." Navarrette cast a glare at the TV helicopter. "Those vultures hovering, filming every last move, don't help the situation."

Tobin studied the yard. "Looks like they've moved all the COs. Maybe to the gym?"

"Fabulous," Navarrette said, his face dark, sour.

Tobin wondered where Navarrette had been when the riot started. Must be eating the guy up—his colleagues, many of them his friends, were experiencing only-God-knew-what out there. And now what? Should the guy just keep his head down? Try to get civilians out? Try to reestablish order?

"How long do these things last?" Livvy asked.

"Hard saying," Navarrette answered. "Can last an hour or two, longer. The longest one, in England, lasted twenty-five days."

She sucked in a sharp breath and her face blanched.

"Really? You had to tell her that?" Tobin asked. "What's wrong with you?"

Livvy's voice fell. "Well, the last time there was a riot of this scale at San Quentin, what happened?"

All three men looked at her.

"There has never been a riot of this scale at San Quentin," Tobin stated levelly.

"In a hundred and fifty years?" Livvy shook her head. "I mean, obviously I knew this was a big deal ..."

Tobin raised a single brow. Livvy fell silent, but he could swear she was trembling.

Even in the shuttered room it was clear that daylight was fading. What would happen when night fell? And what was going on with the others?

For the millionth time, Livvy closed her eyes and prayed by name for all the team members she could remember, then by face. Then for any other hostages—correctional officers, staff, volunteers. And everyone outside the prison, making decisions. And worrying. And everyone in the prison who was scared.

Or hungry. Her stomach grumbled.

No way was she going to complain about being hungry. But were the others being fed? Who controlled the dining facilities?

The creaky old building was drafty. The prevailing wind gusted right through the thin walls. It smelled less like the sea now. It smelled a bit like charcoal. Was that the kitchen? Livvy's stomach complained again.

Tobin rose. "Stay here a minute." He left the room.

A minute? It was beginning to look like she'd be there into the night. And this building would be *dark*. Would she feel safer between Lucas and Rudy somewhere instead of here, even if inmates were guarding rather than protecting?

Smitty and Miles stood. And something unspoken shifted in their room. Fear snaked back into Livvy's muscles. Tobin burst through the door, and Livvy knew before the word left his mouth: *fire*.

Smoke poured in behind him. Livvy lunged for the fire escape.

"No!" Tobin shouted.

But Livvy flung the door open, strewing the security pile she'd built across the floor like so much rubbish.

Smoke billowed up through the fire escape platform. Livvy took a tentative step onto the grill. Below, a cadre of a dozen or so men waved torches—no, lit mops!—and shoved them into the building through broken windows.

Tobin pulled her inside and slammed the door.

"We're trapped!" Livvy screamed. Couldn't go out either door. *Is this payback? For Wade?*

Tobin shook his head and picked up the two-by-four. Like déjà vu all over again, he broke a window on the yard side of the building. He leaned out, gesturing and calling back over his shoulder to Smitty and Miles. In a blink, Smitty swung out the window and disappeared.

It was becoming difficult to see from the center of the room. The acrid stench of burning flesh filled Livvy's nostrils. *No*. Not burning flesh. She shook her head against the mental image of Wade, wide-eyed, a flaming lighter clenched in his fist. *No!* Not this time.

Tobin looked back and grabbed Livvy, then tugged her to the window. Eyes streaming, she bent over the sill.

Tobin was talking to her: "See? The pipes run all up and down the outside of the building. Just make your way slowly. Follow Smitty."

There was Smitty, ten feet down and a couple yards over, standing on rusty pipes, holding rusty pipes. The red brick wall was latticed with pipes running this way and that.

What? Alarm jolted memories from her mind. They wanted her to crawl out the window? It was at least three stories high, given the slope the building sat on. The prison yard waited below, still overrun with running, yelling, and fighting inmates. Livvy's knees buckled. Which was the frying pan, and which the fire?

She shook her head. "Can't!" Then she was gripped with a spasm of coughs as the room behind them filled with smoke.

"I'll be right behind you. Smitty's in front." Tobin was lifting, folding her. Her heart hammered as she realized he was going to shove her out the window.

"I can't!" Livvy croaked, grabbing at the frame.

Miles stood behind Tobin, sucking clean air the best he could. He was a bigger guy than Smitty or Tobin. She realized he was waiting to be the last to test the old, rusty pipes. And she had to leave before either man would.

She could not let another man burn.

Livvy nodded vehemently at Tobin, and he released his grip. She moved her limbs, just like someone who was climbing out a window onto a series of pipes would. A few moments later, she clung to the side of the building. A burning building. In San Quentin maximum security correctional facility. For men. Above thousands of rioting prisoners.

Livvy began to laugh.

It started as a giggle, as she stood, balls of her feet on pipe, clutching another pipe at chest height, shaking. *All I wanted was to get close to Lucas!* The laughter burst forth then, and it was a good thing no one could hear her up there because she was supposed to be a guy. That made her laugh even harder. Giddy, her head light, she imagined how she must look from below in those ridiculous clothes.

Smoke and dust from the rusty pipes burned her nose, eyes, and throat. The laughter morphed into a coughing fit. Tobin, up and to her left, looked alarmed. Livvy wiped her streaming eyes and nose on her sleeve. Well, someone's sleeve. Then she crossed her eyes at Tobin and stuck out her tongue. Still chuckling, she negotiated her way down.

When her feet reached the height of the prisoners in the yard, Livvy stopped laughing. Even in the midst of bedlam, four people crawling down the side of a building got people's attention. Hundreds of faces looked at her. Men, men, men, all of them. Convicted felon each one.

Oh, God help me! I can't do this! Livvy turned, nose to brick. The hands gripping pipe wouldn't release.

Smitty was down there somewhere. But she didn't dare look again. How could she meet any man's eye and not be a woman looking back at him? She was going to be torn apart like a lamb among lions. There wouldn't be enough of her to go around.

Her hands and feet would not move.

Then Tobin was at her side. "You're doing great."

"I can't go down there."

"Well, you can't stay here." Then Tobin was gone.

No—he wasn't gone. He was on the ground, tugging at her heel. So, okay. She did it. Moved that heel and the rest until she dropped to the ground.

"All right!" Men all around her cheered and clapped her on the back. Hard.

Man-up, Liv.

Smitty was there, and Tobin, and then Miles. Her corps of protectors. Or, in the case of Navarrette, fellow protectee.

Livvy was a shrimp in a blue sea. At least that made it easier to avoid eye contact. She had no idea where they were headed next. She just focused on squeezing through the melee, following Tobin's shirt. Out of the corner of her eye, she observed men—

how they carried themselves, jostling, strutting. The chest-out saunter wasn't going to work for her. Instead she tucked her hands under her armpits like they were cold. Not a particularly feminine gesture.

Her mouth was dry with fear. Surely, any moment someone would spot her. Surely someone would notice that she was built all wrong for San Quentin yard.

Hillary Swank, in *Boys Don't Cry*—she played a convincing guy. And Julia Roberts in that scene in *Sleeping with the Enemy*. Gwyneth Paltrow, *Shakespeare in Love*. Katherine Hepburn, *Sylvia Scarlett*.

Livvy'd even had her own breeches role—the pants part of Octavian in *Der Rosenkavalier*. Of course, she'd had a costume department, makeup, hair pieces ...

Shut up, Livvy.

Imogen Stubbs, *Twelfth Night*.

Tobin stopped abruptly; Livvy ran into him. He turned, and Livvy looked up. Except he wasn't Tobin. "What're you following me for, little rat?" The inmate glared at her. "Go hide behind someone who cares." He flicked her on the bridge of her nose. Hard. And told her where to take herself and what to do to herself when she got there. Then he was lost in the crowd, and even her false Tobin was gone.

Chapter Ten

Great. They'd started lighting the place on fire. Anger surged. Lucas tasted blood; he'd bitten his tongue. Impotent, he shuffled single-file behind Rudy as their little group was goaded across the recreation yard. He walked on high alert, watching the crowd for crude weapons, for any threat against their group. The yard was still in chaos, though there was less fighting. It almost seemed like a big street party. Minus the music, food, women, and children. *Yeah. Just like.*

Why would inmates burn down their own buildings? For some reason the senselessness and stupidity infuriated him. He'd watched four guys climb out a window of the burning building and scale down the wall. He hoped to God there weren't any more inside—flames had shot out that same window just moments later.

Lucas's shoelaces bit into his skin where 88 had tied them around his wrists. What he thought Lucas would do with free hands, who knew?

"Where are we going?" Lucas asked the inmate keeping pace beside him. The man just grunted. Maybe they were going to be reunited with the rest of the team. Maybe they were heading for the east gate to be released—some deal having been struck. *Don't get your hopes up.*

Lord, I know that you are in charge even though it doesn't look like it. Please give me wisdom and courage. Shelter us, protect us. Lucas whispered scripture under his breath. He drew upon the Psalms: David knew what it was like to be surrounded by enemies.

Ahead of Rudy, Sean stumbled to his knees, and 88 slugged him in the kidney.

Rudy shouldered his way into the fracas and put his body between Sean and his attacker. "Hitting a guy half your size, with his hands tied? You wanna go? Cut me free!"

Lucas froze. Immobile.

What *would* Jesus do? Really, what in the name of all that was holy would he do now? Lucas had no idea. He wanted to pound number 88. Pretty sure that's not what Jesus would do. Also pretty sure that course of action would merely get himself wrecked.

He prayed through gritted teeth, only barely willing.

One of the inmates in their pack pulled Sean to his feet. He was grimacing but breathing.

Dave pushed in. "You okay?"

Sean nodded.

You should do something. You're the leader here.

Was he? Were all bets off when that first inmate took down that first correctional officer? By virtue of being pastor, was Lucas supposed to be mouthpiece and general, nurse and counselor?

Of course he was. *Lord, help me.* He had a good throwing arm and a solid softball swing. Had the gift of teaching. Pretty much knew his Bible inside and out. But seminary hadn't covered this. What if he misplayed things and got his guys hurt? Killed?

Rudy strode ahead of Sean. And Dave filed behind the two. Then Jim. A shove from behind got Lucas moving. Five of them from the team, still together. The rest were who-knew-where, experiencing who-knew-what. Lucas couldn't protect them, and it didn't look like he was going to be able to protect these guys either.

Livvy began to pant. Her legs twitched to break into a sprint. Flee. But she was corralled by a human blockade. Smitty? Miles? None of her men were near. Just strangers upon strangers. *God be with me!* A scream rose in her throat. She swallowed it, and it hammered behind her ribs: *run, run, run.*

Taut with effort to keep from flying apart, she stumbled along whichever path of least resistance opened up. Miles said she just needed to blend into the crowd, and so she did. She would simply walk and walk with her head down until she toppled over. Twilight was just falling. But at six-to-twelve inches shorter than everyone else, Livvy paced in a darker reality.

Were Tobin and the others looking for her? What an impossible task. At least here in the yard. Where could they find one another more easily? Where would they think she'd go?

The east gate.

The thought lifted her heart a millimeter. Maybe the prisoners didn't hold the entrance any more. Maybe she could get through somehow. Maybe the police were storming the gate right now.

At least the setting sun made it easy to find east. Livvy spun and set out with new purpose. Her foot met resistance, soft, but unyielding enough to send her headlong.

Ouff—her torso landed on something, but chin hit pavement. *Owwwch!* She pushed herself up, half sitting on the thing that tripped her. A body. It was a dead body. Definitely dead. Very dead.

Livvy scrambled, scuttling back and off the inmate, knocking into men. A strangled cry erupted from deep in her chest.

"Hey, watch it!" Someone shoved her from behind.

Someone else laughed. "Did you hear'm scream? Like a little girl. Hey, little girl, come over here!" Laughter. "C'mon sweetheart, you can be my girlfriend." Kissy noises.

Livvy ducked and barreled through the crowd, east-ish, leaving hard laughter behind.

Her chin burned. She daubed it with her shirt cuff. Grit, gravel, and bright-red blood. Down the front of her shirt was more blood. Dark blood, sticky, congealed. Dead man's blood. Livvy's stomach heaved. She clapped a hand over her mouth. A dirty, bloody hand. She doubled over, retched.

Then she stumbled on.

Tobin spun in place, peering into the crush of bodies, scanning for Livvy's thin frame. How could he have lost her? How could he possibly let such a valuable charge slip from his fingers? And whose fingers grasped her now?

This is what horror tasted like. Something like an ashtray coated with bile. His wide eyes burned, but he didn't dare blink.

"Where'd she go?" Smitty asked, looking to Tobin instead of into the crowd. As if Tobin knew.

Tobin glared at Smitty. "Be useful, will you?" He turned on Navarrette. "She was just behind me—how'd we get separated?"

"I don't know. One second she was here, the next she was gone."

"She was right in front of you! Why'd you take your eyes off her?" Tobin wanted to throttle him, CO or not.

"Don't you go ballistic on me!" Navarrette flushed, and he stuck his finger in Tobin's face. "You've been smelling too much of your own musk—"

"Hey, there she is!" Smitty started elbowing away through the crowd.

Tobin barreled past Navarrette and scanned the throng of men in Smitty's path. There was one guy with a beanie, about the right build. Tobin slowed to a stop just as Smitty spun him around. The kid's eyes nearly popped from his head, and he went as white as Livvy's hair, but he was definitely a *he*.

"Sorry, man." Smitty backed off the guy.

Tobin needed to pummel something. His gut twisted tighter than a CO's grip on his key ring. Apparently much tighter. Livvy must be terrified. What would she do? Where would she go?

"Tobin." Navarrette lightly backhanded his shoulder. "Check it out."

Tobin followed Navarrette's nod. There was a single-file line of male civvies being corralled through the yard. Given their clothes, they had to be part of Livvy's softball team.

In unspoken agreement, Tobin, Smitty, and 'Rette fell in beside and behind the group. There were five hostages. Tobin had a sudden visceral, intestinal memory of his first moments in San Quentin. These guys were in way over their heads. The big one looked more pissed than scared. But the others looked like they were going to snap.

Tobin caught Navarrette's eye and raised a brow in silent question. 'Rette shrugged with a slight shake of the head. What could they do for the hostages? For now, nothing.

And what could they do for Livvy? How would these guys react if Tobin went up to them and said, "Hey, we were protecting your little female friend, and then we lost her."

Navarrette drew alongside Tobin. "Okay, so two ways this could go down. In the first scenario, someone notices Livvy and grabs her. What's their game?"

"Man, don't you think that's been going through my mind, nonstop?"

"Hold on." Navarrette was a hand-talker. He tee'd a time-out. "Don't go there—I mean what's the play? Where would they take her? One faction would protect her. One faction would use her for leverage."

And one faction would just use her. Tobin couldn't think

straight for the near panic. He'd lived in San Quentin day in and day out with the tension of knowing man's capacity for violence and how little it could take to spark a firestorm. He'd feared for his own safety. But he wasn't a small guy, and he kept out of trouble. He'd learned to live on high alert.

He'd never been this frightened.

Livvy was an innocent. Maybe there were innocent inmates in the prison. But not Tobin. He deserved the penalty for his crimes. Heck, he deserved the penalty for his sins too—but Jesus had inexplicably wiped his slate clean. Not so the State of California.

But Livvy … Tobin wiped the sweat from his palms across his chest.

"In the second scenario," Navarrette continued, "Livvy keeps her head down and continues to pass. Where does she go? What does she do?"

Tobin nodded. He chewed his lower lip.

"Smitty," he hissed. "You stay with these guys and see where they're taken. 'Rette, I think she'd go to the east gate; she knows that's the only way in and out. Go watch for her. Let's meet up at the canteen."

"Where are you going?" Navarrette asked.

"Gonna check out a theory."

Livvy inched up to the brick wall—the one she'd climbed down. Smoke poured from the high windows and roof, but the entire side facing the yard was a big, red, nonflammable brick wall. At the south end was a ramp, leading from the lower prison yard up to the level of the main prison complex, including the chapel, the quad, and the east gate.

Livvy was midway up the ramp when the crowd roared in a wave from west to east. Some of the men around her high-fived.

Some looked stricken.

"What is it?" she whispered to a grizzled man not much taller than she was.

"West Block just fell. Now we got that, the gym, and the yards."

We? The man didn't look very happy for someone with newly acquired territory. He let out a long breath and scritched his nubby chin. "Remember how Attica ended."

It was a reminder, not a question.

"No! I don't. How?" Livvy strained to keep her voice low.

The inmate looked her over. "Man, don't you belong in juvie? They trying you kids younger and younger. You ain't even shavin' yet."

Livvy ducked her head and rubbed her chin.

"Don't matter." The man was looking west again. "It'll end how it ends."

Men surged up the ramp yelling: "North Block, North Block!"

"Boneheads. They ain't thinking about what they unleashing." The old-timer flattened himself against the cement wall. Livvy was borne with the tide, up the ramp.

North Block housed part of death row. And it was right next to the AC—the Adjustment Center. Those were the ones without chapel privileges. The troublemakers.

Despair shook Livvy: Was there more trouble to be made than this?

Oh lovely. These were *definitely* nicer digs than a classroom with walls and chairs. Lucas paced, as much as he could, within the confines of a ten-by-fifteen chain-link cage. It was basically a kennel in a yard full of kennels between two buildings. No sign of the rest of the team, and—*shocking*—not a glimpse of the east gate.

It was starting to get dark. And if anything, it looked like the riot was gaining steam instead of waning. Prisoners in the enclosure between the buildings were enthusiastically building fires and constructing makeshift scaffolding to reach the external catwalks lining the cellblocks. Why were there no guards on the catwalks? Where had they all gone? Hopefully the cell blocks themselves were locked down. Certainly *some* of the prisoners were still incarcerated, right?

Lucas stood over his men, close to Sean in particular. He tried to pray. Words failed him. A snarling, cursing fight broke out some ten feet from their cage. Gratitude for the fencing that kept them isolated from the inmates coursed through him.

But what were they being kept *for*? Was there a plan for the WBC men? For any of this? If the prison officials didn't negotiate for hostages, what was to happen to them when demands weren't met?

Words still failed him. So he offered up even his wordlessness: *the Spirit helps us in our weakness. We do not know what we ought to pray for, but the Spirit himself intercedes for us through wordless groans*, Romans 8:26.

Chapter Eleven

A phalanx of prisoners led the charge to take down North Block. They were on a mission. More than once, Livvy caught a glimpse of Gant in the pack. A pile of mattresses blazed in front of a double door. The elevated catwalk encircling the building held no officers. Inmates stacked picnic tables, crates, and whatever else they could get their hands on to breach the platform.

Please oh please get me out of here. Livvy didn't recognize anything. Where was the east gate?

Scores of inmates steamrolled on, passing North Block. Livvy went with the current. Now she was going the right direction—the burning building she'd fled with Tobin and the others was ahead on the left.

On the right was a long wall linking North Block and the Adjustment Center. The wall's large brightly-hued mural was the first thing of beauty Livvy'd seen since the portrait of Jesus in the chapel. A door at the end of the wall hung open, askew. Behind the wall, an exercise area filled the land between the two cell blocks. The concrete courtyard was crammed with wire pens. Dog runs? For a canine unit?

With a sharp inhalation, Livvy realized they were for prisoners. High-security inmates must have to stay in cages during their yard time. *What have we done to ourselves?*

Livvy was drawn in like a rubbernecker to a train wreck. There were rows upon rows of pens. Fifteen? Twenty? Each was about eight by ten, most doors bearing heavy locks. A bonfire raged in one. The others were empty, except one—a prisoner guarded a single pen. He had a handgun, the first Livvy'd seen since the chapel.

The chapel—what was she doing? She'd gotten sidetracked. The east gate was back out the door she'd just come through. She spun, but something caught her eye. The men in the cage wore civilian clothes. One had really bushy hair and moustache. Livvy peered. *Rudy!*

And when Rudy shifted, she saw Lucas.

An icy tremor ran through her. Lucas! They were alive. They looked unharmed.

What to do?

She was staring. She shouldn't stare. The other inmates in the courtyard were climbing on pens, lighting fires, scrambling for the catwalk on the Adjustment Center. Livvy paced, weaving through clusters of men.

There were five men in the pen, all from the team. So that meant five or six were missing. Plus four from the worship team.

Trembling, chilled, Livvy tried to circle closer. Certainly she was being too obvious. She had a double target on her back— woman and one of *them.* The prisoners' prisoners. *Don't see me!* she projected at the guard.

But she willed Rudy or Lucas to catch her eye. *Look at me, look at me!* The group wasn't entirely unscathed—Lucas had a shiner. But there was no blood visible on any of them. Thank God they were okay. Where were the others? Were they okay somewhere too?

Are they dead?

No—no, they weren't dead. And they weren't going to be dead.

They were all going to be fine. Livvy's lip trembled violently, unconvinced.

She looked again to Lucas and the others. *C'mon, guys.* There were only so many times she could circle without being conspicuous. She coughed. Rudy looked at her for a split second, then shot his gaze to a fistfight outside his cage. C'mon! She coughed again. Nothing.

The beefy inmate with the handgun in his paw flicked her a glance. She weaved in a different direction. Maybe the guys were safer in there—out of the general population? It was walls again—she wanted a barrier between herself and all these running, raging men. Maybe she should "out" herself? Beg to be let in. Snuggle between Lucas and Rudy. What else was she to do? Even if no one spotted her gender, how long before some ape decided she was just the right-sized guy to be a prison wife? She shuddered again.

Lord, Lord! I need wisdom. You promised—promised!—through your brother James, if we ask for wisdom you'll give it! Gimme, please!

Back around she paced, toward the pen. Rudy looked at her again. Bet her size made it less intimidating to meet her eye. She winked. His jaw dropped, and he ducked his head.

Oh come on! Her disguise couldn't be *that* good, could it?

There! A heartbeat later, his chin shot up. He drilled her with his gaze. She gave a micro nod. He elbowed Lucas.

Careful, guys. Subtle.

Lucas met Livvy's eyes, his as big as plates. The chill that had gripped her melted. Slid down her spine. His concern was so naked. *I'm okay,* she thought to him. *Are you okay? Who hurt you?*

What to do? The east gate should be right on the other side of the AC building. But she knew there was only the remotest chance the authorities had regained control of it. She'd have heard it. The stampede of inmates outside this courtyard would reverse direction.

So the only prospect the east gate offered was Tobin. What could Tobin do for her now—even if she found him? Could he keep her safe from gangs of men intent on devouring her?

Livvy did another large loop, digging fingernail into palm. She *wanted* to be with the men. With Lucas. Wanted to run to the cage and pull on that wire fencing.

But her head said that revealing herself was a bad, bad idea.

If she were James Bond, she'd just rescue the WBC guys and that would be that. Of all days to leave her Walther PPK at home.

Where's that wisdom, Lord?

A huge African-American inmate, in a huddle of huge African-American men, gave her an appraising look. Livvy focused on the concrete in front of her feet. The courtyard was strewn with all kinds of rubbish. As her sneaker trod on a slip of paper, Livvy recognized a handwritten word.

The dirty note was long and narrow. It had apparently been rolled up at some point. The word that caught her eye was a name: *Navarrette.* It was a list of names—first initials and last names. Some of the names had either a number one or a two scrawled after them. There was a *one* after *M. Navarrette.*

Not sure why, Livvy slipped the sheet into her pocket. It disturbed her somehow.

She'd come back around to the guarded pen. With an assurance that was steadying, she made her decision. She didn't have the why, and only a fuzzy where, but she knew the who and a new what. She had to find Tobin and show him that note.

Stealing a glance at the men, she pulled a tight smile. *Don't worry about me.* Lucas seemed to search her expression. His was clouded.

Squaring her shoulders, she set out for the door and the east gate.

And locked eyes with Gant, coming through the door in the wall.

Tobin tried to peer through the library windows without looking obvious. Ancient and grimy, they didn't reveal much of the interior. There was movement inside. That meant people. Probably the same group of hostages Tobin had seen earlier. Possibly the same inmates guarding them.

The question was, was Livvy in there? Had someone grabbed her and tossed her in with her people?

On the spectrum of possibilities, that wasn't the worst thing that could happen. She'd be out of sight. No reason Gant would have any idea where she was.

Tobin rubbed his head. He'd prefer the part of the spectrum where Livvy was safely under his own protection. Or out of the prison. *Of course—out of the prison entirely.*

Tobin squinted again. He couldn't see diddly. He needed to know. *Strengthen me*, he prayed. Then squared his shoulders and shoved open the library door.

Whoosh. Tobin ducked just in time to miss a pipe to the jaw.

"Whoa!" he yelled. He faced a wiry guy, about his own age. "Easy man, I don't want any trouble."

"Then get out," the inmate replied. "This space is taken." He flipped the pipe and caught it *smack* in the palm of the same hand.

"No problem. I just wanted to have a look out the far windows—over the yard." Tobin wasn't wild about taking his eyes off the guy, but glanced beyond him into the moderate-sized room. Bookshelves lined the walls, and books covered the few pieces of outdated office furniture.

"You got a hearing problem or just stupid?" the inmate strode into Tobin's personal space. The muscle in his jaw pulsed.

"I heard they've started an assault—coming in over the southwest wall. I just want to see." Tobin avoided inhaling. The guy had bad teeth.

"They're coming in?" A voice from across the room. "You sure?" A couple of people scuffled to the western windows. Meth Mouth turned too. *He's not going to engrave me an invitation.* Tobin shoved into the room.

Two inmates were at the windows, one trying to rub a clear spot on the pane. The hostages sat in a row on the floor along one of the stacks. They were the same people he saw being escorted from the chapel earlier. The woman, three men, and Dale Peak, plus two COs.

No Livvy.

Tobin's gut ratcheted another notch tighter. He hadn't expected to find her. So why did he feel like all the oxygen had been sucked from the room?

The older CO caught Tobin's eye. Lieutenant Knox—he was a shift captain. He had a cut over his eye, but otherwise seemed to be in good shape. Neither officer had his duty belt, but no one was cuffed or tied.

The woman narrowed her eyes. She looked steely, that one. "Where's Livvy?" she asked. "What have you done with her?"

Multiple emotions slammed Tobin, tangling his tongue. Of course—they'd all seen him take Livvy from the chapel. They couldn't know it was a rescue rather than abduction.

"I don't see nothing," said one of the inmates at the window, now a total of three since Meth Mouth had joined them.

Tobin had only a second before their attention returned to him.

"Where's Livvy?" The woman pushed louder.

Tobin hushed her with his hands. "She's okay," he whispered. *I hope.* "I didn't hurt her. I'm looking for her."

"What do you mean, 'looking for her'? She was with you." Boy, the lady was a *lot* like his aunt Lydia.

Knox and the other men followed the exchange. Tobin shot a glance at the three stooges. Meth Mouth was done with the window and coming his way.

"*She* who?" one of the inmates asked.

"Your mama," Tobin called over his shoulder as he bolted from the library.

Out the door he headed right, toward the canteen. Not two strides along, a familiar form caught the corner of his eye. Gant. He stood, back to Tobin, in the doorway to the high-security exercise yard.

Yikes. That was close. Tobin turned his face away. He didn't need Gant interrogating him about Livvy. But—*thank you, God*—it looked like Gant didn't have her either.

Gant's eyes. Restraining venom that swam like a living creature. Though his skin was a canvas of colors and images, only Gant's eyes revealed anything personal.

Heat suffused Livvy's cheeks. Horror almost rendered her motionless. She faltered but kept walking. Gaze averted, she knew she was sunk. He'd not just seen her—he'd seen into her.

He loomed in the threshold of the door. The madness continued to rage around them—prisoners shouting, shoving, fighting, running. But Gant was motionless, and for Livvy, time stood still.

A couple of inmates rushed up behind him in the doorway. "Move your meat!" one snarled. When Gant swiveled his head, the prisoner blanched, backpedaled, and sprinted away.

Livvy couldn't look at Gant. Doing an about-face would call attention to herself. But, just as she believed that drawing attention to herself no longer mattered, she also knew that there was nowhere to turn.

Wait—the other inmate had a gun! Maybe he was allied with some faction. A faction that was calling the shots and controlling the hostages. Would he lock her in with the guys, away from Gant?

Livvy spun, sprinted to the pen, and skidded to a halt in front of the prisoner. "Let me in! I'm one of them!" She shook the locked door. "Let me in!"

The prisoner-guard trained the gun between Livvy's eyes. She whipped off the beanie, her hair springing free. "See! I'm with them!" The gunman lowered his weapon slightly, but kept it aimed at her. His forehead creased, eyes narrowing.

Lucas and the men inside leapt to their feet, their shouts lost among the mayhem. The activity on the outside of the pen came to an abrupt halt.

"Hey—she's a chick!" Someone shouted. A great chorus of catcalls and wolf whistles went up.

"You need to lock me up with those guys." Livvy insisted. "I'm a hostage too."

A lean, shaggy inmate stepped forward and threw up his hands. "Glory hallelujah, Christmas has come early!" He seized Livvy's arm.

"Livvy!" Lucas yelled. He pounded on the mesh. "Get your hands off her!"

Now Lucas was the only source of noise. The courtyard had fallen still and quiet. Shaggy released Livvy and melted back into the crowd.

Gant was behind her. Livvy knew it as surely as she knew her own gender.

Come on prisoner-guard. Assert your claim. Lock me up in there. Pulse racing, nerves rapid-firing—she should be vibrating, projecting an audible keen of terror.

The man lowered his weapon. He gave a curt nod, directed over Livvy's shoulder. Livvy closed her eyes, hope draining from her like the fading daylight.

"We have North Block," Gant said. "We're cutting off the AC, but not pursuing it now. We'll move Bravo Group, like we said."

"Yes sir."

Livvy opened her eyes in time to see the man jerk his head at someone in the sea of prisoners. Three men came forward and stood, arms crossed, in front of the pen.

The armed man turned to Gant, expectant.

"Come with me." Without looking Gant's direction, Livvy knew he spoke to her.

Lucas slid his fingers through the mesh. His eyes glistened, his face a mask of horror.

Is that my expression? Livvy grasped his fingertips. They were flesh against her stone.

"Let her go, Gant." Lucas's voice was gravel. "Don't make things worse for yourself."

"Worse? This is beyond my wildest dreams. And believe me—I have wild dreams." He stared intently at Livvy, lips slightly parted as if panting, one corner of his mouth uplifted.

The prisoner motioned with the gun. "Move."

But how could she move when she was rubber? String. Incapable of bearing her own weight. Maybe she was going to faint. What a kindness a blackout would be.

Oh, Lord, oh, Lord. Save me. Take this from me. Please, God. Tears coursed down her cheeks, dripped from her nose. The inmate wrenched her hand from Lucas's, and she clasped arms around herself. Behind Lucas, the other WBC men were on their feet, mouths agape.

God-fearing women got raped. Were murdered. From the time humans first made the choice to do things their own way, this big ball of a planet pretty much kept spinning, free will generally playing out. Heinous, vicious acts of volition were perpetrated daily, apparently without divine intervention.

Oh, God, oh, God. Save me.

Chapter Twelve

Oh, dear God. Lucas dropped to the ground, pressed forehead to concrete. *Oh, please God.* He couldn't string together a sentence. Just had ugly images flashing through his brain, a word jumble of vile crimes. *Not to her, Lord. Please.*

Had he ever in his whole life asked for anything with this kind of fervor? *Jesus, you sweated blood. Oh please, Jesus, not this.*

It was Lucas's fault Livvy was even here. She didn't want to come. He could have let her off the hook so easily. But the truth was that he wanted time with her. He wanted to get to know her.

Forgive me.

If ever there were a lion's den, Lord, a fiery furnace, this is it. She's your daughter, your beloved. Do not abandon her.

Just that morning, Livvy had pointed out that God had still been sovereign when early Christians were fed to lions. Would he intervene? Where was the balance between the power of prayer and Gant's free will?

Lucas felt a hand on his back. From the weight of it, it would be Rudy's. His brother knelt with him in prayer. Lucas was aware of the proximity of the others. Whispered pleas, fervent petitions.

Take me, God, if that'll make a difference. Let come whatever you will to me. Just please, don't let that sadist hurt her.

Why was she even still in the prison? Where had she been all this time? Wandering free, alone? She'd been wearing inmate clothing. Where was the rest of the chapel group? There were ten other WBC people out there, somewhere beyond this pen. Lucas groaned. Joan was out there.

Lucas rocked back on his feet and stood. Dragged his arm across his streaming eyes. One of the goons posted outside the pen eyed him with something like disinterest or boredom. Lucas's brewing anxiety bubbled over and spat into fury. He rushed the gate and grabbed the metal links.

"What are you looking at, you filthy scum?" He flailed his fists against the wire. If he could get his arm through, he'd throttle that son of—

Rudy pulled him back. Lucas spun, shaking off his friend's hands. Rudy's eyes were full of compassion. Sean's of fear.

Lucas turned back to the gate and kicked and kicked it. "Let us out! Bring her back! Let her go! You *animals!*"

Spent, he fell back and leaned against the side of the cage. Stupid. Pointless.

Here he'd wanted to reach these guys. Show them hope, forgiveness. They just flung it back in his face like so much excrement.

What would Jesus do? Really? How could God love *any* of them? They were barbaric. He'd seen coverage of that Gant guy. Knew what he was. What he was capable of.

Livvy.

Lucas started pounding the fence again, tears streaming from his blinded eyes. He pictured peeling back the steel latticing of the cage and driving the barbs into Gant's throat. His hands ached to grasp the gun that prisoner had and to shove it into Gant's mouth. How did the man still live? How could someone who'd destroyed so many lives still be permitted to draw air—and to destroy more lives?

North Block was huge. It smelled of sweat, urine, and the monster under the bed. Five open tiers of cells stretched above Livvy, cement and iron volleying sound in collusion to disorient and strike fear.

Livvy was beyond fear. She trembled and sobbed, trailing Gant. The armed inmate followed her, nudging her when she faltered.

A woman in North Block was as much a sensation as the bearded lady at the circus. No one called out, however. They stole their glances at Gant.

On the bottom floor, he stopped. Livvy's heart seized. In an office, several huge inmates bearing swastika tattoos jumped to their feet.

Gant addressed one. "You go with Edwards. Move Bravo Group," The man nodded and left with the armed inmate.

"You two, with me." Without so much as a glance toward Livvy, two gorillas fell in behind her.

Gant led the way to the stairs. Even they were barred around the sides and top—a chute leading up and up. And above the ceiling of the highest visible tier, the sixth and final floor was closed off to the rest of the cell block. Death Row, it held condemned prisoners. In its underbelly Livvy ascended. Perhaps to her own execution.

Gant stopped at the fourth floor landing. Livvy thought she would vomit.

"Clear out the tier," Gant said to the thugs. "I want it to myself. Make sure no one comes on—or off," he glanced at Livvy, "until I say. No interruptions."

Gant hadn't yet laid a finger on Livvy. Had hardly even looked at her. One of the musclemen worked the tier, rousting inmates from their open-door cells. And Gant strode forward. Any prisoners in his way got out of it.

A few yards down, Gant paused, half turned: "Come here."

Livvy shrank. She clung to the railing, quaking so violently her teeth clattered.

Gant turned another quarter toward her.

Slinking, she stretched back with her foot. Around and down to the top stair.

Inmates passing her on the tier and down the steps were a blur of irrelevance. Inches she crept. Lifetimes passing.

Without turning his head further, Gant snapped his fingers.

Steel bands pinioned Livvy. The gorilla behind her peeled her from the railing.

"No! No, no, no!" She babbled and shrieked, incoherent even to herself. Gant continued to a cell and stopped. Livvy kicked off the railing, thrashed and clawed at her captor, her screams bouncing back to her from hard, indifferent surfaces.

The thug threw her into the cell and was gone. Gant slid inside and clanged the metal door shut.

Livvy shrank to the back of the tiny cubicle. Wedged herself between the end of the bunk bed and the sink. Gant switched on a fluorescent light, startling shadows into sharp relief.

For the first time, Livvy got a good look at the man. Coiling around and up his neck and covering his head was the tattoo of a serpent. And on each cheek were two sides of the same—the shimmering scaled head of a snake, jaws open, fangs bared. As if Gant's mouth and the snake's were the same.

Gant crouched at Livvy's level, some three feet away. "So ..." he uttered in a low, calm voice. He smiled slowly. Then licked his lips. The tip of his tongue had been split down the middle. Forked. The cell tilted and Livvy gripped the bed.

"Where's your protector? Mighty Tobin. Jesus with skin on."

Livvy shook her head, wiped her nose on her sleeve. "I don't know."

He took that in. Tilted his head. "Wash your face." He nodded at the sink.

She did, keeping her back pressed to the wall, watching Gant as she washed. The water ran black, and the washcloth stained with the transfer of soot and grime.

"There's blood on your shirt." He stood now too.

Livvy nodded.

"What happened?"

"I fell on a dead man."

Gant nodded as if this were an everyday occurrence. "Take it off. Toss it over there." He indicated the corner opposite her, between the wall and a lidless steel toilet.

He watched intently as she unbuttoned the blue chambray shirt. Heat rose to her throat, cheeks. The clean turtleneck underneath was preternaturally white.

"It's Livvy?"

She nodded.

"You are exquisite, Livvy." His exhalation was a long sigh. He took off his own outer shirt. Down to a white tee.

"Where are you from?"

"San Jose."

"Santa Clara County?"

She nodded.

A grin lifted one side of his serpent mouth. "You know, there are pieces of my girls scattered across all fifty-eight counties in California."

Livvy's knees gave out.

Gant squatted on the balls of his feet. Slowly he leaned into a palm, flattened to the floor. Crawled a pace toward her.

Livvy couldn't draw her knees up any tighter. Couldn't be smaller. Couldn't wish herself away.

"Take off your shoes."

She hesitated. At what point did she refuse? A single tear trailed down her cheek. She unlaced a sneaker.

"What's the name of the last man you let between those knees?"

Livvy's head snapped up. Gant raised his brows and nodded toward the shoes.

"I, uh ..." She trembled. "I've never ..."

Gant rolled back onto his heels. "Really." He breathed deeply, nostrils flaring. "Extraordinary. How lovely. You don't come across that much these days. And here you are, in my home." He marveled with a shake of the head. "Shoes." He nodded at her stilled hands.

Livvy was frozen in horror. Already naked before this snake-man.

"Shoes!" he raised his voice.

Livvy jerked into motion.

"Did Tobin get you those clothes?"

She nodded.

"Is he working with anyone else?"

She shook her head. *Liar, liar, pants on fire.*

"I don't know how you got separated, but I'm sure he hasn't given up looking for you." Gant ducked slightly, examining Livvy's expression. "Tobin is ..." He tilted his head, as if listening for the right word. "Steadfast. Not that he'll do either of you any good."

"You know him?" She wanted more Tobin.

Gant flicked his tongue. "Oh I know him. I look forward to talking to him, once this is ... finished." His mouth quirked into something like the smile of a naughty boy.

Then he straightened abruptly. "Wait here." He left the cell.

Livvy was dumbfounded. She crept from behind the bunk. In the middle of the six-by-ten cell she strained, listening. Where had he gone? She tiptoed further. She couldn't see any of the walkway except that in front of the cell. Maybe she could—

Gant filled the doorway. He chuckled at her shriek. She skittered back to her nook. "Here," he held out a comb. "For your hair." He rubbed his bald head. "Don't own one myself."

He remained that way, arm outstretched, comb hanging in the void between them.

Livvy cringed at the thought of being connected to him through the object. Being a comb's length away from him.

"You can take it," Gant said. "Or I can *give* it to you." His voice rasped like glass ground under a heel.

Livvy snatched it. Dragged it through her hair.

"Did you wonder if you'd see me here today?" Gant asked.

Here? "North Block?"

"At San Quentin. Before you came, did you wonder if you'd see me on the grounds somewhere?"

"No." What was he talking about?

Gant reflected. "Didn't even cross your mind?"

"I don't understand. I didn't know you existed."

He started. "Really? You don't know who I am?"

"I'm learning."

Gant stood, strode to the door and back. He appraised her, arms crossed. "You really are a virgin."

Livvy gritted her teeth against a whimper. She would scoot further back—through the wall, into the floor if she could. This is what they meant about your skin crawling. Every cell of her body wanted away from this man.

Gant knelt, upright, on splayed knees. Now just a foot away from her. "I can't believe you're here." He closed his eyes and leaned in, inhaling deeply. "If only we had more time."

He extended a finger, poised, before Livvy's foot. His hand trembled as he held it there for a beat. Then he touched the tip of her big toe. "We'll have to do things a bit differently. Can't be helped."

He seized her foot. Livvy yelped at the abruptness of it, and he looked pleased. He pulled to extend her leg.

Livvy's mind and mouth babbled simultaneously. "Please don't!"

No use.

"Please!"

Everyone begs.

"Don't hurt me."

Right.

"Please!"

This man is unreachable.

Livvy fought, contracting her leg, gripping with her arms. Gant relaxed his grasp, eyes glassy, breath heavy. "Tell me about the man in alpha group—in the cage on the yard. He's your boyfriend?"

"No," she whispered. He was so close. No longer touching her, but breathing into her lungs.

"Liar. I saw the way he looked at you." Gant peeled her hand from her knee. Turned it over and traced the lines on her palm. "Don't lie to me."

"No, he's my pastor. We—I hardly know him."

Gant pegged her with his gaze. Those eyes. Something from the abyss. Searching her. She looked away. He grabbed her chin. "Don't lie to me!"

Livvy whimpered. Surely it was possible to die from fear—her heart ran so fast and chest fluttered with shallow breath. Saturated in a cold sweat, it was not unlike being in the grip of a panic attack, except this was an infinitely more rational emotional response.

He slid his hand behind her neck. Took a handful of hair and pulled her head back. Above her, his garish face seemed something hell born. He flicked his tongue. She gagged. He smiled.

Gant encircled her, encompassed her. He tugged the collar of the turtleneck away from her skin. Bile rose in Livvy's throat as he ran his tongue up the side of her neck. Then he took her earlobe into his mouth.

And bit.

Livvy screamed, pushed. She was pinned. Still he gripped her lobe in his teeth, breath hot in her ear. Twisting, writhing, her hip came against the bedpost. Something dug into her bone. She fumbled and grasped. Then squeezed her eyes shut, held her breath, and blasted Gant in the face with pepper spray.

He roared back, clutching at his face. Livvy leaped up and over him. He grabbed her ankle and she reflexively sprayed his hand. Then slammed his knuckles with the canister.

She was free. Out the cell door, sprinting down the walk. One of Gant's goons loomed large several yards ahead. Between her and the stairs. Gant stumbled out of the cell behind her, and beyond him goon number two came on fast.

How many sprays did the OC canister hold? Could she bypass an impaired thug on the narrow catwalk? What to do?

A moment of clarity: *improvise.*

Livvy snaked through the bars at the edge of the tier. She climbed and swung to a pole that ran up and down all five tiers. With a nauseating slide she was down to the third tier. Easy-peasy. Until she looked down. She was a good thirty feet above concrete. And, like some sick playground game, inmates on all tiers were swinging onto the monkey bars, closing in.

"Livvy!" Someone shouted. It wasn't coming from Gant.

"Over here!"

Gripping tight, Livvy looked over her shoulder. A tier below her, on the opposite wall, was a gun walk. And praise be to God—Tobin waved both arms at her.

But between was empty air—fifteen feet across and ten down.

"Jump!" Tobin cried.

Crazy. No way.

Tobin twined a leg around a bar and stretched toward her. "I'll catch you!"

Yeah right. Coiled razor wire ran along the bottom of the walk.

But the monkeys were closing in. And they were all rabid. Warmth trickled from her ear down the side of her neck. The alternative was no alternative.

She perched, then launched. Eyes and arms wide open.

And Tobin caught her. One hand under her arm, the other with a fistful of shirt. She slammed into the railing, knocked Tobin back to the wall.

Two feet on solid ground. Tobin's arms around her, her face in his chest. "You came, you found me." She clutched him, certain she'd never held tighter to anything in her life.

"Thank you, God. Thank you, God," Tobin muttered over and over into her hair.

They only separated when Gant screamed. A primal sound of fury. Tobin grasped Livvy's hand and pulled her into a run.

Chapter Thirteen

The floor was cold. Livvy's hip and shoulder pressed into concrete. Her arm curled under her head was almost numb.

And it was wonderful.

Tobin lay facing her, just inches away, the two of them crammed under the lower bunk in some cell. With a sheet draped over the end and side of the bed, the cramped space was their safe haven.

Now that she'd caught her breath, she plied Tobin with questions. "How did you find me?"

Tobin grimaced. "Word traveled fast about Gant's 'bridal suite.'"

Livvy cringed. "He said you'd keep looking for me."

Tobin grunted.

"It seemed like he knows you pretty well."

"In a way. He's my cellie."

"Really!"

"*Shh!*" Tobin brought a finger to his lips.

"Do you guys choose your cellmates?"

Tobin snorted. "What do you think? This is prison, not college. Actually, I hold an unofficial record. The longest Gant's kept a cellie."

"Yeah?"

"Two years, three months, and ... four days."

"Wow." Livvy fell silent. How long had Tobin been at San Quentin? How much longer was his sentence?

And what had he done?

"You can ask," Tobin said.

"What?"

"What you want to know—you can ask."

"What makes Gant such a bad cellmate?"

Tobin chuckled. "Chicken." He rolled onto his back. "Gant talks a lot. I don't mean like he's full of hot air. I mean he is a very sick, twisted individual, and he shares his thoughts, desires and fantasies out loud. It's ... toxic."

"He was surprised I didn't know who he was."

"Classic narcissist. He has a huge ego and loves his fame. He thinks everyone is jealous or wants to knock him off his perverted perch. The guy *is* pretty notorious though. He gets fan mail."

"Fan mail!"

"You'd be surprised."

"I'm already surprised. I'm shocked." Livvy fingered her ear. It had stopped bleeding but was pretty torn up.

Tobin faced her. "Did he ... Are you all right? Is it just your ear?" He shook his head. "I don't mean like it's no big deal. I—"

Livvy put her hand on his. "It's okay. I'm okay. The ear is as far as it got."

Tobin was visibly relieved. He shifted, and Livvy realized that they were holding hands. The realization was accompanied by a current that almost took her breath away.

"This is the closest I've been to a woman in four years. Well, a woman that didn't hold a weapon or a syringe." His tone was light, but eyes weighty.

Four years. "That's how long you've been here?"

"Yup."

It was crazy, so unwise, but Livvy couldn't resist. She traced Tobin's jaw with her finger.

"How much longer?"

"It's hard to say."

"That's what Miles said about the riot."

A grin transformed Tobin's face. "That's the way of prison—time is hard to pin down."

"You should smile more often. It's a good look for you."

Tobin arched a brow, smile still playing at the corners of his mouth. "I haven't spent a lot of time considering what looks good on me."

His world was so different than hers. She'd spent a terrifying day experiencing that firsthand. But now it was something between them. She opened her mouth, but closed it again. For some reason, tears sprang to her eyes. This whole thing sucked.

Tobin grasped her hand in both of his. "You sit tight. I'm going to go check on things and get us some food."

"No, don't leave me!" She grabbed his shirttail.

"I won't be long. Promise."

"What if the guys who live in this cell come back?"

"They're good guys. That's why I picked this one. They were in chapel today. I haven't seen them since, but you'd be safe with them. And anyway, I'm going to be back." He slid from underneath the bunk. "Here, watch the news, see what you can learn." A little TV hung suspended at an angle, tethered to a shelf over the commode.

It shouldn't have been a surprise to see San Quentin's east gate on screen. But it was weird to have a vivid view of what was so close and so far.

The news correspondent was stationed outside the visitor's entrance. That funky little building Livvy'd entered hours ago. Where she'd signed her life into the hands of the California Department of Corrections and Rehabilitation. Which wouldn't be negotiating for her, thank you very much.

As for why and how the riot had started, it sounded like those on the outside were just as in the dark as Livvy. At least the press was. Who knew what official info they were privy to?

The lithe Korean-American reporter was the picture of earnest professionalism. Maybe she was thinking this was the story of her career. "Authorities are tight-lipped tonight about negotiations with the rioting prisoners. They have confirmed that they've established communications with the inmates, but have not yet received any demands.

"However, estimates of the number of possible hostages seem to have stabilized in the last hour. As we noted earlier, the riot began just after visiting hours ended for the day, which clearly reduces the number of hostages. However, there were volunteers inside the prison, as well as correctional officers and staff. It takes over 2,000 staff members to manage more than 5,000 inmates on the grounds. That includes all three watches in a twenty-four hour period, as well as areas of the prison that have not been affected by the riot—the Neumiller hospital building located to the south of the main compound, the industries yard to the north, and H-Unit, San Quentin's minimum-security facility.

"CDCR employees and volunteers who evacuated the prison at the outset of the riot have been accounted for, giving authorities here what they hope is an accurate headcount of those still inside the prison walls. According to the CDCR press liaison, there are between 80 and 105 staff members unaccounted for and believed to be inside sections held by the rioting inmates."

"Tiana," the network desk jockey cut in on the reporter's live feed, "do the authorities consider all of those guards to be hostages?"

Tiana fingered her earpiece. "Well, Jeff, that's uncertain. It is possible that some staff members are in hiding, or even defending areas within the prison. And, to clarify—not all of the CDCR employees are correctional officers. Those numbers include custody staff, support, and medical staff."

"You said there may also be volunteers inside the prison?"

"Yes, we understand there may be as many as twenty volunteers inside."

"Any word yet on the State's strategy?" Jeff asked.

"Not yet. Since the Governor's arrival an hour ago, she's been in closed discussions with Warden Espinoza and CDCR Secretary Kate Hendry, Operations Undersecretary Chris Hartman, and Marin County Sheriff Keith Maraschin. As soon as we have more information on that meeting, we'll get back to you, Jeff."

"Thank you, Tiana." Tiana Jo's feed disappeared from the screen, and anchor Jeff Wiltz addressed the camera. "Operating continuously for over one hundred and sixty years, San Quentin is California's oldest prison."

The network transitioned to a recorded piece with narration voiced over photos and video clips.

"Over the years, many notorious criminals have passed through its gates, including mass murderer Charles Manson, and Sirhan Sirhan, assassin of Robert F. Kennedy."

Livvy's stomach flip-flopped—next onscreen was a photo of Gant, "... one of the highest-profile inmates currently in custody. Many remember the grisly details surrounding his case. Connected to as many as sixteen homicides, Gant was only convicted of two. He confessed to eight additional murders, in order to avoid the death penalty."

Photo after photo flashed across the screen. Livvy didn't hear the women's names, didn't have a chance to read them before the TV dipped and spun. Young. Petite. Short blonde hair, blue eyes— descriptions alone wouldn't suffice to drive the point home. But each picture spoke a thousand words. Any of the women could be a sister. Could be Livvy herself.

"No remains for those additional eight victims were ever

found, however. And the only physical evidence linking Gant to the two homicides—the lynchpin in his convictions—was the discovery of two earlobes, each with trace amounts of DNA from Gant, as well as the women—"

Blood roaring in her ears, Livvy clawed from under the bunk. She made it to the stainless-steel toilet in time to throw up.

A zigzag crack climbed from the floor up the chalky wall. It was a river, splitting off tributaries here, swelling its banks there. It forked into two great rivers, the land between it a fertile plain.

Livvy studied the terrain as a remote, satellite observer. A blotch represented a sprawling city, specks were towns, hamlets. If the river were to overrun its limits, homes and crops would be lost. But in that world everything remained in place. There were no violations of boundaries.

Sneakers crossed between Livvy and the world on the wall. One, two, three, four. Livvy ignored them.

She calculated the best routes to travel from town to town along feathered lines.

Voices, big voices, came from above. They weren't relevant to Livvy or the little world. She didn't need to let them into her mind.

She counted every community, no matter how small. If she lost count, she started again. No one would be left out.

New feet. A face appeared under the bunk, mouth moving. If Livvy focused, she could see beyond the face, through it. That chink was a lake. A reservoir of fresh water as well as a recreation destination.

The face disappeared.

The voices got louder: "What did you do to her?"

Feet scuffled on the floor in her line of vision. She focused harder.

The face reappeared, then two more faces, eyes big and round.

That first face kept talking: "Livvy, Livvy, Livvy."

Livvy put fingers to her ears. She bumped a lobe, tight and distended. Needle-pointed pain streaked, nerve to nerve, through her ear, across the side of her face. She inhaled sharply, and Tobin came into focus. He scooted to her. Livvy fingered her tattered ear. Tobin's eyebrows came together, and he stopped her hand. Took it between his.

"Livvy?"

What was it she needed to say? It was a razor-edged thing, encased in cotton.

"Did something happen? Are you hurt?"

Of course she was hurt. Her ear—

Livvy went rigid. Gant. Those women.

There are pieces of my girls scattered across all fifty-eight counties in California.

Livvy screamed.

Chapter Fourteen

"*Shhh!*" Tobin pressed his hand to Livvy's mouth and pulled her close. "Shh, Livvy, hush."

Even with her eyes closed, Livvy could see the faces of all those women. Those women Gant had torn apart.

"Do you think they heard her scream on the floor?" Tobin asked.

"I think they heard her scream in Folsom," a voice answered.

"Livvy—eat something." Tobin produced a granola bar. "C'mon. It's been hours. And it looks like it's going to be hours more."

Can't you let them all know that I don't belong here?

"Tobe—" a voice from the sneakers. "Gant's goons are doing a sweep. Tier by tier."

Tobin groaned. "Livvy—we have to move. Please eat."

The food awakened Livvy's physical senses. Her stomach fretted for more. Her tongue was a shriveled sponge in her parched mouth. Her bare feet ached with cold.

Tobin dressed her like a toddler. CDCR sweats over the jeans. Turtleneck off, white tee over camisole.

Can't go out there.

Socks. Sneakers on. Sneakers off. High tops on—toes stuffed

111

with paper.

Gant is out there.

"C'mon, Livvy, come back to me." Tobin patted her cheeks, peered into her eyes.

Tobin blurred. Tears overran, dragged down Livvy's cheeks. She hadn't done anything wrong. Hadn't encouraged Gant.

She found her voice. "He's a monster."

Tobin gathered her in his arms. "Our God is bigger than all the monsters," he whispered into her violated ear.

Livvy hiccupped a ragged breath. Nodded into his shoulder.

"Stay with me," Tobin pleaded. Livvy bobbed her head again.

With sweatshirt and stocking cap, Livvy was ready on the outside. But not inside. *My heart has turned to wax; it has melted within me.*

Tobin evaluated her. He swiped his hands down the wall and rubbed dirt on her cheeks.

"Okay. Don't go running off with some other guy this time." Tobin's smile was more earnest than humorous.

Out on the landing, men were scuttling, shoving, swaggering.

Clusters of two and three white inmates bulldozed from each end of the tier toward the middle, swastikas emblazoned on shorn heads. Cell by cell they routed, inspected.

Oh God, oh God, oh God.

It was impossible.

Nothing is impossible for my God.

Livvy's hands shook violently. She tucked them under her armpits. Tobin moved ahead, one of the two cellmates in her corps pressed in from the back.

Then Tobin spun. "I'm a dead giveaway. Cho, you and Agromonte take her. Meet me at the canteen."

The men shuffled. Tobin went left and Livvy was pressed right.

"No!" She reached for Tobin, but Cho knocked her arm down. Wrenched her forward.

Can't do this without Tobin!

I can do all things through Tobin? Or through Christ who strengthens me?

Livvy kept her head down. *My shield, my rock, my protector. Hide me under your wings.* They were on the second tier, about a hundred yards from the stairs. The floor below seethed with moving bodies.

The goons eyed every inmate they passed. How would she get by? She needed a Jedi mind trick: *"This is not the woman you seek."* How did Jesus just slip away from those mobs that wanted to stone him? In Nazareth, at the Temple. *I need some of that, Lord.*

A thunderous blast shuddered the metal under Livvy's feet. A millisecond of silence rippled through the men in the cellblock. Then a second explosion—also out in the night somewhere—was echoed by the inmates' riotous roar. There was a stampede for the exits. Gant's goons were overrun—and in a whisper of prayer Livvy and her escorts were past them too.

Explosion as diversion. *Okay, Lord, that works.*

The night air was chilly. Livvy pulled her hands inside the sweatshirt. No way she was going to get separated from Cho and Agromonte. She was on them like tattoos on an inmate.

Searchlights flashed from the high prison walls, roving over the compound. Prisoners in orange jumpsuits now thronged among the blue—were they troublemakers?

And across the prison, on the lower yard, fire threw copper into the night sky. "Looks like the classrooms," Cho said. But he led them in a different direction. "That's the ISU." He jerked his head toward a small, single-story, fenced-in building.

ISU, ISU ... Oh, yeah. Investigative Services Unit. Where Miles worked.

Not far was a small freestanding building in front of South Block. The canteen had clearly been looted. Broken windows gaped like toothless hags, and ripped packaging carpeted the ground outside.

There, unperturbed by the debris, Tobin leaned against a wall. Livvy resisted the urge to run and wrap her arms around him. Others were with him, heads down in the shadow of the canteen. Smitty and Navarrette! With Cho and Agromonte, their little band had not only reunited, but grown. Astonishing how much affection welled up for guys Livvy'd only known a handful of hours.

"Man, I'm glad to see you, Homes." Smitty grinned. His eyes glowed as he held his fists out to Livvy for some sort of ritual greeting. She left him hanging, no idea what her part of the dance was. Cho stepped in and did the honors. "You 'bout scared the spit outta me." Smitty continued. "An' I thought Tobin was going to have puppies."

"Heard you had a run-in with Gant," Miles said.

"Your pepper spray saved me," Livvy answered. "I'll owe you forever."

Speaking of Miles: *spray ... pocket ...*

"Gant positive?" Miles asked Tobin.

Tobin gave him a withering look.

Positive about what?

"First things first," Tobin said. "Let's just get through this."

"Hey, Miles," Livvy fished out the paper she'd found: *M. Navarrette – 1.* "Do you think this is you?"

Miles unrolled the slip.

"Whatcha got?" Smitty asked.

"Kite." Miles peered, angling the note in the light.

"What's a kite?" Livvy asked Cho.

"A note, passed between prisoners."

"Why don't they just say 'note'?"

Cho shrugged. "Maybe 'cause they're flown with string. From tier to tier."

Miles let out a low whistle. "Of all the hit lists I've intercepted, first time I've seen my own name. That is jacked."

"Hit list!" Livvy leaned in, examining the scrawled names. "How do you know?"

"It's my job. Speaking of which, everyone in my unit is listed as a 'one.' Top priority."

Maybe it was the lighting, but Miles looked a little green. "Wish I knew where these guys were."

"That's quite a list." Tobin observed.

"Never seen one this long. Offing this many inmates and COs would take a pretty major assault."

Their little band was quiet for a moment.

"Like a riot?" Livvy ventured.

"Pretty much just like that." Miles pocketed the kite. "This was well coordinated. ISU's going to have a lot of work to do. If there're any of us left."

Hit lists? Murder targets?

"How come the cops don't just bust down the doors already?" Livvy's voice squeaked with frustration and fatigue. "Land their helicopter in the yard? The inmates are totally outgunned— what're they going to do, throw rocks?"

Miles rubbed his face. "A tactical response is a definite possibility. But the chairborne rangers are likely to exhaust negotiations first."

"The news said the governor was here. Talked about the prisoners having a list of demands. They won't let someone like Gant go free, will they?"

"No. No way that'd even show up on a list of demands. Any inmate knows it'll be a snow day in the Sahara before he'd get a negotiated release from this barbed-wire hotel. But whatever they do ask for, after all this effort, the inmates will need some sort of concession to save face.

"And of course the chance of hostages being harmed escalates if CDCR storms in, guns blazing. So they're out there"—Miles nodded toward East Block, which stood between them and freedom—"working for the most peaceful resolution possible."

"But ... while they're negotiating, people in here are being hunted," Livvy said.

"That about sums it up."

Their band of less-than-merry men remained at the canteen. It was as good a place as any. And better than some.

Huddled against the wall, Livvy yawned. Again and again, until tears streamed from her eyes and she thought her jaw would crack.

"Hey, you." Tobin nodded at Livvy. "C'mere."

The canteen doors were padlocked, but that was no major obstacle. Tobin helped Livvy clamber in through a now glassless window. *Voilà*, a private—albeit trashed—little hut. Shelter from the bay breeze and glaring lights.

Ripped cardboard made for a nice mat, and Livvy hunkered on the floor next to Tobin. Fatigue stole through her limbs, and she curled into a ball.

"What did Miles mean, about Gant being 'sure'?"

"Huh?" Tobin yawned.

"He asked if Gant was sure."

"Dunno what you're talking about."

"Before. Outside. He looked right at you and asked if Gant was sure, or certain—no, 'positive.' You said 'one thing at a time.'"

"Oh. That."

"Yeah." *Yawn.* "That."

"Get some sleep, Livvy, and sweet dreams."

"Hold the phone." Livvy sat up. "I've got you figured out,

mister. If you won't tell me, it's because you think you're protecting me. What is Gant positive about?"

Tobin sighed. "It's not positive *about*, Livvy. It's positive *for*."

Oh.

Well then.

Her ear. He'd bitten her. Livvy's shoulders sagged. "You mean HIV. Does he have HIV?"

Tobin dropped his head back against the wall. "Yeah. And Hep. B or C—I forget which."

"Hep? Hep ... atitis? Wow." Her voice quavered. "Can this get any worse?" So there was this here short-term riot bullet to dodge and potentially a long-term clock ticking too?

Tobin pulled her close. But he didn't say anything.

Nothing to say.

Chapter Fifteen

Tobin was teaching Livvy to downhill ski when someone started shooting.

She bolted awake, trailing a thread of drool from Tobin's chest to her chin. He sat up too, hand poised over Livvy's mouth. But she didn't scream.

There had been multiple shots—four? five?—but they had stopped.

"What's happening? What time is it?" Livvy asked.

"I don't know and 3:17."

"Is this it? Are they coming in?"

Tobin crept to the canteen window. "Can't see much from here."

This was it. The SWAT team and Special Ops and all the stealth ninjas were taking charge. They'd had enough already. Soon, soon, Livvy would be safe. They'd wrap her in an emergency blanket. Maybe give her hot coffee or cocoa while they debriefed her. For the first time in hours, her heart rate increased with hope instead of terror.

Would the media have much immediate access? She couldn't imagine her own face—strained, colorless—plastered across screens, viewed by millions. Those that knew her would try to read between the lines: Grace, their parents, Charlie—if he was sober.

Through the window, the prison lighting cast an amber glow across Tobin's face. Livvy'd definitely put in a good word for him. For all the men who'd sheltered her. She'd make sure it went into their records or files or whatever.

"What will happen to all the inmates when this is over?" she asked.

"Well, everyone will be strip searched. All the cells'll be tossed—inspected for hidden weapons or contraband. Then we'll be on lockdown for a good long while. The riot instigators and participants will be charged and tried. Most likely shipped to different prisons."

Livvy scrunched up her face. How brutalizing to be strip searched. So unfair for a Tobin or a Smitty. And Miles would be one of the searchers—the "us" and "them" decidedly reestablished.

Tobin sank to the floor, leaning against the wall opposite her. He was actually quite good looking. The five o'clock shadow worked for him. Five o'clock in the morning anyway.

When this ended, would she ever see him again? She thought of the electricity that oscillated through her when they'd held hands under the cell bunk. Now he seemed far away. That feeling—it had just been delirious relief at being delivered from Gant. In contrast to the revulsion she felt for Gant, her joy at seeing Tobin seemed magnified to something it wasn't. That was natural.

But she couldn't allow things to get that close again. It wasn't right. And it wasn't fair to Tobin.

Tobin. He was watching her.

The prison was too quiet. "They aren't coming now, are they?" she asked.

"No." The word came out sorrowful. "That was probably a gunner. If it were an assault, they'd be popping gas, using flash-bangs, lights, sirens, flashers—we won't miss it."

Lights, camera, action. Surreal. A prison drama unfolding

around her. Livvy prayed she'd continue to have a bit part—a walk-on. All but forgotten by the time the credits rolled.

The same for Lucas and the others. A shockwave hit her. Dread thumped in her chest. "Could those shots have come from inside the prison?"

"Guess so." Tobin hunched forward.

How many handguns did the rioters have? Maybe she'd just seen the same one twice. How many bullets did they hold?

"Where's Miles?" she whispered.

"Reconnaissance."

Probably looking to warn others on the hit list. Or find out if anyone was already dead. Livvy shivered. "I wish we knew what was going on out there. On the other side of the wall, I mean." The reporter from the earlier broadcast had been a reminder of a world beyond this. A world that cared.

Tobin rubbed his head. Got up and peered out the window again.

"Is it hard for you to be shut up in here with me?" Livvy asked.

Tobin barked a laugh. "This is palatial compared to my cell. And your company is the best I've enjoyed in years."

Livvy's cheeks burned. "I guess I meant away from the action."

He shrugged. "Action is overrated." Then he whistled softly through the window. Smitty appeared and the two spoke in low tones. Smitty handed something to Tobin and disappeared.

Tobin fished around in the debris underfoot. He found what he was looking for, crouched, and flicked forth flame.

"Did Smitty give you a lighter?"

"Uh huh."

"You guys can have lighters?"

"Nope."

"Then how'd he get one?"

Tobin grinned in her direction. "You find it puzzling that a prisoner can get his hands on a lighter, but not a gun?"

"Yeah." Livvy chuckled half-heartedly. "I guess that is funny." She moved to Tobin's side. He'd lit a chunk of cardboard and held a plastic coffee lid over the flame. "What're you doing?"

"Watch and learn, little fish."

"Fish?"

His whole aspect changed when he smiled. "That's what newbies are called in prison. Fresh fish."

"Ah. Yes." As seen in *The Shawshank Redemption* and pretty much every prison movie ever.

"So how do prisoners get guns and lighters?"

"And drugs, and cigarettes, and lots of other contraband ..." Tobin pinched and kneaded the softened plastic. "Where there's a will, there's a way."

"Who's Will?"

"Ha, ha. The stuff gets smuggled in."

"How? I got searched and metal-detected and all."

"Determined and devious minds will always come up with something."

He worked the former lid against the cement floor. "Such as this." The cooled and hardened plastic was now a sharply pointed barb. "From coffee lid to prison shank." He handed it to her. "Just in case. Go for the throat. Or the eyes."

Livvy recoiled. Then she thought of Gant. Yes—she could skewer Gant if necessary.

"Guns, however, that's a whole 'nother ball game." Tobin started on a second lid. "I've been thinking a lot about that. Where'd they get that gun?"

"*Guns*, maybe. I saw another guy with one."

Tobin frowned. "In '71 someone smuggled a 9 mm in to a Black Panther. George Jackson."

"What happened?"

"His attorney was acquitted for it."

"I mean here, with the gun."

"Jackson got six people killed, including him, trying to liberate himself."

How many people had died here in the last fifteen hours? Livvy could only confirm the inmate she'd fallen on. The memory of him made her feel vile. Unclean. He'd awoken, as someone's son, brother, husband, or boyfriend, to just another day, albeit in prison. Now his body lay where it fell. And his soul?

"Couldn't they have taken the gun off a CO?" Livvy asked.

Tobin shook his head slowly. "Like Navarrette said, COs inside the security perimeter don't carry firearms."

"I saw the armory on the way in." Livvy said. "Is that the only place they store them?"

"You know, they just don't keep me in the loop on that kinda stuff, but I'd guess so."

A thump at the wall made Livvy start. There was Smitty again, and he clambered in. "Got it," he said to Tobin.

Tobin took a portable AM/FM radio from him, and offered a lid-shank.

"No way, man. I got my parole hearing in ten days, Lord willing. I get caught with a weapon when this thing self-destructs, it'll set me back years."

Tobin pocketed it instead. "You want news?" he asked Livvy. "We got news."

The three hunkered on the floor, Tobin searching the radio frequencies for a news report.

"—Willowvale Bible Church—"

"Wait!" Livvy stopped Tobin's hand. "That's my church!"

"... issued a statement, saying that the authorities have asked them not to comment on the photos. However, now that the pictures have been made public, many sources have helped identify the people in them."

Photos? Was this even news about the riot?

"Three of the men have been identified in the first picture. The one taken through some fencing. If you're just tuning in now, you can see these photos, apparently captured by a cell phone inside San Quentin and emailed to several media outlets. You can find them on our website, www.ksrq.com. In the first photo, Willowvale Bible Church pastor Lucas Grayson is pictured with Rudy Valenzuela and Sean Mackessy. We don't have names for the other two yet, but apparently all five were part of a team that was playing softball against San Quentin inmates when the riot began. In the next photo, there are six from the church softball team, and three correctional officers." The deejay named the individuals while Livvy shook her head in wonder. A cell phone? Photos from within the walls?

"Aren't you going to ask me how someone in prison has a cell phone?" Tobin needled.

"Hush. I want to hear this."

"Now, in the next picture, there are two correctional officers, San Quentin's Protestant Chaplain, Dale Peake, as well as four more people from Willowvale Bible Church. This group was apparently in the chapel when everything hit the fan."

So they were alive! At least when the photo was taken.

"Huh," Tobin said. "I saw that group in the library earlier."

"You did?" Livvy asked. "How come you didn't tell me?"

Tobin shrugged. "Didn't come up."

What? That seemed like something worth volunteering. What else was he keeping to himself, because it hadn't "come up"? Concern rippled through her—were they not allies?

The deejay continued: "Looks like we have a caller with some information. Who's this?"

"Hey, this is Allen."

"Hi, Allen. What did you want to tell us?"

"Yeah, just that, you know, one of those pictures is taken in the old gas chamber."

"Whoa, what's that?"

"The one on your website with the lady in it, from the chapel? That green round room? Those guys are all inside the old gas chamber. They use the needle in there now, man."

"Allen, are you sure about that?"

"Yeah, totally. My brother-in-law used to work there. Told me all kinds of stories. And anyway, you can find photos of the old execution chamber on the internet. That picture is from the viewing room."

Livvy could feel Tobin trying to read her reaction, while Smitty avoided looking at her. She met Tobin's gaze. Honestly? She didn't know what she felt.

"Where is that?" she asked.

"North Block. In the basement." Tobin answered.

"It's not hooked up to gas, right?"

"Nah. Like the guy said, the state switched to lethal injection in '96."

Grisly. But not inherently more dangerous than anywhere else.

"Do you guys know anyone with a cell phone?" Livvy asked.

"Nope," Smitty answered. "Homey ain't gonna let that be known."

"It'd be cool if we could get our hands on one."

"I was thinking the same thing," Tobin said.

"Then we could let the authorities know about that hit list," Livvy said.

"No." Tobin shook his head. "Then we could get your keister out of here."

Sure, of course. Odd, though, that that wasn't Livvy's first thought. "How would we even do that? It's not like rioters are going to let me pass, or that a CO is going to open a secure door for little old me."

Tobin had his inscrutable mask on. "Yeah. I have an idea about that. But it would be better if someone out there knew you were coming."

"What's the idea?" Smitty asked.

"We're going to need a lot of sheets," was Tobin's reply.

"Toga party?" Livvy's stab at humor didn't jive with the fluttering behind her ribcage.

"Nope. Just a good old-fashioned prison escape."

Chapter Sixteen

With the glaring lights, it was hard to tell if it truly *was* darkest just before the dawn. It was definitely colder. Even in the center of her pack of protectors—Tobin, Smitty, Cho, and Agromonte— Livvy trembled. Each shiver was one part anxiety, one part cold. They were all tucked behind the chapel building, at the base of the north wall. An eternity had passed since she and Tobin had argued in the same spot.

"This oughta work great." Tobin secured a length of wood to the end of a sheet. "It's easier than rope climbing. Use the knots for your hands and feet. Okay, stand back." He swung the board-laden end like a lariat. Then he lofted it high overhead, toward the guard walk on the top of the wall. And missed. Livvy jumped clear as the plank plummeted toward her skull. Again Tobin threw the board. It hit the railing with a clank that echoed through their stone corridor.

"We got some attention." Smitty nodded toward the nearest guard tower. Several marksmen—black clad and helmeted— sighted rifles on the small group. Along the top of the perimeter they ran in a semi-crouch, barrels steady.

Smitty, Cho, and Agromonte held up torn pieces of cardboard. Livvy prayed the officers could read the lettering on them through their scopes.

The lead officer paused. Like Tobin predicted, he seemed to be talking to himself. His microphone connected him to the command center. *C'mon, commander, give us the green light.* Livvy waved feebly. After a moment the officer held up his forefinger, pointed at Livvy, and gave a thumbs up.

Tobin gathered coils of sheet and over-handed the piece of wood like a football. It shot up and over the railing and back down the other side. Feeding lengths of sheet, Tobin lowered the board until Agromonte grabbed it. The two men each wrapped an end behind their backs and braced themselves.

"Okay, go, quick." Tobin urged Livvy.

This was it! So fast.

"Go, Livvy!" Tobin nodded at her ticket out.

"Thank you," she said. "To all of you. I'll never forget how good you've been to me."

Smitty gave her a hug. Cho a salute.

"You can be remembering while you get your keister up that wall!" Tobin barked.

That made it easier to bid Tobin good-bye. Smitty boosted Livvy and she clutched the sheet. She ascended hand over hand. At the first knot, she paused. How high was the wall? Twenty, twenty-five feet? No problem.

A howl went up on the lower yard. Clinging to her lifeline, Livvy watched a cluster of inmates point her direction and come running up the narrow alley in her direction. Small problem.

"Climb!" Tobin roared. Livvy didn't need the prodding. She shimmied up, keeping an eye on the mob.

A marksman positioned himself directly over Livvy's head, and shot into the ground before the onrushing men. That slowed the frontrunners, but not the rest, who bowled them over. Several prisoners in the melee threw things at the shooter. Things which exploded in flame. One spilled fire across the officer's riot gear and onto the sheet rope. Big problem.

Up, or down? Livvy scrambled higher. She could make it.

The marksman above her roared, beating at flames across his chest and arm. Another officer tackled him to the walk, rolling out the fire.

Livvy's focus panned back, off the officers and onto the CDCR-issue bed sheets above her head that were rapidly going up in smoke. *Oh no.*

Part slide, part jump, and part fall—Livvy hit the ground. Still on the wrong side of the wall. The riotous onslaught reached Livvy's gang of four and swallowed them up. Yelling, raging, the prisoners fought for the remaining lengths of sheets, now in two sections.

Livvy scrambled to her feet. No one was interested in her—just in her route. More officers converged above, a couple wielding fire extinguishers. The others bent over the rail, weapons trained. There would be no more scaling that wall.

Tobin burst from the pack and seized Livvy's arm, running.

Rudy was actually snoring. Lucas stared, transfixed. The guy could sleep anytime, anywhere.

Sean remained wide-eyed. He sat stock still, except his head, which turned at every loud noise. Which was often. He looked like an owl. Of all the men, Sean was Lucas's biggest worry. He was only a year or two younger than Lucas, but seemed more. He'd grown up at WBC, in a great family, and had a Christian education straight through his graduation from Biola University a couple of years ago. Nothing had ever rocked the guy. He'd had no storms to speak of. He possessed a serene kind of faith, and more than once Lucas had wondered if Sean ever spent a sleepless hour in spiritual angst or wrestled with a moral dilemma.

Lucas had never seen an expression on Sean's face like the one he wore now.

Across the pen, Jim and Dave, longtime friends, had talked awhile but eventually fell silent. Bleary eyed, they hunched against the cold.

Lucas should have comforting or empowering words for all of them. Scriptures, prayers. All he had was fear. It hollowed him out.

It'd been hours since Livvy'd been dragged off by that sadist. Who knew what had been done to her. What was being done. Repeatedly. Was she even alive? Bile stewed in his gut and burned his throat. Lucas couldn't stay still with the "what-ifs" ping-ponging in his mind. He paced, muscles taut. He ached from the tension in his body. He honestly didn't know what he would do if she came to harm.

If? Who was he kidding? Gant was a butcher.

How would he face her? How could he even *live* with the knowledge—be conscious of the vile ugliness perpetuated against her body, her mind, the very core of her soul?

Of course, that question assumed they would both survive the night.

The night was relentlessly long and cold. In the garden of Gethsemane the night Jesus was betrayed, his disciples couldn't stay awake, even one hour, to pray and watch with him. *How did you endure that? The agony of waiting to be tortured. Knowing what was coming.*

What did Livvy know about Gant? Lucas wished he didn't know details, wished he could scrub his brain clean. He didn't remember where or why he'd watched the news program, but he did remember Gant's voice. His heavily edited description of what he'd done to the women he'd murdered. How long it had taken them to die. Had Livvy watched the same program, years ago? Did she know what she faced?

Lucas couldn't bear it. Was going to fracture. He slid to the ground, hunched with head between knees. He jammed his thumbs into his ears, clutched his head and squeezed. Screwed his eyes closed. But he could still see—Livvy's mischievous smile. Her clear, bright eyes. And he saw things he couldn't keep out. The wide, weeping terror on her face when she'd stood not three feet from where he sat. Blood. Mutilation. The flash of a blade and what it could do to smooth, dewy skin.

His heart raced. He rocked back and forth. If only he could get out of this cage! If he could get his hands on Gant. He could see his own hands, clear as day, clutching the man's throat. He gripped his own skull tighter. *I could kill him. I could so easily kill him.*

In the eyes of the world, he'd be justified. A hero maybe. What if he *did* get the chance to stop the man from drawing breath—and not in the immediate defense of Livvy? That would be murder. Easily explained or excused in these circumstances. Who wouldn't believe it to be necessary, unavoidable? What DA would ever prosecute a young pastor for slitting the throat of a rampaging sadist like Gant? Crushing his skull?

He could use the pistol that inmate had. Lucas practically panted to have the steel, hard and unyielding, in his grip. An accomplice in his intent—built solid and weighty, yet with one soft spot. One moveable piece so easy to bend to his will. Again and again. Making holes in that monster.

Wasn't this the very definition of intent? Premeditation? Lucas trembled. He didn't just think these thoughts. He didn't merely feel the heat of hate. He fed it. Stoked it, higher and higher.

He should turn from these thoughts. These feelings. Cry out to God. God could take his rage, terror. God was big. He didn't balk at the spectrum of man's emotions.

But Lucas didn't want to give them up. He wouldn't forsake them. He would draw from them, suck them dry.

A voice cut through the whirlpool of his mind. That voice. He whipped his head up.

Gant. He approached the pen.

Lucas leapt to his feet. He grabbed the fencing, climbed, peering. Was Livvy with him?

No. The man was alone. His features had changed. He was agitated, eyes wild.

Where was Livvy?

"Where is she?" Gant asked Lucas.

Lucas shook his head. His breath came in short bursts. Had he heard right? "What?"

"Livvy." Gant leaned toward the pen, his face an inch away. "Where is she?"

Lucas frowned, confused. Then it was clear enough. "You don't have her?" He closed his eyes for a beat. *Oh, gracious God.* Warmth flooded him, as if his bottled rage had burst and washed through and out of his limbs.

"Open this," Gant ordered the inmate stationed in front of the cage.

Lucas stepped back, immensely lighter than he'd been moments before. "Yes!" He threw his arms out. "You don't have her!"

Rudy awoke and lurched to his feet. The other three men joined him behind Lucas.

Gant shouldered past the inmate at the door and into the pen, which hardly seemed real because Lucas didn't feel present himself. He laughed aloud before he realized it. *She got away from him. She's safe. Oh, thank you, Jesus!*

Gant grabbed Lucas by the throat and slammed him against the pen. Rudy lunged and put Gant in a headlock. And then the pen filled with bodies. Lucas clawed Gant's hand at his throat, and then at the man's eyes. Rudy was taken down, and the three other WBC men were shoved to the back of the pen.

"What did she say to you? What did you tell her?" Gant breathed in Lucas's face, Lucas himself fighting to breathe.

Gant threw him to the concrete. "Where is she hiding? Where is Tobin?"

Lucas rubbed his throat. "I—" he coughed. "She didn't say anything. You saw everything." He scrambled to his feet. "Who's Tobin?"

Gant's face contorted in rage. He moved faster than Lucas would have believed for his bulk, driving his fist into Lucas's gut. "Tell me."

Lucas doubled over, fell. Again he gasped for air, his body shuddering with pain. A couple of the inmates in the pen grabbed his arms and pulled him vertical. Again Gant slugged him. This time Lucas heard the crack of ribs. The pain made him light-headed for a moment. Gant hit him again and again. Lucas was vaguely aware of Rudy and the guys struggling, yelling.

He clung to one thing. *She got away. Thank you, Jesus. Thank you.*

Chapter Seventeen

Sprinting by the exercise yard of cages, Livvy decided she'd had enough. All these crazed men and this whole accursed nightmare had been pushing her around for hours. Leading her by the nose. She was so close—*this close*—to getting out of this dump, this psycho hellhole, and those rabid dogs ruined it for her. Of all the selfish bilge, they wanted what she had—a stupid rope made out of sheets. And they didn't blink at taking it away from her. With fire. Of course, more fire.

Just a couple strides behind Tobin, she veered off course. Lucas and the guys were right over *there*, through that door, other side of that wall. Fury surged through her muscles. She grabbed a brick. If the inmate with the gun was there, she was going to slam him in the head and take that gun. She'd let Lucas and the guys free, and they would march through the east gate or blow the brains out of anyone who tried to stop them.

"Where're you going?" Tobin was at her side.

"To get my friends."

"Whoa, hold on." Tobin blocked the door. "You can't go in there."

"I can't? *You* say I can't? Get out of my way, Tobin. I'm going to get Lucas and my friends and I'm going to get out of this Godforsaken pestilent sinkhole."

"C'mon." Tobin took Livvy's shoulders. "You need to calm down, let's keep moving."

"I *need* to smash someone's head in. I *need* to not be told what I need!" Livvy elbowed Tobin aside. He shifted his weight to cut her off. She tossed the brick and shoved against his ribcage. "Get out of my way," she hissed.

"Keep your voice down, Livvy."

Livvy slugged him in the stomach. "Get! Out! Of! My! Way!" She punched him again and again.

Tobin grabbed her fists, and the look in his eyes made her want to claw them out. She was not pitiful! Rage filled her lungs and the tendons in her neck went taut. Before she could scream, a hand clapped over her mouth from behind. An arm around her torso pinned her arms. Tobin swept up her feet and she was summarily hauled off.

Not until she was deposited into the canteen was Livvy freed. It was Miles who'd muzzled her. He remained outside, panting slightly, while Tobin climbed in after Livvy.

She pounded on Tobin's chest. Battered it. "What did you do, Tobin? What did you do! Why are you in here? What makes you one of them? They think they can do whatever they want! Take whatever they want!"

Tobin just stood there and let Livvy hit him. That made her madder still. She lunged at him, shoving him in the gut until she backed him to the wall. Then she pressed the heels of her fists into her eyes. Just stood there and bawled.

Tobin enveloped her in his arms. She wept herself ragged. Twenty-four hours ago Tobin didn't exist to her. Now she was getting snot all over his shirt. A convicted criminal. San Quentin inmate.

"Someone did something to you." It wasn't a question, but Livvy knew Tobin was asking just the same.

She nodded. Torn. She didn't belong in his arms. Shouldn't lead him on. But it was the first place that felt right and true and safe in, oh, so long. And it wasn't just in contrast to Gant.

Gant.

"I didn't lead him on, you know." She withdrew from Tobin's arms and jutted out her chin.

"What? Who?"

"Gant. I hadn't even looked at him. I did *nothing* to ask for that."

Tobin frowned. "Of course you didn't. No one said you did."

"People just—they make up their minds to take what's yours. Sometimes it's *you* they want. Yourself."

"What happened to you, Livvy? Before."

"That wasn't my fault either." She jabbed him in the chest with her forefinger.

"Okay."

"I was playing a *part*. Acting out a *role*."

"Tell me."

Suddenly she wanted to. Wanted to expel it. Be rid of it.

"He came to all my performances."

"Who?"

"My 'Number One Fan.'" She twisted the words, bitter in her mouth. "Wade. Then he started coming to my church."

"When?"

"Grad school. And I was thinking, cool, you know? Like I'd recruited one for the kingdom. Then he started dropping by my classes."

"Where?"

"San Francisco. Conservatory of Music. He'd just show up everywhere I was. He followed me in his car. Called and emailed 24/7. Took things from and left things in my apartment. Told everyone I was his girlfriend.

"The cops were sympathetic, but he hadn't broken any laws.

135

That we could prove, anyway. But he stole my freedom little by little. You know the phrase 'death by a thousand cuts'? You can take one—even a deep one. But time after time, little by little, those cuts add up.

"He did creepy things to people in my life—family and friends—to isolate me. I looked over my shoulder all the time. I lost a lead role because I couldn't remember the lyrics. I couldn't concentrate and almost got kicked out of the program. He *stole* all that from me.

"He wouldn't listen to a word I'd say. Why is that?" Livvy searched Tobin's eyes. "What makes a person decide they can do what they want, that they get to decide to mess with your life? That they know what you *mean*, when you've said the opposite?"

"It sounds like he was mentally ill," Tobin said.

Livvy recoiled. "Yeah, well, I didn't *know* that. How could I know that? I was a kid. There's no handbook, you know."

Tobin held up his hands. "Easy there."

"Don't patronize me!" Livvy paced to the window. Miles had been joined outside by Smitty and Cho. Apparently Smitty didn't like the look of Livvy's blubbery face. "You hurt, Homes? That was quite a fall."

"I'm okay." What a relative statement. She ached all over, flu-like. Her belly stewed with adrenal output, acid, and emotion.

"Move over." Miles hopped into the canteen, as did Cho and Smitty.

Tobin remained in the corner, lower lip between his teeth. Smitty looked from him to Livvy. Livvy studied her high tops.

"We interrupting something?" Smitty asked.

"Not at all," Tobin answered.

Smitty peered at Livvy until she shook her head.

"Well," Cho said. "It was a good plan, Tobin. Almost worked."

"So now we're back to laying low," Smitty said.

"No," Livvy answered, pacing the confines of the canteen,

crowded with the bodies of men. She had it all wrong. Her piece in this drama wasn't a bit part. She had a pivotal role, and it was time to be proactive.

"Now we go with my plan."

Say what? Call it a knee-jerk reaction, but Tobin had a bad feeling about this.

Navarrette quirked an eyebrow. "Your plan?"

"Yeah," Livvy said. "The signs you guys held up for the officers on the wall. They worked, right? The guards read them and confirmed who I was, to let me scale the wall."

"That's not going to work again," Tobin said. "We tried the most isolated point on the whole wall. If we couldn't get you out there, there's no better spot."

"We're not going to try that again. We're going to communicate hostage locations to the marksmen on the walls. And tell them about that hit list. That way they'll be able to plan a tactical assault."

"No way," Tobin said. Gant was out there, looking for Livvy. And who's to say she wasn't going to get emotional again, change course, or otherwise put herself at risk? "Let's just keep you under wraps. No more running around the grounds."

"I wasn't asking." Livvy drew herself up in front of him.

Tobin cocked his head. What was with the attitude? Was she mad at him?

"And anyway, who's to say I'm safer in here?" Livvy continued. "Gant could stick his nose in, and then I'm trapped. Or the place could get torched."

"Livvy." Tobin tried a more sympathetic approach. "I understand how you feel, but it's not time to play hero."

"Really, Tobin? You understand how I feel? Do tell." She stood with fists on hips.

"It's not a bad idea," Navarrette said. "It could work."

"It's a lousy idea," Tobin retorted. Did the CO have a death wish? They should all just lay low, keep their heads down until order was restored. "You want us to just stand in the yard holding big old signs for the guard towers? We won't last five minutes."

"We need to get up somewhere high," Livvy said. "And the signs don't have to be huge—the marksmen's scopes are magnified. And after what we did at the wall, they'll catch on really quickly."

"Do we even know where any hostages are?" Cho asked.

"By my count they've got at least twenty-five COs corralled in the old gym," Navarrette said.

"And the radio listed three separate groups from my church." Livvy bounced on the balls of her feet. "Gant called Lucas's group the alpha group. And he mentioned a bravo group." She snapped her fingers. "That must be Joan and the choir guys—they're in the old gas chamber. Gant had them moved there after the rioters gained access to North Block."

"So that leaves one more group," Cho said.

"Good math, Einstein." Tobin rolled his eyes. Were they actually *encouraging* her? "But we don't know if there are additional hostage groups of COs, staffers or volunteers somewhere. And the badges have eyes in the sky—they already know the COs are in the gym. They've probably seen the group in the AC yard. And they can identify the gas chamber just as well as we can. What exactly are you going to be adding to their intel?"

"Hello?" Livvy's tone carried impatience. "The existence of the hit list. So they know they can't just negotiate forever."

Tobin scowled. "Careful what you wish for, Livvy. I'm sure you're looking forward to the guys in white hats busting you out, but an assault will not be pretty. There may be collateral damage on both sides."

"This isn't about engineering my own rescue! It's about helping protect people." She swiveled to face Navarrette. "What time is it?"

The CO blinked, then checked his wrist. "Six forty-seven."

Livvy spun back to point at Tobin. "Six forty-seven. If you nix this, if we don't try to communicate the fact that people are being hunted, anybody on that list who dies from six forty-eight on— heck, I'll give you 'til seven thirty—are on *you*."

Tobin rocked backward. "That's ridiculous." Yet, while a low blow, the force of her words stung.

Smitty held up a hand. "I'm in."

"I'm sure your heroism will look great at your parole hearing," Tobin sniped.

"Ouch, Homes. That wounds." Smitty crossed his hands over his chest.

Tobin sighed and rubbed his face. Smitty was right. That was uncalled for. But why were the guys supporting this nonsense? She was a wisp of a thing, so fragile. She still had a streak of blood on her neck from where Gant had bitten her ear. A weird, physical response gripped him when he thought of her in Gant's hands. An instinct to pull her to his body—part desire, part protectiveness.

"Thank you, Smitty." Livvy leveled a glare at Tobin. "I don't think Tobin or I should go back into North Block. Do you want to take a spin through there and see if you can spot any civilian or correctional hostages?"

"Sure thing, Ma'am."

"Shouldn't we synchronize watches?" Tobin asked.

"So now you're in, Mr. Sarcastic?" Livvy asked.

"Yeah, Livvy, three outta five of us are *in*. For years. Either way." *And longer if we get caught up in some mess.*

A touch of color rose to Livvy's cheeks. And Tobin felt a twinge of anguish. He'd just reminded this beautiful woman, who twenty minutes ago was in his arms, that he was a convict. That when all this ended, she would leave and he would stay.

"I can check out West Block," Cho said.

"Navarrette." Tobin rubbed his crew cut. "What's the word on the ground out there?"

"Quiet. In terms of any sense of orchestration I mean. There's lots of cleaning house. Debts being settled, stuff you'd expect. Didn't see any other COs in dress blues, but there's got to be at least nineteen hundred prisoners loose."

"East and South Blocks still tight?" Cho asked.

"As drums. So is the AC, thank God," Navarrette answered. "If there is some sort of master plan in this goat rope, it included liberating West and North Blocks and the Gym. Does that tell us anything?"

"You tell us, man. You're the investigator." Cho slouched in the corner.

"Do guys on the list live in those buildings?" Livvy asked.

Navarrette cracked his knuckles. "The list has names of COs and inmates. Of the COs, most work in investigative services. I don't see a pattern in the others. Of the inmates, we've got some hard-core gang-bangers. Shot-callers from all the gangs: Sureño, Norteño, Aryan Brotherhood, Nazi Low Riders, Mexican Mafia, Nuestra Familia, Black Guerilla Family, DC Black."

"And these guys all hate each other?" Livvy asked.

"Understatement."

Livvy glanced around the canteen. "We've sure got a heterogeneous group represented here."

"Darn right we're hetero." Cho stiffened.

"Mixed-race, I mean," Livvy said.

In spite of the tension, Tobin snickered.

Livvy rolled her eyes at him. "You guys are all cooperating, in spite of differences."

"Our family is larger than any of those. And more inclusive," Smitty said. "Body of Christ."

"In any case," Navarrette continued, "I don't recognize all the inmates on the list. Of those I do, some live in North Block, but not all. As for West Block and the Gym? That's reception housing."

"Reception is inmates traveling through San Quentin?" Livvy asked.

"You're getting the hang of this. It's short-term housing while new prisoners are processed into the Department of Corrections, evaluated, and classified by security level. Then they're either sent to another institution in the state, or moved to other housing here. If they don't have much time to serve, they may stay in the gym."

"So, those guys are all new to prison?"

Cho snorted.

"Not exactly," Tobin said. "With California's recidivism rate at almost 70%, most of those guys are frequent flyers."

"So why would all those people be on someone's list?" Livvy asked.

"If you recall, that was my opening question," Navarrette snapped.

Whoa. Tread lightly, Liv. Tobin shifted slightly toward her. They were all tired, stretched thin.

"Okay. Where would be a good place for us to broadcast to the guards?" Livvy asked.

"'Rette, come on." Tobin gave the CO a slight shake of the head.

But Navarrette nodded. "Yeah. Let's verify current hostage locations and see if we can identify any more. Smitty, you take North, Cho, West. Then we'll write it up and flash it to the gunners. Livvy, I appreciate your willingness, but I can't permit you to take part in any of this."

"Can't *permit* me?"

"That's right."

"Who put you in charge?"

"That would be the California Department of Corrections and

Rehabilitation. As long as you are our guest, I decide where you can and cannot go."

Tobin fought to keep his expression neutral. He couldn't appear triumphant. It wasn't that he wanted to win the argument with Livvy. He just wanted to keep her the heck out of trouble.

"You've got to be kidding me!" Livvy wasn't going so neutral. "Rome is burning, and you want to keep me behind velvet ropes?" She glowered at Navarrette. "'Guest'? I signed a form. You're released from liability."

"All right, then, let's make this a democracy," Tobin said. "All those in favor of keeping Livvy on the down-low, raise your hand."

All the men were in favor. Excellent.

"All those in favor of Livvy contributing to the safety of her friends and everyone on that hit list, raise your hands." Livvy's was the only arm in the air. "C'mon guys, you can't keep me caged up in here!"

"'Caged up in here'? Really? You gonna go with that?" Tobin cocked a brow.

The other men let it go. Smitty and Cho exchanged glances and left on their assignments.

"I'll scout a good place to flash the info,'" Navarrette said. "Back soon."

And then there were two.

"I'm going to scrounge some food," Tobin said. Hopefully Livvy'd calm down while he was gone. And some food would raise her blood sugar and mood. "You stay put. I won't be long."

"I'm coming with you."

"Not a chance. Word's out there's a woman inside. Guys'll be looking for you." Tobin ducked out the window. "Don't you move!"

Tobin disappeared from view. Livvy's heart hammered. She was all alone, cornered in that small space. Surely somebody was going to peer in and spot her ...

She planted her palms on the sill and hopped out. Hunched, hands in armpits, she trotted after Tobin.

The sky had lightened, though the air still held considerable bite. Livvy pulled the beanie down past her ears.

She caught up to Tobin under the huge aluminum foul-weather roof. He glared at her, but remained silent. All around, men clustered in the clearing. The blue or orange prison garb didn't seem to matter much. Skin color was by far a larger common denominator than uniform color.

Tobin's stride broke. He kept walking, but Livvy tried to read what had changed. A few yards in front of them, two groups of Hispanics faced-off in an edgy detente. The factions seemed about equally sized. Livvy eyed Tobin without turning her head. Were they about to amble through a gang war?

Chapter Eighteen

If Lucas laid on the concrete just so, he could find a position that wasn't excruciating. He could even breathe, albeit shallowly.

Gant had either finally believed that Lucas didn't know where Livvy had gone, or just got tired of whaling on him. Now the five WBC guys were alone in the pen again, guarded by no-necked inmates.

"How're you doing?" Sean asked for the millionth time.

"Okay," Lucas answered. He opened his eyes for a second. It was starting to get light. A new day in San Quentin.

Lucas was oddly at peace. He'd taken one for the team, as it were, and Gant was probably done with him. Livvy seemed safe from the monster. There wasn't much Lucas could do about his situation, and there was nowhere to go but up.

Maybe I'm in shock.

"Rudy," he called. "How many fingers am I holding up?" He waved his right hand at Rudy.

"Uh, five?"

Correct. I must be fine.

"Well look who's here," Rudy said.

Lucas started. *Owww.* He sucked in a breath with a hiss. When his head cleared, he followed Rudy's gaze. Several players from the

San Quentin softball team crossed the walled yard. Expressions were grim as they approached the cage.

Greg's forehead wrinkled in concern. "Oh man. How you doin', Lucas?"

Lucas held up a thumb. "Hanging in there."

"What train hit you?" Roberto asked.

"Gant. He was looking for information I didn't have."

"He's got broken ribs," Sean said, voice heavy with concern. "And he keeps shivering."

I do?

"We brought you blankets, food, and water," Greg said.

"You guys rock," Rudy said.

The inmates passed food through the chain link structure. Granola bars, Slim Jims, candy bars, Red Vines. Bottles of water barely squeezed through. Then there were the blankets. They weren't going to fit. Roberto gathered them and stood. He started for the gate when Greg stopped him.

"No, dude, I better," Greg said.

Roberto glanced at the three inmates at the door of the pen, grimaced and nodded. He handed off the blankets to Greg and knelt to Lucas's level again.

"What was that about?" Lucas asked.

"Nothing. Prison politics," Roberto answered. He didn't look like it was nothing. Lucas maintained eye contact with him.

Roberto shrugged him off. "Those guys are Dissident Nazis. White supremacists, if their name doesn't give it away. Greg's a better shade to be asking them for favors."

Lovely.

"Notice their tattoos—the number 18?" Roberto asked.

"Hard to miss."

"Those stand for letters of the alphabet. One equals *A,* and eight equals *H.* Mean anything to you?"

Lucas tried to focus. Nothing. He shook his head.

"What do they mean?" Sean asked.

"Initials. Adolf Hitler." Roberto answered.

"And 88?" Lucas asked.

"Heil Hitler."

Lucas laid his head back on the concrete. He couldn't imagine being so committed to hatred that he would indelibly declare it with his body. In fact, he didn't think he'd ever hated anybody. Hated sin, maybe, and what it did to people's lives.

Filthy scum. Animals.

With a jolt of pain unrelated to his injuries, Lucas remembered his words from the night before. Yeah. That feeling that had coursed through his body: that was pretty much hatred.

And there was his very real, very physical desire to manually end Gant's life. He'd craved to squeeze the air out of him or bash his brains in.

But look at what they'd done, were doing ...

Uh-uh.

Livvy had said it in the van. Those guys weren't worse than Lucas. All sins were equal in the eyes of God. No scale of "badness." And Jesus, never tap-dancing around truth, had summed up this exact situation. It was easy to love your friends and people like inmate ball players who are kind to you and bring you Twix. It's hard to love enemies that kick the snot out of you and attempt to rape people who are special to you.

Impossible, maybe.

But I can do all things through Christ who strengthens me. Isn't that what he'd told Livvy about facing her fears? How very glib. All Lucas had was quotes from the Bible and hot air. Someone else's words and no character.

Keeping his eyes closed didn't keep them dry. Lying on his side, moisture pooled in the corner of his right eye, pooled on the cement from the left.

His whole body ached. To breathe deeply was to scrape nerve

endings between splintered ribs.

Then there was another question he didn't want to answer: *what if I'd known where Livvy was? How long would I have taken that beating to protect her?*

The group of gang bangers on the right fanned from a focal point. A wiry, knife-edged man commanded the forefront. His skin bore as much ink as any of the rest, his face etched in a scowl.

"What're you staring at, *güero*?" He snarled at Livvy.

She started—she *had* been staring. Reflexively, she grasped the shiv Tobin made for her, thrust deep in her pocket. Her gaze snapped to the inmate's chest, but her mouth wouldn't respond.

"I'm talking to you, whitey," the man repeated.

Livvy sensed Tobin to her left, but what was he to do? This was exactly what she predicted—one savior could not take on dozens of attackers.

"S'matter, Diaz?" An inmate called from the left. "You can't front a Sureño? You gonna take on a punk kid instead?"

The Norteño cursed his rival gang banger. Then he narrowed his focus on Livvy. "You gonna stick me?"

Indeed, Livvy grasped the shiv in her bare hand. She shook her befuddled head. The pack behind the Norteño shifted, bled toward their leader's confrontation. Fear tasted metallic in Livvy's mouth. In a blur of motion, the inmate leapt and struck out at her. Livvy swung wildly, flinging her arm over a flash of silver. The coffee-lid shank arced airborne, free and wide, her grasp lost in a spasm of pain.

Her gasp was cut short, the wind knocked out of her, and Tobin jerked her backward off her feet. Clutching her sweatshirt, he pulled her from the waves of slicing, stabbing Latinos that crashed together in front of her.

"You little fool!" Tobin hissed under his breath as he jerked her about-face and broke into a run. "There are no do-overs in here! Don't you get that?"

Livvy couldn't protest, couldn't deny. Couldn't think clearly. Ragged pain pulsed up her side, warmth soaking layers of clothing. She stumbled to keep up, pressing her hands against the pain.

The din behind Tobin and Livvy grew, and inmates rushed toward and past them to watch. One distressed face in the sea stood out. Miles.

"She's cut," Tobin muttered when Miles stepped in close. Thick crimson beads escaped Livvy's clutch at her side and splattered to the ground.

"Lemme see," Miles said, moving to free Livvy's grasp of the wound. Livvy stared at him, thick and stupid.

"Livvy, let go." Tobin still grasped Livvy's sweatshirt, holding her up like a puppet.

Livvy complied, staring at her bloodied hands. Miles peeled away cloth. Livvy could only see the top of a ragged gash in her right side, below her ribs. The rest of the wound's perimeter was obscured by blood. "It's deep, but short." Miles stared at Livvy, but spoke to Tobin. "She needs stitches."

Every severed nerve ending shrieked to its other half, racing pain up, down, and across Livvy's torso. Each heartbeat pulsed more of Livvy's insides out. Suddenly her stomach tipped and heaved to do the same.

"Whoa, hold on there." Tobin drew her up, tipped her head back, and pointed toward the sky. "Breathe. Deep." The sky was bluing up. Streaks of pink stabbed over East Block. Livvy sucked in air, swallowed down nausea.

"Let's get her to the ISU. I've been keeping my distance, since I have a vested interest in keeping my grape intact. But there's a suture kit there," Miles said.

"In case you hadn't noticed, there's a civil war playing out between us and the ISU."

"Let's go through roadkill cafe." Miles nodded toward the cafeteria. "Come out the other side by the ISU."

Breathe. In, out. It's merely a flesh wound. Livvy closed her eyes.

"No you don't." Tobin shook her. "Stay with me Livvy."

Where did he think she was going? She pressed hands to the hole again. She wanted to lie down. Her knees buckled.

"I have an idea—" Miles backpedaled. "Wait here."

Where did everyone think she was going? Tobin grasped her under the elbows now. No more sky—she hunched over her middle, drawing close around the wound.

"Let me down," she whispered to the concrete with a voice from far away. Her periphery was lost in a muffled tunnel. Which way *was* down?

The world kept spinning. But drowsiness mercifully numbed the pain, stopped her ears, and sandbagged her mind.

Tobin scooped Livvy into his arms and followed Navarrette into the cafeteria. Strewn with debris, the dining area was otherwise empty. Navarrette grabbed a bright orange stretcher mounted to the wall next to a first aid box and fire hose. He dropped the pallet to the floor and helped Tobin ease Livvy onto it. Then 'Rette snatched the emergency blanket from its clip and ripped open the plastic cover with his teeth.

"Here, cover her completely." Navarrette flicked open the blanket and Tobin draped it over Livvy, including her head. That was a disturbing sight.

It's just for her protection. Doesn't mean anything. Still, Tobin's eyes burned unexpectedly.

Stupid girl. Had to go and get herself stabbed. Like things weren't bad enough. She didn't make things easy, this one.

The gang war made for a good distraction. Navarrette was able to open the gate in the fence around ISU as well as the door itself without notice.

Once inside, the CO banged open a metal cabinet and pawed around until he grabbed a good-sized first aid kit. He slammed it open on the desk next to the head of the stretcher.

"Put these on." He tossed Tobin latex gloves and donned some himself. "Pull back her clothes. Put pressure on the wound with this." He held out a wad of gauze. Then he opened a packet with curved, threaded needles in it.

"You've done this before, right?" Tobin asked.

Navarrette didn't answer. He waved Tobin's hands aside and began squirting a clear liquid into Livvy's wound. Then he withdrew a plastic card from the kit. Tobin leaned over. The card had a chart of knots on it.

"Really, 'Rette? You need a cheat sheet? Do you even know what you're doing?"

The CO continued to ignore him. He began cutting Livvy's skin.

"What are you doing? You're supposed to sew her up, not cut her up!"

Navarrette glared up at him. "Tobin, I'm going to sew your fly trap closed if you don't shut it!"

Finally Navarrette began to stitch. With metal tweezers in one hand and the needle in a scissor-like clamp in the other, he sewed the two straight, clean edges of skin together. Tobin gulped a breath and looked ceiling-ward. He'd been in a hurry for this? He was glad Livvy slept through it.

Slept? Was that the right word? She was unconscious. Had fainted. Anxiety gnawed at him. Her face was so pale. But she breathed.

Then she stirred.

"Hurry, 'Rette. She's waking up."

Chapter Nineteen

Fire. She was on fire after all. Livvy cried out and slapped at the flames. But hands closed over her mouth and grasped her wrists.

"Keep her still!" Miles's voice.

"I'm trying!" Tobin's voice was close to her head. "Livvy, you have to keep your voice down."

Livvy panted awake, pain searing through her like a hot tong. She was on a plastic stretcher, resting across desks in a small office building. Miles worked at her side, fumbling near her wound.

"Almost done, Livvy. Hang in there." Tobin relaxed his grip on her wrists. "You're doing great."

"What about me?" Miles grunted.

"I'll bet you were an Eagle Scout," Tobin said.

"I'll bet you weren't," Miles answered. "There." He clipped the suture with a final *snick*.

The stitching may have been over, but the pain wasn't. Clammy with cold sweat, Livvy focused her gaze on a ceiling tile. *Breathe. Breathe.*

Tobin cleaned Livvy's hands with wet wipes, eyes slate pools of concern. "How you doing, kiddo?"

"I'm thirsty."

"No problem." Tobin hustled to a water cooler and back. He

eased her up and helped her drink. "'Rette did a good job. He cleaned everything real good. Gave you a shot of antibiotics."

"Great. Don't want a staph infection on top of the HIV and hepatitis," Livvy mumbled.

Tobin's face was inscrutable.

"Joke. It's a joke." Livvy shifted and winced.

"Livvy, to get through this, you've got to trust me," Tobin said.

Livvy nodded. "I know."

"I don't think you do. Not really."

Miles returned to her line of sight. "Hey, I've got something else for you." He held up a baggie with pills in it. "Oxycodone."

Tobin raised a brow. "Handy."

"Got a whole confiscated pharmacy in here," Miles said and helped Livvy down a capsule.

"What else you got lying around this place?" Tobin pulled out a couple of desk drawers.

"Knock it off, Tobin—you shouldn't even be in here." Miles scooped a teetering stack of files off the desk top near Livvy's feet. He bundled them under his arm, shuffled and grabbed other loose articles, and resettled them on a nearby table.

"Ph-ph-ph-phone!" Livvy exclaimed. She pointed at the telephone revealed by Miles's housecleaning.

He leveled a dry look her way. "Yes, I'm heading for that. Since breaching the ISU marks me number one bullet stopper to anyone watching, I plan to make use of the resources." He snatched up the handset and dialed.

Tobin met Livvy's gaze, brows raised. A smile crept out of hiding.

Miles navigated a few transfers, repeating information until reaching someone out there with some clout.

"Tell them about the list," Livvy hissed.

"Tell them about her." Tobin nodded in Livvy's direction.

Miles waved off both of them, providing his contact with

insider perspective. He read the names off the list and stated their theory. Then explained Livvy's situation. "She's stable, yes."

"He wants to talk with you." Miles held the phone out to Livvy.

"Hello?" Livvy blinked slowly. The pain had receded to a fuzzy throb. And so had her brain.

"Ms. Fischer? This is CDCR Captain Jason Classen. How are you feeling?"

"I've been better."

"I imagine so. I want you to answer a few questions for me right now, with a yes or a no. Can you do that?"

"Yes." Whew. Easy one.

"Are you alone right now?"

What a dumb question. Maybe it was a trick. Livvy double-checked. Miles and Tobin were still there. "No?"

"Is anyone else listening on this line?"

"No."

"Is Miles Navarrette with you?"

"Yes." So far, so good.

"Is there anyone else with you?"

"Yes."

"Are there any inmates with you?"

"Yes." Livvy nodded into the phone. "A guy named Tobin—"

Miles and Tobin waved at her, mouthing, *no! No!*

"It's okay," she told them. "He's been fabulous," she directed to Classen. "He should get an award or something. He totally saved me a bunch of times." She smiled at Tobin. *See there?* He gave her a crooked smile back. But Miles glowered.

"We're going to get you out safely, Ms. Fischer," Classen said. "Could I speak with Sgt. Navarrette again, please?"

Livvy passed off the phone. She gave Tobin a thumbs up. "There you go, big guy, got in a good word for ya."

Tobin shook his head with a wry grin. "Feeling better, Loopy— I mean, Livvy?"

Livvy raised the other thumb. "Peachy."

"What about an aerial extraction?" Miles was saying.

Tobin moved in closer. "Livvy." He edged his shoulder between her and Miles. "I really want you to come through this safely. Could you please promise to trust me, to listen to me?"

"Sure, sure." Livvy nodded. "Totally."

"Liv—" His body blocking Miles's view now, he took Livvy's hand. "I mean, even if you disagree with me again. Even if someone tells you something different. Listen to *me*. Can you promise me that?"

Livvy rubbed her temple. She was so tired. Tobin's hand enclosed hers in warmth. His eyes were earnest. She reached out to stroke his cheek.

Wait, what?

Her hand fell to her side. *What are you doing with this guy?* She struggled to a sitting position, panting through clenched teeth. Tobin steadied her, concern etched in the lines on his forehead.

What do you mean, this guy? *He's been there for you every step of the way. Keeping you out of harm's way and saving you when you threw herself back into it.*

I mean, *this guy—this inmate, this criminal.* He wanted her to sacrifice her own judgment to his? No one got to speak for her.

Livvy looked past Tobin to Miles. Navarrette was the correctional officer. The "good guy."

Oh please, you gonna tell me Tobin is not a good guy?

"Good guys" don't end up in a maximum security prison for Lord knew what.

Oh, shut up, shut up, shut up!

Livvy sized up the man in front of her. Of course he was a good guy. But for Livvy he was *not* a romantic option.

"You in there, Livvy?" Tobin asked.

"Yeah, yeah. Sorry. Look, Tobin, thank you, for everything. You've been so awesome." It was hard to look him in the eye. It was hard to deny that she wanted to keep holding his hand. "But I can't promise to just sign my will over to you."

A muscle in Tobin's jaw twitched. "I get it." He too flicked a glance at Miles. "That's the shining knight, right?" He released her hand. "My armor is a bit too rusty."

"Oh come on. Snide doesn't become you."

"Like I said—I haven't spent much time considering what becomes me." He leaned in close. "Though I have spent a lot of time considering what I've become. I am worthy of trust."

"Of course you are, Tobin. I just can't fall in love with you."

"You can't what?"

Had she said that aloud?

"What?" She shook her head. "I'm so tired."

Miles banged the phone down. "You just had to tell them I let an inmate in here, didn't you?"

Livvy blinked. "The guy wanted to know—"

"Yeah, yeah." Miles waved her off. "Save it." He rummaged through files.

"Are they coming to get her?" Tobin asked.

"No. They're not sending in a bird for just one civvie. I'm to keep an eye on her." He looked at Livvy like she was a two-ton nautical anchor. Then at Tobin. "And you're to keep a distance."

"Come again?" Tobin asked.

"You need to leave the ISU, ASAP. I've got her."

Tobin drew himself up. "Right. Got it. I can't be trusted in here." He flipped over a desk caddy, sending pens and paper clips flying. "Oops—there I go. The out-of-control inmate. What's so important in here, 'Rette? You got your investigations." He hefted a file. "All your evidence. Your eye-witness testimony. You gonna protect Livvy, protect all of this. What about me, Navarrette? What about *my* eye-witness testimony. What about me putting my life on the line, sticking my neck out?"

Livvy hadn't thought about that. About what it had meant for

Tobin to defy Gant. About the fact that he had to keep living here after all was said and done.

"Tobin—" she reached for him.

He jerked his hand away. In a couple of strides he was in Miles's face. "Keep her safe, 'Rette. You better keep her safe."

"Tobin!" Livvy cried out and clutched her side. "Wait!"

"Don't forget to lock the door after me," were Tobin's parting words before he slammed his way out of the office.

Miles stood in the middle of the room with a thousand-yard stare on his face. Then he started muttering to himself, rifling through files.

"You're just going to let him leave?" Livvy demanded. "He's at risk out there!"

And I'm at risk without him. Sure. *Now* you see it, girlfriend.

"He'll be fine," Miles muttered, without looking up from his stacks of paper. He snapped on a desktop computer, still talking to himself as it winked to life.

"What are you doing?" Livvy asked.

"This is the Investigative Services Unit. I'm investigating." Miles pulled out the kite with the names on it and unrolled it on the desk.

"Right now?"

"Look—you're here. This has been no picnic for you. I get it," Miles said. "But I have other things demanding my attention, so maybe you should get some rest."

Wow! Blown off! Maybe Livvy'd just stick with Tobin. Gingerly she set her feet onto the floor and shifted her weight. With a gasp she went down, knees to floor. Leaned back against the desk closest to her.

Miles didn't even notice. Forget him. Livvy reached for the wide roll of gauze and lifted her shirt. Around and around her torso she wrapped it, tightly reinforcing her weakened muscles.

The front door opened with a bang and the small building

shuddered. Miles leapt to his feet. Multiple voices carried over the three-quarter wall partition between his desk area and the front door.

There were men in the ISU, and none of them were Tobin.

Chapter Twenty

Livvy scooted under the desk in the ISU and slowly pulled the chair toward her. Tobin had said to lock the door. But Miles hadn't. Fear cleared Livvy's head. How many men had entered the building? What did they want?

"Oh. 'S'up? Not the first with this idea, I see," a voice said.

"Yeah." Livvy heard Miles clear his throat. "Not much here ... just office supplies."

"Don't worry buddy, we can share." The voice didn't sound like a sharer.

"Scissors," said a second voice, in the middle of the room.

"Nice clock." The first guy again, farther away.

"Check out the phone. Gonna call my girl." The second voice got closer.

Livvy stiffened. The phone rested right over her head. A pair of scruffy shoes overhung by bunched pant legs were visible under the back guard of the knee well. They stopped just a foot from her feet. *Please oh please don't look under.*

"Thought of that," Miles said. "They'll pull the phone records and lean on your girl. She'll dime you out, man. Not worth it."

"Oh man, check this. Come. To. Daddy." The voice above gloated. Livvy hugged knees to chest.

"What?" The first voice was on the other side of the room. Seemed like just the two of them, plus Miles.

"Looks like Oxy. Gotta be fifteen in here."

"Gimme half."

"Find your own, dirt bag."

Quick steps. A scuffle. *Bam!* The desk overhead shuddered. Someone swore.

"'Rette!" Tobin's voice! "You've gotta be kidding me—"

The men feuding next to Livvy's desk grunted as they struggled. One went down on his knees. Livvy shrank away, toward the chair. The pill baggie hit the floor, got kicked under the desk. Livvy froze, tempted to snatch it up, to fling it back.

A hand groped under. Another gripped the first wrist. Now the two men wrestled on the floor. Livvy nudged the bag into one of the flailing hands. But not quickly enough—

"Hey! There's someone under—*oof!*"

The pandemonium escalated. The baggie fell again as more bodies entered the fray. Tobin and Miles.

Not good, not good, not good.

Livvy scuttled out from under the desk. Grabbed a pair of scissors and crawled to a corner behind a photocopier.

Seconds later it was all over except for some grunting and swearing.

"Livvy!" Tobin called out. "Need your help."

Livvy remained plastered to the wall, peering from behind a recycling bin. Okay: Tobin was on top. That was good, yes?

"Livvy!"

She crept out, hunched. Tobin and Miles each kneeled on the back of an inmate, immobilizing them with arms torqued behind. Looked like Miles's signature move. Her own shoulder twinged in memory.

"It's a woman!" One of the inmates strained to look her way. Tobin mashed his face into the carpet.

"Livvy," Miles began. "There's duct tape in—where are you going?"

Livvy circled the melee, ignoring Miles. First things first: she locked the door.

Tobin and Miles soon had the two men cuffed to desks, mouths taped. The inmates craned to watch Livvy though, and she shrank from their stares.

"I can't leave you for a minute," Tobin said, exasperated.

"Were you watching the building?" she asked.

He nodded and gave Miles a shove. "What were you thinking, man? Next time send out invitations!"

Miles turned on Tobin. The two men, still breathing heavily, glowered at each other. "If you want to keep them, keep your hands off me, Tobin," Miles said.

"Gee!" Tobin threw his hands in the air. "Sorry, Boss, so sorry. You want me down on my stomach?"

"Tobin! Shut up!" Miles shot a glance at the two inmates.

"Now you know how *she* feels. You get it yet?" In spite of his tone, Tobin blanched. Livvy didn't believe he meant to expose Miles as a CO.

"What do we do with these guys?" he asked more softly.

"Leave 'em as they are. They're good for now."

"We should move, though."

"Yeah." Miles sighed. He bounced a small item on his upturned palm a few times and then pocketed it. "I think I've got some things figured out." He glanced at Livvy and Tobin but didn't volunteer more.

"We've got to get her out of here," Tobin said. "Call that guy back up, tell him to come get her."

"Be realistic, Tobin. They're not coming in just for her."

"You're talking about a helicopter, right?" Livvy asked. The three huddled and spoke in hushed tones now.

Tobin and Miles nodded.

"Can't we help them rescue the others?" Livvy searched the men's faces, not at all surprised at the resistance she saw. "We could tell Classen a time and place, and spring some of the hostages, and ..." She shook her head. It sounded lame, even to her. Just a few key details missing.

"What did you figure out, 'Rette?" Tobin asked.

"You got me thinking about people sticking their necks out. There's a pattern in those names. You've got the investigators, some shot callers, and there's a handful of informants—some already in Ad Seg, some in general population."

"Ad Seg?" Livvy asked.

"Administrative Segregation," Tobin and Miles said in unison.

"Segregation for snitches, gays, former gang bangers ..."

"And 'shot-callers'?"

"Top dogs in the gangs. The guys who issue all the commands."

"So what's the point?" Tobin asked.

Whew, glad he asked, because Livvy was missing something.

"The point is, the informants were from a bunch of unrelated cases. Unless they aren't unrelated after all. Which, again, points to something big."

This time Livvy didn't point out the obvious: "big" as in "riot-big."

"Okay, well, we need to move her." Tobin repeated.

Her. "Hello? I'm right here," Livvy said.

"Where do you suggest? We're running out of locations," Miles replied directly to Tobin.

"I was thinking, the, uh, basement in building twenty-two."

"Basement? Oh. You mean the old ..."

"Yeah."

Livvy waved her hand in Tobin's face. "*Hellooo.* You mind including me in this conversation?"

Tobin brushed away her hand. "Livvy, there's a pretty secure spot where no one ever goes. I think you'd be safe there. But it's ...

it's not very nice."

"Gee, and the rest of San Quentin is Club Med."

"It'll seem like Club Med," Miles muttered as he strode to a cabinet on the back wall.

"You got a key?" Tobin asked.

"No. I've got this." Miles returned, a small kit in his hand. "How are you with locks?"

"Please." Tobin pocketed the kit. "I'd be embarrassed to reside at the Q if I couldn't pick."

"What is this place?" Livvy asked. "What's so bad about it?"

"It's the original prison. The oldest cells." The fact that Tobin was practically whispering, so that their prisoner prisoners couldn't hear, sharply increased Livvy's growing feeling of dread.

"It's safe?" she asked.

"I think so," he responded. "And I'll be with you."

That helped. A lot. Okay then.

"Livvy, we're going to pass the AC yard, where your friends are caged," Tobin said. "Don't freak out again."

"I won't." Livvy hugged herself, her sweatshirt ragged and damp with blood. It would be nice to at least let them know she was okay. "Are they still there? What about those gunshots this morning. You don't think they would've ..."

"No. Don't go thinking that way. There's nothing Gant and his goons would gain from hurting hostages."

Well, hostages other than *her* any way. Apparently Gant gained something from hurting women just like her.

Livvy was small again. Damaged, weak. "Can't I just stay in here?" she whispered.

Tobin shook his head. "We don't know if anyone knows these guys are here. And I don't want you in the same room with them anyway. Let's head out. It's a straight shot, back toward the chapel. You stay close." Tobin tugged Livvy's beanie down further. "And look male already."

Chapter Twenty-One

Livvy wished she could run. Wanted to reduce her time out-of-doors. As it was, she loped awkwardly. The pain was manageable, but she was glad for the future doses of oxycodone snug in her pocket.

Tobin led her past the AC yard, then the east gate quad. She almost cried out upon recognizing it. So close to the exit. A cadre of goons guarded it, however, in a tense détente with armed CO's on the catwalk above it.

And there was the chapel entrance. Weird. It was almost twenty-four hours since they boarded the vans at WBC to head for the prison. What would she give to warn the Livvy of yesterday to not come!

Tobin studied her with a sidelong look, as if concerned she'd bolt for the gate. But she trod on, following him to the mystery spot.

They arrived at the far end of the now-gutted building where she and Tobin had originally sought refuge many hours ago. It still smoldered where fire had met stone and run out of fuel.

Tobin pulled up short in front of a tall medieval door, latticed with iron and padlocked to the stone wall. He picked the lock and wrested the door open a foot, two feet.

"What is this place?" Livvy whispered. Daylight illuminated the mouth of a hole hewn in stone. Its recesses yawned into blackness. Dread licked at Livvy's imagination.

"Go, go." Tobin nudged her in, none too gently. He followed and pulled the creaking hulk of a door closed behind them, sealing them off from the outside.

A ventilation hole above the door provided the only glow of light. Livvy grabbed Tobin's arm and peered. She could perceive no depth in the ink soup.

"C'mon." Tobin shuffled forward, guiding Livvy with an arm around her shoulders. "Let's go to the rear cell."

"No, Tobin. This is fine."

"I want you away from the door." Tobin was resolute, his arm firm. "No one ever comes into the dungeon, but with it unlocked—"

"Dungeon!" Livvy braced her feet on the stone floor, arms flailing wildly for any surface in the utter black.

"It's just a word, Livvy. Right now think of it as your safe place."

Her safe place. *Riight.*

They reached the back wall. Tobin felt along it to the right, until they reached another wall. "Here," he said, gently guiding her over a threshold and into what must have been a doorless cell. He eased her to sit on the stone floor. "Lean against me."

It was so quiet. Deathly quiet. Livvy reached her arms both directions. She could touch the wall on the right, and if she stretched—*ouch. Don't stretch.* In the darkness, it was easy to imagine the walls being closer than they were. Inching closer, closing in on her. She convulsed in a shiver.

"Here, gimme your sweatshirt. Let's switch." Tobin maneuvered behind her. "You're all wet."

Livvy exchanged with him gratefully. Then her stomach gave a ripping complaint.

"Man, we gotta get you some food. You're so tiny—you're going to digest yourself." Tobin moved as if to rise.

"No! Stop! Don't you go anywhere." Livvy pleaded. "I'm okay. Just stay with me."

"Okay, okay." Tobin settled back and Livvy drew her knees in close for warmth.

"Men actually lived down here?" she asked.

"Yep. They packed them in. No running water. No windows. This is the oldest part of San Quentin. Originally, prisoners lived on a ship in the San Francisco Bay while they built their own prison. California wasn't even a state yet."

Wow. Building your own prison. Each successful placement of rock another barrier to your own freedom. Livvy shuddered. She pictured the men who had been imprisoned in here, completely cut off from the outside world. Bereft of light, bereft of hope.

Then there was Livvy. How much had she kept herself imprisoned, rehashing the past, obsessing about Wade and what she could have done differently? She'd made her world ever smaller. She sniffled.

Tobin encircled her with his arm. Such a strong arm. She leaned into him. She was injured, after all. What would have happened to her if Tobin hadn't been in the chapel, hadn't taken it upon himself to be her protector?

"I thought you were a bully yesterday, when you were staring at me in the chapel," she told Tobin.

He chuckled, a rhythmic vibration in his chest. "You were so defiant."

"What did Miles and Smitty mean about you knowing about the riot ahead of time?"

"I didn't know. I was just worried. Gant was involved in a flurry of gang politics—kites, discussions on the yard. The big tipoff was day before yesterday when he stockpiled a bunch of food. Often means a guy knows a lockdown is coming.

"You know," he continued, "when I saw you up there singing—let's just say Gant has me conditioned. I recognized his type immediately. I'm sorry I scared you when I grabbed you. But when I saw him coming ..."

They were silent for a time. Livvy considered those women. Wondered about their families. Did they have husbands? Children?

"Tobin?" She whispered. "What did you do? Why are you in here?"

She felt his chest expand as he inhaled, his breath on her cheek as he sighed.

"How about you ask me that again when I can look you in the eye."

She pondered that. Did she want to know? She hadn't had much time to wonder, but now the darkness fueled her imagination. Statistically a great deal California's incarcerated were in for violation of some drug law or another. That wasn't pretty, but at least it wasn't violent. Surely Tobin wasn't violent, was he? And whatever he'd done, he was a Christian now, right?

"So ..." She hesitated. None of it was any of her business, really. "Did you learn about Jesus here, in prison?"

"Yup. D.P.—Chaplain Dale Peake—is amazing. He never gives up on a guy."

Sometimes people said prisoners faked religion to get paroled. Tobin seemed awfully sincere. But what did she know about seeing through lies? She was as gullible as they came.

No. She used to be. Not anymore.

Livvy shifted, sat up under her own power. Her eyes were as used to the dark as they were going to get, and it was still utterly black. How odd that she sat here completely dependent on Tobin. There were no witnesses. No undercover CO around to keep an eye on things.

So what had Tobin done? Curiosity was killing her now. Not

just curiosity. Self-preservation. How long had he said he'd been in? Four years? Was that a long time for a drug charge?

"Before, you guys were talking about frequent flyers."

"Yeah."

"Is this your first time here, these four years?"

"Yes."

"Have you been in prison anywhere else?"

"Nope."

"And how long is your sentence?"

Tobin stretched. Now they no longer touched.

"I was sentenced to six years."

Wow. Six years. Two more to go. What had he done to earn that? The silence stretched into the blackness.

"Welcome to prison, Livvy," Tobin said dryly.

"What—why do you say that now?"

"Because now you're experiencing the real torture of prison. Too much time for thinking. You'll make yourself crazy."

Make yourself crazy. Could you make yourself crazy, or is it already in your nature, latent, waiting for circumstance to bring it out? That's how you made someone *else* crazy. You brought it out. Like Livvy had to Wade.

She'd never meant to feed into his particular obsession. It wasn't her fault, exactly, but she had unwittingly played her part to the tee. Her therapist explained it all to her after it was over. She wasn't to blame, not responsible. She was the victim, after all.

But then, Wade was dead and she wasn't. Death was a pretty steep sentence for stalking.

Tobin breathed rhythmically. Was he asleep? She couldn't blame him. She should probably sleep too, while she had the chance. But she couldn't close her eyes against the blackness. She stared into it until it threatened to give her a headache. How long would they stay in here? They couldn't hear anything outside these walls—two thick feet of stone. How would they know if the riot suddenly ended?

"So why did you come yesterday?" Tobin asked, a disembodied voice in the dark.

Livvy started. "I thought you were asleep."

"Even I'm used to a softer bed than this."

"Um. There's not a simple answer to that question."

"I don't need a simple one."

"Well ... You know Wade, the stalker guy?"

"Yeah."

"I haven't been able to sing in front of people since him. To do a lot of things, really. I guess I thought it was time."

"You picked San Quentin to get back into the game?" He sounded incredulous.

Livvy laughed. Then she sighed. "It's kind of embarrassing, really. At first I agreed to come because of a cute guy."

"A cute guy here?"

"No—someone on the softball team." Livvy's ears burned in the dark. *Dope. Why did you say anything?* "It's no big deal. Then I just felt like I was supposed to come. Guess I'm not so good at sensing the leading of the Holy Spirit, huh?"

"Just because things didn't go as expected doesn't mean you're not supposed to be here."

"Well, that's a weird thought. I'm supposed to be in the middle of a full-on riot? Why would God want me here?"

"I dunno. I'm glad you are. I mean—not glad you are in danger, but glad I've been able to get to know you ..." Tobin's voice faded into the darkness.

Livvy reached for his arm and gave it a squeeze. "I'm glad I've been able to get to know you too. I wish—" She cut herself short.

"Wish what?"

Livvy shifted, hugged her knees. "Just that we met under different circumstances. That you weren't in prison."

"There, see, that's what I meant about you."

Livvy chuckled. It was easy to talk to him in the dark. In fact, it was pretty easy to talk to him. Wonder why that was? Usually she got pretty tongue-tied around guys she was attracted to, but not Tobin.

Uh, wait a second. Attracted to? It was so matter-of-fact true that it seemed pointless to lie to herself. She was attracted to him. Good heavens. Where had that come from?

"So whatever happened to stalker-guy Wade?" Tobin asked.

"How about I tell you when I can look you in the eye," Livvy replied. She so didn't want to get into that.

Tobin didn't respond. Now Livvy wondered what he was wondering. He was right about too much thinking.

"I just wish I could figure out what God's will was in all of it, so I could move on," she said.

"How do you mean?"

"Well, I know God doesn't *cause* bad things to happen to us, but he allows them for his own purpose."

"How do you figure that?"

"Well, it's in the Bible."

"Is it?" Tobin sounded genuinely perplexed. "I mean, I'm no scholar, but I've read the Bible through a couple of times the last few years. I don't remember anything like that. It seems like every time someone in the Bible comes against some problem, evil is attributed to the Evil One."

"Well, yeah. That's what I meant. He doesn't *cause* it. But he *allows* it."

"Does he? Every time Jesus saw someone sick, he healed them. He had to deal with sickness, demon possession, even that storm he stopped—a note in my Bible says he used the same word as when he rebuked demons. Seems to me, he sees the devil behind all the crappy parts of this fallen world. After all, Satan is, temporarily, the ruler of this world."

"But that's what I'm saying."

"No, it isn't. It's hugely different. If—in hope that we'd choose love—God really gave us freedom of choice, then our choices have to matter. You can't let someone choose something and then change the fallout from their choice. That's cheating.

"And if our choices have outcomes, the ones we make against his will are going to have outcomes against his will. I think that, for a time, he's given men and angels free will. In the end he's going to wrap it all up, and we'll all have to live eternally with our choices. But for the time being, horrible choices have horrible consequences.

"Do you think God *lets* people kidnap, rape, and murder children? I'm sure he *hates* it. It must piss him off and rip his heart out. I'm thinking that if we are in an unseen war, this stuff happens because of the enemy, and God's side must be fighting that enemy at every turn. If he had some divine purpose behind evil, what kind of God would he be?

"He never promised stuff would make sense. Only that he'll work in the bad to bring about good, and that, above all, he'll stick with us through it. You know that bit that Paul talks about? Not death or life, angels or demons, our fears for today or our worries about tomorrow—not even the powers of hell can separate us from God's love."

Livvy got a chill down her spine. Tobin's words, or the subterranean cool of the dungeon?

If Tobin was right, God didn't *let* Wade torment Livvy. No more than he gave tacit approval of Wade's mental illness.

And that would mean ...

That would mean God had been with her all along. Rather than resting in smug assurance that he knew the reason for all things, he'd wept with her as the smoke rose to heaven.

And that changed everything.

The silence stretched until Livvy felt like it would snap.

"What do you do all day?" Livvy asked. "Play checkers with Gant?"

"Um, not," Tobin said. "Believe it or not, North Block is kinda the mellow block at San Quentin, if there is such a thing. Lotta lifers, lotta guys who've settled in and know how to jail. I've spent a bunch of my time getting the education I was too much of a screw-up to get on the outside. Got my GED and am a few credits away from an AA."

"Wow!"

"Thanks for sounding so surprised."

"It's just awesome that you've used your time so well. What do you study?"

"Renewable and sustainable energy. The idea is to be employable when I get out. Plus, I like the idea of doing something to benefit the earth after all the damage I've done. To create some beauty."

"That's amazing."

"It might surprise you, but the Q is pretty progressive when it comes to programs. Guys want the chance to come here 'cause there's so much you can do."

"So I see," Livvy said dryly.

"Right." Tobin was about to say more, when a metallic squeal echoed through the stone chamber. Someone opened the door to the dungeon.

Chapter Twenty-Two

A sliver of light grew to a swath across the back wall of the dungeon. Tobin moved in front of Livvy, set low in a crouch, silent as a cat.

The door to the dungeon was to their left, on the other side of at least one stone cell wall. But while the invaders weren't visible to Livvy, their shadows filled the gap of light on the wall as they filed into the cavern.

"Go. Get in there." A man barked orders. "Hurry up."

The whisper of shuffling feet filled the space.

"To the right, all the way down against the wall," the same man said. Only his shadow remained in the doorway now. The others must have gathered in the first cell.

The door ground closed again, and the dungeon was cast back into darkness.

As soon as the door closed, the talking began.

"Where are we?

"Man it stinks in here."

"You okay, Mackessy?"

"Yeah. Back just a little sore ..."

Mackessy! That was Sean. He was with Lucas!

Livvy merely thought about moving before Tobin was on her.

His hands gripped her shoulders. "Don't even think about it," he whispered in her ear.

Livvy pushed his hands away. "I'll be careful!" She hissed back and stood. *Oof*—the blood rushed to her head and she put her hand out to the wall to steady herself. Her wound woke from its relative slumber and throbbed.

Tobin wrapped his arms entirely around her, pinioning her to his chest. "This is one of those times, Livvy—you've got to trust me. Do *not* reveal yourself to them."

It hurt to struggle. Livvy stilled. What was the risk? Clearly the guard was on the outside. So it was probably just the guys from the Willowvale team who were in the cage with Lucas earlier. Why not whisper to them? Lucas was *right there*!

"They can't protect you." Tobin read her mind. "You can't do anything for them. Just do me a favor and don't rush this. Let's see what happens."

That was reasonable. Livvy nodded. Tobin relaxed his hold and they listened.

"What a pit." That sounded like Rudy. "I'm going to check it out." Feet shuffled.

"What do you think they'll do to him?"

"Lucas?"

"Yeah, Lucas. How's he supposed to help find Livvy?"

Livvy gripped Tobin's elbow. Hard. What were they talking about? What about Lucas?

"I think he's meant to be bait." That was Rudy again—now slightly separate from the others. "There's another cell in here. Wonder how far back this thing goes."

Bait?

"Bait?" Sean asked.

"Yeah, to attract Livvy. That Gant guy is obsessed to get her back."

"Why Lucas?" Sean again.

173

"Haven't you seen the way they look at each other when they're not looking at each other?" Another voice.

Even in the dark Livvy felt her cheeks burn. She had a weird urge to tell Tobin it wasn't true. But it was true. The main reason she even stood beside Tobin was dimples. She'd been so lame to mention it to him.

"I hope they lay off the guy." That made four voices total. The other four who had been in the cage with Lucas?

Silence fell, except for Rudy's shuffling.

"These cells are tiny," he said. "Must not have held very many people down here. That's six cells on this side so far." His voice was very close now, and his shuffling feet turned the corner. Tobin gently tugged Livvy to the opposite wall of the cell. Rudy seemed to be feeling his way around the entire jail, along the walls.

"Do you think they broke his ribs?" Sean asked.

Livvy inhaled sharply. Tobin tucked her under his arm. *Broke his ribs?* Lucas? What were they doing to him?

Rudy stopped moving. "This place is spooky. Haunted."

Tobin waited until Rudy moved again, then crossed the small cell with Livvy, back to the wall Rudy had already investigated.

Surely she could just talk to Rudy—he was right there!

For the umpteenth time in as many hours, Tobin put his hand over her mouth. His head was so close to hers she felt his silent breath on her ear.

"I dunno. He was in a lot of pain," the men continued. Livvy's eyes brimmed, trickling tears onto Tobin's hand.

"How's he supposed to know where Livvy is? She could be anyplace in this hellhole." That one sounded angry. At her?

"Not like he'd tell Gant, even if he knew. That guy is demonic."

"Well that's the point, isn't it? They know he won't tell them, so they keep whaling on the guy ..."

Silence again. Livvy peeled Tobin's hand from her face. Could she buy Lucas's freedom? Some medical help? In order to do that, though, she had to be in a position to bargain. And that one guy sounded too mad to bargain. Sounded like he might just hand her over.

Rudy returned to his group just as the door opened again.

"Here. Eat up." Scuffling and the sound of things being caught in bare hands.

"'Bout time." Angry man muttered.

"Where's Lucas?" Sean asked. "What are you doing with him?"

"Shut up, pip-squeak." And the door closed again.

Tobin leaned in close. "I'm going to see if I can get some of that food. *Don't move.*"

Livvy clutched at him, but he'd already slipped away into the darkness. Had he taken off his shoes? He was so quiet. He was going to try to steal food from her church-mates in the dark. Livvy didn't know what to do with that. She shook her head. This was so messed up. Her stomach rumbled and she clasped her arms around it. Could the men hear that?

Again the door opened, a hulking form filling the frame cast on the wall. Where was Tobin? *Oh please, Jesus, keep him safe.*

The four men were silent this time. No muttering.

"I see you got lunch." Gant's voice turned Livvy's knees to pudding. She slid down the wall.

No response.

"Preacher man doesn't seem to have an appetite. Maybe you guys wanna help him out? Did Livvy make contact with you again, last night or today?"

"No! Like we said, the last time we saw her was when you grabbed her." That was Rudy.

"What'd you do to her?" one of the others asked.

A sharp electronic trill made Livvy start. A cell phone. A cell phone was ringing. Of all the unexpected sounds.

"Yeah?" Gant answered.

The dungeon door was only cracked now. A slivered beam cut

through the darkness. Gant paced in and out of it, sending stabs of light toward the back like an anemic strobe.

With horror, Livvy realized that he was pacing deeper into the dungeon, toward her cell. Panic welled—an irrational urge to run screaming from her hiding place. Instead, she sat hunched, trembling, in the far corner of the chamber.

"No, I don't think we're gonna get the last few. Badger is still secure. You gotta mop that up yourself. Yeah. No. No. Right."

Gant was at the back wall now. Right at the mouth of Livvy's niche. He was faintly lit by the finger of daylight, but his cell phone glowed brightly. He hunched and muttered into the phone.

"No—not yet! I'm telling you, I want the girl. This doesn't end until I'm done with her. I've given you a nice little retirement gift, helping you clean house before you vacate. You gotta be patient while I get what's mine. You better get my exit visa together and be patient a little longer."

Livvy could see the illuminated Gant. Could he see into her cell? He continued to pace. Livvy's spirit prayed, even while words failed her. All save two: *please help.*

"Yeah. Okay." And with that, Gant terminated the call. He strode to and out the door without another word to the men in cell one. Without seeing Tobin or Livvy. *Thank you, thank you.*

"That guy is psycho. Thank God Livvy got away from him," Rudy said.

"I wonder how she did, and what he did to her ..." Sean trailed off.

Again, Livvy felt the powerful urge to speak out. To let them know she was okay.

"I'm almost glad we don't know where she is," Rudy said. "What if we had to make a Sophie's Choice?"

By the time Tobin returned to the corner of the stale stone cell, Livvy no longer cared whether he brought food with him. She grabbed his arm, clutching tightly before he could even sit next to her. Her painkiller had worn off, and her side throbbed like the heartbeat of its own life force, threatening to take over hers. She curled with her head on Tobin's knee. He was the only one she could trust. None of the other inmates in her posse were as smart or as dedicated to her protection. Miles acted like she was ruining the whole riot for him. And her WBC mates might well throw her to the viperous Gant if given the chance to save Lucas. Or they'd be faced with sacrificing Lucas to save her. Neither choice was life. How could she live with herself if anything happened to Lucas because of her?

And what was she doing? Her tears wet a patch on Tobin's jeans. She was hunkered in the dark, sniveling, while Gant and his goons tortured Lucas.

Lord God, help him. Help us.

Chapter Twenty-Three

Lucas sat in an awkward hunch. With his arms tied to the palm tree behind him, the weight of his upper body forced his lungs onto the pikes of his splintered ribs. He drew a slow breath and held it awhile before letting it out. His upper lip was cold with sweat.

Where'd Gant's goon taken the other guys? Why'd the other inmate—who'd helped force the five from their comfy pen—separate Lucas out of the pack and bind him here?

With as little movement as possible, Lucas turned his head toward the east gate. The sally port was just across the chapel quad. The SWAT team members on the walkway above the door were so close that Lucas could practically see the whites of their eyes. Well, okay, it was a hundred feet and they wore helmets with face shields. Plus, one of his eyes was swollen to a slit. Still. It was crazy. He could see them, and they could see him. True, they'd given him and his escort their full attention. But a gaze from afar wasn't going to help Lucas and his busted ribs any.

So here he sat, in a patch of grass next to a juniper bush. He tipped his head back to let the sun glow orange through his one good eyelid.

Hey Jesus, I'm not equating us or anything, but I'm alone now, like you were after you were arrested.

What did Jesus do, when he was alone and in pain, awaiting his fate? Where did his thoughts go? It wasn't clear in the Bible how long everything took—being dragged from the high priest to Pilate, then to Herod and back again. But Jesus definitely had a lot of time to think. He must have been praying the whole time. Was he planning ahead what he'd say when questioned, or had he just been in the moment?

Was there anything Lucas could say to turn any of this around? Jesus promised his disciples that the Spirit of God would give them the right words to say at the right time. Did he want to speak through Lucas? The Holy Spirit had definitely worked in and through Lucas's sermons. He couldn't explain it, but when he prayed over material, God breathed life into it, during both the drafting and the delivering.

But he'd never been called to speak truth into a completely hostile situation. In his struggle against sin, he had not yet resisted to the point of shedding his blood. This was genuine "pick-up your cross and follow me." Genuine sharing in Christ's suffering. This was no exegetical exercise.

Not that there was anyone to talk to just now. What was with Gant? Was he messing with Lucas because he was a pastor? Or did the psycho really believe he could ensnare Livvy by using Lucas as bait? Wherever she was squirreled, hopefully Livvy was hidden enough that she didn't know *what* was going on out here.

To the naked eye, Lucas must look like pretty easy pickin's, sitting exposed in the courtyard. His personal inmate had left, so no one stood guard.

Other inmates milled about. A group clustered around a little flat-bed utility truck on the road between buildings. One guy sucked on a hose, the other end of which was stuck in the truck's gas tank. Siphoning. They got a flow going and started filling up all kinds of containers. Lucas couldn't make out much detail, his view partially blocked by a guy ripping a sheet into strips. One by one the cloth wicks were inserted into the receptacles.

Lucas groaned and closed his eyes. Was this thing ever going to run out of steam?

"You sleeping, or dead?"

Lucas's eye popped open. "I'm not really sure."

The inmate, a grizzled bear of a man, chuckled and crouched next to Lucas. "Sucks for you, man."

In spite of the pain, Lucas breathed a brief laugh. "That about sums it up."

"You want I should get you some water?"

"That'd be awesome," Lucas answered. "What's your name?"

"Fallon. You're the preacher ball player, huh?"

"Yeah. Lucas."

"I'd say 'nice to meet you,' but somehow that seems kinda mean right about now."

Again Lucas fought a laugh, exhaling into a grin. "No problem." *Also a weird thing to say right now.* "I don't suppose you could untie me?"

"Naw, man. Sorry. The song says the devil went down to Georgia, but I can tell you, he right here. I ain't takin' him on." The man stood. "I'll be back in a minute. Don't you go and die on me."

"Not planning to."

Fallon lumbered off, toward the cell blocks, past the siphoners. He didn't give them a second look. Lucas furrowed his brows in wonderment. Could men really adjust to anything, if given enough time?

Something splattered on Lucas's shoulder. He craned to look overhead. Seagull? A guffaw redirected his gaze to the right. Three men appraised him, two with grins that were one-part sneer. The third, in front, looked like Lucas's uncle's English bulldog—squished face, heavy jowls, creased forehead. His fists were like hams. Just looking at them made Lucas's ribs hurt more.

Not good.

Lucas looked left. His SWAT buddies remained. There was only so much they'd let these guys get away with, right?

Splat. This time it hit the grass just next to Lucas's foot. *Are we really going to do this?* "Something you want to say?" he asked the bulldog.

"Nah. I'm good." The man cleared his throat, hawking a big loogie.

Lucas's stomach turned. He looked away. *Splat.* His shoulder again.

"You should be careful you don't dehydrate," Lucas said. He thought back. Yeah, pretty sure ... This was the first time he'd ever been spit on.

"What're you doing in here, man?" bulldog asked. Apparently the other two men were just window dressing.

"I came to play softball with your team."

"Ain't my team."

"Right. With the San Quentin team."

"Why?" One other guy actually had the power of speech.

"Uh, I like softball? I like meeting and talking to the guys in here."

"What do you talk about?"

Here comes. "I talk to them about what it says in the Bible. That God loves them and wants a relationship with them."

Bulldog laughed. Or maybe it was a cough. "Guess you learned different, huh? God don't come to the Q."

"Sure he does." Lucas jerked his jaw. "He's right next to you."

The inmate on bulldog's right flank jumped, wide eyed, away from the spot Lucas indicated.

Bulldog squinted, his eyes all but lost in folds of skin. He strode to stare down at Lucas. "You yanking my chain?"

"No. No way. Look—God is definitely here, all around us. He's all knowing, ever present, and all powerful. If you don't think he cares about you, I dare you to read the book of John."

"Who's John, and what's he got to do with it?"

"He was a friend of Jesus's. He hung out with him and wrote down his story. His writings are called the Gospel of John, and it's in the New Testament of the Bible."

"That religion crap is for idiots and whiners."

"Yeah? And how are your choices working out for you?"

Bulldog flushed and leaned in. "You better watch your mouth, Jesus Freak."

"I'm just saying"—*c'mon Jesus, bring it home*—"that if I were still making all my own decisions, my life would be a mess. I screw everything up on my own. But God cares about me too much to let me live like that. He loves you too."

Bulldog jerked back. Lashed out and kicked Lucas's foot. *Ow ... right on the ankle bone.*

"Hey, don't you mooks have somethin' better to do?" Fallon approached from behind bulldog. "Fires to set, buildings to loot?" He shouldered through the three inmates, crouched next to Lucas, and held out a bottle of water.

The Aquafina bottle had clearly been reused many times. But to Lucas it was the Holy Grail. Fallon slowly poured into Lucas's upturned mouth. Lucas had a bit of trouble getting his swollen lips to close properly, but despite a little dribbling, the water sweetened his mouth and cooled his throat.

Bulldog remained planted, glaring at Lucas. "Why'd you say that, man?"

"What, that God loves you? Because it's true. He created you. He planned you. He's been chasing you."

The man's eyes widened. "Chasing me?"

"Yeah. He loves you so much, he'll do anything to get your attention, to get you to turn around and get to know him."

"You're crazy, man. You're a freak." Bulldog stalked off, his crew in tow. He shot a dark look over his shoulder. Lucas knew that look: *fish on.*

Fallon waited, ready with more water, but first Lucas grinned. *Yes!*

Livvy awoke stiff and cold. When she moved, her side pierced her with pain. *Ugh.* Should she take more oxycodone on an empty stomach? Could she handle the pain without it?

"Hey, sleeping beauty," Tobin whispered. He sounded like he meant it, so tender in the dark. To Livvy's surprise, she began crying again, snuffing as quietly as she could.

"Oh hey, hey!" Tobin cradled her head against his shoulder. "It's going to be okay. This thing will end soon, and you'll get everything you need. I promise."

The WBC men were quiet. Perhaps sleeping. Livvy tried to keep her voice from squeaking with emotion: "Gant said he won't end the riot until he gets me."

Tobin tensed, but his voice remained calm. "Gant isn't in charge, Livvy. Even if he thinks he is, he's only part of the equation."

Livvy nodded into his shoulder. "'Kay."

Who'd Gant been talking to? He'd been bargaining with the person on the other end. Well—more like demanding and threatening. Everyone else he'd commanded. Had Tobin heard the conversation? Livvy was about to ask, when Tobin whispered.

"I have a plan."

"A plan?"

"Yeah. To get you out of here."

"The dungeon?"

"The prison, goofy."

"Is it a good plan?"

"It doesn't suck."

"Lay it on me." Livvy wiped her cheeks.

"Not yet." He eased her off his shoulder. "You sit tight."

"Wait!" Livvy hissed. "I hate this plan already. Don't leave me!"

"I have to be gone just a little while, to execute phase one. I won't be far."

Livvy clutched his sleeve. "Tell me what you're going to do!"

Tobin sighed. "Me and the guys are going to overpower the guard. Then we'll have enough hostages for the badges to swoop in and pick you all up."

Livvy reflected. "That's a good plan, except a small detail."

"What's that?"

"How are you going to overpower the guard?"

"With a sweatshirt and surprise. But no one knows you're back here until I'm sure it's safe to bring you out. So you sit and be quiet!"

Tobin crept away. Livvy dug a fingernail into her palm. *Be safe. Oh, please be safe.*

A moment later there was whispering, a stifled exclamation and rapid muttering. In spite of Tobin's command, Livvy inched to the opening of her cell and looked toward the faint rectangle of light around the massive door.

A figure moved in front of the light, ducked around the corner from the first cell into the second. Tobin.

Then the WBC guys started yelling.

"Hey, guard! Help!"

"Hey man, we need some help!"

"We got a sick man in here!"

Livvy tucked behind her wall. Someone pounded on the door— from the inside or out, she couldn't tell. But it opened.

Livvy tried mightily to stay out of sight. But she just couldn't stand it. She peeked again as the guard entered pointing a gun at the men. *Oh! He's armed! Abort, abort! Don't do this, Tobin.*

"What's going on? What are you yelling about?"

"Our friend is sick. He threw up," Sean said.

"What do I care?" the inmate asked.

Livvy peeked again. The inmate was no longer visible, having entered the first cell. And Tobin crept out of the second one, sweatshirt twisted long and taut between his outstretched hands. *Oh don't, Tobin! He's got a gun!*

Tobin disappeared into the cell. There was an abrupt guttural sound and scuffling.

"Get the gun!"

"Grab his legs!"

The thrashing, writhing group of men were suddenly silhouetted in the half-closed door as they carried the inmate further into the jail. Livvy jerked back so quickly she almost gasped in pain.

More muttering, bossing, directing. Then relative silence, other than heavy breathing and intermittent scuffling.

"How about one of *us* carries the gun," Rudy said.

"Nope. I've got it," Tobin replied. "And you're welcome."

"Where did you even come from?" Sean asked.

"I was in here when you guys arrived. Now we have to get moving. Stick with me and do what I say."

"Where are we going?"

"Do you mind if I don't tell you in front of this guy, Einstein?" Tobin sounded more wry than annoyed. "Oh man, awesome."

"What?"

"A cell phone. We got ourselves a cell phone."

"Let's go, let's go!" Sean urged.

"Just a minute, I have to get my friend," Tobin said.

Livvy stepped out of the cell. She could barely see the men, much less distinguish any features.

"How many guys do you have back there?" Rudy asked.

"Just me and Shorty. Let's go. Me first, then you," he nodded at

Livvy, then at Sean, then the two men she didn't know. "You're bringing up the rear, big guy," he told Rudy. "Stay together and low."

Tobin edged to the door.

"What about the inmate?" Livvy whispered.

"He's hogtied with his tube socks. He's not going anywhere."

It was a little frightening, the things Tobin knew how to do.

The group of six crept out the door, and Tobin led them down the slope toward the main yard. That didn't seem like a good idea to Livvy, but then, there were goons guarding the quad in the other direction.

The yard made for a stark contrast from the night before. It was mostly empty. A few inmates worked out. A couple played basketball. But mostly any movement took place on the edges, in the same way their little party skirted the base of the brick wall Livvy had climbed down the day before. Fresh air on her face cleared her mind, and her eyes adjusted to the sunlight. But her stomach knotted in hunger, her side in pain.

She glanced back at their group and was startled to see the guys wearing civilian clothes. Of course they were—she'd just forgotten. Eyeing the officers on the catwalks, she wondered what they thought of these two inmates leading four civilians along. She couldn't see the handgun on Tobin. Hopefully the guards with their scopes couldn't either.

Sean caught her looking back. "Livvy!"

"Yup."

"You were in there that whole time?"

"Yeah. You invaded my haven." Livvy smiled, but was surprised at the genuine hardness she felt behind the words.

"Are you okay?" Rudy asked.

"Let's keep moving, folks. We can do the whole 'Reunited' song later." Tobin was in his McGruff mode.

Livvy smiled to herself. He was completely transparent. So

concerned for them.

The small band made its way to the ramp that led to the upper part of the prison. If Livvy had her bearings right, it would come out near the ISU. Was Miles still there? The inmates he and Tobin had subdued? That'd be two sets of prison blues for the four men behind her. Maybe they should've taken the clothes from the inmate in the dungeon.

About a third of the way up the stairs, Livvy faltered. She missed a step and went to her knees. Tobin was by her side in an instant. "You okay?"

"I'm just light-headed. I'll be ok."

"What happened to your pants?" Sean pointed.

The waistband of her jeans spread a deep crimson stain. Livvy lifted the hem of her sweatshirt and shirt. The gauze around her midriff had soaked through, and blood seeped down her skin.

"I'm going to kill Navarrette. What a lousy stitch job," Tobin said.

"What happened? Livvy, are you okay?" Rudy and the others crowded around.

Livvy dropped her shirts, elbowed her way through the men. "Stop looking at me."

"Come on, keep moving!" Tobin hissed.

"Whoa, man, she's hurt!" Rudy took Livvy's elbow. "She needs help!"

"She needs you morons to stop pawing over her and get it in gear! We can't stop here."

"Hey tough guy, thanks for your help back there, but you've got to take it easy on her—"

"No," Livvy muttered through clenched teeth. "He's right. We are sitting ducks out here. We've got to move."

"Livvy, you're going to pass out if you keep going." Sean's eyes were wide with concern.

"Then Tobin will cross that bridge. Get moving." Livvy grasped the railing with two hands and dragged herself upward. Tobin switched to walk behind her, in case she toppled backwards.

At the top of the stairs, Livvy trembled in cold sweat. But she was still on her own two feet.

"Where to, Cap'n?" she asked Tobin.

Chapter Twenty-Four

Miles looked none too happy to open the ISU door for them. "What are you doing here?"

"Just let us in, 'Rette." Tobin shouldered past him, ushering Livvy inside. The two inmates were still handcuffed to desks. Sean blanched slightly at the sight of them.

"We got company in the dungeon," Tobin said. "These guys are from Livvy's church."

Nods all around from the men.

"So get that guy, Classen, on the phone and tell him you have enough hostages for an airlift now."

Tobin eased Livvy onto the stretcher. The hard plastic was not exactly comfy, but it felt good to lie down. He got her some water.

"She needs food, Navarrette. What do you got around here?"

Miles pulled a stash from a desk drawer. Granola bars and cookies.

Livvy chowed through a strawberry cereal bar, then fished an oxycodone from her pocket. *Down the hatch.*

Rudy cleared his throat. "Uh, what's going on, Livvy?" Tight-lipped, he nodded at Miles and Tobin.

"Rudy, this here is my faithful protector, Tobin. And that's Miles Navarrette." She pointed at Miles and added in a whisper, "he's a correctional officer."

"We're going to get you guys out of here," Miles said.

"What about Lucas?" Sean asked.

"Yeah man, we can't leave Lucas behind," Rudy added.

Miles paused, phone half raised. "You're killing me here. Where's this Lucas?"

"We don't know, they took him off somewhere."

"He could be anywhere," Tobin said. "Let's just get you guys and Livvy out of here. I promise to keep looking for Lucas." He wrapped a fresh layer of gauze around Livvy's wound.

Concern was etched across his face. A face that had become very dear to Livvy. But Lucas was too—and he'd been separated out of the pack in order to draw Livvy to Gant. There was no way she could let him get left behind.

She touched Tobin's hand and their eyes met. He shook his head slightly. "If they can come get you, you are going. No matter how cute the guy is."

Livvy's cheeks flamed. She looked away, confused. She almost felt like she was caught cheating ... but cheating on whom, with whom?

"Livvy, where's the rest of the group from the chapel?" Sean asked.

"We got separated. But we think they're in the basement of North Block." Smitty was going to do reconnaissance in North Block. And Cho the same for West Block.

"Tobin?" She searched his face tentatively. "What about checking the canteen for the other guys. They don't know where we are. Maybe they know more about the other hostages."

Tobin sighed. "Let's just focus on you, Livvy, and these guys. I'll bet the badges will send in a chopper for five of you. Then 'Rette and I can keep searching for the rest."

"I don't think you get it, man," Rudy said. "We're not leaving without Lucas." He jabbed his thumb toward his teammates. They nodded their agreement.

"Well, that's just fabulous!" Tobin's voice rose. He drilled Livvy with his gaze. "You need medical attention. And you need to be on the other side of that wall from Gant. ASAP."

Sean looked pained. "He's got a point, guys. Even if we find Lucas, what are we supposed to do? They'll be guarding him and stuff."

"They were guarding us and stuff, and we got away." That was the voice of Angry Man, which went with a tall, gray-haired guy.

"Yeah, with his help!" Sean jerked a nod at Tobin. "And surprise and luck."

"Give us some inmate clothes," Rudy said. "We can at least have a look around."

Tobin snorted. "Right. And when you get lost, confronted, or taken, I'll have to save your keister again."

"Listen," Rudy threw his chest out, "I appreciate your help and all, but I can handle myself just fine—"

"Man, you don't know the first thing—"

"Shut up! Shut UP!" Livvy shouted. "Tobin, off the top of your head, where do you think Gant would put Lucas. Quick. First thing that comes to your mind."

Tobin shrugged. "The box—holding cage. On the floor of North Block. Near his little make-shift office."

"Okay, then—"

"It's just a guess, Liv."

"But it's a good one," Miles said.

"Isn't it at least worth a shot? How about we check it out and if he's not there, then we call Classen about a ride?" Livvy asked.

Tobin frowned and rubbed his head. "Depends on who you mean by 'we.' You're not going anywhere. 'Rette has a target on his back, and I'm a goner if Gant sees me. We were mighty lucky he didn't see us in the dungeon."

Miles looked up, brow furrowed.

"I'll go," Rudy said.

"Man, you don't even know how to walk right in here." Tobin shook his head in disgust.

"Well I've been penned up and pinned down for a day. I'm ready to do something." Rudy strode to a cabinet and flung open the doors.

"Whoa!" Miles was quick to his side. "There's a lot of sensitive stuff in here. What do you think you're doing?"

"Where'd you get those clothes?" Rudy nodded at Miles's prison blues.

"This isn't a department store. We don't keep inmate uniforms here."

Tobin rolled his eyes. "I'll go check the canteen for our friends. No one move until I get back."

"Be back," Livvy said. "Soon."

"I will. And 'Rette—*Lock. The. Door!*"

Miles got ahold of Classen almost immediately this time and filled him in.

A tapping on the door made Livvy jump, but she caught herself before uttering a sound. She scooted off the stretcher and under a desk.

Miles let in Tobin, and with him Cho and Agromonte.

"Smitty's headed back to North." Tobin updated them. "He didn't spot any hostages a few hours ago, but is going to check again."

"No hostages in West Block, far as I could tell," Cho said.

Waiting was unbearable. The men were all quiet except Miles, on the phone with Classen. From Miles's side of the conversation, it sounded like the authorities felt five civilians were worth sending in a helicopter. Livvy struggled to keep the flutter of anticipation repressed, in case things got fouled up. Again. But as the painkillers kicked in and her blood sugar rose, so did her hopes. She could be on the other side of San Quentin's walls in the matter of an hour!

She ducked her head. *Jesus, please help Joan and all the WBC guys still out there. Keep them safe until this is over. And any other civilians, and staff, and COs.* As the list grew, Livvy felt increasingly grateful that she had a ride on its way. *Please, please help us find Lucas. Protect him. I hope he's not too badly hurt.*

Her not-date at Ruby's with Lucas was not quite a week ago. Strange, now, that she'd been so nervous. Life was sure short and unpredictable. They always said that, but it didn't really sink in until you had your own close encounter of the life-changing kind. Then it was like *The Matrix.* You glimpsed beyond the physical construct everyone interacted with on a daily basis and saw into the eternal.

And that's what they called perspective.

If I get a chance at a do-over, I'll do dinner with Tobin very differently. I'll ask him all about his life and tell him about mine. I won't worry about how I'm coming off, I'll—

Wait a second. Was that "Lucas," or "Tobin"?

Because, of course, she'd never have dinner with Tobin.

Livvy glanced around the room. Us and them. Having that line between Tobin and her was beyond sad. And it was going to be redrawn as soon as she got on that helicopter.

Still handcuffed to the desks, the two inmates kept shifting and grunting. They looked so uncomfortable. Livvy rose and got two cups of water and two power bars from the dwindling stash of snacks. When she approached the prisoners, Tobin, playing with the cell phone taken from Gant's thug, arched an eyebrow but didn't say anything.

"If you yell or bite, you don't get anything." Livvy advised the men. Gently she pulled back the tape over the first man's mouth.

He drank greedily and made quick work of the power bar. "Sorry," Livvy said, applying fresh tape over his mouth.

"Hey," the second man said when his mouth was freed. "What other drugs you got in here?"

Livvy frowned. "This is all you get, take it or leave it."

"Nah, man, I'm just saying—" He directed his comments to Miles. "I didn't get my medication, Boss. My Prozac. You got that in here?"

Miles frowned. "I'm not authorized to dispense medication. Don't have it anyway."

"I need my medicine, man." The inmate insisted.

Miles shook his head with a shrug. "It's currently secured in the Neumiller infirmary building. You'll just have to wait it out."

Livvy offered the water. The man never took his eyes off hers as she tipped the cup and he drank. He ate in slow, measured bites. "I ain't no animal," he said after a swallow.

Livvy felt heat rise to her cheeks. "I know that." But she had been thinking about the *us* versus *them*. How the little brigade in the building was such a hodgepodge of men in a tense accord to work together. How out-of-control hundreds of the inmates had been. The prison was much quieter than yesterday. What were they all doing? Why didn't the authorities come in, now that it was quiet? And something new to consider—what percentage of the prison population was off their meds?

Yesterday the TV said the prisoners had made demands. Miles said the authorities would try to negotiate an end to the crisis. Gant talked on the phone as if he had the power to end it or prolong it. So what was going on? Who else inside the walls did Classen talk to? What was left to resolve this madness?

"Get this," Tobin said, tapping on the cell phone he'd taken from the thug in the dungeon. "There's some guy out there, outside the wall, tweeting updates about the riot: nosy neighbor. '@nosyneighbor--Guvnr has coffee break,' and 'Red Cross rep argues with press.'" Livvy looked over his shoulder as he read aloud. "Here's the latest one: 'police chopper warming up.'" Tobin grinned at Livvy. "Guess Classen has some pull."

He tilted the phone so Livvy could see the screen better. "Same guy has a 'hostage watch' on his Facebook page," he said. "Those pictures we heard about on the radio are on there. And look—" He held up the cell.

At first Livvy couldn't tell what she was supposed to be seeing. Then she spotted it: "The Livvy Watch: Where in San Quentin is Livvy Fischer?"

"No way."

"Way." Tobin clicked, scrolled, then read aloud: "'Willowvale Bible Church's choir team is all accounted for in hostage photos except soprano Livvy Fischer, pictured here.'" Unbelievable—a head shot from her conservatory bio.

"'It doesn't take a rocket scientist to see that Livvy Fischer looks just like the preferred victim of serial killer, Gant, leading this blogger to ask, where is Livvy?'"

There were hundreds of comments to the post, people saying they were praying for Livvy. People had started candlelight vigils on her behalf. She was trending on Twitter.

Livvy shook her head. Truly unbelievable.

"So much for not being the center of attention." Tobin observed. "Here: let's tell them you're okay." He pecked out letters with his thumbs.

"Wait! Do we want Gant to know we have access to a phone?" Livvy asked.

Tobin paused. "What could it matter?" But he erased the message. "Guess your public will have to keep wondering for a little longer." He looked at the clock. "A *little* longer. Where is Smitty? I say fifteen more minutes, then we get you guys up on the roof for the helicopter, with or without Lucas."

Cho stood, rubbed his hands on his thighs. "Can't sit here all day. Gonna go find Smitty." He looked to Agromonte. "You in?"

Agromonte nodded and the two left.

"So," Angry Man said to Tobin. "What're you in for?"

"Jim!" Rudy said. "Geez man, show some class."

"What? It's not exactly a secret that the man is a convicted felon. I'm just wondering what for. I don't hold it against you: you seem like a changed man."

Tobin crushed his water cup. Tossed it into a nearby trashcan. "No offense taken." But a small muscle in his jaw worked as he fell silent.

Livvy dug her nails in her palms. Poor Tobin. The us-versus-them line had shifted again, invisible boundaries realigning, stretching between and around those in the room like spider webbing.

A great thumping on the door made all heads swivel to the front of the office. Again Livvy took refuge under a desk. Both Tobin and Miles went to the door, and from the sound of things, that was a good move. A chorus of yells and shouts, thumping and crashing shook the small building.

"Shut the door! Shut the door!" Cho yelled.

"Quick, barricade it," Tobin ordered.

Livvy jumped out of the way as the men grabbed desks, tables, and filing cabinets and shoved them in front of the door. The pounding and swearing on the door continued, but the men inside paused for breath.

Livvy turned to Smitty as Cho explained. "Sm'other guys saw us coming in. Guess they thought it was a good idea."

"What about Lucas?" Livvy asked, addressing Cho, Smitty, and Agromonte. "Did you guys see him?"

They each shook their heads, expressions somber.

"Liv," Tobin said softly. He was right next to Livvy and perhaps meant for only her to hear, but the room went quiet at his urgent tone. "They have Lucas tied up in the quad, by the chapel and east gate. The media spotted him from the air."

Livvy drew her brows together. "How do you know?"

Tobin waggled the cell phone. Rudy drew himself up and faced off with Tobin. "When were you going to tell us that?"

Tobin kept his eyes on Livvy. "I didn't want you to think you can stay and rescue him." He looked truly grieved. "There's no way we can get him. It's totally exposed. Not this little crew, not unarmed."

Tears misted Livvy's eyes. "Did they say whether he was injured?"

Tobin shook his head.

The assault on the front of the building grew louder.

"I guess we're not exiting through the front door," Sean said.

"Okay, 'Rette, how do we get everyone on the roof?" Tobin asked.

Miles shrugged, but cleared off a desk. "Go up, I guess."

Rudy didn't wait for an invitation. He leapt on the desk and knocked aside an overhead tile. With a surprisingly agile leap, the large man pulled himself up. Sean grabbed a flailing foot and pushed to give leverage.

Once up, Rudy disappeared from sight. "Over here," he called. "There's a vent." The ceiling creaked as he made his way around above. Then it shook as he pounded on something. "Come on up!" he yelled.

Sean was next atop the desk, but he turned to help Livvy. Rudy leaned down, and with the men hoisting below and Rudy clasping her arm, Livvy was in the crawl space above the ISU in the span of an inhalation. Dust danced in the dim light, and a hole in the ceiling some ten feet away beckoned her forward. Even before she had her shoulders into the open air, she could hear the thrum of an approaching helicopter. This was it! She was getting out of San Quentin.

Sean crawled through the hole behind her and onto the roof, followed by the other WBC guys. They all crouched as the helicopter approached, wind from the rotors washing over them. The ISU was now an island, surrounded by a throng of pushing, shouting inmates. Someone in the crowd threw something. Fire exploded about five feet from Livvy. Molotov cocktails, like those lobbed during her attempt to escape over the wall the night before. The bombs hit the walls of the ISU, flames catching hold and lapping into the structure.

The helicopter dipped and hovered, just feet from the ISU roof. Would it be able to land? Would the building give way under its weight? Gently, as softly as a fallen autumn leaf coming to rest, the chopper touched down.

"C'mon!" A helmeted officer, tethered by a strap, leaned out, arm extended.

The little rag-tag group needed no second invitation. Projectiles exploded around them, casting shrapnel 360 degrees. Flames now licked up all sides of the building.

Livvy scrambled forward. Movement caught her eye: Miles, and Livvy's cadre of inmate protectors surged through the vent hole onto the roof. One of the SWAT officers leveled his weapon at them. "Stop! Freeze!" he yelled.

Tobin, Miles, Smitty, Cho, and Agromonte all hit the roof. The officer swept his weapon over their backs and paused on Livvy, still on her feet. He raised his rifle a hair, her prison blues surely giving him pause.

"No!" The WBC men yelled in unison, over the deafening rotors. "She's with us!" Rudy reached to push the muzzle of the rifle down. Another officer restrained him, but the first man lowered his weapon and beckoned to Livvy.

There was a loud crack, and the roof shifted. Livvy fell to her knee. Tobin was arguing with the others about something: "trapped" was all she could make out in the din. The two inmates below! They were handcuffed to desks in a burning building. Cho grabbed at Tobin, but was too slow. Tobin disappeared back down the rabbit hole. At that moment, a Molotov cocktail hit the windshield of the helicopter.

"Come now!" The SWAT officer urged, and the guys from WBC were all wide-eyed screams, gesturing at Livvy, the only evacuee still on the roof. She crawled, the roof now buckling and hot under her hands and knees. The helicopter lifted off the roof, hovered a foot above.

Smitty and Agromonte ran to the back of the roof, dove and slid on their stomachs to the edge, and deftly spun and dropped over the side.

Livvy had to go, *now*, but Tobin was down in that inferno, trying to free those two men. She scuttled along the roof, abruptly turning toward the hole. If she could just see him—

"Livvy!" someone screamed from the helicopter. She looked over her shoulder in time to see an explosion of fire illuminate Sean's panicked face, his eyes locked on hers.

The uniform of the SWAT officer next to Sean ignited. Another officer brushed a burning device to the roof and slapped out flames on the man and in the helicopter. "Go, go!" he yelled. The copilot gave the pilot an urgent thumbs-up.

No! They were leaving! Miles grabbed one of Livvy's arms and Cho the other. They dragged and carried her toward the helicopter in a hunched run. Another flaming projectile exploded against the side of the helicopter, and with a *woosh* it lifted off and away.

Livvy screamed, pulling toward where the helicopter had been, then toward the hole down which Tobin had disappeared. The surface she stood on shifted abruptly, and Miles and Cho dragged her to the edge of the roof at the rear of the building and threw her off.

Chapter Twenty-Five

Fire, fire. Fire again.

It would not stop until it consumed her, like it had swallowed Wade. And now it had taken Tobin. Livvy hunched on her knees, a couple of yards from the flaming ISU. She coughed and gagged on the acrid smoke, her side splitting with pain.

Miles swept her up in a fireman's carry. Ran to a chain link fence that trapped them next to the burning building and began to climb. At the top he dumped her down to Cho.

"No!" Livvy screamed, clinging to the fence. "Tobin! Tobin's in there!"

Cho slapped his hand over her mouth. "Shut up! We can't do anything for him now."

The crowd gawked at the blaze. Miles and Cho pushed a way through for the three of them, dragging Livvy along. They were under the foul-weather shed again, heading toward the canteen.

Livvy thrashed and pulled, gasping for breath and from pain. Miles spun her to face him, glaring at her from inches away. "Do you *want* to live?" he hissed. "You have got to be either the stupidest or the most unlucky person I've ever met. All you had to do was get on that helicopter."

Cho tugged on the two of them. "C'mon!"

But Miles wasn't finished. "How many lives are you going to risk for yours before this is over?"

Smitty burst upon them from behind, pulling Livvy into a trot she could barely sustain. He got her back to the canteen. Livvy evaluated the window sill, a yard off the ground. No way she could haul herself up and over that. She was a quivering mess of pain.

Cho and Smitty dumped her inside. She crawled to a front corner out of sight of the window and hugged her knees to her chest. Distant howls went up, perhaps as the ISU finished its collapse.

Was Miles right? Had her choices put others at risk? Was Tobin dead because of her? If she'd stayed put, last time she was in the canteen, she wouldn't have been stabbed. They probably would not have ever gone to the ISU in the first place. If Tobin was dead, it was her fault. The horror of that realization crept over her, chilling her limbs.

Miles paced inside the small space, cursing. "So much lost. I was so close." He fumbled with his shirt and pulled out a couple of file folders he'd stuffed under it.

Smitty slid down next to Livvy. "You okay, Homes?"

Livvy just stared at him. *Okay?* How could she possibly be okay?

Four of the WBC team had made it out of San Quentin. She tried to feel something about that. But Tobin, Tobin ... Could he have made it out? How long would it take to free those two men? She pictured Tobin fighting through thick smoke. Then, unbidden, the image of Tobin's face melting in flame, the smell of burning flesh made her gag. Smitty held her while she cried.

"So much evidence, gone." Miles cursed again.

"Evidence!" Livvy gasped. "What about the lives of three men? What about Tobin? You had time to grab files but not release the men handcuffed in a burning building?"

"The building wasn't on fire when I went up to the roof!" Miles shouted. He blew out a breath and squatted low to the ground on the balls of his feet. "Of course I care about Tobin and those men. I don't know how many lives have been terminated so far. I do know that lots of men, including my team, are being hunted; that means I continue mission. And the intel I needed just went up in smoke."

"Aren't the computers networked?" Cho asked, his voice even.

"Not the data I'm talking about. Although—" Miles reached into his pocket and withdrew a small item. A USB drive. "Maybe there's enough on here."

"So what *did* you figure out?" Agromonte asked.

Miles shook his head. "I can't share details from an ongoing investigation with inmates—"

"Aw, forget you, man!" Cho exploded. He leapt to his feet and shoved Miles in the chest. "I'd take ten Tobins over one of you!"

Agromonte was on his feet too but interceded between Cho and Miles. There was a flash in his eyes when he looked at Miles. It was caution, Livvy realized: *Us and them.*

Lucas gingerly inched to the right, rotating ever so slightly around the tree trunk. Pain streaked through his torso and he pressed back into the palm with a groan that was practically a sob. His breath came in rapid, shallow pants.

It was a wasted effort anyway. He couldn't see any further down the main thoroughfare leading to the cell blocks, no matter how far around he scooted.

Where had the helicopter gone? It'd come over the prison wall and flown out of sight beyond the buildings in front of him. Were the authorities finally launching an assault? Had they landed?

The Molotov cocktail brigade had charged in that direction, and not surprisingly, smoke now billowed from the general area.

Lucas craned to observe the activity on the gun walk above the east gate, but had swiveled too far around the tree. Officers would hopefully be coming through that door any second, and he'd be right in their path of rescue.

Thank you. The God who hears and answers.

Minutes passed. No change. No cavalry.

It's okay. It's all right. He's still the God who hears and answers. *You're. You're still the God who hears and answers.*

But I am so, so tired. And I hurt. Lucas dug his heel in the ground and shifted his weight. He clenched his jaw against a moan. *You're in charge. No matter how things look.*

Things looked like chaos. What was going on behind the scenes? Who was mobilized on the other side of that east wall? *Somebody* had to be talking with a faction of inmates. The Department of Corrections said they didn't negotiate for prisoners. But did that mean they wouldn't dialogue at all?

Of the inmates running amok on the road between buildings, two walked with purpose. They came Lucas's direction, away from the smoke. He didn't want to stare, but there was little else to keep him occupied. They were fifty feet away when he recognized them. They were two of the three who'd guarded the pen last night. Gant's men.

Lucas's pulse increased. On the one hand, being released from this stupid tree was welcome. On the other hand, the less interaction he had with Gant and any of his goons the better.

The men reached Lucas, and without a word, one worked to untie him.

"Where are we going?" Lucas asked.

No answer. The silent treatment? *Oh come on guys, you're going to hurt my feelings.*

"Where are my teammates?"

"Shut up," was all he got in response.

One of the men yanked Lucas to his feet, none too gently.

Lightheaded, Lucas stumbled, caught himself, and stayed on his feet.

"This way," one said. They started back the way the two had come. Lucas struggled to keep pace. He had no interest in being "encouraged" to go faster.

"Where are we going?" he asked.

"Shut your yap." Bulldog's buddies had been better conversationalists than these guys.

They passed the yard with all the cages where Lucas had spent the night with the others. At the corner of North Block, one of Lucas's escorts shoved him left. He shuffled on, but stared at the scene before him. A small, standalone building was in flames, caving in on itself. In the haze of smoke, inmates clustered, some cheering. Fallon stood on his own. He acknowledged Lucas with a nod.

"Looks like some of your buddies made it out," he said.

"They did?" Lucas resisted the inmate shoving him from behind.

"Yeah. You see the 'copter?"

"Don't talk to him," one of the goons ordered Fallon.

"Save it, Adolf," Fallon said.

"How many?" Lucas asked. "Was there a woman?"

"A woman! I didn't see no woman. And I wasn't counting."

"Move!" The inmate punched Lucas in the kidney. Lucas expelled a burst of air with a sound he'd never heard himself make before. Went down on his knees.

"Now how's he supposed to move if you gonna lay him out like that?" Fallon asked.

The two inmates cursed Fallon, grabbed Lucas under his arms, and dragged him through the door into North Block.

A thick, dull fatigue settled in Livvy's joints and spread over her mind like a blanket. She tried to scrabble for a solution—some way Tobin could have made it out of that smoking, flaming building before it collapsed. But he'd gone back inside after the two handcuffed inmates. And the door had been barricaded.

She knew from experience how quickly smoke inhalation could be debilitating. How quickly flames—

She choked in reflex, pressed the heels of her hands to her closed eyes as if she could rub out the mental images of Wade. Not Tobin! Not her valiant protector throughout the last twenty-four hours of chaos and threat.

His six years turned death sentence.

Her own chances of dying in this prison now higher.

A wounded Lucas, separated from his buddies, tied up in the quad and guarded by Gant's thugs.

Gant intent on fanning the riot until he had Livvy in his grip again. She fingered her earlobe.

Miles paced the small space like a caged animal, brow furrowed. He muttered under his breath, stopping periodically to punctuate a thought into the air.

The rest of the group remained immobile. The men sprawled or hunched on the floor, gazes distant. The smell of smoke hung heavy in the air. Was the ISU close enough to any other buildings for the fire to jump? Maybe the riot would end if prisoners had to flee their captured buildings. Like vermin before a flood.

That was an ugly thing to call them. Most of them didn't deserve that. Tobin had proven to be a higher caliber man than many she'd met and even dated. The tears started again and Livvy made no effort to stop or hide them. She was so tired. If only she could go to sleep and wake up after someone put everything right again.

A rhythmic sound slowly penetrated the fog of Livvy's consciousness. A familiar sound. Her pulse quickened—helicopter rotors. They were coming back for her! She limped to the window. The enormous aluminum roof that provided shelter over the foul weather yard blocked all view of the sky. But the sound was unmistakable. They were coming.

Livvy scrambled out of the canteen. The helicopter noise came from the direction of the yard, the other end of the covered pad, where the ISU burned. She staggered towards the sound. Where would they land? She couldn't miss the chance this time. She needed to maintain her disguise while in this throng of men, but be identifiable to her rescuers. Men crowded, ran pell-mell in every direction. Livvy wove through the masses, dimly aware of Smitty on her heels.

A sooty face appeared in front of her. It was one of the inmates that had been handcuffed in the ISU—the second one, who'd asked about his medication. Livvy gasped. He was alive! The man saw her at the same time and registered surprise.

"How did you get out? Where's Tobin?" Livvy demanded. "Did he make it too? Where is he?"

Smitty reached Livvy's side and viewed the inmate with apprehension.

"Tell me!" Livvy cried, grasping the man's sleeve. "Where's Tobin?"

"I don't know." he said. "I could barely see him through the smoke when he uncuffed me."

Livvy would not, could not, cry here in the middle of all these men. Even if the man kept her identity a secret, she'd never pass for an inmate if she started blubbering.

Her eyes welled.

"What're you even doing in here?" The man leaned in close, his breath foul. "You staff?"

A voice cried out. And there was inmate number one. "Hey! There she is!" he yelled.

Smitty stepped in front of Livvy, between her and the man. As if her other three quarters weren't flanked by felons.

The one voice, in the chorus of voices reverberating off that aluminum roof, was all it took. One, two, six, twelve men looked, stopped, pointed. Livvy was an island in a sea of prisoners focused on her.

Most stared, many leered, a few grabbed. Livvy tore away from clutching hands, backing into more hands, arms. She was surrounded by a throng of pawing men. A deer encircled by wolves. She could no longer see Smitty. *Oh God!* This was it. *Please help!* She couldn't move to throw her elbows. Simply clasped her arms around herself, crying out inarticulately.

An ear-piercing blast rang out. A gunshot. It ricocheted off the roof, the echo reverberating. Most men hit the ground. Everyone sought the source.

A few yards away, handgun raised overhead, Tobin stood resolute. "Come here, Livvy," he said. He pointed the gun at the men who remained around her. "Get down." The men obeyed. Livvy picked her way to him, trembling violently. Then she ran. She slammed into Tobin and wrapped her arms around him. The tears overflowed.

Tobin wrapped one arm around her shoulders and cleared his throat. "Hi there." His voice was husky, and he smelled of smoke. He took a few steps backward, sweeping broadly with the gun. There were few men behind them: some twenty yards back the ISU fire raged. And the thrum of the helicopter rotors still approached.

Livvy dragged her sleeve across her eyes. The crowd of men in front of them looked mostly curious. Several grinned like this was big entertainment. A few looked at Livvy instead of the gun, hunger in their eyes. Livvy met one gaze. Miles. He narrowed his eyes. Disapproval? Because of their situation? Because Livvy endangered Tobin? Because Tobin held a gun?

Tobin pulled Livvy further back. Toward the helicopter. He would help her get on it. They backpedaled; they ran. Smoke billowed out to greet them, limiting visibility. Livvy tried to picture the area past the ISU—the entrance to North Block, corridor toward the east gate and chapel quad. Where could a helicopter land? It was so close now that it kicked up wind under the aluminum roof. Livvy and Tobin coughed, waved at the billows of smoke that engulfed them. Between the terrible visibility and the difficulty Livvy had keeping her eyes open in the stinging haze, she might have lost Tobin if she hadn't been clutching his arm.

An odd roar, pitched deeper than the rotors' thrum grew into a great *whoosh!* Sizzles, pops, then an outpouring of filthy water. Debris flooded toward Livvy from the direction of the ISU. Water swept over her feet and rose up her calves, before dissipating again.

And the helicopter flew away.

They weren't coming for her.

They were fighting the fire.

Gant's henchmen dragged Lucas to the man himself. He held court in a small office on the first floor of the cell block. Lucas jerked his arms from the goons on his right and left. He'd stand on his own.

Gant glared at Lucas with his reptilian eyes. With a roar, he seized a computer monitor and heaved it in Lucas's direction. Tethered by cables, the monitor yanked other equipment behind it in its brief period of flight, then all smashed to the concrete. Lucas, still outside the door to the office, kept his ground.

Gant strode to him, nostrils flaring. Something flashed in his right hand—a knife, apparently, that he pressed against Lucas's jugular. "She may have made it out, but you're not going to. You won't see her again either, lover boy. You're gonna die in here."

Mute, frozen, Lucas locked eyes with Gant. His body was ice

cold, except his sweaty palms. *Made it out. Gonna die in here.* Everything beyond Gant blurred, all commotion was a low roar in Lucas's ears. Then adrenaline hit, and he began to twitch.

Gant's lip curled. He pressed the point of the shank against Lucas's throat until Lucas felt his skin pop. Slowly Gant etched a line from right to left under Lucas's chin. "You'll never see her again," he said. Then he stepped back. "Take him downstairs," he directed the two inmates.

Lucas clasped his hand to his throat. It was bloody, but intact. The pain was sharp and wordless, taking over his mind and thoughts. He stumbled along with the inmates, barely aware of their direction as he was herded down stairs and through corridors into the strangest room. It was a quirky shape and held a weird capsule. A pale green, the pod looked like something from a submarine, complete with one of those wheels you spin to seal the door closed.

A window in the side revealed people crowded inside. Lucas could see green correctional uniforms. Then an inmate swung the door open and there was Joan, Hector, and all the guys from chapel. Lucas hurried toward them, but then the purpose of that odd structure slammed his consciousness. He spun, struck out at the inmates. "No way! You can't do this!"

That's why Gant hadn't slit his throat—he was going to kill all of them at once in the gas chamber.

Chapter Twenty-Six

Tobin pulled Livvy away from the deluged ISU. The flames were nearly out, but the area was still full of smoke and steam. *Where to take her?* They had precious little time before guys on this side of the smoke screen made Livvy for a woman.

Tobin went north, Livvy close behind. They ran past North Block, past the high-security exercise yard and the Adjustment Center. Through the quad Tobin led and into the chapel. Down the aisle, up across the stage and through the door across from the one Livvy had thought was an escape route the day before. Only then did Tobin stop, in the small corridor that stretched the side of the chapel and disappeared around the corner on the inside wall.

He stood facing Livvy, so close. His hands trembled. Then Livvy grabbed one. "I thought you were dead."

Tobin pulled off her beanie and twined his fingers in her hair. "I thought you were on that helicopter." He had to swallow down so much more he wanted to say.

"How'd you get out?" Livvy asked.

"The front door," Tobin said. "Why are you still here, Liv?" He gripped her shoulders, then slid his palms over them, down the sides of her arms.

"I—I froze. I saw you go down there, and the whole building

was caving in. The fire spread so fast."

"You should be gone," Tobin said, but he enfolded her in his arms and wished he didn't ever have to let her go.

If she'd gotten on the helicopter he'd never have seen her again. Or would she have come visit him? Could he ask her to? Bring her back to this place, to meet in that colorless, airless visitors' room. Across a scarred table. *To talk about ...*

A great pressure settled on his chest. She'd never consider visiting him. Why would she? She'd have her cute pastor.

Lucas flailed against a swarm of inmates. "You can't! It's sick!" He was no match for one of them, much less four. One twisted Lucas's arm behind his back and shoved him toward the gas chamber. Everyone in there was yelling too, reaching past the inmates who blocked their escape, struggling to get to Lucas.

With a final thrust, Lucas was in the chamber, and that heavy oval door clanged shut behind him. He scrabbled at the steel plate. No handle. Of course. Why would you need a door handle on the inside of a gas chamber?

"Lucas!" Hector grabbed him by the shoulder.

Lucas scanned the ceiling. Where did the gas come in? Would they hear it? Did it have an odor? How long would it take?

"Lucas, honey." Joan cupped his face. "What have they done to you?"

Lucas clasped her hands in his, lowered them, and turned to the two correctional officers among them. "Can we block it? Use our clothing to smother the duct?"

The COs were slow to respond, but Chaplain Peake leaned into Lucas's line of sight. "Lucas, the gas isn't hooked up. It's disabled."

Lucas stared at him for a moment, the words taking a long time to penetrate. "The gas doesn't work?"

"No." The COs shook their heads.

"San Quentin switched to lethal injection years ago," an officer nodded toward the elevated gurney in the middle of the chamber. It was Knox, the CO who had briefed them upon entry into the Q. "This just seems to be a place to secure us."

Oh.

Well then.

Lucas caught his breath. He scanned all the faces, etched with concern. Right: he was a mess. He reached for his throat. It still oozed blood, a fair amount of which had soaked into the collar of his T-shirt.

All of a sudden, he didn't feel so well. He swayed, bumping into Hector.

"Sit down, Lucas." Joan directed him toward the—the what? Bed? Table? Lucas frowned. The execution table was complete with thick straps across to hold down the condemned man and arm rests angled out to give the executioner access to his veins. Creepy.

But it was Joan. "Sit," she commanded. "Gimme that." She tugged on the tie that hung loosely around Hector's neck. Gently she laid it over the cut on Lucas's throat, passed the ends around behind, and secured them in front. Part ascot, part tourniquet, part just plain weird. But effective.

Lucas was slow to take in details. There were seven people in here with him, two others sitting on the gurney. It was quite a squeeze. Everyone looked pretty good to him—Knox was the only one with a visible injury. Looked like he'd taken a blow to the eye.

"Why isn't Livvy with you?" he asked Joan.

Her stenciled eyebrows shot up. "When the riot started, this prisoner just grabbed her and took off through a window!"

"It's okay, Tobin's a good guy," Chaplain Peake said. "He wouldn't hurt her. I'm sure he's keeping her safe somewhere."

Tobin. That was the name Gant had used when he was

pummeling Lucas last night.

"No," Lucas said. "She's not with him. She's out—safe. She got out in the helicopter."

"Helicopter?" Knox asked. "When did that happen?"

"Little bit ago, I guess. Some of the team got out too."

"Oh, thank you, Jesus." Joan exhaled loudly and leaned back against the wall.

"What else is going on out there?" the other CO, labeled *Velasco*, asked.

"Uh," Lucas blinked slowly. "Mayhem."

"Could you be more specific?" Knox asked dryly.

"Not sure." Lucas shifted and winced. He waited a moment for his head to clear.

Joan was on alert again. "What else did they do to you?"

"Gotta couple of busted ribs, I think." Lucas eyed the floor. It was so crowded in there. "I know this sounds weird, but I'd love to lie down if I could."

'Cause, you know, if you're going to hang out in a gas chamber, you might as well make yourself comfortable.

Another confined space of relative safety. Livvy and Tobin huddled in the near dark. Livvy leaned against Tobin's chest.

"I thought you died in that fire."

Tobin rubbed her arm, but didn't speak.

There was so much Livvy wanted to say. She was so confused. She wanted to tell Tobin how she felt. It was hard to admit it to herself. Not hard to acknowledge—the feelings were too strong and close to the surface to deny. Just hard to wrap her head around.

It made sense, on a certain level. He was her knight, her protector. This was some kind of twisted Stockholm Syndrome.

But beyond that? Right now there didn't seem to be much of anything beyond this little hallway, and life outside the prison walls was light years away.

Yet somewhere within these walls was Lucas. Maybe being tortured, *for her*. She was sick with guilt over it. But what else did she feel for Lucas? Was she really this fickle—out of sight, out of mind?

She was probably confusing one feeling for another. She felt comfortable with Tobin. Safe. Like she could tell him anything. The only reason she didn't feel that way with Lucas was because he was first a customer at the café. And then there was the pastor thing. She had to get past that—stop seeing him as a pastor but as a guy.

Wait a minute ...

"We ran through the quad," she said.

"Yeah, so?"

"So, Lucas wasn't there."

Tobin's eyebrows pinched together. "No, he wasn't." He pulled out the cell phone and started typing.

Tobin was the only one who had seen the post about Lucas being in the quad. He wouldn't lie to her, would he?

"What are you doing?" Livvy asked.

"It's time to put our tools to good use. Maybe we can leverage Livvy Watch to put some pressure on the badges to get you out of here."

Livvy read over Tobin's shoulder. He tweeted that she was okay.

Wow. There was an almost immediate onslaught of relieved responses. People praising God for answered prayer.

Then there were a few cynical replies. *Prove it*, they essentially said.

Tobin pecked out words. *Livvy is hurt and in danger.*

"I should take your picture," he said. "Let's show them your wound."

Livvy raised the edge of her shirt and stared into the camera. It seemed too weird to smile. Like a mug shot.

"It's too dark," Tobin said. He cracked open the door and had Livvy stand in the shaft of light until he was satisfied with the shot. "No one should be able to tell where you are. There's practically no background in the frame."

In an instant, the photo was out to the world. If only Livvy could travel with it so effortlessly.

We need your help, Tobin typed. *We need CDCR to extract Livvy, to get her to safety.*

The tweets came fast and furious. A groundswell of responses indignant for Livvy's rescue.

"How do you know how to do all this technology stuff, anyway?" Livvy asked.

"I write for the *San Quentin News*, the prisoner newspaper. I did a series on social media. The more out of touch with technology we get, the further behind we fall."

Livvy nodded. "You know, you're kind of ..."

"Amazing? Handsome? Brave?"

"Surprising. You are full of surprises."

"Well, I wouldn't want to bore you," Tobin replied. "Hey, you know who we should get on your case? Tiana Jo. The reporter who has the San Quentin beat? She'll make you the face of the civilians at risk in this riot. Then the badges will have to go the distance to make sure you're safe."

"So how do you get ahold of this Tiana Jo?"

"Easy." Tobin tapped on the phone like a pro. "Her email address is at the end of all her articles. One of her stories is how I found the tweeting nosyneighbor guy in the first place."

Their hallway was quiet as Tobin worked. Livvy watched his fingers fly. He had strong hands. And a strong body. He must work out. On the yard? Like so many prison movies depicted?

It was weird, having someone take such an active interest in helping her. It made her feel a little indebted. A feeling she didn't like. She could never repay what he'd done for her. He'd risked so much, and for him, the end of the riot wouldn't be the end of his troubles.

"Will you have to cell with Gant when this is over?" What would Gant do to him?

"Nah. He'll be charged with a boatload of stuff in connection to the riot. They'll probably move him to a supermax facility."

Supermax. Sounded like feminine protection. "What's in it for him, do you think? He's gotta know it just makes things worse for himself."

Tobin shrugged. "Gets to be king for a day. And I don't know what kinds of demands they're making, what they're negotiating for."

"What would you ask for?"

"You." Tobin grinned. Ah, he was beautiful when he did that.

Livvy punched him in the arm. "Seriously."

"Better food. Cleaner conditions. And you know the programs I told you about, that a lot of inmates want to participate in? A bunch of those have been or are going to be cut. Budget stuff. I'd demand they cut somewhere else."

"Anything else?"

"Our mail is seriously screwed up. I'm talking delays of weeks for something as simple as a postcard. Even the confidential mail takes forever to get through."

"Confidential—like letters from your attorney?"

"Yup. We have a right to send and receive mail to certain people without it being read. Politicians, attorneys, legal help organizations, people like that. It's still searched for contraband, but not read. The badges are even supposed to open the letters upside down so they don't accidentally read anything."

"But what if someone's waiting for something important from

their lawyer?"

Tobin shrugged. "It's still hurry-up-and-wait."

"I'd complain about that, too."

"Would you riot over it?"

"No. Doesn't seem worth the risk and the return."

"Agreed."

They sat in silence for a while. Miles had said the riot started in several places at the same time. That it was really well coordinated. Gant bossed his guys around, but talked to the person on the phone like he was reporting in. So who was on the phone?

"Hey, here's an email back from Tiana. She says she'll definitely profile you. Huh. She wants to know who I am."

Livvy leaned in. "Tell her you are Prince Charming."

"Right, the felonious Prince Charming."

"You'd still be a prince outside of prison. That's just the kind of guy you are."

"Now, maybe. I wasn't that guy outside of prison before."

"What changed?"

Tobin blew out a breath. "I had to take a long, close look at myself. Stop blaming other people for my screw-ups. I didn't like what I saw. So when D.P. explained that Jesus would not only take me as-is, but make me better than I was, that sounded too good to be true."

"It is a pretty amazing deal," Livvy agreed.

"Indeed. I sure sleep a lot better at night, knowing I won't be roasting in hell for all the crap I've done."

"Just roasting in here."

The corners of Tobin's mouth sagged. "Well, I earned my time. You gotta differentiate between earthly justice and divine grace. A lotta of guys in here will cry innocent, but I can tell you I deserve what I got."

That brought it all back around to Tobin's crime. What had he done? He said he'd tell her when he could look her in the eye. But

Livvy wasn't sure she wanted to dredge it up right now.

"Oh. That's cool," Tobin said.

"What?"

"Tiana Jo remembers who I am. She interviewed me for a story she was working on. Interviewed a few of us from the SQ *News*."

"Oh. *Hmm*," he said.

Had he just angled the phone away from Livvy?

"What?" she asked.

"Nothing."

"Like fun, 'nothing.' She wrote *some*thing." Livvy reached for the phone. Tobin held it away at arm's length, blocking her with his other arm. "Lemme see!" she demanded.

"Easy, don't pop a stitch." Tobin continued to shoulder off her advances, but brought the phone close, held it to his chest.

"Tobin, knock it off. Whatever it is, it affects me. I have a right to know."

"'Right to know.'" Tobin snorted. "Says who?" But he held her gaze. "Tiana forwarded a picture. Lucas is in the gas chamber, with the others."

"Oh. Okay." Well, it was good that he was with others. Good to know where he was. "There's a picture? Let me see."

Tobin kept the cell pressed to his chest. "I don't think that's a good idea."

"Why?" Livvy tried to pry the phone loose. "What's the matter with him?"

"I'm just guessing he's usually more photogenic."

Livvy sized him up. "Tobin, please?"

Tobin rolled his eyes, dropped his chin to his chest. And held out the phone.

The group in the gas chamber was photographed through a window. There were a bunch of people smashed in there. Lucas was looking at the camera—if you could call it looking. Given the swelling, it was likely he could only see out of one eye. Much of his exposed skin was bloody or filthy, mouth purple and distended. And Sean said he had broken ribs?

"Livvy ..."

Livvy couldn't stop staring at the photo. What was around Lucas's neck?

"It's not your fault. It's a prison riot. People get hurt."

"It may not be my fault, but it's my ..."

My what?

Tobin let her think.

Yesterday morning Lucas's baseball shirt had been crisp white with navy sleeves. Now the center was a bloody Rorschach blot, an impressionistic depiction of pain.

Her chest tightened, vocal cords constricted. "It's my mess. And I have to help clean it up."

Chapter Twenty-Seven

Tobin resisted groaning aloud. *Knew it.* Shouldn't have shown her. No—he hadn't had a choice about showing her. Shouldn't have reacted to the photo in the first place.

"Livvy, for cryin' out loud. Right here and now you are safe. Please don't hatch any schemes."

Full, but not overflowing, her blue eyes shimmered. *Not fair.* He was not equipped to resist that. He set his jaw and stared at the wall. "They're in the basement of North Block! We couldn't get to them if we tried. Much less get us all back out."

Livvy nodded. She looked down at the phone. A single tear splashed to the screen, trickled south.

No. Not going to happen. Tobin studied the wall again. "That's why you stayed, isn't it."

"What's why?"

"You didn't get on the helicopter. You stayed for him." He definitely couldn't look at her now.

"No—I told you, I didn't think. I just ... I hesitated too long. I balked."

Tobin nodded. She didn't owe him an explanation, really. Whatever was between her and Lucas wasn't any of his business. But keeping her safe? He was *making* that his business. She wasn't going anywhere.

"You have a gun," she said so softly he almost didn't hear.

"Yeah, and maybe so do they. And maybe there are more of them than I have bullets. And maybe I can't guard everyone with one gun. And maybe I don't really want to shoot anyone anyway." He was almost shouting now.

Livvy sniffled. Loudly.

Way to go, man.

Tobin had never been real good with crying women. Hadn't known many, actually. Aunt Lydia hadn't been much of a crier. But when she *had* teared up, boy howdy, he was done for. Her tears were how he'd first known, at the age of twelve, that something was terribly wrong when he was pulled from class one February afternoon. And it was her face—eyes pinched, lips in a contorted grimace, chin trembling—that was still his main visual from his mom's funeral. Not the casket, not his dad dressed in an ill-fitting suit, slipping out the back door in the middle of the service. Those memories came later.

Tobin hadn't seen Aunt Lydia cry again until his sentencing.

Dang. He hated it when women cried.

"Livvy," he started. Then sighed. He had nothing to say. This guy—Lucas. He better know how lucky he was. He better know how to treat her right.

"If it were the other way around," Livvy said. "I'd come for you."

Uh. Tobin's head dropped. There was the kick to the gut.

"I'm not saying we have to storm the castle," she continued. "I just want to talk things through. With what we have—can't we do *something* to help them?"

Tobin hunched, arms crossed. "I don't know what to tell you, Liv. If Tiana Jo knows where they are, so do the authorities. It's in their hands."

"Well, what if—" Tobin merely shifted his body weight, and

Livvy blew out an exhalation of disgust. She laid back on the floor. "Fine. Let's just bury our heads in the sand until all the problems go away by themselves."

Tobin snorted. "'Snide doesn't become you.'"

"But being an ostrich does?" Livvy fell silent. No doubt she was mentally running scenarios, looking for solutions.

"See, the thing is," Tobin said. "You think like a free person. You think anything is possible."

Livvy wrinkled her nose. "No I don't. And anyway, what's wrong with that? Don't you have any hope? Faith? Imagination? So you've gotten used to walking the yellow line. So what? That's what you do in here, not who you are."

"How do you know who I am? *I* don't even know. I was a stupid, aimless, thoughtless kid when I came in here." Tobin rested his head against the wall. Thumped it against the paneling, once, twice. "Easy for you to talk about hope and imagination. You have your whole life ahead of you. Anything *is* possible, for you. All I know about me is what I've built in here."

"And you've built a lot. With all your studying? When you get out, you'll be able to get a good job. There's a lot of possibility for you too." Livvy poked him with her toe. "You'll just have to improvise."

Tobin shrugged. "Yeah. I guess. It's just ..." He cleared his throat. "Riots aside, it's kinda safe in here, you know? You focus on being a better person every day. And the people that matter— the few you care about—notice. I'm sorta succeeding in here, you know? But out there ... Out there I'll just be an ex-con. My best is going to stack up pretty pathetic alongside the next guy."

"Well, you'll just have to keep doing your best and stick with it."

"Right." Tobin nodded.

Sure. Just do that.

Livvy sat back up, folded her arms on bent knees and rested her chin, staring straight ahead at the wall.

Tobin faced the same direction. *Well that's what he got.* They were always saying—in group, in recovery, in chapel—to open up. To trust people. That there was no shame in having feelings.

Right.

What was he thinking, babbling on to her? *I'm such an idiot.*

A long, silent pause filled the space around them. Suffocating.

"You know, I get it," Livvy said. "We've all got stuff way down deep. Lies we believe. And no matter how much our brain tells us differently, no matter how much progress we make, contrary to all the truths we claim, the deep stuff breaks through. It's like our default programming."

Tobin hardly dared breathe. He stared at Livvy, her profile turned to him. She'd heard him. She'd understood. She'd said what he couldn't.

This was like a moment in an old movie, when the heroine was lit in soft-focus. A spotlight on Livvy right now wouldn't make it more obvious. She was expertly designed, utterly perfect to fit him. To be his partner, his mate.

Which, of course, was utterly, perfectly impossible.

Just a day ago, he'd been focused on serving out the remainder of his sentence. Proud of what he'd accomplished behind bars.

Now someone stood on his lungs. Wrung out his heart. He'd never be content again a day in his life. How could he be? Now he knew. Now he knew what was out there that he could never have.

What had he said to her? That maybe God wanted her to come to San Quentin for a reason. Was Tobin that reason? Was she here so Tobin could see what might have been, if he'd been a different man?

"What?" Livvy asked.

"What, what?"

"You look ... ill. You okay?"

"No, not really. No."

Lucas jerked awake. He stretched his eyes wide, blinked, and pulled his surroundings into focus. Then wished he were still asleep.

The eight of them hunkered, curled, and perched in the stuffy chamber. Stretched along the wall opposite the door, Lucas took up the most space.

The CO, Knox, was watching him. "So what did you do to piss someone off so bad?"

"Nothing, really. This guy—Gant?—was taking out his issues on me. He wanted to get his hands on one of our friends."

"Livvy?"

"Yeah."

"And she escaped, on a helicopter?"

"Looks that way, yeah."

Made it out.

Gonna die in here.

Why hadn't Gant killed him? He sure seemed to want to. What was he waiting for? What use was Lucas to him alive?

"So listen," Knox leaned in. "I've had a lot of time to think about getting us out of here." Lucas followed his gaze around the chamber. Most everyone was dozing or lost in a thousand-yard stare. "Maybe out of the prison, but mostly out of these guys' clutches. There are a ton of places in this old rat trap where we could hide."

"Yeah?"

"Wouldn't that be pretty risky?" Joan's voice floated down from above. She peered down from her perch on the execution table.

"There's always a risk," Knox replied.

"I think we should just stay right here. They haven't mistreated us." Joan gave Lucas an apologetic look. "Well, the rest of us."

Knox was an imposing figure even at rest. The displeasure in his face at Joan's two cents was an intimidating sight.

Should I tell them what Gant said? He didn't want to frighten Joan unduly. Plus, maybe Gant was just threatening Lucas—not all of them.

"We're their ace in the hole," Knox said. "If they don't have us to bargain with, they'll surrender that much sooner and this whole thing will be over."

"I thought the state won't bargain for us?" Now Hector chimed in.

Knox grimaced. He cursed inaudibly, his lips quite readable. Apparently he wasn't interested in a public hearing. Had he been looking for Lucas's support before broadening the discussion? Had he anticipated making a plan and executing it without debate?

Knox stood. "Look, people, the guy calling the shots—Gant—he's not going to give up easily. Or happily. If he has the chance to take out his rage on someone, he will. On us. Clearly, some of your friends understood that and took enough risk to get themselves to safety."

Todd cocked an eyebrow. Nodded.

"But there are a lot of other inmates out there," Joan said. "Who knows what they'll do, if given the chance."

"I'm aware of that." If Knox's tone were any dryer, he'd spontaneously combust.

Hector nodded at Lucas. "You even able to move?"

Lucas could feel Knox's gaze boring into his skull. "I'm not up to taking on a ropes course, but I can walk."

"I think it'd be too hard on Lucas." Joan pressed her lips into a firm line. "I'll stay here with him. If some of you want to go, go."

"That's out. Anyone left behind is going to get pummeled, or worse. We aren't splitting up," Knox stated.

Lucas had to agree with him. He'd just been reunited with this group, he didn't want people splintering off. Besides, he didn't want to be left behind, still under Gant's thumb.

"So listen," he began. "Gant told me I'm not leaving this prison alive. And I found him to be quite convincing. I don't know what he has planned for everyone else, but if there's a chance for me to get out of his grasp, I should take it."

Joan looked at him long and hard. Black smudges creased under her eyes—yesterday's makeup. *What was he getting her into? He was her pastor—would she follow him just for that reason? What if he was making a bad decision?*

"Okay, Lucas. I'll support whatever you decide," she said.

Knox lifted one side of his mouth, nodded.

"Let's pray about it," Lucas said. "And then hear the man out." The WBC group nodded and shifted ever so slightly, adopting an attitude of prayer, a physical posture that demarcated conversation from petition.

Knox scowled and sat. At his side, Velasco sought the older officer's eye contact, but Knox remained stone faced.

I know you're in charge, Lord. So you'll have to help me in the event that your will doesn't line up with Lieutenant Knox's.

"Don't get mad," Livvy said.

Great. Was there ever a time when anything following those three words was *not* infuriating?

"What?" Tobin asked.

"Just hear me out," Livvy held him off like a traffic cop: *stop.* "Gant is supposed to be holding onto Lucas to bait me, right?"

"Yes."

"So, what if we bait *Gant.*"

"With what?"

"With me."

"Say again?" Tobin knew he was going to hate this.

"Let's tweet that I'm somewhere in the prison that I'm not. And Gant will go looking for me or will send his thugs. Either way, that would take manpower away from guarding the group in the gas chamber."

Tobin briskly rubbed his short hair. "No. That's just ..." He sighed. "I'm not mad, I'm reasonable. We don't know how many guys he's got guarding the chamber. It's in the basement. I don't even know where—or who or what we'd have to go through to get there."

Livvy turned to face him, grasped his arm. "We could watch North Block. See if Gant leaves and how many go with him."

"Livvy." *Not mad. Not mad.* "I get that you want to help. It's just not possible."

"What if we get Smitty, Cho, Agromonte, and Miles to help?"

"We don't know where they are."

"We could check back at the canteen."

"Do you hear yourself?" Tobin turned too so they sat face-to-face cross-legged, nearly knees to walls on either side. "You barely got away from Gant, were stabbed. Almost got served up for dinner to fifty inmates. You're not going back out there."

"Okay. How about this. We tweet that I'm here. Then I don't have to go out. And when Gant comes, we hold him hostage. Make him call his guys and let the others go."

Tobin reared back. "Are you crazy? You want to invite the wolf to the—to the place where the sheep live? The man is psychotic! I'm not just talking a couple twists short of a Slinky. You cannot expect him to react like a normal, rational human being. We'd lose control of the situation so fast you'd get dizzy."

"Then I'd shoot him. *I* would—not you, so it wouldn't affect your time. It would be self-defense for me."

Tobin opened and closed his mouth like a landed fish. Shook his head to clear his ears. "Do you hear yourself? You think you can take a life just like that?"

Livvy inhaled deeply. "No." She closed her eyes. "No, of course not. Not as in trapping him." She clasped her hands in her lap. "You're right. I just wanted to brainstorm a little."

"That was like a brain typhoon."

"Well, if you'd work *with* me ..."

"Okay. I'm with you." Tobin placed his hands on his knees. Looked Livvy in the eye. Open body language.

"We don't have food or water," Livvy said. "No hiding place is guaranteed to stay safe. What if this lasts twenty-five days like the riot Miles told us about? Tobin, I can't make it twenty-five days."

Tobin's jaw dropped.

Duh.

No wonder she was scheming so much. "Oh man, Livvy, it didn't even cross my mind you were thinking that. No way this is going to last twenty-five days. That's just ... there's just no way."

"What if it lasts five days?" Livvy asked, her face open, unguarded. Frightened. "Doesn't it seem pretty amazing that I've survived this long? Think about all the stuff you just listed that's already happened to me. That's after, what? Maybe thirty hours? I can't stay in this hallway for days, Tobin. I won't survive."

Chapter Twenty-Eight

The chamber was suffocating. Lucas's hair plastered against his skin. Nobody spoke or moved much.

Guess when you constructed a gas chamber, you didn't include a ventilation system. By design the capsule was airtight.

"There's one," Hector said.

Closer to the window, Todd pounded on the glass. "We need some air!" he yelled to an inmate who'd finally come to check on them.

A moment later, the chamber shuddered with the squeal of the turning wheel. And the door opened, exchanging fresh air for stale. Perspective was funny. North Block air—which smelled like death well past its expiration date—was sweet in Lucas's lungs.

"We need another bathroom run," Knox told the inmate in the doorway.

The inmate grunted, then yelled over his shoulder. "Edwards!"

Lucas's breath hitched briefly when the inmate entered. Edwards was the man guarding Lucas's pen when Livvy begged to be let in. The one who turned her over to Gant.

Ripped, white, bald, and tattooed, Edwards looked like an especially large version of Dissident Nazi. He withdrew a pistol from his waistband. He beckoned to Knox, who stood at the forefront of the hostages.

"C'mon, old man. Let's go," he said.

Knox strode from the room in front of Edwards. The CO had a ramrod bearing that Lucas admired. So the guy was terse and commanding. It was still great to have him on the same team.

Joan gripped Lucas's wrist. Her eyes were wide, darting from the door of the room, to the inmate outside the gas chamber, and back to the door.

Calm down. She was practically telegraphing her thoughts. And the others—staring at their shoes, exchanging glances. Didn't they seem glaringly obvious to the inmate?

If the guy was concerned that something was up, he didn't register anything. Not until he faced the barrel of the gun Knox pointed at him.

"Everyone out," Knox ordered. "And you—in." The inmate glared, seethed. And did what he was told. Velasco sealed him in, and the group turned to Knox, expectant.

"This way. Single file. Be silent." Knox took the lead.

Lucas's heart jack-hammered. How much adrenaline could a guy's body handle in a thirty-hour period?

The group crept up stairs. At the top, a corridor gave them a right-or-left choice. Knox led right. They passed an alcove—a doorway—where Edwards's body slumped, his neck at an impossible angle. Lucas closed his eyes briefly. He hoped Joan didn't see.

The hallway didn't seem like a great choice for sneaking around. Someone was bound to bump into them. But Knox stopped at a brown metal door. He eased it open and nodded everyone in.

It was an electrical room. And at the end, another door. A narrow passage—grated floor, scaffold ceiling—stretched before them. "Maintenance alley," Knox whispered. The group filed in behind him.

It was very *Escape from Alcatraz*, this passage behind a wall. Aluminum heating ducts rose rectangular out of sight into the dim expanse above. Black sewage pipes. White PVC tubing. Metal electrical conduits. And the eight of them, creeping away from Gant.

Thank you, God.

Knox stopped at another metal door. Where did this one lead, and how could they know whether it would open into a room filled with inmates?

They filed into a cramped storage room. Which was off a corridor that led to a passageway. That narrow cement tunnel stretched long. Lucas was completely turned around.

"Where are we going?" he whispered to Knox.

"This way," Knox hissed back.

Helpful.

The door at the end of the corridor was framed in white, daylight penetrating the cracks. Anxiety constricted Lucas's breath even more than his sore ribs did. He hadn't had a lot of great experiences out and about in San Quentin during the last day.

"Maybe we should go back and hide in the maintenance alley," he whispered to Knox.

"Trust me," the CO replied and inched the door open. "Okay, now. Now!" He stepped out and shooed the rest along.

They were right next to the high security exercise yard, coming out between North Block and the Adjustment Center. Lucas had gone in sort of a circle.

"C'mon." Knox dashed across the road to a decrepit building, flinging open another door. Wordless, everyone followed.

It was a library. Floor to ceiling, shelves crammed the small space.

"Help me," Knox ordered Velasco. They rolled a book cart in front of the door and blocked the wheels. "Bring those big volumes," Knox said to Hector and Todd.

Ah so. Instead of being trapped in a small space by inmates who wanted to keep them in, they were strategically hidden in a small room, keeping inmates out.

The door shuddered with rapid pounding.

Already? This place was safe for 0.07 seconds.

"Knox!" A voice called from the other side. "It's Miles."

Knox pulled stuff away from the door. "Open it!" he ordered Velasco.

The door flew open and several inmates tumbled in. Lucas took a step backwards.

"It's okay, L-T," one said to Knox. "They're okay."

Knox nodded, and Velasco secured the door.

The inmate that had vouched for the others shook hands with Knox, then they clapped each other in a hug. "Good to see you, man. You're the first friendlies I've seen yet." Then the man turned to the now-crowded room. He pointed at Lucas. "You have *got* to be Lucas."

"Miles Navarrette," the man held out his hand. "Sergeant. Don't let the clothes fool you." He indicated his prison uniform.

"You're a CO?" Lucas asked.

"Affirmative. And I've heard a lot about you."

"How's that? From who?"

"Livvy, mostly, and some guys from your softball team. They're all very loyal, by the way."

"You were with Livvy?" Joan approached.

"Was, yes."

"Did you help her get out, on that helicopter?" Joan's eyes glowed. She looked Navarrette over like she was sizing him up for his superhero uniform.

Navarrette snorted. "Help her? Yes. Get on the helicopter? No."

He caught Lucas's eye. "That woman is a left-handed football bat."

Lucas frowned. *A what now?*

"Well, however it happened, I just thank God that she got on and got out," Joan said.

Navarrette shook his head. "No ma'am. That's a big November-golf: a no-go. She didn't make it onto the helicopter. It bugged out without her. Four of your guys made it though."

Lucas chilled to his marrow. "Livvy is still in the prison?"

Navarrette nodded.

"Where?"

The CO lifted a shoulder. "She's gone Elvis."

"She's with Tobin." Another one of the men spoke up. African-American. An inmate? Guess you couldn't assume by the clothing. Course COs probably didn't sport long dreads.

"Smitty," the man said, patting his chest. "This here's Cho and Agromonte." The men nodded in turn. "So anyway, Tobin pulled a John Wayne, waved his pistol in the air, pulled Livvy out of a jam, and took off with her. Went North from the ISU."

Tobin again. What was up with this Tobin?

"Pistol?" Knox approached from behind Smitty.

Smitty's eyes bugged a little. He shot a look at Navarrette.

"Where'd he get a weapon?" Knox asked Navarrette.

"Liberated it from one of Gant's men." Navarrette answered.

"True Gant busted your ribs?" Cho asked Lucas.

Weird. This was just weird. Who were these guys?

"Hold on—" Lucas held up a hand. "I think we have a lot of catching up to do. Think we can sit down for this conversation?" *Or lie down?*

"Shame Livvy ended up with all the oxy—seems you could use you some," Navarrette said.

"Oxy—codone?" Maybe this whole messed up San Quentin experience *was* a dream, after all. "Why would Livvy have oxy?"

"Well, Navarrette could hardly give her the meth, could he?"

Smitty grinned wide. He waved at Chaplain Peake. "Oh, hey D.P.! You in here too? How many you got back there?"

Lucas must have looked as stupid as he felt, because Agromonte leaned in a little. "Navarrette gave her the oxy for pain. After she got stabbed."

"Oh!" Joan put her hand to her mouth.

Joan should probably sit down.

Lucas kinda crumpled to the floor.

That was masculine.

Joan fluttered over him.

See that was the plan. Gave her something to do.

"Could someone please fill me in from the beginning?" Lucas asked, pressing his hand to his side.

"You let a prisoner keep a loaded gun?" Knox scowled at Navarrette. "What's wrong with you? Didn't I teach you better than that?"

This was getting decidedly more complicated. COs dressed like inmates. Inmates that were "good guys," some of them armed ...

And Livvy was *still* in San Quentin, stabbed, and with Tobin.

"Maybe if we get that group out of the gas chamber, the helicopter will come back," Livvy said.

Tobin rocked his head side-to-side, in a sort of "yeah, maybe" kind of way.

"What?"

"What, what?"

"You were going to say something."

"No, no. I'm working *with* you."

"C'mon Tobin," Livvy said. "What hole are you going to pick in that idea?"

"Just that I don't know how we'd alert Classen to send in a

helicopter. The ISU is gone, including the phones."

"We have *our* phone."

"You're right."

"What now?"

"No, I'm saying you're right: You. Are. Correct. Getting ahold of someone about an airlift is probably the easiest part of that plan."

Livvy could feel her nostrils flare, but Tobin held up a single index finger. "Easy there, I was thinking that baiting Gant is actually not a bad idea."

"Wow, thanks. As in, 'Gee, your idea doesn't totally suck'?"

Tobin grinned. "Yeah. Something like that."

That grin melted something inside Livvy a wee bit. *Okay. No more snarking.*

She rubbed her temples. She had a low, dull headache. "You know what I really want right now?" she asked.

Tobin raised an eyebrow. "I can think of about a million things you must be wanting right about now."

"Coffee. Hot, fresh coffee."

"Lemme guess—you like girlie coffee. Lots of foam."

"Nope. I like it strong."

"Like your men." Tobin grinned and went back to the phone.

Livvy gasped. Pressed the heel of her hand to her heart. *Grace.* The waterworks started up again.

"What?" Tobin shifted and stared, dazed. "What just happened?"

Easy, Liv. It's just coffee.

She swallowed so her voice wouldn't squeak. "That's a joke with my sister. We always say I like my coffee strong—like my men. It's twist on a line from *Airplane*."

"Yeah, that's where I got it."

It's not just coffee. It's Grace.

"What if I never see her again?" Somehow that thought was

worse than the fear of dying. She drew in a quick, hiccuppy breath.

Tobin took her hands in his. "You'll see her again. Soon. She's probably on the other side of that wall and is going to give you a big hug as soon as you are too. And a cup of strong coffee."

Tobin's hands were warm. Hers were filthy. She was beyond disgusting at this point.

Funny thing, dying. Maybe it wasn't really that long of a separation from loved ones. From the ones who have the assurance of heaven anyway. The passage of time in this earthly realm probably had no meaning in heaven. Maybe it'd be like seeing Grace again in a matter of minutes.

So it would be Grace left behind, missing Livvy. *Poor Grace.* Livvy sniffled.

The phone in Tobin's pocket pinged. He looked relieved to fiddle with it a second. "Looks like someone leaked the names of the four guys on the chopper to the press."

Livvy wiped her nose on her sleeve. "'Kay. I don't know why that should be some sort of secret."

Tobin shrugged. "I'm just reporting. Tiana Jo posted your photo on her network's website. And nosyneighbor tweeted it. Hopefully the governor is getting slammed with demands to send a SWAT team in for you."

Livvy pursed her lips. "They wouldn't know where to find me."

Tobin glanced up at her. "I was just ... Don't get your hopes up too high."

"No, I know. I'm just wondering if we should tell Tiana where I am, secretly, so she can tell the authorities."

"We ran right by the boys on the wall."

"Oh. Yeah."

"See." He flicked her on the arm. "You forget they are always watching. You think like a free person."

Livvy narrowed her eyes. Peered at him through wet lashes. "You're right."

"I know I'm right."

"I mean, if I'm going to beat Gant at his game, I need to think more like him."

"Whoa. Don't go there. Believe me, you do *not* want to put yourself in that man's head. That's, like, Dante's worst level of hell. The ninth circle."

"Wow. You are well read."

"Lotta time on my hands." Tobin tapped his knee with the phone. "I have half a mind to send the guy on a wild goose chase just to mess with him. But, if we're going to do this, we need to be clear about our objective."

Livvy nodded.

"There are other hostages," Tobin observed.

"Yeah."

"That report we heard last night said there was a group of ball players and a couple of COs in one photo."

"Yeah?"

"If we could find them, they should be enough for your helicopter."

Livvy pondered. Nodded slowly. *True.*

"You don't like that idea."

"I didn't say that. I'm thinking."

"You're thinking about how you'd rather fly off into the sunset with Lucas." Tobin's tone was biting.

"Don't tell me what I'm thinking. I hate that." But she had been zeroed in on freeing Lucas. There were other WBC hostages. And lots of COs and San Quentin staff. It wasn't like she could make anything happen under her own strength anyway, right? Maybe it would be a good idea to ask God what he thought. Maybe she was too narrowly focused.

But Lucas had been hurt for *her.*

So why did she suddenly feel guilty, asking Tobin to help her help Lucas?

What had Miles said? *How many lives are you going to risk for yours before this is over?*

Chapter Twenty-Nine

"Wild," Hector said when Smitty and Navarrette finished their tale.

Lucas nodded. *No kidding. Understatement.* He was boggled. Livvy had endured so much in the last day. And had done so much! Lucas tried to reconcile the feisty "football bat" Navarrette described with the easygoing Livvy he'd spent time with. Granted, not a lot of time.

Hopefully there'd be more time.

Velasco practically tripped over Lucas on his way to the windows on the east side of the building. While the windows on the west side, overlooking the main prison yard, were a couple of stories high, the windows on this side were at ground level. Velasco shifted bookcases and books to block the panes.

Why bother? They were so old and filthy, who could see in, anyway?

But Velasco pressed on. Maybe he wanted to look good to the other officers. Which he may have, until he tripped over Lucas again.

"*Gah!*" Lucas burst out.

"Sorry!" At least Velasco apologized. And he seemed genuine enough.

Navarrette commandeered a few long-sleeved shirts, reducing Cho and Agromonte to tees. He ripped along seams—here, there—then bound up Lucas's ribcage. The counter-pressure provided some relief. Lucas didn't have to concentrate on every inhalation. For a few minutes at a stretch, he even forgot he was breathing.

When he was finished with Lucas, Navarrette sat next to Knox. The older CO had dismantled the handgun he'd swiped from Edwards, peered down the barrel, clicked this and snapped that. It was reassembled now, resting in his lap.

"So check this, L-T." Navarrette fished something from his pocket. "Livvy found it."

Knox unrolled a narrow slip of paper. "Huh," he muttered.

Velasco wandered over from the window. He crouched next to Knox.

"'Zat you?" Velasco asked Navarrette, pointing at the paper.

"Looks that way." Navarrette nodded.

Did Velasco pale a little bit?

"What's that?" Hector asked Lucas out of the side of his mouth.

"Beats me." And he was reluctant to ask. Reluctant to intrude on what seemed like official business.

"What is that?" Joan asked Navarrette. Good ole Joan.

Cho and Agromonte looked at her, at each other, then at their shoes, the ground.

"You see any of these guys?" Navarrette asked the other two COs, again pointing at the paper.

Velasco shook his head.

"I haven't seen anyone, until you," Knox answered.

Chaplain Peake approached, stood over the huddle.

"Dale?" Joan asked.

"It's a list of names, Joan," Peake answered. "It's probably a list of targets."

If Lucas hadn't been looking at Navarrette he would have

missed it—the man scowled. Shot a dark look at the chaplain under heavy-lidded eyes.

"You see the commonalities?" Navarrette asked Knox, voice low.

"Sure."

"But what's the connection between the sets? And there's this guy—you know who that is?"

Velasco edged forward to read the name Navarrette indicated. Abruptly, Knox folded the paper and stuffed it into his pocket. "We'll pass these on when we get a chance."

"I already did," Navarrette said. "To that Classen of the negotiation team."

"Good thinking," Knox said. "They have any theories?"

"We didn't get into it."

"Hey! Come take a look!" Todd called from the windows overlooking the exercise yard.

Hector was next to him. "What are they doing?"

The COs were to the window in a flash. Lucas wasn't feeling very flashy. "What is it?" he asked from his spot on the floor.

"Some inmates are leading a group of officers and staff across the lower yard," Chaplain Peake answered.

"Who are the guys in brown?" Todd asked.

"Food service workers," Peake replied.

"Where are they going?" Hector asked.

No one answered.

Everyone was huddled at the windows now. There wouldn't be room for Lucas even if he hauled himself over.

"Are they letting them go?" Joan asked.

The room was quiet. Lucas could hear intermittent shouts behind him—from the corridor on the east side of the library. But no sound came to him from the west. Including the group at the window.

Then someone let out a low whistle. Navarrette and Knox

stepped back and high-fived.

"They let them go?" Joan asked.

"Yes. That's the gate to the industries yard. It's held by our guys." Velasco answered. A grin spread across his face. Chaplain Peake laughed and clapped him into a hug.

Lucas raised himself to his elbows. "How many?"

"Maybe a dozen?" Hector answered.

"Thirteen," Knox said. "Seven COs and six staff."

"Is that good?" Sean asked. Then he made a *duh* face. "Of course it's good. But does it mean the riot is ending?"

Knox shrugged.

"It's not a bad sign," Navarrette said. "It tells us someone is communicating with someone. Thing is, you can't always tell if inmate negotiators actually speak for the prisoners. Or, specifically, for the faction making the most trouble."

"Did you see what building they came out of?" Knox asked Todd.

"That one, the low white one."

"R and R," Knox said.

"What!" Lucas cupped an ear. "We got the gas chamber, and they got R and R?"

"Receiving and Release," Velasco said.

"Release is right," Jim muttered.

"Thank you, God," Joan whispered in an exhale.

Heads nodded.

Yes! Way to go. *Could you get Livvy safely out next?*

"Yes!" Tobin's exclamation jolted Livvy from a doze. Befuddled, she stirred to rise.

Tobin pulled her to his side. "Nosyneighbor says hostages were released."

"Yeah? Who?"

"Staff and personnel. No civilians. Thirteen."

Sweet. "Did he say why? What happened?"

"Nope. Nobody's talking." Tobin snorted. "Except the governor. She's taking credit."

The phone pinged.

"It's an email from Tiana Jo." Tobin tapped rapidly.

"What did she say?"

"She just asked if I know this guy. An inmate."

"Why?"

Tobin shrugged.

"Do you know him?"

"Yeah. Used to work with him on the newspaper."

"When Tiana Jo interviewed you?"

Tobin raised his head, cocked it in thought. "Yeah, guess so. Anyway, guy got himself mixed up in some yard politics. Now he's in the hole."

The hole. There had been no one in the dungeon. So the hole was ...

"The Adjustment Center," Tobin filled in her blank.

"That's the building that shares the high security yard with North Block?" The troublemakers.

"You're getting a feel for the place."

Great. Just what she wanted. A working knowledge of the layout of San Quentin. "Gant said they were 'cutting it off, but not pursuing it,'" she remembered aloud.

"That's good. Maybe he has some sense after all." Tobin's gaze lingered on Livvy's earlobe. His face clouded. "Or not."

The phone pinged again.

Tobin read the message. Then held the phone out for a moment, staring. "Huh."

"Now what?"

"She ..." Tobin rubbed his chin. "She says Roberts—that's the guy—tipped her to a story. He wanted to run it in the *San Quentin News*, but knew it would never fly."

Livvy waited. Tobin chewed the tip of his thumb, his hand fisted. Livvy rolled her eyes and took the cell from his other hand.

"A 'Green Wall' at San Quentin?" she looked up at him. Had she seen any green walls? There was the one wall with the mural.

"Yeah. You know what Green Wall means?"

"Isn't that at Fenway Park?"

Tobin pulled back a corner of his mouth in a lopsided grin. "Impressive. But while that is *a* green wall, it's called the Green Monster." He took the phone back. "What Ms. Jo refers to is the green of the correctional officer uniform. A green-walled code of silence."

"'Kay." Livvy squinted. Surely she'd clue in. Any second now. She was just so tired that she couldn't quite track his point. She shook her head. *Nope. Nothing.* "Could you explain, please?"

Tobin rubbed his short hair. Blew out a breath. "Well. I'm not sure exactly what she means. Or what she thinks Roberts meant. But originally the Green Wall was a group of COs at the state prison in Salinas. They were kind of a rogue gang that beat on guys and stuff. Basically ran the prison with fear and intimidation, and anyone who tried to complain got stonewalled by the muckety-mucks and pounded by the COs. Finally someone blew the whistle and it all came out."

"So, is that happening here?"

"No. I don't see it." Tobin typed a message.

"Then ..."

"I said I don't know what she means. But it is kinda weird. Roberts was maybe looking to expose something, then landed in the AC? He never was one to mix it up. I remember thinking at the time that it was odd."

"So, are you saying there's some sort of conspiracy or cover-up?" Livvy struggled to nutshell the nebulous.

"*I'm* not saying anything." Tobin clicked on Tiana Jo's new email before the *p-* got to *-ing.*

"It's a link," he announced.

"To an article." He peered at the tiny screen.

"She wrote two months ago." He read silently, lips moving. "Seems some criminal justice student, working on a thesis ..."

Click. Scroll.

"I'm going to rip that out of your hand," Livvy muttered.

"Yeah ... sorry. Can't walk and ... chew ..." He lowered the phone and stared at the wall. "Huh."

"You said that already."

"So this student was looking into the reach of imprisoned shot callers—the gang leaders. He wanted to see how much power they wield from a place like the Q, where most of them have contact with other prisoners, visitors, lawyers, and stuff, compared to a supermax like Pelican Bay, where they are in solitary for twenty-three hours a day.

"He found that not only did the gang leaders in San Quentin seem to exert more power than shot callers at Pelican Bay, but more than at any other prison he studied. Like a statistical anomaly."

"How do you study a thing like that?"

"Interviews of guys who debrief—drop out. Number of retaliations and hits. Witnesses killed. Both inside and outside the prison walls."

Livvy winced. "A guy can order that from prison and have it done?"

Tobin nodded, his mouth a grim line.

"How?"

He waggled the phone at her. "And they pass word along through someone getting paroled, through a visitor, through the mail."

"Doesn't the prison listen in? Read letters?"

"Bangers use code. Like a letter congratulating someone on the birth of a baby means something totally different. 'Do this' if it says baby boy, 'do that' if it says baby girl."

"That's nuts. Just think what these guys could accomplish if they used their powers for good instead of evil."

Tobin almost smiled. Nodded. "So all the stuff I just said—that goes on in prisons all the time. But the hinky thing is this spike in San Quentin's numbers. And Tiana Jo talked to a federal forensic accountant."

"An accountant for ... dead people?" *I really need coffee.*

Tobin snickered. "A financial specialist that investigates money trails. Looks for evidence of fraud, illegal payments, money laundering. That kind of stuff."

"Wow. I don't even balance my checkbook."

"There's money changing hands. Payments that may be linked to hits. Accounts that were frozen that got unfrozen, or got around being frozen, or something."

"What does this have to do with that Roberts guy and a green wall?"

"Dunno."

"Why is Tiana Jo telling you all this, now?"

Tobin cocked his head. "Dunno." He got busy typing.

"And don't say 'huh.'" Livvy cautioned.

"*Hmmm.*"

Livvy punched him in the shoulder.

"You know how I said you weren't going anywhere?" Tobin asked.

Livvy nodded.

"I may have changed my mind."

Chapter Thirty

Lucas studied the library ceiling. A couple of the guys napped on the floor, but he was too uncomfortable to sleep.

Joan read *The Last of the Mohicans*. Lucas eyeballed the shelves of books. It would be too hard for him to read lying flat on his back.

Officer Navarrette flipped through papers in a file spread across the floor in front of him, muttering aloud every so often. "Hey—Velasquez," he beckoned the young CO.

"Velasco." The officer scrambled to his feet.

Navarrette looked up, a pen clutched in his teeth. "*Oorph.*" He removed the pen. "Sorry about that. Can you see if you can find a Bible for me?" He waved at the stacks.

Hello? Lucas held up a hand. "Can I be of any help?"

"Not unless you have Deuteronomy 40:25 memorized."

Lucas frowned. "I don't think Deuteronomy has a chapter forty." Exodus ended with chapter forty, and only a handful of books were longer. Was Deuteronomy one of them?

"According to this letter it does," Navarrette said.

"Here you go." Velasco handed him a tattered volume.

"Deuteronomy ... Deuteronomy," Navarrette muttered.

"Genesis, Exodus, Leviticus, Numbers, Deuteronomy," Joan

recited without looking up from her hardback.

"There is no chapter forty," Navarrette said, drawing out the words as though they communicated something of significance.

Lucas smiled. *Random stuff memorized while father was preaching, for $100 please, Alex.*

"Just a screw up." Knox waved it off. "The meathead meant four or fourteen."

"Is that an inmate's letter? Why do you have inmate mail?" Joan asked, looking up from her book.

"It's a copy of the correspondence of a known Sureño shot caller. Chief gang banger. Prisoners know their mail is monitored." Navarrette scribbled something on a notepad. He didn't see the glance Cho and Agromonte exchanged. Looked like they *loved* having their personal mail inspected.

"A gang leader included a scripture reference in his letter?" Joan set her book down.

"Oh, glory hallelujah." Knox waved his hands in the air. He leaned over to peruse the letter. "It's to his mother. He's trying to convince the old lady that he's turned over a new leaf and is on the straight and narrow."

Navarrette remained silent, scratching out notes. He didn't look so convinced. What was he looking for? Theories about secret messages encoded in the Bible had cropped up and been debunked plenty of times in the last couple of millennia. Did the CO think he was onto a new one?

Shoulda left her behind. She was safe in there.

But Livvy wouldn't have stayed. Not without him. And if he'd returned to find her gone? Tobin checked over his shoulder. She was right on his heels. She lifted her face to him and lit up with a brief smile.

She trusted him.

Why on earth did she do that? Who had ever trusted him before? He thought back. No one. That's who. A fleeting sense of panic fluttered in his chest. He should warn her about what he'd done. Who he *was*. She was all that was good and right and had no business trusting him.

They rounded the brick corner of ancient, empty building twenty-two. And Tobin ran smack into a burly man half a head taller than himself.

"Watch yourself, cowboy." The man put out a hand to steady Tobin.

"Hey, sorry man." Tobin gave him a nod. He side-stepped in front of Livvy, which blocked the other man's path all the more.

The inmate jerked a nod toward the officers atop the perimeter wall. "You keepin' your head down?"

"Yeah. No doubt." Tobin drew the back of his hand across his mouth. Glanced sidelong at Livvy. Hands in her pockets, she slouched with her focus on the dirt.

Tobin looked back to the man. He had followed Tobin's gaze and continued studying Livvy.

"Well. Stay outta trouble," Tobin said and made to edge past the man.

The inmate didn't move.

"Me and Jack are heading to the laundry," Tobin heard himself say. *What? Where'd that come from?* He willed the guy to stop looking at Livvy.

"You don't say." The man sucked air in through his teeth. "Maybe I'll come with you."

Tobin could feel the gun tucked into the back of his jeans, pressed hard in the small of his back. *You know I don't want to use that*, he prayed. Never. Ever. He'd hurt too many people in his life already.

But he looked again to Livvy. Her chin must have been about

touching her chest. All he could see was the top of her beanie. She could trust him in one respect: if she were with him and he still drew breath, he would not let anyone hurt her.

"Suit yourself," Tobin replied. The three stood at an impasse for a brief second. Tobin wanted to put himself between Livvy and the man. But he couldn't let Livvy lead—for one, she didn't know the way. Tobin sidled past the man, his muscles on taut alert and Livvy closer than his shadow.

The three stuck to walls, walking single file around the squared perimeter of the lower yard. Tobin resisted looking back too often, but couldn't go long without a glance.

You are broadcasting. Your body language is screaming.

Maybe the guy would just chalk it up to tension from the riot. This wasn't exactly your standard walk in the park.

They approached Receiving. A group of inmates loitered in the doorway and in the darkness inside. The inmate behind Livvy closed the distance to her by half a stride. Tobin's heart hammered. If the guy grabbed her and tossed her to his homies? Tobin hadn't handled guns much. But he could put a hole in a guy at this distance. He glanced at the top of the perimeter wall. The SWAT officers were as poised and focused as lions. As soon as Tobin pulled the handgun they'd drop him. That was a chance he might have to take.

He stepped to the side, waved Livvy in front of him. She searched his face as she passed, but didn't break stride. Neither did the big guy, who seemed intent on sticking to Livvy. Tobin shouldered his way between.

It was all of about forty-five seconds, and they were past R and R. Forty-five seconds. The stress of it probably took a good forty-five minutes off Tobin's life span.

At the laundry door, Tobin nodded Livvy to enter, but blocked her tail. Maybe being willing to face down a dozen prisoners and several high-powered laser-sighted rifles went to his head. He tapped the big man on the chest. "Look, buddy, I don't know what your apparel needs are, but get what you want, quick, and get out."

"Easy, cowboy." The man slowly appraised Livvy, who had retreated into the dim facility, and sized up Tobin. "You want I should give you some privacy?" He drew himself tall, towered over Tobin. "I don't think so." He shoved his way in.

Lord, oh Lord. Don't let it come to this. Tobin didn't want to even reveal the gun to the guy. But he reached back, hand under shirt, and wrapped his fingers around the grip.

The inmate approached Livvy, stopping two feet in front of her. "How you doin'"—he looked back at Tobin and grinned—"*Jack*?"

Livvy maintained eye contact with the linoleum. She shrugged.

The man leaned over her. Tobin felt nauseated. The differences in their sizes—the guy could snap her like a toothpick. Tobin edged the gun out of his waistband.

"Your friend was lookin' for you." The man spoke softly, but Tobin could hear him clearly. "He was right worried about you." He straightened and glared at Tobin. "And for good reason. Don't you worry about this jack rabbit. I ain't gonna let 'im hurt you."

Livvy lifted her chin. Brows pinched, she looked from the man to Tobin. She cleared her throat.

No, Livvy! Tobin took a large stride forward.

But she spoke, "What're you talking about?" Part croak, it was an unconvincing attempt at a tenor.

The inmate grinned broadly. Shoved his hands in his pockets. "The preacher man. Lucas. He asked about a woman getting on that chopper. But fact is, you never made it, did you?"

Livvy's jaw dropped. "You spoke with Lucas?" she asked in her normal voice.

"Sure." The man held out his hand. "Name's Fallon."

Livvy looked to Tobin, who was frozen, gun still gripped behind his back, half out of his jeans. She slipped her hand into Fallon's big mitt. "Livvy."

"Right pleased to meet you, Livvy." Fallon turned to appraise Tobin, who stood agape. "So how 'bout you collect your marbles and get on out of here. Today's not your day, cowboy."

"No, it's okay." Livvy slipped past Fallon and wrapped her arms around Tobin.

Tobin fought to collect his thoughts and feelings—slipping, tripping wild. He slid the weapon back into his waistband and rested an arm across Livvy's shoulders.

"Ah," Fallon nodded. "It's like that, then. Well good. This ain't no place for an unchaperoned lady." The man's eyes held a twinkle when he looked at Livvy.

"Where did you see Lucas? When?" Livvy's words tripped in her haste to get them out. Tobin resisted the impulse to withdraw his arm. His arm around another man's girl.

"Right after that 'copter took to the air. North Block. He was being escorted to meet Gant."

"Was he okay?" Livvy asked.

Fallon's eyes were somber now. He met Tobin's gaze. Then smiled at Livvy. "He was happy, thinking you'd made it. So what you gotta do now, is you gotta keep safe so he don't have to worry."

He jerked a nod at Tobin. "You want I should stick with you? Strength in numbers."

That was probably a good idea. But Tobin did have the ace up his sleeve. Gun in his pants. "I've got a friend. Some friends."

"Right then." Fallon shook a finger at Livvy. "You be safe." The man blocked the fading light for a split second when he filled the doorway, then was gone.

Livvy looked up at Tobin. "This is a weird place," she said.

Tobin laughed into a grin. "You better believe it."

Livvy's face was as open as a still pond. "Weird he thought he had to protect me from my protector."

Tobin had nothing to say to that. They still stood with his arm around her shoulders and hers around his waist. He hadn't noticed before—she had copper flecks in her eyes, ringing her irises.

This is not ... Tobin swallowed. *Not ...*

Livvy stared deep into him. He needed to break this connection before she read his thoughts. Racing, racing thoughts.

Tentatively Livvy reached high, then brushed her palm across Tobin's crew cut. A delicious shiver traveled his spine.

"I've really been wanting to do that," she whispered, her smile shy.

Tobin was mute. He tried to catch his breath, to stop the spinning.

Livvy lowered her hand, stroking, then cupping his cheek. He started to shake his head, but she was firm. With her gentle tug and tiptoed stretch, Livvy closed the gap between them. A gap that was more than four years old, that was taller than the walls of San Quentin. She pressed her lips against his. Tobin closed his eyes and was lost. Lost in tenderness, in hunger. He held her close, uncertain which was his heartbeat and which was hers, caught in the thrumming blood-pulse rhythm.

Chapter Thirty-One

I kissed Tobin.

To call that a kiss was to call the Statue of Liberty a figurine.

Technically, it was a kiss.

What had she been thinking?

Duh—that I wanted to kiss Tobin.

Standing in a rolling laundry cart, Livvy gripped a tabletop with both hands, pulled herself close, then pushed hard and sank cross-legged to the bottom of the basket.

Spin, spin. Like my thoughts.

Thud. Livvy's basket collided with a washer.

Never in my life have I known a kiss like that.

Livvy stood and pushed off the washer. Dropped back into the rolling canvas bin.

It's not real. What was that Sandra Bullock line from *Speed*: "You know, relationships that start under intense circumstances—they never last." Great. Her mind was Hollyweird instead of holy-wired. Shouldn't she be considering God's will in this?

Thud.

And Lucas?

Livvy pushed off an industrial-huge dryer and rolled free.

Fallon saw Lucas going into North Block. That means Fallon

saw him before the photo in the gas chamber, yeah? Then maybe Gant was done with him when the photo was taken.

Thud.

Hopefully Gant was done with Lucas, period.

Push.

Lucas thought I got on the helicopter. Does Gant think that too? Maybe the creepazoid isn't looking for me anymore.

Thud.

Tobin had told her to count to nine hundred and ninety-nine. Said he'd be back from the *San Quentin News* office by the time she got there. She'd stopped counting around one hundred sixty something. So what number would she be at now?

Push.

Roll.

Thud.

She'd start again at two fifty. She probably would have been at a higher number, but this way it was even more likely Tobin would be back before she got to nine hundred and ninety-nine.

Push.

Then she wouldn't run out of numbers and have him still be gone.

Roll.

Stop.

No thud.

Livvy looked up. Fingers wrapped round the edge of the basket. He was back already? Way before nine—

A face peered into Livvy's confines. Snake eyes narrowed.

Horror slammed Livvy in the chest. Snatched her breath. Then she screamed herself empty. She gasped a lungful of air and screamed more.

Gant stood and laughed. A genuine, deep belly laugh.

Livvy stilled. Her nostrils flared as she breathed rapidly. Shallowly. She slid down. Cowered in the bottom of the bin. To escape the basket was to go up. To go up was to go to him.

"Don't you know that San Quentin is a living, breathing organism?" Gant asked. "Its eyes and ears are mine. Do you think you can move without me knowing?"

He feinted a lunge at her, and Livvy clawed at the cloth wall. He laughed again, shook her dizzy in the basket, then sent it careening, spinning.

Livvy pulled up, flung herself over the side of the pitching basket, and slammed into crates of detergents, her wound shrieking in pain. She scrambled and ran. Away from Gant. Away from the door, into the vast darkening laundry room. Her slapping footsteps echoed off the cement floor, the cement walls, the cement ceiling. She scuttled under a table.

Where'd he go?

"Livvy ..." he called to her in a singsong voice.

Over there. He was coming around that row of washers. Approaching slowly. Slithering.

"Livvy ..." His voice gave her goose bumps. "We thought you made it out of here, me and lover boy did. Thought you got on that helicopter."

Turn the other way, she willed him. *Go down that row there.* If he did, she could double back to the door.

But he wound in her direction. "Thing about the news cycle these days: fast, fast, fast."

What a stupid place to hide. Under the long, wide table, behind piles of laundry.

"They talk about how no one really owns the news anymore. Some guy on the street lucks into catching a photo, sells a video to the highest bidder. Things get leaked, posted, emailed, tweeted. They get *out*."

Livvy trembled with the urge to run. To claw through the clothes and sprint screaming away from that voice. But she held herself still. Quiet. To let him pass her by so she could scurry the other direction. To the door.

"So, when someone with happy fingers shared with the world the names of the men that got onto that helicopter, *I* knew you were still here."

Still, Livvy. Still.

"Here."

He was at the foot of the table now.

"Waiting."

Keep going!

"Waiting ..."

Please, oh, please, oh please.

"... for *me*!" Gant roared and lunged under the table. He gripped Livvy's ankle and dragged her. She screamed, kicked, grappled for a table leg as she slid past it.

Gant gathered her up and slammed her onto the table.

"At least lover boy died thinking you were safe." Gant's face was inches from hers. "I slit his throat, Livvy." He drew his finger across his neck, from one ear to the other.

Livvy went blind. Eyes flooded. "Nine hundred and ninety-nine!" she screamed. "One thousand!"

"What?" Gant drew back. Laughed.

Lucas. Lucas. Lucas!

"Tobiiiin!" she screamed.

"No shortage of lover boys." Gant seized her around the neck and slammed her head back onto the table. Livvy blinked, crystals popping white in her peripheral vision.

Gant leaped onto the table next to her. She hammered at him while he straddled her. "Do you think that guy—the one with the flying fingers—will ever know that he actually became *part* of events here? Will he know that he got you killed?" Gant panted. With one hand, he pinned Livvy's wrists to the table over her head.

"Please, please, please," Livvy sobbed.

"Please what, Livvy darling? Just ask me for it, and I'll give it to you." Gant's voice went deep, guttural.

The rubber soles of Livvy's shoes gripped the table surface. She dug in hard. *Push away, away, away.*

Gant lifted her shirt.

Away!

"Who did this!" Gant reared back, releasing Livvy's wrists. His face went purple, rage pulsing at his temples. "Who did this?" he shrieked, pointing at Livvy's bandaged wound.

For a split second the chaos stopped. Livvy stared, open-mouthed, confused.

"Who did this to you?" Gant looked like he was going to pop.

"I don't ..." Livvy stammered.

Then she lunged. Buried her nails deep in Gant's eye sockets.

He roared back, fell off the table. *Broke his neck, broke his neck.* Livvy's thoughts skittered as she sprinted through a maze of machines, boxes, carts, piles.

Then she stopped, listened frozen, lungs bursting to pant.

Nothing. Silence.

She crept to a row of huge industrial dryers. Gently, gently, opened one. Crawled inside. Covered herself with denim. Denim on top. Denim between her and the door.

Breathe. So quiet. So very quiet.

He didn't call her name this time. But he was out there. And he was going to find her.

Lucas! Livvy clutched denim to her mouth and nose. Tried to silence the raspy inhalations.

Sob later!

She saw the body she'd tripped over in the yard. Lucas was that body now. Lifeless. Dead weight.

You cannot do this now.

She panted into the shirt scrunched to her face. It smelled like Tobin. She'd kissed Tobin and gotten Lucas killed.

"Are you Tobin's special little pen friend now, Livvy?" Gant's voice echoed through the room, reached Livvy inside her denim-padded cell. "Big, strong Tobin! Did he tell you what he did? What he's in for?"

Doesn't matter. Doesn't matter. Livvy screwed her eyes closed.

"You think he's so different than me? Did you let him touch you?"

Was his voice getting further away? It was hard to tell, with the echoes, the muffling of the clothes, the acoustics of the dryer drum.

"Your knight in shining armor is the same as me, Livvy. Him and me—we're here for the same reasons."

Not true. Don't listen.

"He's a murderer, Livvy. Did you know that? He took a man's life, using the same hands you want him to touch you with."

No! Gant's a liar. The father of lies.

"And he was convicted for violating California penal code number 261. Do you need to look that one up, Livvy? Let me help you. That's rape."

That word reverberated.

"Did you hear that, Livvy?" Gant shouted. "Tobin is a rapist *and* a murderer."

Not true. Livvy's eyes streamed. She shook her head violently. *No. Liar. He wants you to give yourself away. Don't listen.*

"They didn't even get *me* on rape. But Tobin's doing time for it."

Not true.

"You think he's so brave, your hero. Did you let him *touch you*?" Gant screamed again. He sounded closer.

Slam! "Where are you, Livvy?"

Slam! Definitely closer.

Slam! What was he doing?

Slam! Livvy's dryer shuddered.

Slam! The metal drum vibrated.

Slam! The dryers. He was coming down the row of dryers, slamming open the doors and searching inside them.

Slam! She was going to die.

Slam! But not quickly.

Livvy could hear him breathe.

He was outside her dryer. The only one with the door standing ajar.

"Tell me who cut you, and I'll kill him before he sees another dawn," Gant whispered. The air around her couldn't have stirred, she was so mashed into the clothes, but Livvy felt as if his breath lifted the hair off the nape of her neck.

"Marring such a pristine canvas. What is his *name*?"

There was a stirring. The pile of shirts shifted slightly.

"Does Tobin know who? He'll tell me. He'll want the man dead too."

The clothing on top of Livvy slipped inches.

"Livvy ..." Gant whispered.

A shirt under her shoulder tugged, dragged away through the twisted tumble of cloth between Livvy and Gant. And another.

Dear Jesus. Help me, please.

Had Lucas prayed the same thing?

The pile got lighter. Thinner.

And then there was nothing. Livvy pressed to the back of the drum, clutching the last shirt to her nose and mouth. Soaked with tears and mucus.

Gant stood with the door wide open. Blood from the gouges at his eyes muddled his macabre mask.

"Livvy," he whispered. He licked his lips with his forked tongue. Livvy closed her eyes. Maybe it would be easier if she didn't look. If she didn't fight. Nausea welled. Would he be repelled if his pristine canvas vomited?

A slam and a grunt startled Livvy's eyes open. Gant was gone. The dryer door swung slowly towards her, a red slick streaked down the center glass.

Another slam, and a crunch.

Livvy quivered violently. Waited wide-eyed.

A sigh floated into the drum. And then a hand reached in.

"C'mon, darling. It's over. That snake has slithered his last." Fallon leaned into the drum.

Fallon?

His mouth pulled into a knot. "Poor little kitten. He really did a number on you, didn't he?" He stretched his hand further. "C'mere."

Livvy took his hand. Let him pull her to the edge of the dryer.

"Best not to look down and to your left," Fallon cautioned.

Livvy swallowed. "Is he really ..."

"As a doornail, kitten."

Shouldn't she feel something about that?

"C'mon. Let's get you back to your people. I know where some are stashed."

Livvy let Fallon guide her, ignorant of her path or surroundings. She still clutched the shirt in her fists, pressed over her mouth, when they arrived at a closed door.

Fallon pounded. Tried the handle. Pounded again.

Livvy watched and blinked. Now where was she? What if she was the spoils and Fallon the victor she'd so readily gone with? She swayed on her feet.

"I know ya'll are in there," Fallon called. "I got one of yours. Open up and give some sanctuary already."

A voice called through the door. Asked something.

"I think it's best for everybody if we don't use no names," Fallon spoke to the door. "I tell you what. You don't like what you see, you can kick me in the teeth."

After a scuffle, the door opened a crack. Livvy watched Fallon. "What'd I tell you," he spoke into the building.

Gently he took her by the shoulders and steered her to the

door. Livvy stepped up and in. Lots of faces gaped.

Joan. Joan wrapped her in a hug.

A pat on her back. "Now I best go find your cowboy. He's gotta be worried halfway to crazy by now."

The door thumped closed.

From a place deep, deep within, Livvy began to sob.

Chapter Thirty-Two

"Liv?" Tobin hissed into the gathering darkness. "Where are you?"

Maybe she was hiding. Playing with him.

Right. Because she was sick and twisted enough to think that would be funny in this particular setting.

You were gone too long. Had she panicked? Gone looking for him? Tobin studied the view out the door.

It was dark now—the yard and outdoor areas of the prison took on an anemic pallor under the penetrating beams of ballpark-scale electric lights. Disfigured shadows cast their reach across the grounds and stone walls.

No. She would not go out there alone.

Some exterior light glowed into the laundry. Inside, a few auxiliary lights gleamed, but the structure was outmoded and far from any kind of code.

Tobin stepped carefully. Quietly. Were those crates scattered like that before?

"Livvy!" he called softly. She probably just went to the back of the room, to hunker down 'til he returned.

If you'd accepted Fallon's offer, she wouldn't have been left by herself.

But he'd wanted to be alone with her. Wanted her to himself. Remembering the kiss that followed flooded him with heat, almost made him gasp aloud. How was it possible that she'd kissed him? It hadn't been a dream. She was more flesh and blood than anyone he'd known.

But where was she?

To his right, a bank of dryers stood open, rounded doors gleamed dimly metallic in the faint lighting. Against the rules to leave the doors open like that—potential for accidents and all that. Tobin cocked his head, peered fully around, and crept past a table used for folding clean clothes. Not all the doors were open. The floor was strewn with clothing spilling out of the dryers. At the last open door, a larger pile. And, crumpled on the floor—

God, no!

No—no. The shape was much too big to be Livvy. Tobin closed the dryer door, peered down at the man. He dug in his pocket for the lighter Smitty gave him, flicked it to life.

Gant.

Tobin reeled. Panic surged, streaked through him. "Livvy!" he shouted. He began running, opening washer and dryer doors, digging through piles of clothing. "Livvy!"

Gant dead? What did it mean? A fight—over Livvy? Winner take the prize?

He never should have left her! He should have given her the gun. Why hadn't he thought of that?

If she were with him and he still drew breath, he would not let anyone or anything hurt her.

What a load! He'd failed her. Again, a visceral memory of their shared kiss, willingly given. What was someone violently taking of her, *right now*?

Tobin gagged and spewed a mouthful of bile onto the concrete. He snatched up a crate and hurled it into the darkness. Screaming inarticulate as he battered a dryer.

"Easy, cowboy."

Tobin whirled, hand to gun. He couldn't make out any features in the dark, but from the voice and the stature, that had to be Fallon.

"Take it easy. She's safe."

"What?" Tobin wiped his eyes on his sleeve. "Where?" He gestured toward Gant's inert form. "Did you do that?"

"Won't confirm or deny. C'mon. Cowboy up. Your girl needs your shoulder."

Trailing Fallon, Tobin clenched his hands into fists to stop their shaking. As much as it killed him to have to part with Livvy, he had to get her out of this prison.

Lucas rolled onto his forearms, pushed to his knees and stood.

I don't believe it. There she was—Livvy, just a couple of yards away, her back to him, gripping Joan like a life preserver.

Lucas steepled his hands, pressed fingertips to forehead, and closed his eyes. *Thank you, Jesus. Thank you for hearing our prayers.*

Livvy withdrew from Joan's embrace. Lucas's breath quickened. So much to say. No place to start.

"Smitty." Livvy reached for the inmate, clutched him in a hug.

"Hey, Homes," Smitty whispered into her hair. "I was worried about you." Livvy nodded. "My man Tobin okay?" Livvy nodded again.

She released Smitty, turned profile to Lucas and greeted the guys from the choir. Sniffled as men patted her on the back and welcomed her.

She stepped further into the library, moving toward Lucas. When she saw him, her eyes fluttered wide. Her mouth formed a perfect oval. Then she burst into tears again.

"He lied!" she wailed. "Of course he lied." She crossed her arms over her chest and bent double. Then dropped to the floor and bawled.

Lucas opened his mouth. And closed it.

"Hey, hey, honey." Joan patted Livvy on the shoulder. And raised her brows at Lucas. Nodded down at Livvy's bent head.

Yes, Joan. I'm getting there.

Lucas knelt in front of Livvy. Joan withdrew and the others cleared back as well.

She's right there. What's wrong with you?

What was wrong was that he wanted to pull her into his arms and hold her and rock her. What was wrong was that he wasn't her boyfriend. He was her pastor.

Lucas extended his hand. He rested it on her back, rubbing her shoulder with his thumb. "Livvy," he whispered. Then she melted, just sort of poured forth so that he was sitting back on his heels and she was curled half on him. It really hurt. But there was no way he was moving.

He had no idea what to do. So he prayed. Sat there holding her while she shook, just praying out a lifeline.

"He said you were dead." Livvy snuffled. She sat up. "Gant said he slit your throat."

"Well, he did." Lucas fingered the tie bandage around his neck. "But I'm not dead."

Livvy's gaze searched his face; she appraised him all over.

"'I'm getting better,'" Lucas continued. "'I think I'll go for a walk.'"

Livvy's eyes were puffy and bloodshot, face smudged. "Did you just quote Monty Python at me?" She had dried blood on her chin, under a swollen lip. He wanted to wipe it off.

"Yeah." *Really Lucas? When push comes to shove you quote* The Holy Grail?

But Livvy laughed. It might well have been the most beautiful thing Lucas had ever seen. He was flooded with feelings—many of them contradictory, some without name.

"You're looking more than a little macchiato," Livvy said. She cupped her hand around his distended cheek.

"Right." She was too. She'd been through so much, endured who-knew-what kind of pain and terror. And it was all his fault.

"I'm *so* sorry," they both said in unison.

Lucas recoiled. "What do you have to be sorry for?"

Livvy wiped her nose with a shirt she clutched. "I almost got you killed! Did Gant really break your ribs?"

"I think so. But he never would have touched *you* if I hadn't talked you into coming. You wouldn't be here if I'd just listened to you."

Livvy shook her head. "You didn't talk me into coming." She searched his face with red-rimmed eyes. "It's not your fault."

Right.

"I wanted to be with you. And he's dead now," she said.

"Really?" Wow. Lucas wasn't exactly aggrieved. *Wait—with me? Specifically?*

"Who's dead?" Navarrette asked from the far side of the room.

Nice. Guess you didn't have the expectation of privacy in prison.

"Miles?" Livvy shifted to address the CO. "Gant is dead."

Knox straightened, leaned out from the wall he sat against. "Gant is dead?"

Livvy nodded. She gave sort of a weak smile, which melted into a tremulous line.

"Did Tobin kill him?" Navarrette asked.

Livvy's forehead wrinkled. She looked from Navarrette to Knox, then to Lucas, where her gaze lingered, searching his eyes. Something clouded her typically transparent expression.

What? Lucas didn't know how to read her.

"No. Tobin didn't kill him."

"Did you?" asked Navarrette at the same time that Knox spoke: "Who did?"

"I didn't kill him." Her face hardened and eyes narrowed. "I wish I did."

She looked to Lucas. *Defiant.* Did she expect him to judge her for that? Images flooded him—visions he'd had of obliterating Gant. Lucas had a new appreciation of what he was capable of. What was Livvy capable of? Would she lie about it?

"Who killed him?" Navarrette asked.

Livvy exhaled a deep sigh. "I think that's on a need-to-know basis. And you don't."

Lucas laughed. He hadn't meant to—she'd surprised him. The correctional officers all glared, but Joan nodded. "Let the girl be. Let her get her head on straight."

"Livvy—we talked before about justice, you remember?" Navarrette asked. "That's all I'm looking out for. Who took out Gant? What went down?"

"He got justice, Miles. That's what went down." Livvy wadded up the denim shirt she held and threw it into a wastebasket. She wiped under her eyes with the backs of her hands and ran her fingers through her hair.

Navarrette didn't look like he was going to let it go. But before he could speak, the door thundered with blows from outside. The three COs ran to meet the threat. Knox pulled the handgun he'd taken off Edwards.

Livvy scooted away from the entryway wall and crouched behind Lucas, her hands light on his shoulders.

Yeah. That's right. I'll protect you. Lucas frowned. What use was he? He covered her hands with his.

There was muffled yelling, more pounding, and apparently, a decision in the alcove by the door. The door opened and two inmates were allowed admittance. Fallon led. His eyes traveled over the group of people and came to rest on Livvy and Lucas.

The other man was agitated, intent. He swung around, poised to confront. When he saw Livvy, he pulled up short. Then he looked down at Lucas like a man unsure of his footing.

"Tobin!" Livvy stood.

"Liv—" he shifted something from one hand to the other. A manila envelope. Tossed it onto the floor. "I shouldn't have left you. When I saw Gant ..." He jutted his jaw, nostrils flared. He flicked a gaze around the room and took a step closer to Livvy, shouldering the others out.

And there was Lucas, sitting on the floor between them. Holding Livvy's hands. *Don't mind me.*

"I'm so sorry," Tobin spoke to Livvy in just over a whisper.

Seems to be going around.

Tobin glanced down at Lucas, leaned in closer to Livvy. "Are you okay? Did he hurt you?" He reached out a hand, extended his fingers toward her puffy lip. But then he stopped. Stood immobile. He flushed, fisted his hand and withdrew it. He swiped a palm over his hair and looked up at Livvy from the ground. "Are you okay?"

"Yes." Livvy's whisper was more of a breath. A flutter of communication from her to him. Over Lucas's head.

This was Tobin. *The* Tobin. And clearly there was more to the story than had been related to Lucas thus far. It wasn't surprising to see desire in a man's eyes when he looked at Livvy. But there was something more in Tobin's expression than mere desire.

An additional feeling—an ugly one—stirred in Lucas and rose above the others. This one had a name: jealousy.

Chapter Thirty-Three

Tobin had never felt more imprisoned. He didn't even have the privacy of his own intimate thoughts. Surely his feelings were naked on his face. The COs and Livvy's friends were all packed close in the reception area of the small library. Tobin would probably never have another unmonitored word with Livvy again. The pain of that thought ripped open all the deep places where he'd hidden his private feelings and stuffed his vulnerabilities. He shuddered. Reached back to the wall for support.

"Are you okay?" Livvy took a half step toward him. Then seemed to realize she was holding hands with the man who could only be Lucas. She colored and folded her arms across her chest. "Tobin, this is Lucas. Lucas, Tobin's been protecting me this whole time."

Right. The whole time. Like when he left her alone in the laundry, and she was attacked by the scum who clearly struck her in the face. Who could have sliced her to ribbons.

Lucas nodded and moved to stand. He gasped and put his hand to his side.

"Don't get up," Tobin said. He extended his hand.

Lucas shook it. "Thanks for taking care of Livvy. I hear you're a real hero. I—we all owe you a lot of gratitude for keeping her safe."

Great. The guy had to go and be classy. And he had a firm handshake.

Tobin was at a loss for words: *You're welcome?* He hadn't protected Livvy for Lucas or for any of the others. At first it had been instinct. Then so much more. *It was nothing?* It was everything.

"Tobin!"

Tobin started. Looked around the room. The voice came from Knox. "Are you carrying a weapon?" the CO asked, eyes pinpoints.

Heat flooded Tobin's face. "Yeah." He started to reach behind for the gun.

"Hold it, inmate," Knox pulled a handgun from nowhere and leveled it at Tobin. "Put your hands on your head and turn around."

Behind Knox, Smitty closed his eyes for a beat. Shook his head and dropped it forward.

Tobin exhaled long and set his jaw. He raised his hands, palms forward, fingers spread, then interlaced them behind his head. Slowly he turned to face the eastern wall of the library, studiously not seeing any of the eyes glued on him.

Someone, had to be Navarrette or Velasco, approached and patted him down. He pulled the pistol from Tobin's waistband and continued to frisk him. The CO found the shank Tobin made out of the coffee lid and took that too. Great. That would be fun to explain.

"Okay," the CO behind him said. Tobin turned. It was Velasco. Navarrette, just beyond him, was impossible to read. But even in inmate clothing, 'Rette clearly belonged more with Knox and Velasco than with the rest of them. At least he had the character to meet Tobin's eyes.

"He only had those to protect me," Livvy said, her voice urgent. "He's not in trouble, is he? He didn't hurt anyone—he kept me safe. Plus four guys from our church that he helped get onto a helicopter."

Tobin's shame burned hotter. He shoved his hands in his pockets. "Never mind, Livvy. Don't worry about it." He couldn't even look her direction. He and Knox glared at one another.

Knox slid his gun into the waistband of his uniform and held out his hand for the pistol Velasco gripped. A shadow flickered across the young CO's face.

Good. You get to feel your place in the pecking order too.

Velasco handed the gun to Knox, who pocketed it.

"That's all," Knox said to Tobin with a curt nod.

For some reason, that was the worst. Tobin had been dismissed. He fisted his hands, but kept them at his sides.

"Are you injured, Tobin?" Dale Peake asked him. Tobin had hardly noticed the man until then. Tobin eyed the Chaplain. Was he trying to ease the tension? Interjecting himself to remind Tobin to keep his head?

"No," he bit off. "I'm okay."

Just peachy.

Please don't do anything stupid, Tobin.

So far, Livvy had not seen Tobin lose his cool or act irrationally. *You know—in the vast amount of time I've known him.*

But now he stood rigid, coiled, staring down Lt. Knox. He looked ready to fly at the man. That would be an epic mistake. Knox was a *them* if there ever was one.

Did Livvy really even know what Tobin was capable of? Gant's words came back to her. She was riveted by Tobin's clenched hands. Hands that had held her while she sobbed. Caressed her while they kissed. Had those hands taken someone's life?

Focused on Tobin, Livvy didn't see Joan move until the woman reached for Tobin's fist.

"Thank you," Joan said. She smoothed out Tobin's hand and clasped it between her own. "I was rude to you earlier. I'm sorry about that. I've heard about everything you've done to keep Livvy safe. Thank you."

Tobin inhaled sharply. He blinked several times, then nodded. "Yes, ma'am. You're welcome."

"I'm Joan."

"I'm Jasper." Fallon stepped forward and held out his hand. "I helped too."

Joan burst out laughing. She shook his hand. "Hello, Jasper."

The tension in the room drained dramatically, like someone letting the air out of a tire. Even Tobin grinned. Until he looked at Livvy. Then his face stilled and eyes clouded. He gave her a little nod and looked away.

Livvy swallowed hard and pressed a fist to the knot in her chest. Smitty studied her, his dark eyes awash in compassion. For whom? Her, or Tobin? She turned and stumbled blind down a row between bookshelves.

There was no going back. This riot—which had nothing to do with her—had enmeshed her, had caught her, heart and soul. To leave was to leave Tobin, that kiss—that weak-kneed kiss—never to be recaptured. And, *oh Jesus!* could Tobin be a rapist? It wasn't possible, was it? He'd been so gentle. He'd let her beat on him in impotent anger. Could he have taken a woman by force? Could he have taken a life?

You change us all. Our old selves are dead, we are made new in you. Was this Tobin so new, the former Tobin so different that he'd been a killer and rapist?

Livvy's cheeks were raw from tears and the wiping of them. She leaned back into the shelving. Dropped her hands open to her sides, tipped her head back, and closed her eyes. *Lord I can't take much more. If I can do all things through you who strengthens me, then strengthen me!*

She breathed. Just breathed.

There was a commotion on the other side of the stacks. "They're letting more hostages go," someone said. There was a flurry, people moving to the window.

Livvy breathed.

Wade had cut her off from everyone. Since he'd taken his life, she'd been like a mummy shuffling among the living, wrapped in invisible layers that restricted, muted, suffocated.

The last day and a half had stripped all that away, plus the top layer of her dermis. She was raw, flayed, her nerve endings receptive to connect with anyone and everyone. She felt *so much*. As if, having been frozen, she was dropped into boiling water to thaw.

I don't want this! I can't take this!

She breathed. Just breathed.

"Look at the moon," one of the men said. "It's silver."

Oh Silver Moon.

My moon.

She was flooded with memories. Memories carrying images, smells, feelings. Memory of songs and the breath that brought them to life. Breath that filled her chest, the husk around her heart.

My Italian moon. My moon of Santa Barbara, of San Francisco.

Eyes still closed, Livvy began to hum. Not the *Rusalka* of her hideous audition. Not the *Rusalka* that Wade had taken from her. The *Rusalka* of possibilities. Of beauty so fierce it ached.

"Oh moon in the deep, deep sky," she sang, softly at first, the Czech more expressive to her than her native tongue. "You roam around the wide world, peering into men's homes."

A cappella her voice rose and fell, the library hushed with expectation when she took breath.

"Oh, moon! Stand still a moment!" Tears rolled down her cheeks, her voice soaring high and clear. "Tell me, tell me, where is my beloved?"

Tobin stood on the other side of those shelves; Lucas listened too. But neither heard.

"Tell him, oh tell him, my silver moon, that my arms embrace him." No one in earshot knew what the words meant. She poured out her heart for all who listened, but for the moon alone to hear.

"Moon, oh moon, don't disappear!" After some five minutes, Livvy fell silent. Her heart beat at its normal pace. She hadn't broken into sweat. She'd sung the aria all the way through for the first time since Wade lit himself on fire in front of her.

What *was* that?

No one in the library moved. Lucas couldn't say for certain, but it seemed they all held their breath as he did.

He turned, looked down the aisle where Livvy had disappeared. He had no idea what she'd sung, but it had broken his heart.

He still had goose bumps and was reluctant to speak, but Joan caught his eye. Hers were brimming. "Did you know she could do that?" he whispered.

Joan shook her head.

"Why is she pouring coffee?" he wondered aloud.

Tobin—hunkered against the wall opposite Lucas—frowned. "'Cause of what happened."

"What happened?" Lucas asked. Bet he barely beat Joan to the punch.

Tobin scowled. "How do you not know that? Aren't you her boyfriend?"

Say what?

"I thought you were her boyfriend," Fallon said to Tobin.

Say what?

"What happened?" Joan asked Tobin.

Tobin shrugged. "Not my place to say."

Lucas could swear Smitty smirked. Apparently Livvy and Tobin had had a fair amount of time to chat.

Boyfriend? Why would Tobin think Lucas was her boyfriend? And why would Fallon think Tobin was? Lucas recalled his conversation with Livvy in the van, when she'd said women who fell in love with incarcerated men had problems. Did they? Had she?

There was that jealousy again. It burned like reflux. *Odd.* The only impediment to dating Livvy he'd considered was not wanting to be creepy. Was this guy Tobin actually in play?

Lucas studied the inmate. Guess he wasn't hard to look at. A bit sullen, maybe. Just then Tobin lifted his gaze, looked over Lucas's head. The man's face came to life, eyes bright. Livvy's faint footfalls reached Lucas's ears as she approached from behind.

"Hey," Tobin said gently.

"Hey yourself," she replied, her tone cautious. She sat lotus style to Lucas's right, Tobin's left, leaning against the eastern wall.

"That was amazing, Homes," Smitty said.

Livvy colored, but a sweet smile stole across her face. "Thank you."

"Where'd you learn to do that?" he asked.

"Oh, you know, correspondence courses."

"Honey, are you pursuing singing professionally?" Joan asked.

"*Pffhht.*" Livvy bobbled her head. "In fits and starts." She cleared her throat and reached for the manila envelope on the floor. "So. What did you find, Tobin?"

Tobin glanced at the three COs clustered against the wall to the right. "Nothing much."

Livvy opened the envelope and fished around inside.

Tobin winced. He looked to Smitty, then reached up and gave a tug on his earlobe. And at that, Smitty, Cho, and Agromonte all moved. Smitty flanked Livvy on the floor to her left, Cho on the right. Next to him was Tobin, then Agromonte and Fallon. If Livvy thought this was unusual, she didn't let on. Lucas raised a brow at Joan, who pursed her lips.

"Did you unearth anything?" Livvy asked, voice low.

He shook his head the tiniest bit. "Birds on the line, Liv."

Liv?

"Huh?" Livvy crinkled her nose.

"Five-oh," Cho said.

"Phone's off the hook," Fallon whispered.

"*Hay moros en la costa,*" Agromonte said.

Livvy continued to look as blank as Lucas felt. She held up open hands in query.

"Oh for the luvva—" Smitty did a face palm. He looked sideways at the three correctional officers and then pointedly at the envelope in Livvy's lap. "Ears!"

"Oh." Livvy slid the envelope behind her back, between her and the wall. "Birds on the line ..." she muttered. "Wait"—she looked to Agromonte—"did you say 'there are Moors on the coast?' What the heck?"

"Yeah. From back in the day, when the Moors kept invading Spain." He shrugged. "My Spanish *abuela* used to say it when the adults started talking around the little kids."

"Ah."

"You speak Spanish, Homes?" Smitty asked.

"I took it in high school. And I know Italian, so I can pick up some."

Tobin hunched, elbows on knees. He spoke behind folded hands. "Roberts was sure there was a CO hooking up send-outs and street-to-street action."

Lucas squinted. *Huh?*

"He name anyone?" Cho asked.

Tobin shook his head. "Said requests are funneled up. Only one convict in the Q worked directly with Casper."

"*Casper?*" Livvy mouthed to Smitty.

"The friendly ghost," he whispered in reply.

"Seems a red light special—on the bricks—went south. A little kid was killed. Doer was caught and willing to trade up. Said the order and money came through a CO. But the guy was shanked before he could dime out."

Joan waved at Tobin. "Back up the truck, guys. I don't know *what* that was. Was it supposed to be English?"

"In a nutshell," Smitty leaned forward, as did Livvy, Lucas and Joan, "a hit—on the outside—went bad and a kid died. The killer said he'd make a deal and give up a CO at the Q who is lining up hits, sales, and communications between guys in prison and their people on the outside."

"But the hit man was stabbed before he named the CO?" Lucas guessed.

Smitty nodded.

"So, who is Casper?" Joan whispered.

"The CO, because no one knows who he is—he's a ghost," Livvy answered.

"The greatest trick the Devil ever pulled was convincing the world he didn't exist," Joan whispered.

"Kevin Spacey. *The Usual Suspects*," Livvy said.

"C.S. Lewis," Lucas said.

"Charles Baudelaire," Joan said with finality.

"Right." Cho frowned. "Anyhow, Casper only works with one inmate—all the orders go through the one lag to Casper."

"*Worked*," Tobin said. "I didn't get through everything, but Roberts's notes say it was Gant."

"So"—Joan raised a single manicured finger—"Gant was the only inmate that knew who the crooked officer is?"

Cho emitted a low whistle.

Navarrette raised his head. He studied the group, then strode to the edge of their circle. Back to the other COs, he planted his feet shoulder width apart and hooked his thumbs into belt loops.

"What're you all bumping your gums about?"

Livvy peered up at him. "Just chatting."

"Uh huh. Chatting." Navarrette's eyes narrowed. "Wanna tell me what about?"

Knox and Velasco perked up too. Lucas felt his ears burn. He wasn't good at duplicity. And he wasn't necessarily following all this. But he was pretty sure it wasn't a great idea to tell COs about evidence pointing to a crooked CO.

Chapter Thirty-Four

Livvy was at a loss as to how to answer Miles. Which was weird. Hadn't he been on her team since the beginning?

"Just shooting the breeze, Officer Navarrette," Tobin said.

Ooh. *Officer* Navarrette. Did Tobin feel it too? That hesitation? Or was that for the benefit of the other birds on the line?

Miles dropped his voice a scintilla. "Did you gain new intel?"

"*Sabes que ...*" Agromonte addressed Navarrette, then eyed Velasco. Barely audible, he resumed. "*Sabes que algo huele mal.*" Livvy worked to conjugate: *you know something stinks.*

"*Lo sé.*" Navarrette's forehead wrinkled and he lifted a shoulder. *I know.*

Livvy would have translated for the others, but didn't want to open her mouth.

"*Alguien huele mal,*" Agromonte emphasized, steel in his voice. *Someone stinks.*

"*Ya. Lo. Sé.*" Navarrette drilled Agromonte with his gaze. *I know already.*

Lucas leaned into Smitty. "How's your Spanish?"

"Taco," Smitty whispered.

"Yeah. Me too." They looked at Livvy, but she pinched her lips together.

"What's going on over there?" Knox called across the room.

"Just politics and rumors." Navarrette stepped back to bridge circle and CO. He cracked his knuckles. "What a snafu all is this. Bet you wish you'd retired just one week earlier, eh L-T?"

Livvy gasped like she'd been doused with water. Her eyes flew wide. And Knox was looking directly at her when they did.

That one-sided phone conversation of Gant's she'd overheard—he said he'd given the listener a retirement gift. Did he mean the riot? Could he have been talking to Knox?

Knox's facial expression was cast in steel. His eyes seemed to have the power to pry open doors in Livvy's mind and extract information.

Lots of people could be retiring, right? Gant could even have been talking to someone outside the prison. But Livvy's hands and feet began to ice up. She dug nails into her palms. What could she possibly say or do?

"So, um." Her mouth started, brain slow to catch up. "What are you going to do with your retirement?" she asked Knox all in a rush.

"What?" Knox asked.

"If it were me, I'd have old-movie marathons. I love old movies. And vintage cartoons."

Tobin's Livvy radar seemed to be pinging. He searched her face. Tipped his head slightly in query.

Get it? Livvy thought to him as loudly as she could. *Vintage cartoons? Casper the Friendly Ghost?*

Knox looked at her like she was a loon. "Haven't really thought about it."

"Well, no rush I guess. Right?" Livvy sounded goofy, even to herself.

"Right," Knox said. He continued to watch Livvy. "Talk about bad timing. Pretty bad day to visit Bastille by the Bay."

"Definitely," Livvy said.

"At least you don't have to worry about Gant anymore." Knox appraised Tobin. "Tobin, Livvy wouldn't admit that you killed him."

"No man, wasn't me," Tobin said. "Though I'd have been glad to, if I were there."

Knox's left eye narrowed the teensiest bit, for a fraction of a second. Like a tic. "So you were alone with him?" Knox asked Livvy. "That must have been terrifying."

"What did he say to you?" Navarrette asked, ever the investigator. Knox watched her closely.

Livvy shook her head. She didn't want to remember. Didn't want to speak it. She'd probably have to relive it in therapy at some point. In hours and hours of therapy. But she didn't want to bring life to Gant here, in this place. In front of all these men.

All of whom were looking at her. A lump pressing into her shoulder was a reminder of the envelope behind her back. Surely Knox's penetrating stare could see it, right through her. What evidence did it hold? She needed to protect the envelope until the riot ended.

"What do you *think* the animal said to her?" Tobin asked. "Use your imagination. But leave her alone."

Thank you, Livvy thought to him, loathe to speak under Knox's scrutiny.

What a mess. She looked at her hands in her lap. Whatever was going on in the prison was for the authorities—and maybe the press—to sort out when the riot was over and all the hostages safe. She didn't need to be Nancy Drew.

Wait—Knox couldn't be Casper. He'd been locked up with the others. What day was it? It was Monday night or Tuesday morning. Was it possible her time in the dungeon had just been earlier that same day? Livvy's thinking was getting muddled. She rubbed her temples.

"What's happening out there now?" Joan asked the men over

by the western windows.

"Lots of SWAT guys are lining on top of the perimeter wall," Jim said.

Was this going to end soon? Livvy would just hand off the envelope and tell her theory to someone. Maybe Captain Classen. Maybe him and Tiana Jo.

"You two made contact with Gant earlier today, too." Miles stated, pointing at Tobin and Livvy.

Tobin looked blank. Then started. "Oh, in the dungeon. No, no contact. We were out of sight, he was on the phone."

Livvy's heart sank. She couldn't help but look at Knox. He didn't appear to be breathing. Expressionless, he met Livvy's gaze. His left eye twitched. "Who was he talking to?"

"Dunno." Tobin shrugged. "Couldn't hear." Livvy pressed her lips together and looked to the floor. It wasn't an actual nod.

All that time with Tobin in the dungeon, in the chapel corridor. Had she not told him what she overheard? Was she the only one who had the two and two to put together?

It didn't really matter anyway, did it? Gant's comment and Knox's retirement hardly amounted to proof. It was just a starting point. The investigators could investigate.

"Was it Gant who stabbed you?" Knox asked.

Livvy shook her head. "I was just in the wrong place at the wrong time." She could see Gant's face, purple with fury. His desire to know who'd marred her so he could kill the man. Her hands trembled.

Knox was watching them.

Livvy crossed her arms, pinned her hands to her sides with her elbows.

"Maybe it would be a good use of time to interview everyone now, Navarrette." Knox said. He tipped his head toward the group bunched on the floor. "Memories are fresh. Nobody's going anywhere."

Miles seemed to size up the group and the idea.

"I could help—we could split the group up," Knox said. "You take statements from people you haven't been with, I'll do the same."

Miles shuffled items on the desk. "That's an affirmative." He gathered pens and paper. "I'll start with you." He pointed at Hector. "Grab a chair—let's rally in the far corner for privacy."

"I can help," Velasco said.

Knox seemed to have forgotten Velasco. "Yeah. You sit with Navarrette and watch him work. He's the pro investigator." Knox stood. "Livvy, I know this has been a long ordeal for you. What say you go first and get it over with." He held his hands out to usher her toward a small table near the western windows.

That didn't really seem like a question. The chills moved to Livvy's spine. What was he up to?

Lucas gave her a thumbs up. But Tobin was sober, peering into her eyes.

Oh! The envelope. Knox would see it when she stood. For once she remembered to keep her poker face.

"Sure thing," she said, straightening her crossed legs. "Oh! Ow." She grabbed at her knee.

"What?" Tobin asked.

"Just a cramp. I must have been sitting too long." Livvy slowly hunched into a crouch, stretching her leg. On either side, Smitty and Cho fussed over her, took her elbows and half rose too. Once on her feet, Livvy brushed herself off. "Thanks," she said to Smitty and Cho. Between them, where she'd been sitting, was clear. No envelope in sight.

Way to go, guys! Livvy smirked. *I'm such a covert operator.*

But the look on Knox's face wiped the smile off hers and dismantled her defenses.

What if he *was* Casper? What wouldn't he do to protect himself?

"This isn't anything to worry about," Knox said. His posture and hyper-focus on Livvy told a different story. "We just want to go over things while they're still fresh in your head. Things are going to start happening pretty quickly around here, and you'll need immediate medical care. So let's use this time to review what you've experienced and observed."

Livvy nodded, then was overcome by a jaw-cracking yawn.

"Where did Tobin take you from the chapel?"

Livvy fought to keep things straight. Knox wanted to know who they'd been with and what they'd done. Should she tell him everything—the *whole* truth? Miles had been angry when she told Classen that Tobin was in the ISU. She had no idea what kind of misery she could unwittingly bring upon her friends. She wished Tobin was with her.

"Don't worry about him," Knox said, catching her looking over her shoulder. "Just tell me in your own words. When you were with Gant, did you see him give men orders? Did he seem to be in charge?"

Livvy nodded. "Definitely. He called one guy by name." The guy with the gun. She tried to picture his face. "Edwards."

"We don't need to waste any breath on him." Knox's tone was dry. "Did you see or hear Gant *take* any orders?"

"Not really."

"'Not really'?" Knox's gaze bored into Livvy, drilling access to the vault of her mind.

"No. No, I didn't." She regarded her hands, folded on the table. Scraped, scabbed, and filthy, they were silent witnesses to the past thirty-six hours.

"Livvy, this could be important. You need to be clear."

"I know. Sorry. I'm just really tired."

"Of course. Now, maybe you heard something odd that Gant

said. A name, a nickname? Maybe his tone of voice gave you a *feeling.*"

Livvy shook her head.

"Tell me about the dungeon."

A shiver went down Livvy's back and she quaked involuntarily. Knox continued to skewer her visually. *You are so hosed. The man is trained to spot liars.* Good *liars. Which you are not.*

She tugged her beanie down, covering her ears. It was cold next to the windows. Sure, *that's* why she shivered. "I don't remember much. Sorry. I'm just so beat."

"This is important." Knox grasped her wrist lying on the table. Hard. "Later on your memories might get mixed up. You might find your mind playing tricks on you—misinterpreting things, twisting them until you aren't sure which memories are false and which are true."

Livvy focused on his hand encircling her wrist. Narrowed her eyes and looked up into his. If she thought she'd cow him into letting go, she was wrong. He gripped her harder.

"You might find that the people you love—your family and your friends," Knox said, "they'll want to help you. They won't understand what you're going through. It could get very painful for all of you."

Livvy's jaw slackened. Did he just *threaten* her? Or was she becoming incredibly paranoid?

"Or maybe you're covering for Tobin," Knox said. "In a situation like this, it can be easy to lose perspective of who's on the right side. Remember, Tobin is only out for Tobin. He may seem like your hero. But trust me, he isn't incarcerated for helping little old ladies cross the street."

Livvy wished Knox would stop talking. She was getting so confused. Wouldn't it be true that someone suffering from something like Stockholm Syndrome wouldn't know they were?

"If you tell me exactly what you saw and heard in the dungeon, it will go better for Tobin. Things will look bad for him if your stories don't agree."

Knox wanted to know if she heard Gant on the phone. And *that* didn't have anything to do with Stockholm, Shanghai, or Silicon Valley.

"I think I can tell who is on the side of right," she said. "Let go of my arm."

Knox straightened one finger at a time, releasing his grip. His stare never wavered. He eased back in his seat. And slid his hand into his right pocket. The one with the gun. "Tell me what Gant said to you. Everything."

"Are you going to shoot me? Here?" Livvy gestured at their surroundings. "How do you plan to explain that?"

"Don't be ridiculous. I'm not going to shoot you." Knox tipped his head, his line of sight directed over her shoulder.

Tobin. He was going to remain at San Quentin. A CO could probably do anything he wanted to an inmate, or get someone else to. That guy—Roberts—he ended up in the hole for just looking into corruption at San Quentin. When Livvy walked out of the east gate a free woman, Tobin would be rounded up and locked down.

She couldn't even prove anything. All she had was a sketchy theory, born of a half-functioning mind. *Half?* Sleep deprivation, low blood sugar, blood loss, injury, terror. She would be lucky to count on half.

"I'm sure you've noticed," Knox continued, "in any riot you've got your inmate perpetrators and inmate nonparticipants. They all get sorted out later, based on evidence and eyewitness testimony. Some of the cons here have spent the last day and a half under their bunks. Not your friends. They've been mixing it up. Carrying weapons." Knox shrugged. "It's difficult to say how that could affect their sentences."

Maybe Knox was just playing bad cop. Wouldn't any CO sitting across from her want to know what she witnessed with

Gant? Navarrette asked the same questions.

But Livvy's gut didn't trust Knox. While her whole body cried out in one way or another—pain, hunger, fatigue—her gut clamored for attention the loudest. If she'd learned to read people at all, she had to believe that Knox was Casper.

Knox rang. He flinched and slapped at his left pocket. It continued to trill, and he fished out a cell phone. Staring at the display, his brows knitted.

Interesting. It was the first time Livvy had seen Knox look flustered.

The phone continued to ring.

"Aren't you going to get that?" Livvy asked.

Knox scrutinized her, silent while the phone pealed in his palm. He looked up, and Livvy checked over her shoulder. Tobin strolled their way. He held aloft the cell phone he'd taken off the prisoner in the dungeon. With an exaggerated swipe, he terminated the call.

Knox's phone stopped ringing.

The smug look was on Tobin's face now. One side of his mouth lifted in a sardonic grin. "Hope you haven't gone over your minutes in the last couple of days."

"I took this off a prisoner," Knox said.

"Yeah." Tobin pocketed his. "Me too. It's the one Gant used in the dungeon."

"Give it to me," Knox ordered.

Tobin shrugged, withdrew the phone, and tossed it to the CO.

Knox placed the cell on the floor. Then stomped it to smithereens with his thick-soled duty boot. He rummaged through the debris and pulled out the SIM card. Which he bent double and back until it snapped.

"Thanks for turning over evidence, inmate," Knox said. He leaned back in his chair and flicked the SIM card pieces at Tobin, hitting him in the chest one at a time. "Now go back and grab some floor with the others."

Tobin saluted with two fingers.

Don't leave me here! Livvy scrunched her face, willing Tobin to read her thoughts. An easy smile spread across his face, almost taking her breath away with its honesty. *You're going to be okay,* it said.

Livvy drew a deep breath. They'd get through this.

Then the building shuddered. The walls rattled and dust rose as something smashed the east wall of the library. Another smash shook the door. Someone was coming in.

Chapter Thirty-Five

The ancient timbers of the library quaked with another assault on the door. Instinctively, Tobin tugged Livvy to him, then hustled her behind the desk and against the west wall. He bent low to shield her with his body.

Everyone else seemed to naturally fall into position—Joan was passed to the rear of the group, the COs in front. The noise level outside had swelled to a roar. There was a lot of yelling, some over a bullhorn or PA system. Tobin cocked his head to listen.

"They're coming in," he murmured.

"Do you think we can stop them?" Livvy asked, her voice trembling.

"No—the badges are coming in. They're retaking the prison."

"Oh!" Livvy's eyes popped. Her expression only showed surprise. No fear, relief, or enthusiasm.

"That's a good thing." Tobin reminded her.

She nodded and gripped his elbow. Which didn't escape Lucas's notice. The pastor watched them openly. He gave Tobin a casual chin-jut of acknowledgement. *Way* casual.

Didn't they understand that this was over? Maybe they were all numb. Shell-shocked.

"Tobin," Livvy hissed. "I need to talk to you."

"Better do it fast," he muttered. 'Cause pretty soon it was all gonna go sideways.

The door splintered. Those in front shouted, met by shouts from outside. Knox plowed away from the entrance, back through the crowd. "Okay," he yelled. "Civilians first. Exit slowly. Keep your hands visible. The officers outside will get you to safety."

The gang from WBC lined up. Hector drew Joan into the middle of the pack.

"Come on, Livvy." Lucas held out a hand.

Livvy didn't move. She squeezed Tobin's elbow. "I think Knox is Casper," she breathed into his ear, her face tipped away from the CO.

"Yeah, yeah," Tobin said, nodding vigorously. "Go with your group." Hands on her waist, he moved her around the desk and toward Lucas. Touching her was like picking up a live cable. Would he ever put his hands on her again?

"Tobin," Livvy hissed.

"Livvy, this is *it*. You have to go." Tobin handed her off to Lucas. The pastor met his eyes, and an understanding passed between them.

"But, *Tobin*!" Livvy reached for him.

With all his being, Tobin wanted to pull her back to him. To fold her into his arms and not let go. He had to force down a swallow before he could breathe. "Livvy, I know. I *get* it. Later, okay?"

Livvy nodded. Her face released its mask of tension. She let Lucas usher her forward, his hand on the small of her back.

This was it. Just like he told her. She was going to make it, going to get out safely, if somewhat harmed. A fierce sense of pride fought a wave of grief for control of Tobin's heart. Livvy was going back to her natural environment and he to his.

Here, in his world, his fellow inmates shuffled from one foot to another. Expressions ranged on their faces—from fear to resignation, fatigue to dread. But something was off. Was someone missing, hiding in the stacks? Tobin did a quick review. All the cons were there. But no COs. That's what was wrong. Nobody remained to sweep the library, to bird-dog the convicts out.

Tobin had been sure Knox would be riding him.

Ahead, just exiting the front door, the CO had wedged himself into the throng, between Hector and Livvy.

Panic surged. It was over—but Knox didn't know it yet. Didn't know that Tobin had photographed the evidence he'd collected and emailed it to Tiana Jo. Didn't know that everyone had compared notes while Knox questioned Livvy. That the others told Tobin the CO had been singled out and dragged from them earlier and returned with a black eye. That Livvy could be right—Knox could have taken Gant's call. He could be Casper.

Knox still believed he could clean up his mess.

"Move!" Tobin hollered, startling inmates and civilians out of his way. He shoved through the group. At the door, he shoved in front of Hector.

"Hey! Watch it!" Hector pushed back.

"Livvy!" Tobin hollered. His voice barely registered in the bedlam outside. An announcement looped over the loudspeaker: "... surrender immediately. Lie facedown where you are. Place your hands on your head ..."

The main artery that passed in front of the library to the rest of the prison was controlled chaos. The control marched in riot gear—tactical squads in wedge formation. The chaos either dove to the ground and lay prone in surrender or went head-to-head with the officers at the point of the wedge. The officers beat their way through, hauling resisting inmates down the line to COs positioned behind the formation who immobilized them with restraints. The perimeter wall was shoulder-to-shoulder SWAT snipers, poised with rifles.

Tobin took all of this in with a sweeping glance. "Livvy!"

She turned. Her face first registered confusion at seeing Tobin. Then fear when she realized Knox loomed over her. She recoiled at something in his expression.

"Knox!" Tobin yelled. "Leave her alone!"

Knox turned his attention to Tobin. "On your face, inmate," he growled.

Tobin started to comply, when Knox pulled the pistol from his pocket. Tobin froze: he, Knox, and Livvy a tense triad in the melee. Officers to the right and to the left enfolded the civilians into protective custody, hustling them toward the east gate.

Something flickered in Knox's eyes, and Tobin knew what he'd decided. Anyone could see, but no one watched. Tobin's focus pulled in, from Knox's face to the barrel of the handgun.

It really was over.

A blur in the corner of his eye, Livvy darted toward Knox. *No!* She pulled the second pistol from the back of Knox's waistband and leveled it at the CO.

"Hey, Casper!" Livvy yelled.

"Livvy, don't!" Tobin screamed. Knox looked astonished. And then, as he lowered his own weapon with exaggerated slowness, satisfaction pulled his mouth into something like a smile.

Tobin was motion before thought. He heard the crack as he tackled Livvy. It echoed off the stone walls at a different frequency than the yells of men. It still echoed as the sharpshooter's bullet pierced Tobin. He smashed into Livvy, crushing her to the ground—Livvy, still in her inmate blues, holding a gun on a correctional officer.

Livvy struggled to breathe, but her lungs wouldn't work right. Panic set in at the periphery, then clawed front and center to her consciousness. A second passed and her respiratory system kicked back into gear. Tobin had knocked the wind out of her. And slammed her head against the ground. And rammed the wound in her side.

"Tobin!" she gasped, shoving him. "Get off me!"

Tobin groaned.

"Tobin." Livvy shook his shoulder. There was blood all over her hand. Where had that come from? Her wound? She stared at her hand. The bedlam that rang in her ears began to penetrate her brain.

"Gunshot wound!" officers yelled.

What? Livvy was awash in horror. Had she shot Tobin? She didn't pull the trigger—did she? Maybe when he tackled her? She was trying to stop Knox from hurting him when he'd flattened her.

Officers barked orders, pulled Tobin off of her, laid him back on the pavement. Livvy scrambled to her feet, but an officer grabbed her from behind, swinging her off the ground.

"Wait! She's with us!" Lucas appeared out of nowhere, waving wildly. "Stop!" He snatched the beanie off Livvy's head. The officer set her on the ground. He peered at her through his faceguard and then bellowed. "Get her out of here!"

Another officer—indistinguishable from the other Stormtroopers—swooped alongside Livvy and wrapped his arm around her. "It's going to be okay," he yelled. "It's over—you're safe now."

"Wait!" Livvy strained against him. "Tobin! Tobin! He's been shot!" she screamed at the officer. "He needs help!"

"It's okay," the officer repeated. "He's getting medical attention."

But none of the people around Tobin were attending to him. Smitty, Agromonte, Cho, and Fallen were all stretched out on the cement on their bellies. A CO kneeled on Smitty's back, who was yelling, jerking his head in Tobin's direction. Agromonte's eyes were closed and he lay like a statue.

"Stop—I have to go back!" Livvy clawed to escape the officer's arms.

"Ma'am, I understand," he said. But clearly he didn't, because he continued to all but carry her away. "It's going to be all right."

"Tobin!" Livvy screamed. Bodies closed off her view—helter-skelter figures in black and blue. Then all was awash as her eyes filled. "Tobin!"

It was not going to be all right.

Lucas swayed on his feet in the triage area. He focused on Livvy, ten yards away, struggling with paramedics. Stretched on a gurney, she flailed to get up. "Stop!" she screamed. The wound in her side had opened up and soaked her shirt. Still she battered at the people trying to help her.

Lucas couldn't hear Joan, but he could see her lips pursed, *shh, shhh,* as she tried to stroke Livvy's hair.

A paramedic held a hypodermic needle vertical. He flicked it a couple times. Then, with help from EMTs who held Livvy down, he injected her in the arm.

"Knox is Casper!" she yelled, eyes wide. "You have to stop him! Help Tobin!"

After a few moments—just short of forever—Livvy crumpled back against the stretcher. Joan continued to stroke her hair and murmur in her ear. Two paramedics worked over Livvy in orchestration, hands moving with certainty and speed.

"That's a nasty cut," a paramedic approached Lucas and nodded at his eye. "And what do we have here?" She worked at the knotted tourniquet Joan had fastened around Lucas's throat.

Lucas struggled to bring himself present. He pulled his mind back from someplace distant and hazy. "A couple broken ribs."

But the paramedic still examined his neck, where the tie had adhered to dried blood. "Oh my." She left the makeshift bandage in place. "Sit down, please." Lucas sank into a plastic chair. "Gurney!" the paramedic called over her shoulder.

Even with eyes wide open, Lucas could see the look on Livvy's face when she'd first seen him alive. How he'd tried to make light by quoting Monty Python.

"It's merely a flesh wound," he mumbled.

"Uh huh." The medic knitted her brows. "Here we go. Upsie daisy. Now lie back." Lucas obeyed and then started to tremble. Someone covered him with a blanket.

In his new position, he couldn't see anyone he recognized. It was a war zone under the glaring emergency lights in the lot outside the east gate. This, the medical area, was a canopied zone of medical personnel and equipment. Other command posts were stationed in the staging area, and personnel in various uniforms rushed everywhere. Not a person in sight stood still or moved slowly. It made Lucas tired. He couldn't stop shaking.

The paramedic cut open Lucas's tee shirt, skimmed her gloved hands over the shirts binding his ribs.

"All right, let's move him out," she said to someone. An EMT appeared, and the two began rolling Lucas's gurney. "You're going to be fine," the medic said. Her forehead creased when she offered Lucas a faint smile. She was quite pretty.

The gurney ride was short. They wheeled him to the rear of a waiting ambulance. *Snap, snap, whoosh, slam*—Lucas was inside and the ambulance rolled out.

With the doors closed, the roar of the chaos was mercifully muted. Was it really over? The whole WBC gang had gotten out of San Quentin relatively unscathed.

Relatively.

"My friend," he said to the paramedic next to him, "she's hurt too. Will we go to the same hospital?"

"Yup. Marin General." The medic slipped a blood pressure cuff onto Lucas's arm.

Good. Lucas closed his eyes. *Give Livvy some peace. And comfort.*

He couldn't believe she'd pulled a gun on Knox. Little Livvy, holding a gun. It had all happened so fast. When the rifle shot rang out, Lucas couldn't tell who was shooting at whom. When Livvy went down ... Lucas grimaced. If Tobin hadn't intervened, that bullet would have struck Livvy square in the chest. She could be dead right now.

"An inmate was shot," he said. "Do you happen to know how he is?"

The young man shook his head. "Nope." He clicked a pen and wrote on a clipboard.

"Where will they take him?"

He shrugged. "Depends. If he's alive, they might treat him onsite in the medical wing. Or they could take him to a local hospital, treat him there under guard."

Lucas nodded.

"Guess he should have thought of that before rioting," the paramedic said. He hung a clear IV bag at the head of the gurney and uncoiled a tube.

Lucas started. "No—he's a good guy."

"Right. They all are."

Huh. Lucas was at a loss. Tobin *was* a good guy. He helped protect Livvy and others. May have sacrificed his life for her. And here this guy just saw him as another criminal. The injustice of that was bitter in Lucas's mouth.

And then it hit him.

That's what Jesus *did* do.

Chapter Thirty-Six

Friday a.m.

Grace didn't say a word, but Livvy could read her like a book. Better, in fact, than the book that lay open, inverted, on Livvy's chest as she lay on the couch.

"I'm really tired," she said to her sister. "And sore."

"Okay." Grace wiped down the island between Livvy's kitchenette and postage-stamp living room. "All I said was that it's a beautiful day."

Right. And all she didn't say was that the doctor told Livvy to increase her activity a little each day. At Marin General they'd given her a few more stitches and a lot of antibiotics. It turned out that Miles had done a decent job sewing her up. Her blood loss hadn't required a transfusion, but the doctor warned Livvy that she was "a quart low" and would be extra fatigued for a while.

She burrowed further under her fleece blanket. "It looks beautiful from here."

No reply from Grace. She faced the other direction now, but Livvy knew her lips were pursed. Mother hen.

Their own mother, off to the grocery store for Moose Tracks ice cream, babied Livvy like there was no tomorrow. Livvy glanced at the clock. She should be back any time.

"Lucas called while you were in the shower," Grace said.

"So you said."

"Aren't you going to call him back?"

"I'm reading." Livvy picked up her book.

Grace snorted. She strode to the couch and snatched the novel out of Livvy's hands. "What's the name of the main character?" She leafed through the fifteen or so pages Livvy had read.

"Grace, leave me alone."

"You don't know, do you? Liv, you need to talk about stuff. You can't keep everything bottled up inside."

Livvy rolled her head toward the back of the couch.

"I get that you don't want to talk to the reporters. But isn't Lucas a good choice? He was there! He's a pastor *and* your friend."

Livvy picked at a knot in her blanket. "I don't have anything to say." Fat tears rolled down her cheeks. She had no idea why.

Grace sat at her feet. "Just start somewhere. You'll get around to what needs to come out."

Start somewhere. Images, memories flashed. The journey to San Quentin. Lucas grinning. Tobin staring at her in the chapel. Then fear—utter, imageless terror—gripped her. She gathered the blanket and pressed it to her face, breathing rapidly. The threat was gone, but the fear was with her every moment, waking or sleeping. How do you face your fear when it's free-floating, amorphous?

Grace rubbed her foot. Patient.

"I sang. *Rusalka.*"

Grace's hand stilled. "You did?" She processed. "Wow."

Livvy peeked out. "I know, right? Why—in the middle of all of that—was I able to sing it through without a panic attack?"

Grace shook her head side to side, slow. "What do you think?"

"I don't understand anything. I don't know why I don't want to call Lucas back." Her chin trembled. "I feel like I owe him something."

"What about Tobin?"

"I owe him everything."

"Then maybe he's the one you need to talk to."

Over the three days since the riot ended, Livvy had told Grace—in chunks—everything that had happened. Except one thing. She didn't tell what Gant said about Tobin's crimes. The thought would barely nudge Livvy's consciousness and she'd push it away. Bury it under Moose Tracks, the *Princess Bride,* and sleep.

The panic welled greater. Livvy's hands shook. "I don't know if they'll let me."

"You can try." Grace brought her the phone. "You must have the number practically memorized by now." Livvy'd been calling Marin General for updates on Tobin's progress. They'd been hopeful they could bring him out of his induced coma today.

She clasped the phone. She didn't want to talk to Tobin over the device—hearing his voice while seeing her wall. But she did want to know how he was. She dialed.

"He's off the pentothal," the nurse in the ICU told her. "Once the sedative is out of his system, we'll take him off the vent and see how he's doing."

Livvy scrunched her face. *Vent?*

"And when he's off the ventilator and breathing on his own, he should wake up. He'll be groggy at first, but there's no reason he can't talk on the phone or have visitors. Well," the nurse hesitated, "no medical reason."

Right.

Just the he's-a-criminal-with-no-freedoms reason.

Lucas heard the bicycle coming, but apparently Livvy didn't. When it whizzed past on her left, she jumped and gripped Lucas's arm with rigid fingers. He guided her across, to the far right of the Los Gatos Creek Trail, and took the passing lane position.

Livvy gave an anemic grin. "Thanks."

"No problem," he said. Half holding his breath, he slipped his hand around hers. The chill of her skin made him want to take her into his arms. Well, more than he already wanted to.

He didn't know how to act with her. She used to be open, flirty, and direct. At least with a barista counter between them. Now storm clouds gathered behind her eyes, and he had no idea how to find his footing. The time he'd spent with Joan, Rudy, and the guys in the week since the riot had been pretty good. Healing even. But this little walk was ... complicated.

Maybe that was partly from learning so much about her lately. He had a sense that her mother and sister buffered her from the stories in the paper and on network news. She made for pretty good headlines—*Beautiful Soprano Stabbed in Prison Riot. Beautiful Soprano's Tragic Past.*

"So"—he cleared his throat—"like I was saying, my dreams have been pretty weird."

Livvy nodded. "Mine too."

Lucas waited, but that was all she offered. "How long are your mom and Grace staying with you?"

"My mom leaves tomorrow for my dad's cataract surgery." She shrugged. "It's cool. Pacific Grove is only an hour and a half away. I may head down next week."

"And Grace?"

"She's gone to Fremont the last two nights to sleep at home. She goes back to work Thursday, so I guess I officially regain independent-adult status then."

Lucas smiled. "You okay with that?"

"Sure. I'm not made of porcelain."

Urp. Had he irritated her? Did he owe her an apology?

But her brow smoothed. "And you? When did the doctor say

you'll be ready for skiing?"

"Ah—Tahoe needs some snow before I worry about that. I should be okay by the time the slopes open."

Joan had told him that Livvy's blood tests came back clean. But also that with HIV and hepatitis, you had to retest after weeks and even months. Uncertainty could be hanging over Livvy's head for as long as half a year. Did that weigh on her?

Autumn leaves crunched beneath their feet.

Lucas had often wondered: when you experienced an awkward silence, did the other person necessarily feel it too? Occasionally it was clearly all-around uncomfortable. But maybe sometimes the other person was completely copasetic while Lucas was sweating a lapse in conversation. What was Livvy thinking? Had she talked with Tobin? Seen him, maybe? Did she plan to? *Heroic Inmate Saves Beautiful Soprano.* Even as he held Livvy's hand, Lucas wondered where her heart was.

"So—" they began at once.

"You go," Livvy said.

"No, you." *Please give me some idea what's going on in there.*

"I guess they're going to prosecute Knox for a bunch of stuff," she said.

"Yeah, I saw that. Looks like more evidence and witnesses survived the riot than he thought would."

Livvy nodded. "I wonder if Miles will get a promotion for linking all the cases back to Gant and Knox."

All too soon they had returned to the playground, picnic area, and parking lot in downtown Campbell. Lucas didn't want to let go of Livvy's hand. Who knew when he'd get her to ditch the phalanx of paparazzi to spend time with him again? A cloud covered the sun, and the morning light took on a somber hue.

Some twenty feet ahead, between them and the parking lot, a burly guy stood watching them. He sported a backwards baseball cap and a hefty video camera slung over his shoulder. A petite

Asian woman on the park bench next to him followed his gaze. She rose.

Great.

Livvy stiffened. Lucas rubbed the back of her hand with his thumb.

"Hello, Livvy. We haven't formally met. I'm Tiana Jo." The reporter's smile was disarmingly kind. Livvy shook her outstretched hand.

"Hello, Lucas." Tiana Jo turned her smile on him now. "I hope you are recovering well from your injuries."

Lucas nodded. The woman had an engaging smile and kind eyes. She'd blown open the whole Gant / Knox mess. Still, he had an underlying feeling that Team Livvy shouldn't be too chummy with the press.

"I'm sorry to intrude." The reporter addressed them both but focused more on Livvy. "I was hoping to ask you some questions."

Livvy had grasped Lucas's hand again and stood close enough to brush shoulders. "I don't know."

"I understand that your experience was very difficult and you may be reluctant to talk about it. It doesn't have to be on camera."

"I'm not ..." Livvy looked to Lucas, then back to Tiana. "I do want to thank you for your help during the riot. And your investigative reporting since. It was—is—really nice knowing that there's an unbiased person looking into the whole mess. Trying to make things right." Livvy's last statement ended like a question.

"Well, that's partly what I'd like to talk about." Tiana Jo glanced at Lucas's and Livvy's clasped hands. "Pardon me for asking, but are you two romantically involved?"

Livvy's eyes widened briefly. She slipped her hand from Lucas's and slid it into the pocket of her jeans.

"We're not sure what we are," Lucas said. He certainly wasn't.

"I understand," Tiana said with her calming smile. "In any case, Livvy, I was wondering if you were aware that the governor is considering clemency for Tobin?"

"What? No." Livvy's brows came together. "What does that mean?"

"Given Tobin's actions during the riot—how he put himself in harm's way to aid others—the Governor is considering waiving the rest of his prison sentence."

"She can do that?" Livvy asked. She was a reed in a breeze. Lucas guided her to the bench.

Tiana sat on Livvy's other side. "Yes, she can. You've answered my first question—clearly you didn't know. Do you think he should be granted clemency?"

Livvy nodded, face impassive. A gust of wind lifted curls off her forehead.

"If called upon, would you testify at a clemency hearing?"

Livvy stood abruptly. "I don't ... I need to go now. Excuse me." She strode off. Away from the parking lot.

"Uh ..." Lucas waved at Tiana Jo and dashed after Livvy.

"C'mon. This way." Arm around her shoulders, he steered toward her car.

"Livvy." Tiana was on their heels. "You should read this." She held out a manila envelope.

"I think she's done for now," Lucas said.

"I know." Tiana leaned across him and put her hand on Livvy's arm. Her face was earnest. "Livvy—please take this and read it. I think it may hold some answers for you."

Lucas frowned. How could some document possibly offer Livvy answers? He still didn't have a clue what the questions were.

Chapter Thirty-Seven

There wasn't enough Moose Tracks ice cream in the world. Livvy licked her spoon clean and let it clatter into the empty bowl. Then she lay her head down, the counter cool under her cheek.

What was wrong with her? How could a thirty-six-hour event send her reeling so hard? She wanted to go back to how she was before the riot. She'd been starting to get it together. Things with Lucas had been looking up.

Yeah. And you sprinted from your Opera San Jose audition like Mephistopheles himself was on your heels.

The front door shook. Livvy hauled herself off the barstool and cranked back the deadbolts. Her mother and Grace blew in with their arms full of groceries. A knot of reporters remained at bay behind them, loosely corralled by the apartment complex's security guard. "Livvy!" "Livvy!" they called and snapped photos. Livvy slammed the door and leaned against it. Funny how quickly she'd gone from hiding in her apartment to being trapped in it.

Mom appraised her over a brown paper bag. "How you doing, baby?"

Livvy shrugged. "Fine, I guess." She peeked in a sack. "Hello? There's only one of me. How do you expect me to eat all this?"

"Most is nonperishable. And you can freeze for a rainy day."

Mom set to emptying bags and placed a ball of Mizithra on the counter.

"*Mmmm.* Browned butter spaghetti and Mizithra?" Livvy picked up the cheese and cradled it next to her cheek.

"What's this?" Grace slid Tiana Jo's envelope across the counter.

Livvy spun it a couple of times. "Answers."

"To what?" Mom paused, jar of olives in one hand and box of granola in the other.

"Search me."

Maybe the answer to why she'd been able to sing "Silver Moon" through without hyperventilating. Perhaps an explanation as to how she could go for a walk with her dream guy and think only of a convicted felon.

A felon who might get his remaining sentence commuted.

She peeled back the flap. Withdrew a stack of papers. The top section was a poor quality photocopy of some official document. She skimmed: *Transcript of Proceedings. The People of the State of California v. Tobin James.*

Her hands began to shake. Tobin's trial transcript.

The People of the State of California—she was a person of the state of California. They'd prosecuted Tobin in her name. Livvy v. Tobin. She backed to the wall and slid to the floor.

"Liv?" Grace said from very far away.

Appearances ... witness lists ... exhibit index ...

In the name and by authority of the State of California, the District Court of Santa Clara County presents in the first count that Tobin James, hereinafter called the defendant, did unlawfully cause the death of David Greer, hereinafter called the decedent, in violation of Penal Code section 192(a).

The Moose Tracks that had gone down so easily churned in Livvy's stomach.

It is further presented in Count Two that the defendant did rape

Alicia Ivers, hereafter called the complainant, while she was intoxicated, in violation of statute 261(a)3.

Livvy closed her eyes and breathed deeply to quell a wave of nausea. She had a name: Alicia Ivers.

Grace sat beside Livvy on the floor. She let out a soft gasp. "Oh honey. You don't need to read this." She grasped the papers. "Don't read this."

A flash of yellow caught Livvy's eye. "Wait." She tugged the stack back. At the bottom of the page was a small yellow sticky note: *Livvy, Keep reading. ~Tiana Jo.*

Why would the woman want Livvy to read Tobin's trial transcript? What could she possibly gain from it? She grimaced. *Answers.* That's what Tiana Jo had promised. But did Livvy really want those answers?

She leafed through the stack. In addition to the trail transcript there were arrest reports. A bunch. Great.

"Who's David Greer?" Grace asked, pointing at one of the pages. Livvy frowned. They were Greer's arrest reports? Tobin's victim? *Assault. Burglary. Armed robbery. Narcotics possession. Possession with intent to sell. Domestic battery.* What a prince.

Wait a second—the victim's name on the domestic battery report had originally been redacted, but then penned in: initialed T.J. The victim was Alicia Ivers. Alicia Ivers was romantically linked with David Greer? And he beat her up?

Livvy organized the documents around her in stacks on the floor. Copies of Tiana Jo's handwritten notes. Trial transcripts. Articles. Arrest reports. A page from a high-school yearbook—say what? Two students' pictures on the page were circled: Alicia Ivers and Tobin. They'd gone to high school together. Weirder and weirder.

Livvy was starting to get a headache. A paroxysm of wind slammed the window above her and she twitched. Rain lashed against the glass like it wanted in. Maybe it would chase away the knot of reporters.

Grace picked up the pile of Tiana Jo's notes and leafed through. Livvy eyed the trial record. Perhaps the reporter knew what she was talking about.

Livvy'd never seen a court transcript before, but it read pretty much like a script. She just had to figure out the players. *Mr. Scharf for the defendant.* That would be Tobin's attorney. Livvy flipped back to *Appearances.* Scharf was a public defender. No deep pockets for a private attorney. Not a surprise there.

Just a minute. Scharf? Livvy looked through her stacks. There it was—an advertisement for a commercial landscaping contractor. The man's name was circled: Ben Scharf. And there was a date handwritten on the ad—about six months after Tobin's trial. So the public defender had left law to become a landscaper? Odd. Was Tiana Jo implying that Tobin's representation had been incompetent? Or just that he liked shrubbery?

Livvy skimmed the first page of the court transcript, then the second. *Blah, blah, blah.* What was she even looking for? Some of the jury instructions were highlighted. What was Tiana Jo trying to tell her?

The phone rang. She tensed, but Mom, ever the screener, answered before Livvy moved.

"May I say who's calling?" Mom looked dubious. "And will she know what this is regarding, Mr. Landucci?"

Livvy gasped and shot to her feet. She grabbed for the phone.

"All right, all right!" Mom released it to her.

"Hello, Maestro," Livvy said. Her mother and Grace froze. They faced Livvy with wide eyes, inclined slightly to hang on every word.

"Miss Fischer?" The conductor's rich voice rumbled through the phone. "I hope you'll forgive me for intruding on your privacy during what must be a difficult time for you."

Livvy nodded. Then shook herself. "Oh, of course. It's no

problem." She flashed back to the look on the conductor's face when she'd choked so spectacularly during her audition. Remembering her sprint through the emergency exit brought heat to her cheeks. Having Grace and Mom gape at her didn't help.

"Let me be direct, Miss Fischer. We've filled the soprano opening in Opera San Jose's Resident Artist Program. But we anticipate another one in six to eight months. We'd like you to consider auditioning for it."

Say what now?

"Well, I … Are you sure?" *Way to sell yourself, Liv.*

"That is if you are still interested and think you're ready."

"I … I don't know what to say." Livvy turned her back on Mom and Grace. "After the last audition …"

"Yes. Well. We were quite impressed with your *Sempre libera.* And as for the *Rusalka,* we … We're aware of the circumstances surrounding your previous performance of that, as well as your experience at San Quentin. In short, Miss Fischer, we believe you are gifted and anticipate that if you can master your stage fright, the world of opera will be better with you in it."

"Thank you, sir." Livvy sat on the arm of the couch, hardly daring to breath. *Don't break the spell.* "I appreciate that."

"I won't keep you. I just wanted to encourage you to watch for the coming auditions."

"Thank you, sir," she repeated stupidly. "I will."

Maybe her life would get back to normal after all. Maybe even more normal than it was before the riot. She'd sung the aria through. She had another shot at her dream. And she clearly had Lucas's attention.

She assessed the papers strewn across the floor. Maybe she didn't need to dig into all of this. What was Tobin to her, really? Her hero in a brief, bewitched, upside-down world. A kiss. Okay, a *great* kiss.

"Olivia?" Mom approached and rubbed her shoulders. "You're

trembling."

Livvy nodded. "He encouraged me to audition for their next opening."

Grace clapped her hands together. Mom caught Livvy in a hug. "That's wonderful!"

Livvy nodded. She kept still, rooted. Why would they give her another chance? Because they felt sorry for her? They'd seen the coverage of her experience at San Quentin and the accounts of the conservatory fire and figured she deserved a break? Earned and unearned. Part talent, part grace.

Second chance, unexpected opportunity—that sounded a lot like Tobin's clemency. Of all people, didn't he deserve it? Hadn't he been reformed?

Livvy swallowed her anxiety and sought the feelings that ran deep underneath. She was glad for Tobin. Glad the system would give him a chance at a new life.

Certain that Jesus had given him a new life.

But what about her? Could she forgive what he'd done? Was that even the right word—do you forgive someone for something they didn't do to you?

Could she testify on his behalf at a hearing?

Could she let him close to her heart?

Could she kiss him again?

Livvy was out the door and halfway to her car before she realized it. What had she even mumbled to mom and Grace?

I have to go. *I have to.* A husky rumble of thunder rolled overhead like wordless confirmation. She had so much to say to Tobin.

The taillights of the last news van pulled out of the parking lot. Certainly God didn't send the storm just to chase them away for her ... *but thanks, Lord, all the same.*

A jeep, revealed by the van's departure, rolled into the lot. Through the rain, behind the wipers, the driver started when he saw Livvy. Then he waved.

Lucas.

What was Livvy doing standing outside in the rain? Lucas parked, overcome with disquiet. Already a bundle of nerves, the unexpected sight of her unsettled him even more.

Oh well, I guess there's no turning back now. He strode toward her. *Okay, Jesus: just like we rehearsed.*

Blue eyes, rounded in question, met him and completely erased the speech he'd planned. Livvy's gaze, open and clear, invited nothing but directness.

"Here's the thing," he said. "I have no idea what's going on in your head. Things have gotten really complicated." Not to mention her complicated past, which he'd only just learned about. "This probably isn't the best timing, but I can't live with the second-guessing anymore."

A faint smile lifted the corners of her mouth. Her pretty little mouth.

"I think it's obvious we've each felt ... something ..." Was it obvious? What if, like a one-sided awkward moment, he alone felt romantic tension? All the words of thought and speech collided and jammed up his brain. Livvy waited, chin raised, rain running rivulets down her cheeks.

Too much thought.

He stepped to her, cupping her face in his hands. He leaned in, she rose to her toes. His lips barely brushed hers, when she made a soft choking sound and pulled back.

"I'm so sorry, Lucas. I'm so sorry," she said.

Then she was gone, and he still stood, cupped hands filling with rain.

Chapter Thirty-Eight

In the end, it was pretty straightforward.

When she'd kissed Tobin, Livvy's thoughts had been filled with Tobin. When Lucas bent to kiss her, her thoughts were filled with—Tobin.

Now her heart raced. She made no effort to check it.

"Fourth floor, please," she called from the back of the crowded elevator.

Her mind remained a blank—a state she'd vigorously maintained on the hour drive up to Marin General. Singing, praying—anything but analyzing.

Her heels clipped down the white tiled hallway. What would she say? What would he say? Did he resent her for putting him in the sniper's crossfire?

Room 426. A uniformed officer sat on a folding chair outside the door. Oh great. She hadn't thought of that.

"Hi, um, I'd like to visit Tobin? I'm—"

"I know who you are." The officer stood. "But I'm going to need to check your ID anyway."

Livvy fumbled for her wallet. What did that mean, he knew who she was? In a good way, or a bad way?

So much for not analyzing.

"I'm glad to see you on your feet," the officer said, handing back her license.

"Thank you."

"He's got a visitor, but you can go on in."

Livvy nodded and tucked damp hair behind her ear. A visitor? Maybe she should wait. She didn't want to intrude on family.

Did he *have* any family?

There was so much she didn't know about Tobin. This was ludicrous. What was she doing here? She dug fingernails into cold palms.

"Not that anyone asked, but I think he'll be happy to see you," the officer said behind her. "Not that anyone asked."

Livvy smiled softly, took a deep breath, and pushed.

The room was a double. The first bed stood empty, the second hidden behind a curtain drawn in an oval. A low male voice came from the other side.

The pattern of the words rang familiar before Livvy recognized them. It was scripture: "And he took bread, gave thanks and broke it, and gave it to them, saying, 'This is my body given for you; do this in remembrance of me.'" It was communion—she was interrupting communion. Livvy stood frozen. She should leave, return later.

The door closed behind her with a soft *whump*.

The curtain drew back, revealing Dale Peake, open Bible in hand. "Livvy!"

Heat rose to her cheeks. "Hello, Chaplain. I'm so sorry. I didn't mean to interrupt."

"Interrupt? Your timing is perfect." Dale looked to the head of the bed, out of Livvy's line of vision. "Join us."

Her shoes were extraordinarily loud as she crossed to the bedside. Dale pulled the curtain open to include her. "Hi there." He gave her a hug. And just like when she'd first shaken his hand, Livvy felt grounded in his embrace. "It's great to see you," he said.

"You too." She let go with some regret.

And then there was Tobin. Raised to a sitting position, he was completely alert, and besides an IV, free of frankentubes.

"Hi," she said.

"Hi yourself," he responded. In a white hospital gown and white sheets, his skin held the warmth of a healthy tan. His face was bright and clean shaven.

He was beautiful.

He offered her a brief smile, then cleared his throat and worked his jaw. "I can't believe you're here."

"Really?" Why would her visit surprise him? "I was going to apologize for taking so long."

"I just figured—you needed to heal too. And you've got your life ..." His voice hitched a little on the last word.

"Which I owe to you."

"Nah." He shook his head.

"I'm not going to argue about it," she said. "I'm right and you're wrong."

He laughed. *Ah bliss.* His face lit up.

"How you been?" he asked.

"Pretty good. Healing."

"That's good. Looks like you've had to outrun the paparazzi." He nodded at the TV suspended from the ceiling. "There's one benefit of incarceration. No news hounds in the joint."

"Yeah. It hasn't been too bad. My mom's mother-bear claws are finely honed. And don't get too comfy—you may have to deal with the inconveniences of life on the outside pretty soon yourself."

Tobin looked at her blankly.

"Clemency?" Livvy raised her eyebrows and used her best *no duh* voice.

"Clemency?" Tobin looked from Livvy to Chaplain Peake. "What?"

Dale shrugged. "Guess that cat's out of the bag."

314

Livvy put a hand over her mouth. "Oh! Was I not supposed to say anything?"

"No, it's okay." Dale waved her off. "The news was going to break soon anyway. Tobin, the Governor is considering it. There's going to be a hearing." Dale glanced at Livvy before continuing with Tobin. "You should know, I've been talking to Alicia Ivers. She wants to testify on your behalf."

Tobin looked dumbfounded. "Alicia? How is she?"

"She's good. She's clean, getting an education. She carries a lot of guilt for the way things went." Again Dale looked to Livvy.

"*She* carries guilt?" Tobin asked.

Dale bobbed his head. "She says her early versions of what happened, including her testimony, were based in anger. I think it would be good for you both to speak to one another."

Livvy was simultaneously invisible and a big pink elephant in the middle of the room.

Dale picked up his Bible. "Livvy, we were just sharing communion. Would you like to join us?"

She nodded. "If Tobin doesn't mind?"

Tobin shook his head and seemed to wrest his gaze from her to the chaplain.

Leaning against the bed, Livvy closed her eyes. The familiar words. The familiar act of worship. Renewed gratitude beyond words. The room was so quiet, so intimate, as the three took the bread and wine together.

Jesus's sacrifice had never been so palpable. His bloody, painful death—Livvy forced herself to mentally look at it. Thought about the pain she'd seen and felt at San Quentin. Jesus had walked into torture—willingly. Volunteered to take it on as the only way to make things right again between God and man. Did it for Tobin, who had taken a life, just as much as he did it for Livvy, who'd let a man die, among a multitude of hateful and repellent things. Because he passionately loved them both.

If he offered his own life as an expression of love, as a payment for those things, how could she not receive it? And if she received it for herself, how could she not accept that it extended to Tobin as well?

Dale read aloud Isaiah 1:18: "'Come now, let us settle the matter,' says the Lord. 'Though your sins are like scarlet, they shall be as white as snow; though they are red as crimson, they shall be like wool.'"

Tobin stood clean and forgiven before God. Who was Livvy to persist in seeing him stained by his crimes? What arrogance!

A silence lingered for a few moments after Dale prayed. Tobin was the first to break it. "Atonement through Jesus's blood takes on new meaning when you've spilled someone's blood," he said, eyes on Livvy.

Livvy nodded gravely.

"So you know?" His forehead creased deeply. "What I've done?"

"Pretty much."

His sharp intake of breath startled Livvy. He jutted out his chin and nodded, staring at a far-off point.

Dale touched Livvy's shoulder. "I'm going to leave you two alone. Tobin, I'll be back tomorrow. Livvy, if you need to talk, please feel free to call me any time."

The door *whumped* behind Dale. Tobin wouldn't return Livvy's gaze. She waited. Was he unwilling to speak, or unable?

She lowered the bedrail and sat on the edge of the mattress. At that, Tobin finally looked at her, brows pinched in surprise. She picked up his hand and held it in both of hers. And his face crumpled. He grasped a pillow and held it to his face while he sobbed.

Impotent, Livvy wrapped her arms around herself. To have him so close and so unreachable. If only she had the power to reach in and touch that place—that deeply rooted seat of pain. To relieve his suffering.

She'd been unable to do that with Wade. Unable to reciprocate his affection, then unable to stand his presence every time she turned around, picked up the phone, or opened mail or email. It still kept her awake some nights—could she have reached him? Explained things somehow in the *right* way, in a manner that he'd hear?

But it had been impossible. And his pain was such that he'd doused himself with gasoline and lit himself on fire. On stage during Livvy's senior recital at the San Francisco Conservatory of Music. Right in the middle of "Silver Moon" from *Rusalka*.

Livvy rubbed Tobin's foot through the bed sheet. He lifted his head, face anguished. "How could—? Why did you come here? Why would you even speak to me again?"

"Tobin—weren't we just taking the same communion in remembrance of what Jesus did?"

Tobin ran his hand through his hair. "Well, he's ... God. But you ..."

"Am not God, so much," Livvy finished dryly.

"I mean, there's Christian forgiveness, and then there's ... I mean, as a woman ..." Tobin paled. "Oh. Duh." He rolled his eyes. "Idiot."

Clearing his throat, he straightened his shoulders. "Of course. You came to see how I am. To see if you'd gotten me killed off." His grin was lopsided.

Really? What a dope.

"Not because of any other reason, or expectation—"

Livvy leaned and kissed him on his dopey mouth. After a second, Tobin slipped a hand behind her head, fingers entwined in hair. And kissed back.

Oh my, yes. This, ladies and gentlemen, is a kiss.

Livvy took a breath. "One of these times you're going to have to be the one to initiate that."

Tobin twisted a lock of her hair. "If you say so."

"I say so."

"I can't quite believe that," he said, searching her eyes. "Why are you here?"

"I couldn't stay away. This feels like a 'we' now." An all new, unexpected *us* and *them*. "I don't want to go back to life without you."

"What about your cute pastor?"

"He wasn't ever *mine*." Livvy countered.

"Yes. He clearly was. Is. For your taking."

"Are you trying to change my mind?"

Tobin shook his head. He still held her hair, as if to tether her to him. "Just making sure you know your mind."

"I seem to know it best when I'm with you."

"What about all the rest? You really see me mingling with your opera friends? Am I the guy you want to take home to the parents?"

"Why do you do that?" Livvy pushed against his shoulder. "Why do you define yourself by what you've done?"

"Please, Livvy, don't play dumb. The world does and will always see me as a felon. Clemency isn't a pardon—I'll still be an ex-con. More importantly, I still did what I did."

"And I've done what I've done! The world loves you! You're the darling of the media—a true-blue hero. And Alicia Ivers wants to testify on your behalf. Doesn't that tell you anything?"

Tobin drew back. As if he couldn't hold Alicia Ivers in his head and Livvy's hand at the same time.

"What about you, Tobin? Do you know your mind?"

He was somber. "It's a little rattled right now."

Was this for real? Was he going to turn her away? Had she simply been a warm-blooded female for him—and he now on the cusp of a world full of warm-blooded females? Maybe he wanted someone who'd never seen him in his prison blues. Who could pretend he'd never been at the Q.

"What did you do, Tobin?"

"I thought you—"

"I need you to tell me. You can look me in the eyes now."

Tobin pulled his lower lip in between his teeth. He nodded. "Fair enough." He shifted and took a deep breath. "Alicia was my first love. I didn't deal well with our breakup. I'd dropped out of school, no future in sight, and no Alicia."

Livvy nodded.

"I started partying a lot—drinking, getting high. Just pot." He grimaced and repeated with air quotes: "Just."

"Alicia's new boyfriend was a dirt bag." He colored slightly. "Well, he had made some bad choices."

"I've seen the arrest reports," Livvy said.

Tobin started. "What? How's that?"

"Tiana Jo gave me a bunch of stuff."

"Ah." He nodded. "She's been telling me my lawyer was incompetent.

"Anyway," he continued. "Greer was a small-time dealer. He got Alicia hooked on meth. One day she calls me over, says she wants to leave him but is scared. Being the brilliant individuals we were"—he scowled—"we rolled some of Greer's pot and smoked it."

He finished and looked at Livvy.

"And?" she asked.

"And that's it. That's the last thing I remember of that night. According to the evidence, Alicia and I had ... were intimate. But she claimed it wasn't consensual. That she'd been too high to consent."

"She accused you of rape?"

Tobin closed his eyes and let out a long breath. Then he held Livvy's gaze. "She was pretty upset with me, since I'd also killed her boyfriend."

Livvy raised her eyebrows. Nodded. "Yeah. Okay. Why'd you ... How? What happened?"

Tobin shrugged wearily. "No one who was there at the time can say. Greer is dead, and his stash of pot had been laced with heroin. Neither Alicia or I remembered what happened."

Livvy frowned. "If Alicia was too high to consent, how come you weren't too high to be responsible for your actions?"

"*Phhh.*" Tobin made a face. "Intoxication isn't a defense. I'm still responsible. But that is what Tiana Jo is all fired up about—says my public defender should have gotten me off or at most involuntary manslaughter."

Livvy studied Tobin's hands, like she had in the library at San Quentin. They'd taken a man's life. How, exactly? No—she didn't want to know right now. This was enough for today.

Tobin searched her face. "You can still leave." He nodded toward the door. "It's not too late. Not for you, anyway."

Livvy's thoughts whirled. Involuntarily she pictured Alicia Ivers, the fresh-faced high school student in the yearbook photo; a young Tobin; a heated fight. And she saw Tobin, the grief and compassion across his face when she'd pounded on him in the canteen, demanding to know what he had done—what it was that made him like the other men in San Quentin.

"What do *you* want?" she whispered.

"Are you kidding? I want door number three. I want the clemency and the diva. But I know I don't deserve it."

Livvy winced. "Do any of us deserve anything?"

Did knowing any of this undo what Jesus had done? Certainly not. Did it change that shifting landscape of a future that she could almost glimpse—the one with Tobin in it? Her extremities were room temperature, palms ungouged. If anything, talking about the big bad secret had actually defused its power.

She kissed Tobin.

"Hey wait a minute! You're not giving me much of a chance to initiate anything."

"Guess you better be a little quicker."

A grin spread across Tobin's face. "Is this for real?"

Livvy nodded.

"So, how will it work? Clemency or no, how are we supposed to do this?"

Livvy rubbed her hand across the top of his head, short blond hairs springing back into place.

"We improvise."

Chapter Thirty-Nine

The steam from the espresso machine was no match for the steam emanating from Kimi's ears. "This is a place of business," she snapped at the umpteenth reporter of the day. "Order something or get out."

Livvy grimaced. Maybe she should take off more time until the media frenzy died down. Working behind the scenes at Cuppa Joe instead of the counter helped, but didn't prevent contact by the most aggressive of the paparazzi.

"Let me get that for you." Charlie lifted the twenty-five-pound bag of whole beans from her shoulder, sliced through the burlap, and poured the beans into the roaster.

"Thanks." Livvy wiped her hands on her apron front. And looked up just in time to meet the gaze of a young man dawdling at the cream and sugar station.

He brightened. "Livvy, how do you feel about Tobin's rape victim recanting her version of events?"

Livvy winced. Rape. Such an ugly word.

"Step off," Charlie said. "Go bug someone who chose to be a celebrity."

Livvy grabbed a broom, grateful for an opportunity to lower her eyes. Alicia Ivers recanted? What did that mean? Was that a formal, legal process, or did she make some comment to someone? With Tobin's clemency hearing three days away, this could be a major turn of events.

"How are the nightmares?" Charlie asked, almost under his breath.

Livvy shrugged. "Technicolor." She almost wished people would stop asking. On the one hand, it was a great comfort that they cared. On the other, she'd started to feel almost obligated to put a positive spin on her answer. Like enough time had passed that she should be showing some improvement.

"Sure you don't need me to come with on Friday? I'll hold your hand, your purse, whatever ..."

"Nah, thanks. Grace is coming, and some of the WBC people."

Charlie's face darkened. "Like Lucas."

As far as Charlie was concerned, Lucas became persona non grata at Joe's when the media started pairing him up with Livvy.

"Yes, Lucas is going." *Oi.* What a pouty baby.

Truth be told, Livvy's gut tightened, anticipating the hearing. Seeing everyone. Reliving the events. Having Lucas and Tobin in the same room.

Charlie went quiet.

Whatever, pouty baby. *You know what?* Livvy couldn't be responsible for his feelings. She had a hard enough time sorting out her own.

Lucas drummed his fingers on the chair's wooden armrest. He had a million things he could be doing besides meeting with Walter. But WBC's lead pastor had asked him to come in and talk. Again. What was the point? Lucas had already talked through the events of the riot with him—a two-hour session with tears and prayer. Almost a week later, Lucas was back in routine. Why did Walter need a one-on-one outside of the staff meeting?

"Hey, Lucas." Walter opened his office door. "Thanks for your patience while I wrapped up that call."

Walter's office had a scholarly feel, like a professor's. Today it seemed crowded.

"Lucas, I asked you to come by because I'm worried about you."

That was one of the things Lucas appreciated about Walter. He got straight to the point.

"You seem ... unsettled. Distant. Irritable. This is entirely natural, given your experience. I think it would be wise to continue to talk about it. It doesn't have to be with me—perhaps an elder, therapist, or mentor?"

"I don't—" Lucas fought his knee-jerk reaction. He took a deep breath and started again. "I appreciate your concern. I have talked about it and continue to work it through with the team."

"Yes, but as their pastor. You need someone to shepherd *you* through this."

"I think I've made my peace with it."

"Then why are you pacing?"

Lucas stopped. When had he risen from his chair? He sat, gripping the seat. "Okay, maybe I'm a little distracted. And I'm not sleeping great." He knew what was front-and-center on his conscience. But he'd confessed it and prayed. He was confident of God's forgiveness.

So why did he still feel like crap?

He jiggled his knee. Cleared his throat. "It's just that the experience—the riot—it's like it took the lid off a witch's brew of emotions, and they won't go back into the pot."

Walter nodded.

Lucas stood. Walked behind the chair and gripped the seat back. "Just saying how I felt, how I feel, seems so ... The words feel flat and empty, compared to what's going on inside me."

Walter returned his gaze, unflinching.

"Fear. Panic. Hate. Rage. Gant's dead and I still want to kill him with my hands. It's a very physical desire. I want to smash things."

He took a deep breath, letting it out with a gust. "I failed my people. In the middle of the storm, I lost my way." His voice caught. "I've never felt so powerless over a situation and over my own emotions. They take me by storm."

"You *are* powerless, every day," Walter said. "Maybe that's why transitioning back is so difficult. The veil's been torn away. In one way, it's a gift to so clearly see the hand of God at work and experience complete reliance upon him. But it's a process that goes against every bit of our humanity. You're having difficulties because this is very difficult."

Lucas nodded. These were things he knew. But there was value in speaking them aloud.

There was standing room only in the small hearing room. Testifying witnesses got dibs on the front seats behind the barrier dividing counsel from gallery. In the back were the lookee-loos that got on the admission list and the few press who'd received passes by lottery.

Grace squeezed Livvy's arm. The governor had entered the chamber. She approached the WBC people, who occupied most of the first two rows.

"Good afternoon." Impeccably groomed, the tall Latina shook hands down the row. "I'm so sorry for your ordeal. Thank God you all made it through safely." When she shook Livvy's hand she covered it, clasping it between both hands.

"Thank you," Livvy murmured. Did she really thank God? Or was that just something politicians said?

The governor took her seat, and Tobin was ushered into the

courtroom. He wore an olive suit, his gray eyes tinged with green when he looked Livvy's way. They exchanged shy smiles.

Livvy tried to stay focused on the proceedings. She half listened to character witnesses and testimony about Tobin's actions during the riot. But mostly she stared at him. At his profile. She had stroked that jaw, kissed that mouth.

Tobin turned and looked at her full in the face. She jumped a little. He smiled, slow and soft.

"Go on, sweetie." Grace nudged her. "It's your turn."

Oh. Livvy collected herself and walked to the witness stand. *Just be yourself,* Tobin's attorney had said. Answer questions, relate your experience.

What weight would Livvy's statement carry? Surely her testimony of Tobin's bravery and selflessness would count for something. Or would the panel and the governor take it with a grain of Stockholm Syndrome salt? Would they see her affection for Tobin and dismiss her biased input?

Seated, Livvy swept the gallery with a glance. Grace smiled widely at her, raising brows in encouragement. Joan pressed her lips together and focused with rapt attention. Dale Peake nodded reassuringly. The press waited in the rear, poised with notebooks—paper and electronic—in hand. No photography allowed. One woman swept her hand across her open pad, eyes flicking back and forth from page to Livvy. Was she sketching her?

Livvy swallowed, trying to force down the roar in her ears.

Lucas sat in the gallery just behind Tobin's place at the defendant's table. To look at one was to look at both. Livvy's breath tightened.

Tobin's attorney walked her through the formalities: "Understand you are not under oath ..."

At first, Livvy didn't know where to look. To whom she should direct her comments. Holding the governor's gaze was a little heady. Gradually she came to focus on Tobin. Peace stole over her as she answered the questions and her voice grew stronger. Panic subsided as she recounted her story from center stage.

Listening to Livvy's testimony was tougher than Lucas had thought it would be. He'd heard the majority of her ordeal, but mostly second- or thirdhand.

Once again, he marveled at all she'd endured and the lengths Tobin had gone to protect her.

As Livvy's gaze settled on Tobin and she visibly relaxed, Lucas began to squirm. The ants came marching on, and he couldn't remain in his seat. He was halfway out the door before he realized his brain had told his feet to move.

Right, then.

He headed to the men's room, relieved to find it empty. Planting his palms on the edge of the counter, he pressed against it as if to push the sink and the whole San Quentin experience away from him.

Lord, I want to be open to what you are doing in me. What are you doing?

A deluge of conflicting emotions washed over him: he needed to break something or break apart himself. His mind's eye flashed to a scene: Jesus on the cross, forgiving those who had crucified him. Those who had flogged him to within an inch of his life. Who had driven spiked thorns into his head from a crown of mockery, struck him, spit on him.

Lucas sank to his knees, shook his head. He could say the words, but could he mean them? Did his forgiveness of them matter? Gant was dead. Edwards was dead. Knox faced judgement.

Jesus. Lucas bent over his knees. *Forgive them. Help me to forgive them for what they did to me, to Sean, to my people, to Livvy. Help me to let go. Take from me this burden that I can't carry.*

He'd been forgiven for his rage and hatred, but they still surged through him. How was he to be a healer of his people if he was so deeply wounded himself?

Suddenly that vision of the cross tilted slightly, offered him a new perspective. Not only was Jesus loving and gracious and just plain God enough to forgive those who hurt him, but here was the thing: he was not so focused on his own suffering that he was unable to help others.

Wow. Just wow.

Lucas fumbled with his phone. He pulled up his Bible app and went to 1 Peter 2:19: *For this finds favor, if for the sake of conscience toward God a person bears up under sorrows when suffering unjustly.*

Bear up ... Lucas quickly tapped his way to Galatians chapter six. Why was the church in Galatia instructed in verse two to *bear* one another's burdens, then in verse five to each *bear* his own load? It was no translation glitch: the same word was used both times in the original text.

Lucas stared off into space. Jesus had borne the suffering he'd been given, and the statement he'd made by doing so remained as extraordinary today as it had when the centurion stood at the base of his cross and confessed, "Surely this was a righteous man."

If Lucas hadn't already been sitting, he'd have had to hit the floor. Freedom—ultimate, eternal freedom had been granted in those moments of sacrifice. God was faithful to usher in hope and peace right smack dab in the middle of Jesus's worst suffering. Suffering that he bore in order to lighten the load for all.

Was that what Lucas was called to? What had Jesus said to Peter in Luke chapter twenty-two? *Satan has demanded permission to sift you like wheat; but I have prayed for you, that your faith may not fail; and you, when once you have turned again, strengthen your brothers.*

Lucas inhaled deeply and stood. This was the moment. He would turn again—return—and in bearing the suffering he'd been dealt, he would strengthen his brothers and sisters. He could be wounded and still be a healer.

The bathroom door slapped open, and Lucas started. So did Tobin, entering with a CO close on his heels.

Tobin shifted, paused. He and Lucas stood some six feet apart. Wordless, the CO sized up the situation. Then he walked between the men, checked the empty stalls, nodded at each of them and exited the washroom. *Probably not protocol.*

"What's the word?" Lucas's tongue unstuck.

Tobin shrugged. "They'll be making a determination within the next few days."

Abruptly Lucas was flooded by a strong desire that this man be granted clemency. That he be given freedom, a second chance, grace. He held out his hand. Tobin stepped forward, grasped it, and was visibly surprised when Lucas clutched him into a back-slap hug with the other hand. "We're all praying. I'm praying."

Tobin's brow furrowed and he nodded. "Thanks, man. That means a lot. I thought maybe …" He lifted a shoulder. "Maybe you weren't so wild about the idea."

It was such sweet relief to be able to answer honestly. "Oh, I'm wild about it. I look forward to see what's next for you."

"Where's D.P.? I thought he was picking me up?" Tobin glanced around the bus station's small parking lot. The edge of his nervousness had dulled on the ride from San Rafael to San Jose, but now it sliced cold and sharp once again. Livvy was all he'd thought about since his clemency had been granted. Now she stood not five feet from him, and he could barely meet her eye.

"He's not far. There's been a change of plans." She smiled

enigmatically.

"Okay. What's going on?" Tobin frowned. He'd made arrangements with the chaplain just that morning.

"Don't worry. Don't you know how to improvise?"

He felt the worry lines on his forehead relax as he smiled. "All right. Lead the way." He slung the small duffel over his shoulder.

"That's it?" She nodded at his scant possessions.

"That's it."

Livvy gestured in their direction of travel and turned on her heel. Tobin fell into step beside her. They headed not to a car, but through the city streets.

"Is it weird?" she asked.

"In so many ways."

She nodded. Wordless.

They walked slowly, their shadows stretching behind and then ahead as they passed under streetlight after streetlight.

"You going to tell me where we're going?"

"Just a little coffee shop I know."

The evening had a nip to it. Livvy's hand was just there. Maybe a foot away. This woman whom he'd held, carried, hugged, bandaged, and kissed. Separated by uncertainty and the forgotten dance of How We Do This.

"What are you thinking about?" she asked.

"I feel a little ... off balance."

She stopped under the denuded canopy of a tree, light from a silver moon strafing through the few leaves autumn hadn't yet claimed. "Could I maybe help you with balance? You don't have to do this alone."

She inclined her head toward a brightly lit café just down the sidewalk from where they stood. Cuppa Joe's was bustling in spite of a *closed for a private event* sign in the window. Tobin started when he recognized Dale Peak through the glass, laughing at something with Joan from Willowvale Bible Church. And there stood 'Rette, strikingly normal in street clothes. Even the newly paroled Smitty had made it, sitting on a tall stool in earnest conversation with Lucas.

"Surprise," Livvy said shyly, waving spread-fingered jazz hands in muted celebration.

Tobin opened his mouth. Then closed it. He dropped his duffle to the pavement.

"I hope it's not too much." Livvy crinkled her nose, looking up at him. "But everyone wanted—"

Tobin reached and pulled her to him. He brushed the curls back from her cheek. Then he initiated the kind of slow, unhurried kiss for which a free man has all the time in the world.

~ The End ~

Acknowledgements

No Turning Back is not the first book I started writing. It's just the first one to make it this far. That's not unusual for a writer, but the thing of it is that I've got a ton of people to thank. And I'm gonna go ahead and do it.

I'm so grateful to those who contribute to the Crime-SceneWriters Yahoo group who give their time and knowledge to help non-LEO (law enforcement officer) types like me to get the facts right. Certainly anything that misses the mark are my own errors. The things I get right are thanks to those who answered my questions, such as Lee Lofland, who started the Yahoo group, Orblover, David Brollier, Derek Pacifico, and others.

I also gleaned lots of procedural knowledge from attending the incomparable Writer's Police Academy, 2013.

Dan Higgins' patient and generous answers to my prison questions were invaluable.

High school buddy and now LEO Doug Gerbrandt gave insight into how someone on a crisis negotiation team might respond to a phone call from inside the locked-down prison.

I had a chance encounter, if you believe in such things, with a fellow writer at the 2011 ACFW (American Christian Fiction Writers) conference in St. Louis who turned out to be an opera singer. Thank you to Kristen Johnson for insights that helped me bring Livvy's opera world to life.

Friend and Fremont, CA, motorcycle patrolman and SWAT officer Kelly Snow paved the way for me to attended the fun and informative citizens police academy, provided me with helicopter insight, as well as let me fire his AR-15 on full auto at the range, which had nothing to with research for the book but was stinking fun.

The plot inspiration came from friend and pastor Tim Ruiz who has led softball teams into San Quentin and Soledad prisons. He told me about signing the prison release forms and the advice to "hit the ground in case of gun fire," and I was off and wondering what the fate of a beautiful young woman might be in such a terrifying situation. Thanks, Tim, for oodles of things, including the seed that grew into a novel.

It's been my good fortune—or more aptly, divine blessing—to have been mentored and coached by some pretty cool people along my journey. And so I'd like to thank all the SCUM who helped make this possible. John "Just-Finish-Something" Olson has been a hugely helpful coach and friend, and thanks to the rest for input and support: Lori Arthur, Candy Campbell, Jan Collins, Karen D'Amato, Tasra Dawson, Donna Fujimoto, Ellen Graebe, Nancy Hird, Kim Lavoie, Carl Olsen, Amy Olson, Patty Mitchell, Lynne Thompson, and John Zelaski.

To the Winklings, I say thank you and please file this under "about-stinking-time": Katie Cushman, Jenn Doucette, John Olson, and Jim Rubart.

The Mount Hermon Christian Writers Conferences afforded me access to some great writers, teachers, and mentors, including the not-so-pesky Randy Ingermanson, Brandilyn Collins, and Jim Bell.

To the San Jose Christian Writers group and Orchard Valley Coffee writing partners, thanks for beaucoup input, hours of shop talk, and above all, your cherished friendship: Shelley Bates,

Kristin Billerbeck, Helen Bratko, Becky George, Marilyn Hilton, Susanne Lakin, Dineen Miller, Susan Mitchell, Pamela Walls, Camy Tang, and MaryLu Tyndall. Loren Peake has been a great sounding board and inspired Chaplin Dale's last name.

Cathleen Armstrong and Kathi Lipp are two of the best critique partners and writing encouragers ever.

Susanne Lakin graciously gave me some of her valuable time and helped me hone the characters' emotional arcs.

Thank you to beta readers Lynn Domke, Kate Mackessy, and Jennifer Wickland, and to Carrie MacMahan who went above and beyond to print out the manuscript and read it through twice!

Bestie Nicole Jolyn was with me throughout—encouraging, plotting, reading, and suggesting. Several lines that she penned made it into the manuscript.

Church of the Chimes has been a loving, safe community for God to keep working on my heart and character for over sixteen years. There are many there, in my eternal family, who have encouraged, shepherded, and blessed me over the years. And just plain put up with me. I wish I could thank you each by name. I'm grateful I can hug you individually whenever we are together. Pastor Lee Graham's message on the Wounded Healer helped unpack Galatians six for me and for Lucas, both of whom needed to hear it on the same day.

I owe my love of reading to my mom, who read to my brother and me and who has always encouraged me. I share a quirky love of words—origins, meanings, and bad puns—with my dad. I thank them both for their love and my good education.

Words fail me when it comes to thanking my husband, Loren, for supporting and encouraging me to pursue writing "for real." Thank you for never making me feel like I was wasting my time. Thank you for providing a home so rich in love and laughter and for fathering and "dadding" the two best kids ever.

Author Notes

I took my sweet time getting this book finished and published. In the years since initial idea and research, there have been some changes at the Q. I'm sure I've made some errors as well: there was only so far my secondary research could take me. Plus, I took some license with other facts.

- Building number twenty-two, which was built before Lincoln was elected, was torn down, and in 2010 a new hospital building was opened in its place with fifty beds, fourteen doctors, and one hundred nurses. The former hospital, the Neumiller building, was also at one time a women's cell block.
- I believe the armory has been moved. Similar to Tobin's experience, they just don't keep me informed on these things.
- During the period of the prison's peak overcrowding, the gym was used for housing. More than 360 inmates lived in essentially one huge cell, bunkbeds laid out in rows, dormitory style.
- The California clemency process does not include a hearing, much less a public one.
- The dungeon does still exist but has been fitted with lighting and reinforcements, and I believe it is used for storage.
- San Quentin was built to house 3,082 inmates. At one point, more than five thousand men resided there. The population (and staff needed to manage it) has declined after legislation aimed at reducing overcrowding. As of November 30, 2016,

there were 3,816 inmates at the Q for a capacity of 123.8 percent.[1]

- All California executions—male and female—are carried out at San Quentin. A new execution chamber and separate viewing rooms for family, victims, and press were completed in 2010. I don't know what they've done with the green capsule-like gas chamber.
- For photos and discussion of some of the locations that figure into the story, please see my author page on Facebook.

Check out my website at
katievorreiter.com
for *No Turning Back* discussion questions
and to sign up for my newsletter.
You'll receive info about new releases,
insight into the writer's life,
and special offers!

---

[1] State of California Department of Corrections and Rehabilitation, Offender Information Services Branch, Estimates and Statistical Analysis Section, Data Analysis Unit. *Monthly Report of Population as of Midnight November 30, 2016.*